Declan emerged. He had on his leather bomber jacket, and while the rain fell on him, he didn't run. No, he stalked to her front door and pounded instead.

Looking down at her old Patriots sweatshirt and lacy red boy shorts, she thought, *oh what the hell*. He was the one showing up early at her cottage. She hadn't expected any visitors but Ellie or Brady.

She swung the door open, wincing as rain splattered her face and cold rushed over her legs. "I'd say don't wake the neighbors with your pounding, but there aren't any. I guess you'd better come in since it's pouring, but you should know, I'm not sure I'm happy to see you this early."

She was such a liar.

He shut and latched the door after they stepped inside. "Seeing you in that outfit, I'm glad I decided to run over here this morning after some early training. Is that lace on your shorts?"

His hand skimmed her thighs, and she swatted it away as her body flushed with heat. They needed some ground rules. "What are you doing here, Declan?"

"We need to be friends. Whether we do more is something we both need to consider. Hard. We should talk about that kiss, Kathleen."

He didn't sound too happy about it, so she went with snark. "What kiss?" she quipped, laughing as his face darkened. "Oh, *that* kiss! You want to do it again?"

PRAISE FOR AVA MILES' NOVELS
SEE WHAT ALL THE BUZZ IS ABOUT...

"Ava's story is witty and charming."

BARBARA FREETHY #1 *NYT* BESTSELLING
AUTHOR

"If you like Nora Roberts type books, this is a must-read."

READERS' FAVORITE

"If ever there was a contemporary romance that rated a 10 on a scale of 1 to 5 for me, this one is it!"

THE ROMANCE REVIEWS

"I could not stop flipping the pages. I can't wait to read the next book in this series."

FRESH FICTION

"I've read Susan Mallery and Debbie Macomber... but never have I been so moved as by the books Ava Miles writes."

BOOKTALK WITH EILEEN

Along Waters of Sunshine and Shadow

The Friends & Neighbors Novels

A feast for all the senses...

The House of Hope & Chocolate

The Dreamer's Flower Shoppe

The Dare River Series

Filled with down-home charm...

Country Heaven

The Chocolate Garden

Fireflies and Magnolias

The Promise of Rainbows

The Fountain Of Infinite Wishes

The Patchwork Quilt Of Happiness

Country Heaven Cookbook

The Chocolate Garden: A Magical Tale (Children's Book)

The Dare Valley Series

Awash in small town fabulousness...

Nora Roberts Land

French Roast

The Grand Opening

The Holiday Serenade

The Town Square

The Park of Sunset Dreams

The Perfect Ingredient

The Bridge to a Better Life

The Calendar of New Beginnings

Home Sweet Love

The Moonlight Serenade

The Sky of Endless Blue

Daring Brides

Daring Declarations

Dare Valley Meets Paris Billionaire Mini-Series

Small town charm meets big city romance...

The Billionaire's Gamble

The Billionaire's Secret

The Billionaire's Courtship

The Billionaire's Return

Dare Valley Meets Paris Compilation

The Once Upon a Dare Series

Falling in love is a contact sport...

The Gate to Everything

Non-Fiction

The Happiness Corner: Reflections So Far

The Post-Covid Wellness Playbook

Cookbooks

Home Baked Happiness Cookbook

Country Heaven Cookbook

The Lost Guides to Living Your Best Life Series

Reclaim Your Superpowers

Courage Is Your Superpower

Expression Is Your Superpower

Peace Is Your Superpower

Confidence Is Your Superpower

Happiness Is Your Superpower

Children's Books

The Chocolate Garden: A Magical Tale

AFTER INDIGO IRISH NIGHTS

THE UNEXPECTED PRINCE CHARMING BOOK 4

AVA MILES

www.avamiles.com
Ava Miles

To unsung heroes in our communities—the butchers at the meat counter—who give kindness and connection, most especially Ciro in New York, and the trio in my recent hometown in Ireland that include Eric (who also boxes like Declan) and the father and son team of Alan and Martin. I'd be remiss if I didn't also mention the generous gifts from butchers in Dublin, Cairo, and Arles.

These men represent what I call unexpected Prince Charmings.

The course of true love often has its twists and turns...

One can expect bumps in the road.
When they come, as they surely will,
There will be help—
As Ireland is a land that believes in true love.

A heroine will remember the joys of loving,
And learn to believe in happily ever after once again.

And the hero will forget his woes,
Only to remember he's a Prince Charming,
If an unexpected one.

CHAPTER ONE

Nothing rocked Kathleen O'Connor's world more than a girls' trip.

Ireland's rolling green hills zoomed by, dotted with soaring ancient stone ruins that made her heart trip. She nudged her best friend, Ellie Buchanan, who was singing off-key with Prince about partying in 1999. "OMG! It's so freaking gorgeous I want to pinch myself!"

"And it never gets old," Ellie replied as she navigated another death-defying narrow turn. "Some days I wake up and think, I must be on vacation."

But Ellie lived here now, and so did Kathleen—for the next four months. Clenching the car's grip handle, she reminded herself there was plenty of crazy driving back home in Boston. It didn't ease her nerves as her friend zipped around another turn. "Promise me I'm going to get used to the driving. I didn't expect it to be even crazier than back home! I mean, we have crazy drivers but not crazy roads and driving on the left. Jeez!"

Ellie laughed darkly and shot her a grin as she took another insane turn. They were at the end of the nearly three-hour car trip from Dublin airport to Caisleán. She could grit her teeth through this last bit. Of course, she'd been here once before, to visit Ellie, but it felt different now that she was coming to stay.

"You're having way too much fun scaring the hell out of me, Ellie."

"I'm keeping your mind occupied," her friend shot back, her Southern accent making the words drip like pecan syrup on buttermilk waffles. "You've never been away from your family for longer than a few days. I know how big this is for you. You said your pop and all seven of your brothers about cried when you left after Easter dinner. That kills me."

Seeing those crumpled male faces had made her sneak off to their ancient bathroom and mop her face so they wouldn't see her crying. O'Connors weren't criers. Still, as tough as Kathleen was, taking the bull by the horns and leaving Boston for the first time in her life had taken real courage.

Only the competitive artist residency she'd won through the Irish Arts Council could have lured her away from home—and even then, a big part of why she'd come was because Ellie was here. Being back with her best friend was going to be awesome. She'd missed her former roommate. "Pop and my brothers are so proud they could bust a button. They'll handle it."

Her family was as tight as they came, even more so after her mother had died when Kathleen was five. Her pop and her brothers had raised her tough, but they'd also given her wings. She planned to fly.

"It's not just my residency. Pop is thrilled to have an O'Connor back in Ireland."

Her parents' ancestors had left this beautiful yet troubled place for a better life, landing at Ellis Island and settling in Boston, specifically Southie. As with so many Irish immigrants, tradition ran strong in her family. Their family pub, O'Connor's, was considered one of the best Irish pubs in the city.

"You'll have to pick your Irish dancing back up," Ellie said with a grin. "I'll bet you looked like a cutie pie in the outfit."

"The wig itched, and it threw my timing off when I had to scratch." She shuddered. All these years later, she could still feel the nylon wig. "I was booed at the St. Patrick's Day parade one year. Of course, the guys who were doing it shut up after I threw a rock their way."

"That's why I love Southie." Ellie laughed as she downshifted to take a crazy narrow turn, making Kathleen bite her lip. "No polite bullshit or backtalking. Everything is out in the open and in your face."

Being a Southern girl, Ellie hadn't experienced much of that directness in her childhood, so she'd embraced the rough honesty of Kathleen's neighborhood. "Stop reminding me of home. You'll make me tear up."

"Wait! I'll take your mind off it again. Hang on to your butt."

Kathleen winced as her friend took another hairpin turn. They might as well have been careening down a fluorescent crazy straw. "Driving here isn't for wimps. You're doing pretty good for someone who's only been here four months. I mean, you don't even slow down when we come to a curve in the road." Her knuckles might be white for days after this.

"I hear the censure in your voice. You get used to the curves and the speed. Out here along the Wild Atlantic

Way, people usually lurch to a stop if they meet another car around a bend."

"Then someone has to back up and find a place to pull over on the turnout," Kathleen said, giving in to the urge to clutch both her seat belt and the handle as they thundered around another curve. "I've noticed. You and the Irish could teach the crazies in Boston something about driving, especially on the Pike."

Ellie pointed an accusatory finger across the dashboard. "With Massachusetts having the highest car insurance rates in the States, I doubt that."

"We don't have ditches on either side of the road in Boston—or escaped animals. Only the breakdown lane."

Her city girl was showing, and she knew it. She peeked out the window at the deep ditch to her left. They had obviously been designed to keep animals of all kinds—sheep and cows mostly but also horses and the cutest donkeys alive—from overtaking the road after clearing the aged aluminum wire fencing, sometimes barbed and downright gnarly.

As a metal sculptor, she knew her metal. She'd used barbed wire in her most acclaimed work to date—the *Heartbreak Series*. The knotted, twisted metal had perfectly showcased her theme. Love sucked when it was laced with betrayal, and damn it to hell, did it leave deep wounds. She was mostly over hers, but once bitten, twice shy.

An image of the man who'd most recently made her crazy came to mind—Declan McGrath. He'd popped into her mind several times since their insane, lust-inspired meeting on her last trip to Caisleán—at a reception at the Sorcha Fitzgerald Arts Center, where she'd be working for the next several months.

Her knees had gone weak the minute she'd seen him standing against a wall, a whiskey in his large hand. He had an arrestingly handsome face framed by blue-black hair and a hard muscled body, dripping with attitude, the kind she never could ignore. She'd almost dropped her own whiskey, and her skin had sparked as though the wires on a car battery had touched.

She didn't believe in love at first sight anymore. But one thing she did know—he fired up her senses like no man had since her ex, Axl. The rare feeling he induced tantalized her.

Apparently, he'd felt the same way because they'd launched themselves at each other and shared a kiss unlike any she'd ever experienced. If they'd been metal and not flesh, they'd have turned white hot, that rare temperature when heat becomes incandescent.

She'd railed over her impulsiveness after she'd left Ireland and finally come to the unassailable truth—they were combustible.

In her art, metal forged by that kind of heat was never the same again. People seemed to be the same way, and that had her thinking about him. More than might be wise since he was the twin brother of Ellie's fiancé.

She looked out the window, wondering how she was going to feel when she saw Declan again. And how he would react when he saw her. *Crazy thoughts, O'Connor.*

Ellie drove past a pasture filled with the infamous spray-painted cows depicting words like Romance and Forever in blue, so she knew they were close to Caisleán.

She studied those giant lumbering cows with their romantic words. Whoever had painted them could write Valentine's Day cards. Good for him, but she was past her romantic phase.

She'd only worn her heart on her sleeve once, and it had been a mistake—the devastating kind. She didn't want to end up drowning in a puddle of her own tears again. She'd spent six years with Axl, dreaming about girly happily ever afters, only to discover he'd been cheating on her all along. Dickwad. She wasn't going to be that screwy again.

Have fun. But play it safe. That was her new model.

The thought of enjoying Declan during her stay enticed her, but she'd have to keep hold of herself and not get swept away by the heat between them. If he was of the same mind... She couldn't wait to find out. Shit. Butterflies fluttered in her tummy. She released her death grip on the seat belt and tried to calm them. Nerves over a boy? This early? Not okay.

"You're thinking about Declan, aren't you?" Ellie asked softly.

She looked over quickly at her friend and saw only quiet understanding on her face. "How did you know?"

"You got abnormally quiet. You're clenching your hands. And your cheeks are flushed like you're getting hot and bothered. He's really gotten to you."

She and Ellie shared everything, the way best friends should. "It's still weird not knowing how he feels, and it's even weirder since you're marrying his brother."

"I don't think it's weird. I like Declan a lot. He's had his heartbreak and then some, so you're both in the same boat, so to speak. As for how he feels... Brady thinks he's been in a dark mood lately. Liam says he's abnormally sullen, and he's one of Declan's longtime friends, so he'd know. I don't have the same scope, but sullen is a good word. He storms around Summercrest Manor and slams doors."

Sullen was interesting, God help her. "You still like living at Summercrest with the boys?"

"Yes, until Brady and I can figure out a more private living situation. There's a terrible shortage of houses and rentals, and most of the ones that *are* available have the damp or need more renovations than I want to handle. The county council is really strict about granting more planning permission for new houses, and it doesn't allow outside labor. Daddy's trying to figure out a plan."

And he would. Lincoln Buchanan was a force of nature. "How is Papa Linc?"

"Good, although he's traveling right now. But we're digressing... Back to Declan."

"I told you my plan." Kathleen unclenched her hands and placed them on her thighs. "I'm going to play it cool. See how he acts. I don't have the time to deal with a sullen Irishman, regardless of how attracted I am to him."

"I'm glad you didn't use past tense."

"I know myself too well for that." Kathleen had worked hard to be attuned to her emotions, especially after her mother died. As an artist, she had more to say because of it.

"That's one of the many reasons why I love you," Ellie said, warmth in her voice. "By the way, if you look across the pasture, you'll see our girl."

Kathleen turned her head to the right and couldn't help but let out a soft sigh as she beheld the killer orange and red sunset illuminating the Sorcha Fitzgerald Arts Center on the majestic green hills. "My God, it's beautiful. You did good, giving it a million smackeroos."

Her very rich friend snorted. "Thank you," she said dryly. "Becoming a public benefactor has been a little weird, but considering the kinds of additions the center can make now—as well as the independence it's gained—I'm glad I did."

Ellie had spent most of her adulthood concealing that she was an heiress, the daughter of the billionaire king of windows, Lincoln Buchanan. In the beginning of their friendship, she'd hidden it even from Kathleen. Of course, Kathleen didn't care how much money anyone had. People were either good or they weren't. How light or heavy their pocketbook was didn't factor into her estimation of them unless they acted like it made them better than others.

But Ellie had been burned before, burdened with a mother who only wanted money, first from Ellie's father and then from her, and a deadbeat ex-fiancé who'd happily jilted her for a payout. "I'm glad it's out in the open for you, but if someone steps wrong, I've got your back."

"Appreciated."

As they zoomed along the paved road leading to the center's parking lot, her hands began to sweat. "Is that my studio out back?"

"Shed, in Irish. Newly constructed by Liam and a few others. I hope you like it."

The dull gray aluminum *shed* around back might look ugly as a cracked sidewalk to some, but to her it was heaven. "It's a wicked pissah."

Ellie coughed out a laugh. "God, I've missed that one. People around here say 'class' for awesome."

She'd have to learn the lingo, but that could wait. That shed was all hers, and she planned to use it to create a metal sculpture so evocative, so wicked, it was guaranteed to rock the art world.

As soon as Ellie pulled her car to a stop in the empty lot, Kathleen threw open the door and embraced the fragrant spring breeze rushing over her face...or that was the idea. She coughed as the smell hit her nose. "Jesus! What is that?"

"Welcome to the land of forever beauty and sometimes ordure. Someone just slurried their fields. Ugh! I'm going to gag."

She lifted her shirt over her nose. "Slurry what?"

"They put cow shit in a blue tank, fill it with water, and spray it everywhere." Ellie covered her nose with her hand as well. "Those wavy grasses don't happen without a little TLC."

"God, don't say any more. Let me enjoy my moment minus the smell. Dammit, I'm going to kill it here."

"Yeah, you are," her friend said, grinning at her. "I'm so glad you're here. Even though we've been talking every day, it's not the same as when we lived together in Boston."

Those days were over, and they both knew it. Ellie would be staying here in Caisleán —she was getting *married* —but their friendship would never change. Some people were like that. From the moment Kathleen had met Ellie to interview her as a roommate, she'd felt like she'd known her forever. They were sisters all the way and always would be.

"We're going to have a blast here. I'm so psyched." She shimmied her hips to celebrate but kept her nose covered. She must look like an idiot. She dropped it and tried not to inhale.

"Come on," Ellie said, toughening up too and taking her hand. "I'll show you the shed. Not that there's much to check out yet. You'll see what I mean."

They walked around the three-story white building that had been originally built as a massive house. Everyone in Caisleán knew the story—after his wife had died tragically young, Carrick Fitzgerald had built her dream house as part of the grieving process. Then he'd donated it to the town to be used as the arts center.

The large picture windows gleamed, and through the ones on the first floor, she could see the painting studio where Carrick's new wife worked and taught. She'd already met both Angie and her sister, Megan, a potter who taught at the center. They were both from the States. As was the director of the center, Betsy O'Hanlon, whom everyone called Bets. Ellie's fiancé said it was an American invasion in the best way. Kathleen was excited to be a part of it.

The mowed grass around the center was damp and gave under her feet as she walked next to Ellie. The shed was a short distance away from the main center—a mindful choice that had been made both for fire safety considerations and because of the noise of her tools.

Ellie tugged on the metal door, grunting like an old man, and Kathleen nudged her aside. "You stained glass artists have no muscle."

She pulled the heavy door open, pleased it was well oiled. Her eyes squinted to make out the dark interior of the shed before Ellie flicked on the overhead lights. The concrete floor was still white and pristine, but that was all.

"It's empty."

"The items you wanted haven't been delivered yet," Ellie said with a hefty sigh. "I was hoping they'd arrive this afternoon. Bets has been at them for days now. One thing about Ireland: stuff doesn't always run on time, and Customs can be a bitch."

Kathleen had done her best to select equipment from Ireland, but some of her most specialized tools—like her English wheel, plasma cutter, grinder, and Pullmax metal shaper—came from suppliers in Sweden and Germany.

She'd planned on starting tomorrow. Unlike the other residents, she wouldn't be teaching. Her entire time here would be devoted to making her sculpture, and she needed every minute of it. She lifted her chin and told herself to suck it up. "It'll show up. I'm not letting this get me down."

"Your design is awesome! I can't wait to watch it unfold.

I might even bring some of my stuff out here and work alongside you so we can talk as we go."

Kathleen swung her arm around her friend's waist. "That would be nice. We didn't have enough space for that in our art studio back in Southie."

No, in their converted warehouse studio for nearly twenty artists, they'd had only a small dedicated space apiece, although Kathleen had shared the machine shop with a few other artists.

Here she wouldn't have to share at all, and everything was brand new, courtesy of both her residency as well as Ellie's donation to the center. The arts center had put forth half the money for the shed and supplies, hoping to bring in more metal artists in the future.

Instead of kissing the concrete floor in sheer happiness, Kathleen gave in to the urge to do a little jig from her Irish dancing days and laughed at herself for being so out of practice.

"I'll tell Brady we've got tonight's entertainment at the bar covered," Ellie said with a grin, joining in. "If we're lucky, the Lucky Charms will invite us to dance with them at the pub when they put Bon Jovi on."

"I've only seen the videos you've sent of Bets and her girlfriends dancing. I love that they've added you and Angie to the mix. Man, I want to be dancing like that when I'm sixty."

"Me too! It's totally cool. Brady loves watching me, and I'll bet someone he shared a womb with will love watching *you*."

She didn't need to say Declan's name. Kathleen's skin tightened thinking about having his eyes on her as she moved her body. God, she was getting hot.

Her phone bleeped then, signaling a text. Good. It

would be her oldest brother. Hearing from him would be like taking a cold shower.

"Five euros it's Billie," Ellie said with a wink. "He won't be able to give a car his complete attention until he knows you didn't die in a plane crash. I've never heard anyone bitch and moan about airplane crashes as much as he does. He only thinks cars are safe, which makes sense since he's a mechanic."

"Except Robbie always reminds him how many car accidents there are a year." Kathleen shook her head. "It's gonna be Robbie. He got my brothers to agree he'd be the main point of contact so they don't text me all the time."

"You're kidding! Robbie is the best older brother ever."

"Until he starts driving me crazy. He never stops thinking like a cop. Did you know he wanted to have my address, the center's address, the names of the people I'll be spending the most time with, and the make and model of my rental car? I swear, he was planning to look everyone up. Meanwhile, he and my other brothers keep teasing me about falling into the fairy world. They don't want to admit how much they're going to miss me."

"From my experience, that's the Irish way too. They're crazy superstitious, and they talk about bad luck and death all the time. You'll see, but I know one thing. You're going to fit right in."

"I don't doubt it. I felt the pull of my Irish roots when I came last time."

The Irish had different accents and used different words. They certainly dressed differently, and God knew this place was remote as hell. She'd never seen a real cow or sheep before coming here—only a horse, and even then, it had been a police horse. But she still felt a thread of familiarity with the people and knew it to be the bond of Irish heritage. It was a wicked pissah.

Her phone bleeped again, and she pulled it out and held it up for her friend. "Yep. It's Robbie."

You alive? I've got a salvage boat ready to come after you if you're on some flimsy inflatable raft in the middle of the Atlantic.

Typical snarky message. She teared up as she replied.

The raft wasn't too bad, but I had to pay for those little liquor bottles like we'd get at a packie. I'm at my shed, well away from the ocean. It's magic.

He texted her back instantly.

Seen a leprechaun yet? If you do, knock him out at the knees like I taught you, put him in a box, and ship him back to Southie. We need a short guy with a pot of gold around here. Send pics of the shed. I'll tell Pop and the rest you enjoyed the raft as a bad April Fool's joke. Love ya.

She had to swipe her eyes with the sleeve of her black coat. "He's such a moron."

"Your brothers are the best," Ellie said, hugging her. "I'm still proud y'all adopted me. I told Brady he's going to have to meet them, especially since he also runs the family bar like your brother does."

"Pop and a few others might come to Ireland someday—"

"What if I flew them over for my wedding?" Ellie asked, lifting her brow.

Kathleen knew where this was going and made a face. Ellie and Brady hadn't set a date yet, so they had time to figure everything out. "You know how proud we O'Connors are. We make our way. They'll want to be there for you—"

"But it's expensive." Ellie heaved out a breath. "All right. We'll talk about it later. Is it time for a drink?"

Kathleen gave another dance. "God, yes!"

"I'll tell you right now... The entire village is showing up at the pub to welcome you. If we were back in our old neighborhood, I'd called it a rippah. Hope you're not too jet-lagged."

Like her family always said, *You can sleep when you're dead.* "Your Boston accent still needs work, but bottom line: I can handle a big party." They linked arms and headed back to the car. "Damn, but it's good to be back together."

"You bet it is! Let's head over to my sweetie pie's pub and get this party started."

She took a last look at her shed and then followed Ellie to the car. When they arrived in the mostly full lot, Kathleen couldn't help but grin at the sight of the pub. Or, more specifically, the sight of her best friend's new stained glass window over the front door of the Brazen Donkey.

"Your pictures didn't do it justice, babe. Oh my God!"

Her brilliant design was a colorful, cheeky depiction of the pub's name. A floppy-eared donkey stood in profile in front of a whiskey barrel, which he was peeking into with obvious delight. The design was captivating, not kitschy. Because seriously—a stained glass donkey? Typically, the only time art elevated that animal was in nativity scenes.

"You struck the perfect balance between the old and the new."

Art was all about creating something universal—classic, even—while making it unique and timeless.

"Stop, you're making me blush."

Ellie was still getting used to praise, so Kathleen let her off the hook, her job done. "Got a verdict yet about whether Brady's pub is better than O'Connor's?"

Her family's Irish pub in Boston kicked butt, only it wasn't on the so-called *hallowed* ground of Ireland. Legend, she'd read on the flight over, boasted that the whiskey and beer tasted as if the angels and fairies themselves had crafted them.

Ellie made a face. "My current answer is that they're different in the best ways—like an apple and a pear. I love both."

"Brady and my brother can't take offense at *that* answer," she said with a laugh. "One thing is for sure. I plan to do my own form of study. I can already taste my Guinness. Before we get to that, I have to tell you again—your window, babe, is a real wicked pissah."

"I think so too."

Kathleen glanced down the small main street of Caisleán, with its brightly colored stores and shining windows. The town was downright cute but tiny as hell. It didn't even boast a stoplight, only one of those roundabouts filled with a large circular planter overflowing with red tulips and yellow daffodils. "There's no garbage on the street like there is back home."

"Or broken glass. You don't need to clutch your purse or make a beeline down the street."

"No bad boys congregating on the corners..."

She broke off as she caught sight of one particular bad boy exiting a shop across the street.

Declan McGrath.

Her body instantly sizzled with heat as she watched him stride purposefully toward them. His edge, his reserve, and his flat-out hotness rocked her back. Their eyes locked, and she swore his mouth curved to the right.

"Oh, boy, here we go." Ellie waved him over like they were in junior high. "Hey, Declan! Look who I've got."

"Cut it out," she hissed. "You're going to make this weird."

"I can't help it," her friend whispered back. "I saw how he looked at you and then how you looked at him and... Whoa! You two! I'm going inside. You'll do better without me."

Kathleen couldn't agree more—her friend's face was blushing three shades of red. "Go."

"Tell him I had to pee after the trip from Dublin," Ellie said in an undertone as she ran to the front door.

"Why are you still standing here?" Declan called out as he came closer. "Didn't you want to run inside too? I've never seen Ellie run away like that. Looks like she was getting out of the way."

Busted.

Her skin turned hot under her clothes despite the spring breeze as he took her in from head to toe. She planted her feet, knowing she'd need her balance as she gave him the same treatment.

Lordy, his looks should be illegal. Midnight black hair. Blow-torch-blue-flame eyes. A rock-solid jaw. Hell, every-thing he sported was rock solid—from his shoulders to his hips to his legs. Declan was built and tall and as tough as they came.

She cocked her hip, knowing how to handle boys like this. "I wanted to admire my best friend's window a little more. Ellie raced inside to tell everyone we'd arrived. I hope no one's jumping out of a cake."

His brows slammed together. "Cake?"

"Apparently there's a party brewing," she explained.

"To welcome you, yes." He ate up the remaining distance between them, all badass male in a brown leather bomber jacket, faded jeans, and workman boots nicked with wear.

Come to mama.

He touched her short brown curls the moment he was near, sending off a shower of invisible sparks along her skin. "Your hair looks even shorter than last time."

She made herself knock his hand away. "I just got it cut. You got some problem with my head, Ace?"

God, they might as well be kids back in her neighborhood. No one passed notes asking if someone liked you with a box to check. When you had it bad for a boy, you kicked him in the shin or threw a rock at him on the playground to get his attention. He pulled your hair and chased you around the school. Then you teased each other until he grabbed you in kiss tag and planted one on you. After that, you went steady.

"No problem. Only commenting." Declan's wicked mouth curved as he raked her with another lusty gaze.

She cocked her hip, bringing his amused eyes back to hers. Yes, he was as delighted with their game as she was. Her belly went liquid with heat. "What's got you working so late on a Friday night?"

"Ordering, Kathleen. My boss has turned that task over to me and ruined my life."

She had to lock her knees at the way he said her name in his Irish accent. He might as well have lit a trail of gunpowder inside her. "Ruined your life, huh?" She tried and failed to contain her smile. "If it's ruined, fix it. Only you can, you know."

He snorted. "I already live with Yoda, in the way of Liam O'Hanlon, who has turned the dungeon at Summercrest Manor into a meditation room, God help me."

"Oh, you've got it so tough, Ace, living in an old place like that." When she'd visited Ellie, she'd had to hold in her sighs at its beauty.

"It's a grand place, for sure, and I have a grand living as well, but a man can vent, can't he? Or don't they do that back in Boston?"

"They do. I'm sure you'll figure things out." She gestured to their family's pub. "Your brother did when he finally got to take over the Brazen Donkey from your dad."

"He did at that, and with much help from his one true love." He pointed to the window over the front door. "People have been coming to Caisleán to see her design. Not that the pub needed the advertising, but it's brought new fame to the Brazen Donkey. She's got one hell of a gift, that Ellie Buchanan."

"She does indeed," Kathleen agreed. "She's been killing it."

"I imagine you'll do the same," Declan said, shifting on his feet. "With Ellie as your herald, everyone in town is high on you."

And you? she wanted to ask. She waited a beat. He met her gaze with pure potency.

"That's nice. It's always good to have friends, especially in a new place."

"You certainly have that. And more."

The word *more* lingered in the air, like a piece of paper waiting to catch fire from the sparks going up between them.

She poked first. "Lucky you happened to come along right as I pulled up. I'm guessing that was your butcher shop you left?"

He inclined his gorgeous chin in acknowledgment. "That's right. It's called the Last Chop."

From the vantage point of the shop's front window, he'd be able to see the lot of the pub. Could Declan have been waiting for her? "That's a funny name."

She made a slicing motion with her hand. Giddy like a schoolgirl because a boy she admired *liked her*, she started laughing.

He joined in, his laughter a rough rumble of sound, before saying, "I find it pretty amusing myself, but I'm told I have a dark sense of humor, even by the Irish."

"I don't mind dark."

"Good to know." He held her eyes again.

She waited another moment. Wasn't it weird they were talking this much? Especially when there were a bunch of people inside waiting to welcome her? Surely he was still standing here because he wanted to flirt. But did he want it to go beyond flirting?

Time to find out. She patted his broad, muscular chest. "I should probably head inside. You want to buy me my first true Irish beer?"

The silence between them grew again, charged with power. Dammit, he knew how to draw things out. He started to smile, holding her gaze still. Oh, he was working it.

Answer me. She poked at his chest when he didn't budge. She wasn't going to draw this out forever. "Forget it! I can buy my own damn beer."

As she brushed past him, he closed a hand around her

wrist, the touch shocking her nerve endings. "Now wait just a moment—"

"Kathleen O'Connor!" a male voice shouted from the pub's front door. "You're wanted inside."

She didn't need to pull her arm away. Declan dropped his hold instantly, but her flesh still sizzled. Wishing she could take a deep, cleansing breath, she gave her full attention to the ninety-three-year-old man bustling toward her. She'd met him on her last trip and had fallen totally in love with him. He had the soul of an artist, although he'd only begun to put it into practice recently.

"Eoghan O'Dwyer! You look even more handsome than you did when I last saw you."

He gave her a cheeky wink as she kissed his weathered cheek. "Thank you, my dear. You're as welcome to these eyes as a fine whiskey on a cold day. Ellie said you were coming along, but now I see the way of things. Is this one bothering you?"

Declan glowered. "We were having a chat, is all, you old codger. When did that become illegal in this country?"

She laughed, delighted Declan seemed put out by the interruption. She wondered if Ellie had sent Eoghan out. She'd have to ask her friend later. "He's not bothering me. Much."

Declan gave a rude snort.

"I'm kidding, Eoghan. Ace here and I were shooting the breeze and talking about Ellie's window. I'd seen pictures but—"

"The real thing looks as if it were created by angels themselves," Eoghan said with a sigh. "I can't wait until I can make a window such as hers."

"First pottery and now stained glass," Declan said,

shaking his head ruefully. "Eoghan, you'll have to live another few decades to master it all."

Eoghan fitted his hand through her arm in the way of an old gentleman. "Who says I won't, Declan McGrath? I feel younger every day. Now then. Come inside, Kathleen, and have a drink. I'm buying your first round."

Declan caught her gaze. His shrug seemed to suggest he wouldn't object.

The butterflies in Kathleen's tummy fell to the ground in disappointment. Still, she bucked up and said, "You coming, Ace?"

His blue eyes fired with heat, the long scorching kind a guy gave to a girl to make sure she understood him. "I'll catch up with you. I need to make a call."

She took Eoghan's arm more firmly as they walked to the front door of the Brazen Donkey. She was ready to party.

Declan McGrath might have taken a step back, but he wasn't immune to her.

Not one bit.

CHAPTER TWO

Declan waited until Kathleen and Eoghan were inside before shoving the phone he'd taken out for show back into his pocket. Her effect on him was just as potent as it had been last month, what with her long legs and slender neck and the hot siren-like call in her big brown eyes—a call he seemed incapable of resisting.

Is this what she'd reduced him to? Faking a phone call so he could have a moment to breathe again?

Fuck this. He started for the front door.

"Not so fast."

Declan jumped at the voice, an incredibly strong one for someone who was dead. "Dammit. Not again."

"I'd hoped for a more pleasant greeting now that Kathleen O'Connor has returned," Sorcha Fitzgerald said, appearing in front of him in the same white dress she'd had on the last few times she'd materialized out of thin air and scared the life out of him.

For fuck's sake, why did his best friend's dead wife have to pester him? She kept coming to him, insisting Kathleen was his soulmate. It was a load of nonsense, and he wouldn't have it. "I'm not talking to you, Sorcha."

The scent of oranges saturated the air around him, so overwhelming that it tickled the back of his throat. He started to cough. How she'd continued to smell like oranges as a spirit, he'd never know, but it had been her signature scent before she'd died in a senseless car accident over three years ago.

The scent didn't dissipate. No, it only seemed to grow stronger, like a million oranges had exploded around him. "Are you trying to kill me?" he accused between hacking up his lungs.

"That was for ignoring me the last two times I tried to talk to you," she said, narrowing her green eyes.

"Take a hint," he shot back. "*Go away.*"

"That won't be happening, Declan McGrath, even if you fell to your knees and begged me." She laughed heartily, her brown hair fluttering as if a gentle wind were ruffling it.

Only there wasn't any wind to speak of. He wasn't a man to grow faint—he was a butcher, wasn't he?—but he leaned against the nearest car in the lot as weakness overtook him. "Leave me alone, Sorcha."

"I knew this assignment might be one of my toughest, seeing how hardheaded you are, with a heart barred shut like an abandoned cottage. But I intend to help you and your soulmate come together, and I won't be denied."

"I don't want your help," he ground out. "And stop calling Kathleen O'Connor my soulmate. She's an incredible woman, I'll grant you, and I might be interested in her as any warm-blooded man would be, but that's all."

"If that were true, you wouldn't be afraid to kiss her again." She let out a royal snort. "Declan McGrath, I've known you since you were a boy. Will you deny that the only reason you fear being with Kathleen is that you know she is more than a mere object for slaking your lust?"

He was not going to admit that. Nor was he going to admit how much he'd enjoyed flirting with her before Eoghan interrupted them.

"I don't like you pushing me toward her. How do you claim to know such things? You're dead." He didn't care what the Irish tales said about ghosts and their uncanny ways. Those stories had never interested him.

"I'm dead, yes, but I know what's true." She reached for him, and he flinched as her hand passed through him.

"Jesus, stop that."

"I won't." Her chuckle was hair-raising. "I will pester you until you give in. You can ask Carrick. Didn't I help him find love again with Angie?"

He'd expected this argument. "I understand you wanting your husband to be happy again." He pressed a finger to his brow. "But why torture the rest of us?"

"Kade doesn't look tortured with his new wife, and your brother is happier than ever with Ellie, and that's saying something since he arrived in the world with a smile on his face."

Declan knew the tale. They'd been born minutes apart like most twins, but according to everyone in the delivery room, Brady had been smiling when he came out. Declan had never been as happy as his brother, sure, but his heartache had only made him more closed off. Humiliation did that to a man.

He pushed away from the car and stood tall in front of her. "You're wrong about me and Kathleen."

She grinned. "Then you've nothing to fear about becoming her fella."

He'd put his foot in the puddle, he surely had. "I don't

want to be anyone's fella, and I'm not sure she wants that either."

"Really? You didn't see the way she was looking at you? Like she wanted to devour you?"

His body reacted to that confirmation. He'd suspected she still wanted him. But they'd both undoubtedly considered the complications. Setting his heartbreak aside, he was Brady's brother, and if anything went wrong, it would be uncomfortable for everyone involved. "If we do anything—"

"Yes, *that* will definitely be on the agenda." She held up her hands and fire danced on her fingertips, making him step back. "Sparks fly between you. But your connection could run so much deeper, and that's what has you scared."

He glared at her.

Her face softened. "She made you laugh, Declan."

When she mimicked Kathleen's slashing motion, laughter tickled his throat again. "That doesn't prove anything."

"Name another woman who's done that. Certainly Morag never did."

No, she'd inflamed other senses, he could admit now, the kind that made a man lose his head. He didn't want to let that happen again.

"Ellie has, and my mum," he managed to say after the fire disappeared from her fingertips—saints preserve them.

"Those women aren't romantic interests." She patted his shoulder, although her touch didn't land. "You're being stubborn, but I expected it. Morag was a right bitch, and she hurt you terribly. Of course, I didn't know she'd slept with your old boxing nemesis back then although I suspected something along these lines. You didn't refute her story that she'd decided she wasn't ready for marriage and wanted to move to Dublin and work on her career."

"Perhaps that was part of the truth for her actions." He felt the weight of his friends guessing such things, but they'd known him well enough to not speak of it. "I want your word you won't speak of her betrayal."

"You have it." She only let out an exaggerated hum of a sound. "Carrick said to leave it be when you were hurt, but it's gone on long enough. It's time to put the past behind you. Consider me your helpful matchmaking ghost."

He only wanted to wake up from this nightmare. "I don't want any of this, dammit. Leave me alone."

She tapped his nose like she might have when they were kids, except her touch didn't land. "Like I told Carrick, we can do this the easy way, or we can do it the hard way. You know what I used to be capable of, Declan. Think of what I might do now that I'm a ghost."

That was a ball-shrinking thought if ever there was one. Sorcha Fitzgerald had been beautiful and bold, in her actions as much as her famous poems. She hadn't been one to mess with in life. He'd always loved that about her. But he had to push back. "She's not my soulmate."

Her lyrical humming seemed to echo in his bones. "Like I said, then it won't matter if you kiss her again...and more. Will it?"

She let the silence grow. He met her gaze dead-on. A smile curled her mouth and mischief filled her green eyes. He knew to brace himself.

"I don't like to show off, but you seem to bring it out in me." She laughed before raising a delicate brow. "Seamus is going to ask you tonight about buying the butcher shop in that roundabout way of his that used to drive me mad when he was my father-in-law."

The news was like a bucket of cold water. "No— He said he'd work forever."

Another laugh stole around him along with the scent of oranges, softer this time. "The string of retirements amongst his friends, your father included, has him thinking about a new path. Don't believe me? You will. Then maybe you'll have the sense to believe me about other things."

She disappeared.

He let himself sink against the car and wiped his brow. Seamus retiring? The man had said he'd cut meat until his hands withered or he was in the grave, whichever came first.

Declan wasn't prepared for this—financially or emotionally.

Carrick's father had been a beloved father figure growing up and then a mentor once Declan decided to give up boxing and settle down with Morag and have a family. Only Morag hadn't been ready to settle down—or so it seemed from her wild actions before their wedding.

Jimmy Slavin and Declan had been well matched since they'd first faced each other in the ring at eleven years of age. Only...Jimmy was willing to fight dirty—so much so that he'd seduced Morag before their last time in the ring, knowing it would give him the edge to beat Declan. Indeed, it had—it had broken Declan clean through. Jimmy had knocked him out in the first round, ending his boxing chapter in shameful failure.

Heartbreak and humiliation were bitter pills to swallow for any man.

He felt a chill as he thought about those dark days. Many said anger was hot, but Declan's never had been—his anger was like the ice along the shore in winter. He never wanted to experience anything like that again. With Kathleen, he felt a kind of unbalancing intensity, one he feared could lead him back to those frozen shores if he weren't careful.

What a tangle. He looked back at the pub. Well, he might as well go inside and face the music. Going home would be the coward's way.

He hoped Sorcha was wrong about Seamus. He wasn't ready for his life to change again. As for Kathleen, he still felt at sea. She was the powerful riptide, and he the boat.

He gave himself another moment, seeing as one woman had made him fake a phone call for peace while the other had made him lean against the nearest vehicle in weakness. Then he strode to the front door of the pub and let himself inside, wishing to wrap himself in the sense of home it always gave him. The familiarity of the pub gave him the balance he desperately craved.

Except comfort was the last thing on his mind when Kathleen's gusty laughter reached his ears. Something in his chest popped before a surge of warmth rose up inside him unbidden. Jesus, she had a great laugh. Sorcha's words resounded in his mind about her being the only woman who could make him laugh. More rubbish...although he couldn't deny he was back where he'd started, in her thrall.

"Hello, brother!" Brady cried as people he'd known all his life called out greetings to him. "'Bout time you arrived. The rippah—that's a party in Boston speak—has begun."

"*Slainte*," a chorus of familiar faces cried out, one of which belonged to Kathleen herself, grinning as she downed her whiskey.

A bunch of tables had been pushed together to create what looked like a head table. Kathleen was sitting at the end, surrounded by his friends, with Ellie on her right and Eoghan on her left.

At the next table sat his parents and their friends. When Declan lifted a hand in greeting, his dad raised his glass. Declan's mum, beside him, was knitting what looked to be a baby blue jumper, one of Brady's new girly cocktails in front of her. Next to them, Betsy O'Hanlon was holding court. She looked red in the face, likely about the arts center, something she was passionate about, God knew. Donal O'Dwyer was listening to her every word, a whiskey in hand. Killian and Nicola Donovan sat at the end of the table, their heads tilted together about something, and Seamus and his wife were planted in the middle. Declan sent him a wave in greeting, hoping again that Sorcha was wrong.

From there, the cluster of tables fanned out, every one of them packed, the pub as full as Declan had ever seen it. One thing was abundantly clear—everyone was fixated on Kathleen.

He couldn't fault them.

"Come pull up a chair," called Liam. He sat beside Jamie, one of the two Fitzgerald boys, the other being Carrick.

Carrick, whose first wife was haunting Declan.

"The new Yank is filling our heads with tales of Boston and the promise of unveiling her design for the arts center," Liam continued.

"I'm holding my very breath," Eoghan said, patting down the thin strips of his gray hair.

"Don't hold it too long or you'll be six feet under by the moon's rising," called out his cousin Fergus from his perch on the other side of Ellie.

Kathleen held his gaze for a moment—yes, he could both feel and see her siren's call—before she turned to Ellie and the two shared a laugh.

God, he was going to have to sit through this agony and pretend she didn't affect him. There only one thing for it. "Brady, I need a whiskey!" He grabbed a chair from the corner, scraping the floor, and brought it to the table.

Liam made room for the chair, and Carrick, leaning back to look at him, asked, "Why in the world were you working so late?"

For a moment Declan thought about telling him everything and asking him to get his first wife to leave him be, but that would only invite questions. "I was catching up with the ordering."

"*Ordering?*" Jamie slapped him on the back as he sat down next to him. "Dad would never want you to work so late, especially when there's a...what's the Boston word again?"

"A rippah," said their friend Kade, who sat across the table. His Yank accent was so bad it made his American wife laugh.

"That's about as bad as my Irish accent," Megan declared.

"What Irish accent?" Angie asked with a chuckle. "Megan, you've got to try and talk like the female version of Mark Wahlberg."

"I love Mark Wahlberg!" she exclaimed, her face brightening. "He was so good in *Good Will Hunting*."

Kathleen barked out a laugh as Angie groaned, saying, "That was Matt Damon, Megan."

"It was?" her sister asked, this time prompting Kathleen and a few others to start laughing.

"Donal," Bets cried out from the other table, jostling him playfully. "You lived in Boston for a year—"

"Ages ago," Donal said, already shaking his head. "No, for the love of God, don't ask me to do the accent. No offense, Kathleen, but when I was a server there in my youth, sometimes I had to ask people to point to a menu

them as he signaled to Brady at the end of the bar. "I wonder what our girl Sorcha will be up to now that she's seen Brady settled with his soulmate."

Declan hissed. "Enough of that talk." Sometimes his friend's Yoda act made him want to bash his head against a wall.

Jamie's earnest eyes widened. "With that tone, I'm half-afraid you're going to make me stay after school, Declan, and I'm the teacher here. Why are you so cross? Don't you want the new Yank to like you?"

Liam fingered his gold pirate earring. "I imagine you'll come to the way of things, Jamie boy. Now, let's do as Declan says. He knows his own mind."

With Liam, there was always a hidden message under a comment like that. "You have something more to say?"

Brady slid three whiskeys toward them. Throwing a thanks his way, Liam turned back to Declan. "With a new whiskey in our hands, I might wax poetic about the knowing of one's heart, but in your mood, you'd as soon knock me out."

"You have the way of it," Declan said, lifting his drink to them and then downing it.

Another waft of oranges tickled his nose, and he sneezed, kicking off a herald of Gaelic and other blessings for his health and good fortune.

"You should see your face," Liam said, chortling. "I'm guessing Sorcha wanted the last word. On that note, I'll take myself back to the crash course in Boston slang. Come on, Jamie."

But Jamie continued to stand there, empty drink in hand, his eyes wide as he studied Declan. "You mean you're next? Sorcha's here for *you*? Jesus, Mary, and Joseph. She's gone mad after the dying then."

Liam laughed and then covered it with a cough. "Jamie, let's be off before Declan grinds down all his teeth and has to subsist on baby food for the rest of his days. Declan, when you're in the mood to talk, you know where I live."

Declan only shook his head while Jamie said, "That's a good bit of *craic*, it is, Liam, seeing as how he lives with you," as they walked away.

Brady slid back in front of him and refilled his glass. "I would have brought your whiskey."

He didn't need to tell his brother he was impatient. Everyone said he'd been born that way. He certainly didn't feel like telling him why. "You have your hands full."

"Come on. Back to your seat. I have something in mind."

Declan took himself to the head table of sorts, glaring at Liam, who was grinning like a smug old codger. Brady topped off Kathleen's drink, then Ellie's, then a few of the other people who sat closest to them. By God, but Kathleen had a way about her. Everyone was eating out of her gorgeous hand. Himself included.

"A toast to our new friend, Kathleen O'Connor," Brady called out. "May her happiness here be long and her friends be many."

"Thanks, Brady," she said, rising and kissing his cheek. "That's a beautiful toast."

Everyone took a drink.

"To having my best friend in the wonderful village of Caisleán," Ellie added, making the whole crowd cheer.

Those who hadn't already downed their drinks took another sip.

"To all you beautiful people for welcoming me with such kindness, and to all the possibilities in this beautiful place," Kathleen said, a challenge in her smoldering eyes as she gazed at Declan. His heart sped up at the look. "*Slainte*."

"*Slainte*," everyone echoed before downing the last of their drink.

Conversation and laughter sparked all around the room after that. Brady pulled Ellie out of her chair, only to settle her onto his lap as he poured more whiskey for the group closest to him.

Kathleen leaned her elbows on the table. "So I have a question. I've never lived on my own before, and Irish cottages have a reputation for being haunted. Who's on speed dial if a ghost starts to howl outside my window?"

Declan jolted in his chair.

Would Sorcha do such a thing? Surely not...

"We can't have you fearing for your life and not sleeping, Kathleen," Brady said, making a face. "What kind of friends would we be? You should stay at Summercrest Manor with us."

Declan almost fell off his chair.

"That would be awesome!" Ellie exclaimed, turning to her friend, who only blinked. "I'd be the happiest girl in the world."

"Making you happy is my daily joy, *a stór*," Brady continued.

Declan's head started to pound.

Kathleen's face remained neutral as she picked up her whiskey and took a long pull. She appeared to be biding her time.

"You *do* have plenty of room," Jamie said, glancing from Brady to Declan, then Liam.

"We have the room and more," Liam confirmed, biting his lip. "I'm sure all of us would love to have another roommate at Summercrest."

For God's sake. His friends were trying to set him up, weren't they?

Everyone turned and looked at him, Kathleen included. He gazed at her, trying to discern her thoughts.

"And you, Ace?" she said with a gleam in her eyes. "You want me to stay there too?"

He was stuck and he knew it. To refuse would be the rudest of gestures.

He never should have gotten out of bed this morning. Hell, he shouldn't have stayed late at the butcher shop so he could catch Kathleen the moment she arrived at the pub. He'd have done better to go home and watch a fight on the telly.

The smell of oranges tickled his nose again, pushing him to answer, which only made him compress his lips together.

The entire table was staring at him, and he knew it. He coughed to clear his throat.

"Oh, don't stress yourself out, Ace," Kathleen said with an edge.

Give a man a chance to form his own mind!

Wanting her was one thing. Having her sleeping under his very roof when he wanted to *sleep* with her wasn't a mere idle request. She damn well knew it.

Someone kicked him under the table. He jolted.

Her luscious mouth curved. "It's a sweet offer, you guys, but I've been dreaming about living in my own quaint Irish cottage ever since I decided to come here."

"You have?" Ellie asked.

A look passed between them, and then Ellie nodded enthusiastically. "Right. Of course. I mean, after apartment living in Boston, who wouldn't want their own cottage?"

In that instant he felt certain she hadn't wanted to stay

at Summercrest any more than he'd wanted her there. Maybe he'd misread her. Maybe she didn't want to follow through on this mad force between them.

Why did that make him want to growl?

Enough of this madness. He needed to go home.

But Brady caught him as he pushed out of his chair. Leading him over to the bar, he said, "Let me pour you another drink, brother."

After ducking under the bar top, Brady did just that and then leaned on the wood. "How could you be rude to Kathleen? You should have told her you'd roll out the welcome mat to have her come stay at Summercrest Manor. That woman is the best friend and sister of the woman I'm marrying."

Clearly Ellie hadn't told Brady what had happened between him and Kathleen. That was a relief. Since Ellie had run off earlier, he assumed she knew about it. Still, his brother was right. He'd been rude. "I'm sorry," he said softly.

"Good," Brady said, pouring himself a drink and lifting it in his direction as an olive branch. "I mean, you might be sullen lately, but this was unlike you. I couldn't reason a cause."

The scent of oranges surrounded him again. Wouldn't you know...

Brady's brows shot to his hairline. "*Oh, Jesus!*" he exclaimed, glancing around. "Sorcha's been seeing you? But that's wonderful! You and—"

"She's wrong," Declan declared flatly.

"*But she's never wrong,*" his brother shot back.

Just then, Seamus came up behind Declan and put an arm around his back. "The McGrath men seem to be making a lot of changes these days," he said in a booming voice. "First, your dad, and now your brother. Have you thought about what might be next for you, Declan?"

His legs turned to jelly. *Jesus*. Sorcha had the way of it. For a moment, Declan could have sworn he heard the ghost's laughter.

Brady only smiled and wandered off, humming a romantic ballad.

Declan wanted to bash his head against the pub wall.

"You know I love the shop and all," Seamus continued, "but a man can't work forever, can he? Well, he can, but me and Brigid might be wanting some of the fun the others are having, the ones who are retiring, your dad and mum included. You know how much we love going to Portugal for the sun."

Every Irish person longed for the sun—complaining, rightfully so, that they never saw enough of it at home. "You should do what you want, Seamus. Of course."

"I know you just bought Summercrest Manor, but I'd work with you as best I could—if you had the mind for taking over."

His bank account was as light as a feather right now. "I'd find a way to pay you what it was worth." He braced his knees and said what needed saying. "If you wanted to sell the shop to me."

"It's been my dream to turn it over to you since you first started working with me," Seamus said, gripping his shoulder. "It's proud I am to do so, you being like a son to me."

His throat clogged with emotion. This was really happening.

"I'll find the money, Seamus. That's fair. You think up a price."

The man nodded, his round face split with a wide grin. "Good, good!" He paused, giving him a sly glance.

"You know... I was chatting with Cormac earlier this week."

Declan waited. There was nothing unusual in talking to Cormac. Only he wasn't just a villager. He was the local bookie.

"He mentioned the county boxing scene could use a fresh injection of competition."

Declan's heart about exploded in his chest. Jesus, to step into the ring again. It had been right for him to stop at the time, but he'd missed it something fierce. At first, he'd planned to give it up for Morag and the family they'd spoken of. After, he hadn't wanted to face the ring or Jimmy, or all the chattering about his humiliating loss. Things like that tended to stick for a time.

But Jimmy was still in Dublin, so they wouldn't meet. If he only did it awhile, strictly local matches...that would be like heaven. He missed it, so much so he'd wake from dreams of being in the ring, expecting to have his boxing gloves on.

Nothing satisfied his body in the same way, except sex.

Seamus clapped him on the back. "A few good purses—"

"Would give me enough—"

"To buy my shop." He gripped his shoulder. "You think on it."

Seamus had worked this all out, the whole angle about the boxing. Emotion clawed hard at Declan's heart. Even in this, Seamus was helping him find his way.

But by God, was he crazy for thinking he could fight competitively anymore? He was thirty-three now. He hadn't fought in five years. He hadn't even worked out beyond some running and lifting sides of beef at the shop and punching them when no one was around.

"Maybe I've been out of the game too long," Declan said, all while his heart drummed in his chest.

"The club will get you ready with a fierce training regimen, don't worry. We'll all take part." Seamus steered him toward the table where his parents and their friends sat. "How about we start tomorrow? Five o'clock suit you?"

He said it as if the others knew what he meant. Had the older crowd had a meeting with him as the main agenda?

Declan's dad looked up and grinned at him. Yes, he knew. From the smiles on Killian's and Donal's faces, along with some of the others, he was sure they were all co-conspirators.

"Why didn't you just put your gloves on and knock me out, Seamus?" Declan managed with a laugh. "My God, man!"

Seamus' mouth twisted. "When I saw the way your face lit up at the mention of fighting again, I knew you still loved it. Come. Let's have a whiskey."

"I probably shouldn't have more. I'll be training." And just like that, he was a boxer again.

Seamus grinned and then shouted for everyone to hear, "Declan's going back to boxing. And the lot of us old bastards are going to help him train."

"Hurray!" a number of patrons called out.

"Cormac," his father called, loud enough to be heard over the hushed conversations, "I'll be making the first bet on my son's first boxing match."

Someone took Declan's hand and pressed a whiskey into it—Liam, wide-eyed and smiling. "Jesus, Declan, when you jump into it, you do so with both feet. First Kathleen and now this? You're in for a wild ride of transformation, my friend. It's lucky I am to be alongside you for it."

Oh, Yoda, he thought. *I might end up in your meditation room at this rate.*

"Here's to Declan taking life by the horns," Seamus said, lifting his whiskey. "*Slainte.*"

Declan's eyes tracked to Kathleen. She lifted hers—a trace of amusement and admiration in her gaze—and finished her drink. He couldn't ignore the toast or the challenge. Bad luck came from such things. He downed his whiskey.

He could feel the pull to go to her, to pour her another whiskey—hell, to pull her onto his lap and feel her body against him.

He ignored it.

As the villagers went around and congratulated him for reentering boxing, he was swept away. Inside Declan, the burn of old ice was receding, replaced with a new warmth he barely recognized: an excitement for life and hope for the future.

Then a gusty spark of her laughter rocked him down to his toes, and he was sure the earth had shifted underneath him. Everything that had been up was down.

Sorcha had been right about Seamus.

His heart raced as the next question arose in his mind: *was* she right about Kathleen?

CHAPTER THREE

Bets knew boxing fever when she saw it.

Donal's deliciously muscled body—a body she quite enjoyed—fairly pulsed with it. She couldn't wait to get him home tonight. The air in the pub was charged with an exciting energy that translated very happily into the bedroom. At the moment, they needed a boost. In the bedroom and out of it. Since his retirement and their talk about keeping things as they were for the time being—not moving in together and not getting married—they'd been listing a little. Maybe this would help.

"I believe we've found another way to keep ourselves occupied during the day," Donal said to the other men at their table as people in the pub continued to congratulate Declan. "And... The women will be delighted we have another part of our retirement figured out."

Bets glanced at her fellow Lucky Charms, and they made sure to roll their eyes in unison. "I thought you guys already had your retirement figured out. You've sure said so often enough."

"Yes," Gavin said with a rude sound. "But when I look

over my shoulder, I can still see the bumps in the proverbial road. With Declan fighting again, we'll have more hours to fill our days. Linc is going to be pleased to hear this news when he returns from his business in the States, completely retired as well. Maybe he'll even join us for the training."

Bets didn't want Linc focused on boxing training. She wanted him to concentrate on the arts center, her baby. Ever since she'd first come up with the idea of opening the arts center, it had given her new purpose. Although the men around her were talking about retiring, as far as she was concerned, she was just getting started with finding a purpose outside of being a wife and a mother.

Nothing was going to get in the way of that. And despite some opposition from her sister-in-law and nemesis, Mary Kincaid, and Mary's minions, one of whom was head of the county council, nothing had.

The Sorcha Fitzgerald Arts Center had grown to a level she'd only dreamed about, and she was going to make sure the ship kept running, so to speak. Linc had promised to help them further operationalize the trust they'd set up for his daughter's million-euro donation. They now had tons of money, which brought a slew of new possibilities as well as legal issues that boggled her mind.

Linc was an expert in such things, having been involved with numerous art establishments over the years. She needed him to make the center everything it could be. The men were not going to distract him with their testosterone-driven training plans.

"I'm not sure Linc has ever boxed. I just don't see him doing that." She wouldn't say he had more sense than to get his face bashed in.

"Ellie, girl," Gavin shouted to the next table. "Did your dad ever box?"

Leave it to Gavin to check. Bets held her breath.

Ellie broke off her conversation with Kathleen at the next table, turning toward them. "Not that I know of. Why?"

"They're wanting to punch his face in," Bets joked, finally able to laugh about it now that the danger was over. "Go back to talking with Kathleen. I'll be over in a while to chat. These men are plotting more of their retirement."

Ellie brightened. "That's great news!"

Truthfully, it was. Mostly. Bets and her other friends had been worried about the men wanting to up and retire without a plan. Visions of them sitting around with nothing to do, wanting to be entertained and waited on, had sent them all into a frenzy.

Frank discussions had been had, and Bets and Donal had almost split over it. But now the men all understood the need to have things to do, hobbies included. Linc, being from the States—where planning for retirement was more of a norm—had further helped them, thank God.

"I know you have your boxing club," Bets reasoned, laying a hand on Donal's arm, "and helping Declan is further motivation. But do you really envision punching each other until you're Eoghan's age?"

She and the other women had discussed it before, and they'd envisioned it as a man's club where they hung out while strutting around in boxing gloves and their green boxing robes, crowing like roosters.

Every male at the table stared at her before Donal said, "What do you mean? My father and his cousin, Fergus, and a few others still get into the ring."

"*At his age?*" Bets was sure her voice carried. This was news!

"It's good for him," Donal said, and the other men

46

nodded briskly. "It's like Roberto 'Hands of Stone' Duran said, 'Getting hit motivates me.'"

Seriously? This was how men thought? Bets had three boys, and she still didn't understand men sometimes.

"I've always liked the quote by James Corbett," Seamus said, hooking his hands on his sweater. "'To become a champion, fight one more round.'"

She and the Lucky Charms shared another look. Yes, these were their men, God help them. At least they'd be doing some good, helping Declan come out of retirement.

"Maybe you aren't wired to understand it, Bets." Donal patted her arm. "This is men stuff."

What could she do but nod? Some women would probably understand, but she wasn't one of them. "Carry on," she told them.

Donal laughed. "So it's agreed then. We'll all help with Declan's training. Gavin, you're the best at footwork. Seamus and I can handle the punching. My dad will have something to add, I'm sure. After all, he taught me. Killian, I know you'll still be raising your horses, not in full retirement like the rest of us, but you're a model at the proper stance."

"He's never going to give up the farm," Nicola said, some aggrievement in her tone, no surprise.

"But I'm cutting back my hours and hiring another trainer, so I should be able to help some," Killian said before looking pointedly at his wife. "And you, my dear, had promised to give more work to our beautiful daughter with the plan to let her run the bookshop in a year or so."

Bets waited for this response. All of the women save Brigid Fitzgerald, who'd worked her whole life as a teacher, had been out of the work force until after their children were raised. Bets wasn't the only one who wasn't ready to give up her purpose.

Nicola's eyes narrowed. "We'll be seeing when the time is right for me to make those changes at One More Chapter, Killian Donovan. I did call it that for a reason."

Bets wanted to yell *Amen*.

Gavin tilted his head to the right, where Siobhan sat beside him. "That's what this one said about cutting down her hours at her and Bets' knitting shop and hiring another helper. The only thing that makes her contemplate taking time off is—"

"Portugal," Seamus said with a laugh. "I was just saying as much to Declan. Every Irishman loves to go there for vacation."

Bets didn't. She and Bruce had gone with the others a couple of times, and sure, it had beat cold, rainy Irish days. But they'd stuck to tourist sites and beaches, and something had been missing. Art and culture, she now realized.

"I dream about the hot sun on the beaches," Brigid said with a sigh.

"Me too," Nicola said, closing her eyes a moment as if the sun itself was on her face. "And then there's the wine and the food."

"Bets dreams about Paris," Donal said, putting his hand on her knee and squeezing it. "We still haven't found the time to get to Paris, have we, Bets? Every time I ask, she says she's too busy with the center. I don't know how Linc convinced her to go the first time."

He knew how busy things had been. "I didn't know Linc was taking me to Paris. It was supposed to be a simple dinner."

Linc had suggested dinner spontaneously, and she'd gone along, little expecting what he had in mind. She hadn't realized he was interested in her, but thank God that was behind them. Linc was just a friend, and Donal had come to consider him one too. In fact, one of the things on their to-do list was finding Linc the love of his life, a tall task seeing as he had three ex-wives.

But they'd find her for him. The local matchmaking ghost Sorcha was on their side.

"Maybe I need Linc to corral you to go again," Donal said, pinching her playfully in the side. "I could probably handle him coming to Paris with us since I'm the one you'd be going back to the hotel with."

Oh, these men and their posturing.

"That's my cue to go talk to Kathleen," Bets said, rising. "Her shipment didn't come in today. That's the fourth day I've been at that company to have her stuff delivered."

"You know how things are here," Gavin said. "Even the alcohol isn't always delivered on time, and this is Ireland."

"Yes, if the alcohol is late in this country, there's no hope," she said in an aggrieved voice and went over to join Ellie and Kathleen.

"The life of the party arrives at last," Ellie said, leaning over to kiss Bets' cheek as she lowered into a chair next to them. Kathleen sent her a smile.

"Dad texted earlier. He's coming back in a few days, and he wanted me to ask if you need anything from Paris? He didn't think Donal would mind."

So Donal wasn't the only one who intended to keep bringing that up. Bets decided to laugh. *If you can't beat them, join them.* "Tell your dad to bring some arnica cream for the men. They have boxing fever."

"I thought they were only going to train Declan," Ellie said with wide eyes. "Aren't they a little old to be boxing?"

"They're Irish, girl," Eoghan said, leaning his elbows on the table. "It runs in our blood. And don't be insulting men

49

of a certain age. Fergus and I still get into the ring from time to time and go at each other."

"You do?" Ellie's shock was as evident as Bets' had been.

Eoghan and Fergus both put up their fists and grinned like loons. "We do!"

"That's wicked cool," Kathleen said with a laugh. "I'd pay good money to see you two fight."

"That can be arranged, dear Kathleen," Eoghan said, patting her hand. "At the club, we mostly spend our time chatting, dancing around in the ring—"

"And drinking," Bets and Fergus said at the same time.

"It's easier to take a punch in the face if you've had a whiskey," Eoghan said philosophically. "I'll be sure to remind Declan of that."

"Go off and tell him now before you forget," Bets told the older man with a wink. "I want to talk to Kathleen without you interrupting."

"Me interrupting?" He waved a dismissive hand at her and made a rude sound. "I don't know what she means, Fergus."

"I do, cousin," he said with a snort. "You suck up more air than a vacuum some days. Let's leave the women be and go speak of our grand Irish boxing traditions with Cormac and the others."

"God help us, but it will keep the men occupied, which is what we wanted," Bets said as she took Eoghan's vacated chair. "Now... I'm sorry your things haven't come yet, Kathleen. I've been at the delivery company for days."

"I told her, Bets." Ellie grabbed a sweat-lined water glass devoid of its former ice. "She's trying to live in the moment, but I know my girl. The minute we stop partying, she'll be at her work calendar, fretting over timelines."

Kathleen pursed her lips before saying, "It *is* a big

project for four months. I had it laid out to my last day here."

"We'll make it work," Bets said, giving her a reassuring smile. "And if you need to stay longer to finish, we have the money. No need to ask the Arts Council for more."

Ellie and Kathleen shared a look before her new artist said, "It's not that I don't appreciate that, but I don't want to delay my return for too long. My pop is getting up there, and while he won't admit it, he's slowing down. Plus, my brothers will be as lost without me as I am without them, although we'd all rather have our faces bashed in than cop to that."

"Kathleen is the only girl," Ellie said, resting a hand on her friend's arm. "They're a tight family."

"I probably wouldn't have come if Ellie weren't here," Kathleen said, nudging her friend gently with a smile.

Bets nodded, thinking they sounded like a real nice family, the O'Connors. "Understood. We'll figure it out. Is there anything else I can get you as we wait?"

"Some sheet metal and a hammer?" Kathleen said, miming the action of it pounding on the table. "I'm joking. Mostly. I've finalized my design, as you know. When do you want me to share it with the village? There was some talk of doing it tonight, and Brady has the printout in the back."

"Let's do it," Bets said, her feet tapping under the table as excitement rushed through her.

"Right now?" Kathleen asked with shining eyes.

"There's no time like the present." Bets stood up and clapped her hands until the talking died down. "If you have a minute, Kathleen would like to share her design with everyone. This is something we've never done before, but given that she's locked and loaded, we thought it might be fun to get the village excited. Hint: I think you're going to love it."

Kathleen's chair scraped the pub's ancient floor as she rose. "Since I was lucky enough to have a back door into your village, so to speak, through Ellie, I talked with some of you about what made Ireland great. What symbols or figures loom large. This country has one of the most powerful reputations for magic, as you all know."

"Did they suggest the fairies to you?" someone called out.

She didn't miss a beat before saying, "They did, but I thought you might want a bigger metal sculpture than a mere sewing thimble."

People roared with laughter, and Bets found herself charmed. She'd only met Kathleen once in person before—when the young woman had flown in briefly for the reception celebrating Ellie's donation to the center—but they'd talked on the phone and emailed back and forth. The young woman was snarky and no-nonsense, and Bets was delighted to have her with them, if only for a short time.

When the crowd quieted again, Kathleen continued. "A leprechaun seemed too obvious and a giant shillelagh sticking out of the earth, well... Too phallic." She winked, sending them into fits of laughter again. "The one thing people kept coming back to were the days of the pirates. Not far from here is the home of the female legend, Grace O'Malley, as you know, and I got to thinking... Wouldn't it be a wicked pissah if I built a pirate ship with the Irish sea cresting at her hull for all to see?"

There was a stunned silence.

"I have the drawing right here," Brady declared, crossing to her with the rolled-up design in hand.

When she unrolled it, a few people gasped while others

got soft smiles on their faces. Someone started humming an old pirate shanty Bets' boys had loved to sing growing up.

"I can already see it rising above the ground, dear Kathleen," Eoghan cried out, pressing his hand to his chest in his charming dramatic way. "It's going to be grand, girl. Thank you for bringing it to our village. In fact, let's thank all our Yanks for coming to Ireland and bringing their artistry with them."

He started to applaud and others joined in, until the whole pub was rocking with clapping and whistling.

Bets didn't get emotional too often, but her throat thickened as she cheered with the others. This was another reason she loved these people.

"All our resident artists," Bets called, gesturing to them. "Stand up!"

They all rose, Megan blushing, Ellie wiping tears, and Angie softly smiling, her arm resting on Carrick's shoulder. Kathleen, though, grinned like the Boston Red Sox had just won the pennant.

When she'd first thought of starting an arts center in the middle of the countryside in County Mayo, Bets had hoped for this kind of influx of new people and ideas and art, knowing the teaching of it would be a gift to the area as much as the art created.

Not even a year later, the arts center exceeded her every imagining. That was also something she wanted to talk to Linc about when he returned. What more could they do here in Caisleán? As far as she was concerned, after Ellie's gift, the sky was the limit. Still, she didn't fool herself into thinking her nemesis, Mary Kincaid, had given up her one-woman mission to destroy the center. Her kind didn't like to admit defeat.

"It's quite a moment, isn't it?"

She turned her head as Liam put his arm around her. Her son had encouraged her through it all. "Yes, it sure is. I've never been happier."

He kissed her cheek. "If you ever wonder if the Universe is working, you have only to look at your own journey. First, you had the vision of opening an arts center, and then Angie lost her job in Baltimore when the funding was cut. She brought Megan along to help her with her grief over losing her husband. And then Ellie came along and up and gave the center a million euros. Today we have Kathleen, the newest resident, announcing a grand pirate ship to be built for all to behold. Not bad, Mum."

Of course, all three women had met their beloveds and would be staying, which suggested they'd been meant to be here in some cosmic way. Bets wondered what might be in store for Kathleen. Or if Sorcha would be involved.

Playfully tugging on the gold earring everyone joked made him look like he himself was a pirate, she smiled. "Thanks for the reminder and for helping yourself. You've been there from the beginning, cleaning out the first shed we used."

"I still shudder when I think of the mess of cobwebs," he replied with a chuckle. His mouth tipped up a little more. "I have a feeling this party is going to go well into the night. I hope you're up for it."

She cocked her hip. "When the time's right, the Lucky Charms will show you just how much."

"I love seeing you happy, Mum. Come on. I'll buy you one of Brady's new cocktails."

He ordered the drink for her, and Bets grabbed his hand, awash in that messy feeling of loving her son to distraction. Liam wasn't just her son, though. He was also her friend and teacher, and she was more than grateful for that too.

She sipped her cosmopolitan after Brady finally set it in front of her, looking a little harried. There was a crush at the bar, and Bets thought he could use a second bartender in such a moment—she recognized the rhythm from her own bartending days over thirty years ago—but Brady would figure out his own way of doing things.

They all were.

Declan was to box again, and sure enough, he was surrounded by Donal and the other men. She was sure they were talking up a storm. After the ups and downs with both the center and her new relationship with Donal, she would be glad for some easy sailing. Like the vision of Kathleen's soaring pirate ship.

When Bets smelled oranges, she lifted her glass and made a silent toast to Sorcha, the namesake for the arts center.

Someone was looking out for them, after all.

They were in good hands.

CHAPTER FOUR

E llie was a doll! When Kathleen stumbled into the cottage's tiny kitchen the next morning in desperate need of caffeine, she discovered her bestie had stocked the cupboard with her favorite coffee.

Kathleen didn't get choked up too often but seeing that touch of home grabbed her by the throat as much as the handwritten note taped over the orange Dunkin' Donuts bag.

While it won't be the same, this original blend should do the trick. BTW, I'm glad you're here.

Helping her shake off that crazy rush of emotions was another note on a clear glass pot with some kind of plunger.

Boil water. Dump grounds. Two inches. Pour water to half. Wait two minutes. Press plunger down and pour. Have fun with your first French press!

She planned to. God, she needed coffee. She had a good

head for whiskey and beer, thank God, or she might be sporting a headache. The rippah had run until three in the morning. Most of the villagers had gone home by then, but Ellie and Brady and most of their friends, plus Bets and Donal and some of theirs, had stayed until the end. So had Eoghan and Fergus, who'd slapped their wrinkled cheeks repeatedly to stay awake and waved off suggestions they seek their beds.

Declan had left around midnight with many of the others, citing boxing training. Her skin tightened, thinking about him. She'd dreamed about him. They'd been walking on a wild swath of beach. Upon awakening, she'd had the feeling he was still holding her hand.

She shivered again.

That wasn't mere lust. That was romance.

"Dammit," she said out loud.

Kissing someone was one thing. Holding hands implied a relationship.

They were *not* going to have a relationship.

While it was sweet of her friend and Brady and even Liam to invite her to stay with them at Summercrest, there was no way she'd take them up on it. She'd told Ellie as much when they'd gone to the pub's bathroom after that weird exchange. If she and Declan *did* get it on, they needed to keep things separate, including separate residences.

After the disastrous end to her six-year relationship with Axl two years ago, she'd kept things light with men. While she was wiser now than she'd been at twenty, when she and Axl first got together, she still didn't want to take another deep dive. Her two divorced brothers agreed with her.

Love was good when it was good, but when it went bad,

there was little worse. Only losing her mother to cancer so young had been worse.

She didn't do bad or worse anymore—if she could avoid it.

Enjoyment. Pleasure. Respect. Those she could do.

After last night, she still wasn't sure what Declan wanted. But he was clearly interested in *something*. She'd think about that later though. Right now, she needed coffee.

She ripped open the Dunkin' Donuts bag and followed Ellie's directions. The plunger was harder to work than she thought, and in her force, some of the hot liquid gushed out of the pot. But she didn't care. The smell of roasted beans and caramel and vanilla filled her senses, and soon she had a cup poured and was searching for the sugar and the cream. The local cream had a thick top on it, almost like ice cream, which Kathleen imagined meant it was closer to the cow than the kind she had in Boston.

Closing her eyes, she savored the taste of her doctored coffee, only for homesickness to smack her in the face. She told herself it was natural, but the feeling was almost painful. On a morning like this back in Boston, she'd text her brothers to see which of them were up and about, and they'd make a coffee run and hang out.

She walked into the next room, the silence a new sound to her. The tiny parlor didn't inspire much comfort. She found her phone on the small dining room table in the corner with its cushioned benches.

She had a 'how're ya doing' text from Robbie, along with the craziest request. *Take pictures of your doors.*

She shot back a snarky reply. *You develop a door fetish?*

Three dots showed he was typing. It was the middle of the night back home, but she wasn't surprised he'd added her to his emergency list—the numbers allowed to contact him even if his phone was on silent mode. Oh, jeez. She wouldn't text him again his time in the middle of the night. *No fetish. I want to see your locks.*

She should have known. Still, she was going to tease him. *Ellie says everyone leaves their doors unlocked here.*

His response was immediate and typical: *No.*

God, she loved that moron.

Then another text: *Don't make me track down an Irish locksmith.*

He would do it too, likely through Ellie. That was her life. Her brothers pestered her. She snarked back. Usually they got their way because they were being protective. That was their version of love, Pop always told her. She needed to accept it. After all, hadn't she been born as the only girl in a family of tough guys? She couldn't disagree.

Instead, she rose and took photos of her doors.

Robbie replied he was satisfied with her locks for now and going back to bed. When he sent a heart emoji and told her Pop missed her, she got a little teary-eyed. Pop wasn't a texter. They'd agreed she'd talk with the entire family every other Sunday, after family dinner at the house. Everyone religiously showed up, even in a blizzard armed with snow shovels. Those were great days, actually, with snowball fights and roughhousing and Irish coffees to stave off the cold.

God, she was getting maudlin. She was in Ireland! She'd had the time of her life last night. Today, Ellie and Brady were going to take her sightseeing around Westport, a big local tourist draw, and more interesting to her, the former pirate stronghold where Grace O'Malley had reigned. More inspiration for her work.

It was after nine, and with no text yet from Ellie, Kathleen imagined her friend was sleeping in or enjoying a morning romp with her fiancé, as she should.

She stole over to the front window, noting the pouring rain. The wind was a lively force, making the ivy-ridden tree branches undulate like a belly dancer. Green was everywhere, mixed with the gunmetal gray sky. Weirdest of all, there wasn't a soul in sight. No cars honking. No person jawing at someone for double-parking on the street.

Last night, she'd been so tired she'd practically fallen face-first into bed after taking off her clothes. She hadn't noticed the quiet. This morning, the sense of remoteness was a pointed reminder that she'd come to a different world.

City girl that she was, she was eager to explore it. She would manage the homesickness.

Her ears cocked as a car pulled to a stop in front of her cottage. She took a few steps toward the window. Declan emerged.

She almost spilled her coffee.

He had on his leather bomber jacket, and while the rain fell on him, he didn't run. No, he stalked to her front door and pounded instead.

Looking down at her old Patriots sweatshirt and lacy red boy shorts, she thought, *oh what the hell*. He was the one showing up early at her cottage. She hadn't expected any visitors but Ellie or Brady.

She swung the door open, wincing as rain splattered her face and cold rushed over her legs. "I'd say don't wake the neighbors with your pounding, but there aren't any. I guess you'd better come in since it's pouring, but you should know, I'm not sure I'm happy to see you this early."

She was such a liar.

He shut and latched the door after they stepped inside. "Seeing you in that outfit, I'm glad I decided to run over here this morning after some early training. Is that lace on your shorts?"

His hand skimmed her thighs, and she swatted it away as her body flushed with heat. They needed some ground rules. "What are you doing here, Declan?"

He sniffed the air. "You have coffee. It's an Irish custom to offer someone a cup."

She devoured him with her eyes, the slightly dripping hair now jet black, the smoldering blue eyes with long lashes now framed with mist, and the positively wicked curve of his mouth that made her think of kisses. His kisses. "I'm American. We only offer coffee to our friends."

"That's why I'm here. We need to be friends. Whether we do more is something we both need to consider. Hard. We should talk about that kiss, Kathleen."

He didn't sound too happy about it, so she went with snark. "What kiss?" she quipped, laughing as his face darkened. "Oh, *that* kiss! You want to do it again?"

He scowled, looking very much like the sullen man Ellie had described to her. "I tossed and turned all night. I still haven't decided."

"*Seriously?*" She nudged him with her hand like she would the boys back home. Not a thing a girl wanted to hear.

"We don't have the time or luxury to hedge." He blew out a harsh breath. "Not after last night. Yes, I've thought about it, since practically the moment your lips left mine. I've had the day of your return firmly in my mind. Every morning I tore aside the day on the calendar at the butcher counter and thought of you."

She locked her jaw so her mouth wouldn't gape. "You still don't look happy about it. Did it unsettle you too much, Ace?"

His level stare made her smile.

"All right, I'll throw you a bone. You're a butcher, after all."

He didn't blink at her humor.

She steeled herself for honesty. "That kiss unsettled me too, and I've thought about you. I'm tempted by the pleasure, but I want to bypass anything too intense. I'm not into discomfort anymore."

His rude sound filled the air. "Your *Heartbreak* series is a study of discomfort, is it not? The metal men and women are all twisted together with hard edges and agonizing expressions."

Color her surprised. "I had something to express, and I expressed it. Kind of my way of doing a post-breakup purge."

His dimples flashed—God, he had dimples! They'd transformed him in an instant to the boy next door. Her heart up and sighed on her. She had her weaknesses, God knew, and they included Dunks coffee, cuddly puppies, and bad boys with dimples.

Shit.

She was doomed.

"The purge, eh? I like that. When my ex tossed my heart to the crocodiles, I worked like a dog and thought things not fit for polite company."

She admired his honesty. Some tough guys—her brothers included—wouldn't cop to being hurt. "I like that image. It's fitting. I won't lie. I had some thoughts about taking my blowtorch to my ex's unmentionables. It's how my design for the series came together in the beginning." But after she'd pounded out the anger, she'd dropped into the hurt—and ultimately the healing.

His blue eyes fired. "Are you over him?"

She didn't need to think about it. She'd searched her heart every day for a year to finally have her *I'm over him* victory. She didn't think about Axl anymore, and oh how that would piss him off. "Who?"

He laughed, the sound dark and rich like an Irish coffee. Speaking of which, she should probably pour him a cup...as soon as she managed to look away. She was riveted by the change his humor brought to him. His blue eyes had turned cerulean. The hard edges of his face had softened. Not all tough guys had humor, and she found that attractive.

Just like that, he'd become less like a hot guy to drool over and more like someone she wanted to know better.

Double shit.

"You're funny, Yank. Not too many people make me laugh."

His voice held a rueful note. Yeah, she was becoming a person to him too. "Are you over her?"

The humor drained from his face. "Hard to answer. Do I still love Morag? No."

Morag? That was a name for the ages. "But?"

He rubbed the back of his neck. "The wreckage she left isn't completely gone, and that makes me terribly cross."

"Scar tissue takes a while to heal—"

"It's always there," he finished with quiet determination.

"Sometimes it fades." She said it for herself as much as him. "Time. Vitamin E. You know..."

"Vitamin E?" His dark chuckle stirred something within her. "Another bit of *craic*. You're full of them. It's compelling, and I'm not easily compelled."

"Is that why you're not sure you want to kiss me again?" Best get it out there. "Because I'm not sure either."

His mouth twisted. "It's good to be on the same page. We're both conflicted."

She put her hand on his chest. "I want you, and I seem to be starting to like you, but I have wondered if this is a good idea. I'm not looking for a relationship or anything serious."

"That's a man's line." His mouth tipped up on the right. "You're as honest as they come, aren't you?"

Honesty wasn't just a word to her. It was a way of life. "I hate lies and liars and don't have time for drama. I don't see why people dick around or hurt others when they can just put it all on the table. It's pretty simple."

He rubbed the back of his neck again. "I want you as well, and I am starting to like you. But there are other factors, and that's why we must be friends. You're Ellie's best friend. She's marrying my brother, whom I love even though he's going to probably drive me mad after last night."

"What happened?"

He was silent a moment before saying, "Brady wants me to be happy. He might think you're part of that for reasons best left unsaid."

His grimace might as well have been a death mask. Oh, he was mysterious. She couldn't read him now. "I see."

"Beyond that, everyone knows your business in this village, and if we get together, they'll be thinking things again about me that I don't want resurrected. The man I used to be with Morag is dead."

She swallowed the tightness in her throat, suddenly sad for him. "I understand rising from the phoenix ashes and becoming someone new. I prefer to think it's a better version, personally. I also get that there are drawbacks to tight communities."

They were stacking up every obstacle, and if she were to

weigh it all, they were coming down on the side of not going there.

"I can withstand the temptation of seeing you for four months, especially now that I've starting my boxing training."

Withstand the temptation of seeing you.

The words stole her breath. Yes, that's exactly what they'd have to do. "And I have an installation to build. We should be able to resist each other."

He looked her dead-on again. "Especially if I don't see you in those shorts again."

Her belly tightened. She made herself laugh. God, it was too bad they couldn't launch themselves at each other just once and then forget it happened.

Only she knew neither of them would be able to forget. Memories like that stayed with a person a long time.

"This outfit won't leave my little cottage, I promise." She crossed her heart for good measure, making him smile. "As of right now, I'm flipping the switch and will only treat you as a friend. Shall we shake on it?"

He held up his hand as if blocking her. "No. Better not to have any contact, I think."

Apparently his skin sizzled too. "Yes, you're right." She nodded briskly, trying to look at him like she would one of her brothers.

She couldn't do it.

The whole idea was wrong. She'd have to try another approach.

He rolled his massive shoulders, and they cracked. "Well, it seems we had a good chat."

Had they? "I never got you a cup of coffee. Ah... Do you want one?"

"No, thanks. I'll be leaving you to your morning." He

inclined his chin. "I know Ellie and Brady and many others will be taking care of you, but if you need anything, you let me know. Ellie will be my sister-in-law, and you're like her sister. That makes you family."

It did, but the thought of trying to be that kind of family with Declan formed a hard knot in her chest. "Yes, it does, I guess. I'm glad we thought that far ahead. Because, to our minds, we are sisters, and that means I'll be around—"

"For the rest of my life," Declan said, his jaw locked. "Every holiday, likely. I thought about that last night. Couldn't expunge it from my mind. Hell, we'll probably be godparents to their children."

She had a glimpse of his torture. "I'll be Aunt Kathleen and you'll be Uncle Declan."

"Exactly."

The idea of those sweet children should have made her smile, but it only cemented the daunting task ahead of them. They weren't just protecting themselves from hurt. They were protecting Ellie and Brady and their family. That kind of incentive was stronger than a cold shower.

"And birthdays too," she added. "I always celebrate Ellie's birthday with her."

His mouth shifted to a morose angle as he studied her. "Is it awful of me to say that I hope you grow uglier as the years pass?"

She laughed. She couldn't help it. The words were so unexpected. "So long as I can say that I hope you get fat and puffy in the face and—" *Stop smelling so delicious,* she silently added.

"We'll work on looking ugly to each other then," he said after a moment with a crisp nod. "Very ugly. In fact, I'm going to start telling myself I don't like women with short brown hair."

Declan stepped a few inches closer and touched her hair softly. Everything stilled inside her. She could feel his body heat.

"You clearly don't lack confidence," he said, tipping her chin up while studying her face. "Only a woman brimming with it could clip her hair as such and wear it so proudly. It should make you look mannish."

Her throat went dry. His touch was even hotter than she remembered. Lucky for her, she was used to heat. Fire was part of her profession, her art. "My brothers tease me about that too, saying I'm trying to fit in with them."

"Then there's your jawline." His fingers slid over the bones. "It sticks out even more with your hair this short."

God, she wished she could laugh as they tried to convince each other they were unappealing. "When you frown, you look like a thug. And your eyes turn small—like a weasel's."

She wasn't telling the truth now. They might be the most captivating eyes she'd ever beheld, ones that could inspire a work of art.

"I'm glad we're finding reasons not to find each other pleasing." He inhaled harshly, as if the sound was forced from deep within him. "We're going to need it in the coming days. I'd best go before I find more reasons you aren't beautiful."

Beautiful? He thought she was beautiful? Guys in her neighborhood always told her she was *hot* or *smoldering* or *wicked sexy*.

Never beautiful.

She watched him walk to the door. That damn lump rose in her throat again. "Declan..."

He stopped and turned.

"I wish we were strangers who'd met on vacation."

His eyes held hers for a long moment. The quiet seemed to chill her skin, and she longed for the heat between them. But it was gone, snuffed out by their mutual decision.

"So do I, *mo chroí.*"

With that, he left her, heading back out into the rain.

She shouldn't look up the words he'd used. She knew the phrase was Gaelic. But if she couldn't follow through on her temptation with him, at least she could follow through on this small wish. When the meaning flashed on her screen —*my heart*—she felt the pang deep in her chest.

She thought back to her dream, of them walking along the beach, holding hands. Deep inside her, she knew there was greater emotion with him. His endearment suggested he knew it as well.

His heart.

She sat on the uncomfortable wicker settee and tucked her feet under her, unbearably cold and very lonely.

CHAPTER FIVE

His training couldn't have come at a better time.
Declan dove into it as if he would be fighting Muhammad Ali or Joe Louis back in the day. He had eight weeks to prepare for his first match, according to Cormac.

While his return to boxing had been about reclaiming something he'd loved and earning money for the shop, it was more about avoiding Kathleen now. It was bad enough knowing she was close by—he could almost sense her in the air—but she seemed to be everywhere he was: at Summercrest, at the pub, in town.

Seeing her all the time was breaking him down more than being pummeled by a cadre of large men, all of whom seemed eager to whip him into shape. The giddiness of his trainers swept them all away for the next week as they began their strength and conditioning plan. He rose at five for a few hours of training in the early hours before work and then rushed to the boxing club after he closed the butcher shop at five. He often trained until ten.

They ran miles and full-out sprints, jumped rope, hit the speedball and bag, and sparred with each other amidst workouts dedicated to leg lifts, crunches, pull-ups, push-ups, and multiple rounds of holding plank.

His muscles burned. His body sweated. His heart pounded.

He got used to seeing bruises on his body and ugly scrapes and cracks on his hands and face.

It was miserable. It was elating. It was hell.

On the rare occasions he managed not to think about Kathleen, Sorcha appeared. She'd watch as he beat the bag senseless, arms crossed over her chest, but he didn't break his rhythm. He ignored her until she went away.

He fell into bed every night, exhausted. He barely spoke to his roommates. He was hardly home.

He ran with Donal, Seamus, his father, and Killian on occasion. Sometimes Fergus and Eoghan walked briskly behind them, and sometimes they tootled behind on ancient blue bicycles Declan was sure had sped through the countryside before Ireland was a republic.

There was an instant male comradery. They had the fever, that was true, but they suffered through the pain with him. The older men complained to high heaven about getting old even as they gritted their teeth and trained like they hadn't in years. They all gasped for breath after a round with the speedball, and they laughed when someone screamed from a cramp.

Brady didn't trouble him about Kathleen, thank God, but the villagers shared news about her when they came to the butcher shop. He listened with gritted teeth, determined not to react. She was part of the fabric of the community, and people were bound to talk about her and her work. More troublingly, he realized he was eager for news of her.

That was how he'd learned Kathleen's equipment had arrived at last, and the Yank was beginning her project. Lisa

Ann, who took pottery classes at the arts center, told him the sheer power and noise coming from Kathleen's shed was like nothing she'd ever heard.

He saw her life through their eyes and was heartsick at not seeing it with his own.

When he was alone, her visage came to mind unbidden, that siren call in her beautiful brown eyes. He looked on it as more training, the kind of exercise that built more of the mental toughness every good fighter possessed.

When she was visiting Ellie at Summercrest one evening, he heard her laughter floating from the parlor. He fashioned his response as he would to another fighter, one of emotional resilience. Her laughter was not going to pull him or sway him to temptation. He gritted his teeth, breathed, and used his training until sanity returned.

She'd laugh if she knew he was using her to hone his concentration and toughness. Actually, she might not, he thought, remembering how sad she'd looked when she'd said she wished they'd met as strangers on vacation.

If only...

They were star-crossed, he came to realize. The idea grew in his mind, and he started to intentionally think of her as he trained. She tested his willpower. She pushed him to the edge. She gave him the courage to keep going when he was exhausted—body, mind, and soul.

Over the next couple of weeks, he worked on coordination, footwork, and agility. Eoghan brought out an old Irish boxing trick of throwing stones for him to catch to improve his hand-eye coordination. When Declan mentioned that most people used tennis balls now, the older man punched him in the shoulder, a pretty good punch for a man of ninety-three, and informed him that no one would fear a man who trained using tennis balls.

Declan caught the stones.

He remembered how to take a punch, and he remembered how to give one. Donal and Seamus could knock him a good one back, while his father's speed and footwork wore him down, teaching him the age-old lesson that muscle mass doesn't always win fights.

He went from two miles to four, and it was agreed he would run five days a week, come rain or shine. He went from one hundred sit-ups to five hundred, with one of his older trainers sometimes holding his feet if they were on the red mats at the boxing club.

Everything burned, including that part of him that ached for Kathleen.

He worked through that burn, the fatigue, and the pain from the training. He got so used to wearing gloves again, he was surprised when he saw his bare hands slicing meat at the butcher shop from time to time or washing salt and sweat off his body.

When Eoghan pulled him aside after a brutal bout of punching the bag and told him that a good fighter worked on not only his body and mind, but his heart, he stilled where he stood, dripping sweat. "You have something you want to say?" he rasped.

"I have eyes, don't I, as much as a sound mind and knowing heart?" Eoghan grabbed a bottle of water for him, which he took and guzzled down fiercely. "You can't work her out of your system, my young buck. Many have tried that path and failed."

Declan glanced over his shoulder. His trainers were chatting by the boxing ring, thick as thieves, yet somehow he knew they were aware of them. "Were you sent to talk to me?"

"I sent myself after much discussion," Eoghan said,

"seeing as I'm the oldest and you likely wouldn't take a swing at me for saying such things."

Declan upended half the bottle of water over his heated head and grabbed a towel. "I wouldn't hit anyone for speaking their mind."

"Good." Eoghan pursed his lips a moment. "Then I should add the additional item I wanted to mention. The smell of oranges in your vicinity from time to time."

He reeled. Eoghan might as well have punched him in the face. "You'd be knowing what that means?"

"I do," he said, slowly nodding. "Donal's smelled it too and knows the significance. Your father and Seamus do not. Yet."

He took his time answering. "Sorcha has her opinions, but Kathleen and I are agreed. We aren't pursuing each other."

"Sorcha has her *opinions*, does she?" Eoghan crossed himself like a good altar boy. "Jesus, Mary, and Joseph, you're a bold one, disrespecting not only a ghost but our dear Sorcha Fitzgerald. My young buck, you have a fine head on your shoulders, but in this, you're wrong down the line. If Sorcha says you and the new Yank are meant, you're meant. Fighting against it will only weaken your body, mind, and heart and make you a pitiful fighter and man in the end. Is that what you want?"

Emotion backed up in his throat like dammed water in a bog. He'd have preferred Eoghan to beat him until he was blue. "I'm not the only one in the mix here. She's agreed to this. You know she's going back to Boston to her family. What would you wish for her? Heartache?" He wouldn't speak of himself.

"What's important is that you're meant for each other." Eoghan waved his hand dismissively. "The details work themselves out. To deny it—for either of you—would be pure folly, like our Irish myths say. I wonder if her art will suffer for it."

They both smelled oranges then, and the hairs on Declan's arms rose in response.

"Well, there's your answer." Eoghan nodded.

He didn't want to hear any of this. "Maybe Sorcha needs to appear to Kathleen then," he said, dropping his arm. "I'm wrecked. I'm going home."

"You think on what I said, Declan McGrath. It was uttered with the best intentions, mind you. I respect how hard you've been training, but you can't be a winner if you continue like this. Your first fight is going to be as tough as they come. Paul Keane is tireless. He'll use every weakness you possess. Shadowboxing the new Yank and your desire for her certainly is a weakness."

He shifted on his tired feet at the mention of his boxing siren. "How I train is my business," he said caustically.

"You know that's not how it works." Eoghan clapped him on the back. "I know those were hard words to hear, and I'll hope you'll remember the feeling with which they were said. If it's any consolation, I agree with Sorcha."

His breath arrested in his chest.

"You and the lovely Kathleen *do* seem like the perfect match. Good night, my boy."

Declan couldn't run out of there fast enough. He gave perfunctory farewells, grabbed his stuff, and headed home, but no matter how fast he moved, the words Eoghan had spoken followed him.

Summercrest Manor was lit up like Christmas when he arrived, so warm and inviting one would never have thought it had a reputation for being haunted before they moved in.

The presence of Kathleen's car in the driveway made him lower his head against the steering wheel.

He couldn't handle seeing her tonight. It was hard enough to resist her when he was in top shape. He was raw meat after his encounter with Eoghan.

But he was no coward. Besides, they'd agreed to be friends. He could give her a simple greeting before going upstairs and showering.

He let himself inside quietly. Immediately, he heard the two women laughing in the parlor. He locked his muscles and walked to the doorway.

The very sight of her, sitting on the floor in black jeans and a skintight red shirt next to her friend, sent his troubled heart racing. Their eyes met and held, her brown ones looking larger than usual in her oval face.

"Evening, ladies," he managed.

Ellie shoved off the floor next to her friend and rushed over to him. "Declan, you look exhausted."

His mouth curved. "That's good to hear. Boxing training is supposed to be miserable. If I looked good, I'd be doing it wrong."

He swore he heard Kathleen muffle a laugh.

Ellie only wrung her hands. "Have you eaten? Brady's still at the pub, but Kathleen and I managed to make a pretty good bowl of pasta."

"Thanks, I'll grab some before I head upstairs and crash. How are you both? Work going okay?"

"I'm good," Ellie said, her mouth lifting into a small smile. "My window for the center is coming together. Kathleen is the one you should ask."

His breath arrested as Kathleen sat up straighter. So she was facing her own fight. Well, he could pity them both.

"I only mean," Ellie managed after an uncomfortable silence, "that she is working as hard as you are."

"No, I'm not, Ellie," his beautiful siren said, standing and holding his gaze. "Otherwise, I'd look something like Declan here, and I certainly wouldn't have been shooting the breeze with you since six."

"Yes, but when I teach my night classes on Tuesday and Thursday, you work until after midnight."

He glanced between the two of them, aware of the sudden subtext in the room. Ellie, it seemed, was worried about both of them.

"You know I like to work late," Kathleen said, resting her bottom on the edge of an armchair. "You should grab some dinner, Ace, before you fall over."

"Declan, let me heat it for you." Ellie took his hand suddenly, making him wince. "Good God! Are your hands supposed to look like that?"

"He's punching people, Ellie," Kathleen said, coming off the chair. "It happens. Right, Ace?"

He could hear the edge in her voice when she used that nickname—the one that kept distance yawning between them—but he appreciated her alleviating Ellie's worries.

"Wouldn't be called boxing otherwise," he agreed. "Ellie, you don't need to heat my supper. I can manage."

"Nonsense," Ellie said, dashing for the doorway. "I'll see if we have enough ice in the trays for an icebag. Kathleen and I used some of it for drinks."

"A bag of peas will do just fine, Ellie, but really, I can take care of all that."

"Grab a seat, Declan." Her voice wasn't sugary now. "Kathleen, sit on him if you must."

Ellie raced from the room while Kathleen studied him quietly. "I'm glad the boxing is going well. Although if the stories about you using stones in your training are true, you Irish are a hell of a lot more brutal than the boys I know back home who fight."

He wasn't surprised she knew fighters. "Eoghan said such stories inspire fear and create mystique. Boxers love stuff like that."

"Like Boston Strong Boy—"

"John L.," he continued, "who wore a supposed magic stone given to him by his mother under his sash along with his signature green trunks. His parents were Irish, you know."

"Some of the best boxers were and are," Kathleen said, crossing to him with her long, endless legs. "I love the story about Eoghan tossing stones at you for training. I even mentioned it to my brother, Robbie, who used to box. But I have to say, I know when a man looks like he's training too hard, and that, Ace, is how you look to me."

"Can you never simply call me Declan like everyone else?" he asked, his emotions frayed at last.

She let her hands fist at her sides. "I'm not anyone else, *Ace*. You must be tired to take offense."

Angry at himself and the desire to hear his name on her lips, he lifted a hand in entreaty. "I'm poor company. Tell Ellie not to bother with supper."

"But you need to eat," she said, stepping even closer to him. "Declan, you're pushing yourself too hard."

Sweat broke out along his temples at the mere thought of taking her into his arms. "I'm working out my temptations."

Her breath was audible, a whisper of desire between them. Their eyes met. He could feel the heat coming from her. This was madness.

"Are you working too much, like Ellie said?"

He watched as she bit her lip. "Maybe a little. I don't like being cooped up in that cottage. It's too quiet. There's not much to do when Ellie isn't around. She needs her time with Brady too. We're finding a new rhythm."

"You're lonely." He clenched his hands into fists to keep from comforting her, which made him wince. His muscles had stiffened after the battering he'd taken tonight.

She took a moment, but he watched her swallow thickly, the long line of her neck bared by her shirt. "You aren't supposed to know things like that about me."

He laid a hand on her shoulder, unable to withstand the temptation to make a brief, if impersonal, connection with her. The moment he touched her, he couldn't deny the truth. Nothing between them was impersonal. It couldn't be. "You aren't supposed to know I'm training too hard."

"What am I, an idiot?" She laid her hand over his, her palm soft and warm yet rough with calluses from her work. "I could probably knock you out right now, you know."

He chuckled. "Do you think so?"

"Absolutely." She moved in, making a fist with her other hand and pressing it into his abdomen. "Nice abs, Ace."

He met her fist more firmly by moving forward another half step. She was within the circle of his arms, smelling like hot steel and sunshine. He wanted to drown in her scent. "I'm glad you approve."

Her tongue wet her lips. "But I don't like the way your face looks, as if one of the local tractors ran over it."

"Does it make me uglier?"

She lifted her hand and touched his jaw. "No, unfortunately."

The feel of her fingers stroking his jaw was pure bliss. Part of him wanted to close his eyes and give in to her touch, but he couldn't bear to lose sight of her beautiful face. "You don't look unpleasing to me either. Work on that, will you?"

Her mouth tipped up to the right. "I'll try. You should cut back your workouts. Or I'm going to have to come by your boxing club, grab the stones Eoghan uses, and throw them at you."

Was there any woman more arousing, more perfect? "You could try, I suppose, but I'd have to use my superior strength to stop you. I'd pin you beneath me, and you'd never be able to rise again." He imagined she wouldn't want to leave, any more than he would want her to.

She laughed, the sound loud and rich, as she ruffled his hair. "If I weren't so nice, I'd put you on your butt this minute and stomp that macho talk into the dust. You're lucky though. I *like* the macho stuff—to a point. I grew up with it. It comforts me and makes me feel warm and gushy inside."

"It's official," he said, deciding to test the waters and trace the graceful arch of her cheekbone. "You're sick in the head. I wish it made you more unattractive."

They let their hands roam, their eyes holding contact. "What can I do that's unappealing?"

"Screech," he said after a moment. "It's one of the few things I can't abide. When kids do that in my shop, I want to pick them up by their scruffs and deposit them on the sidewalk outside."

She smiled softly, and the impact of it made his heart swell. "I can't screech. Ellie will get freaked out. Liam too maybe."

"Where is Yoda?" Declan asked, wishing they could remain alone as they were.

"He's meditating, I think." She rubbed the back of his head, making him groan. "He got home early from a less

AVA MILES

than inspiring date, as he called it. Wanted to clear his head."

"Liam's dates usually go better than that," Declan said, turning his head to prolong her touch.

"He says maybe the tide is turning here, whatever that means." She turned her attention to his right shoulder, her ministrations making him groan. "You need an ice bath."

"God, no. They're brutal."

She dug her finger in harder on the perfect spot. "But effective."

"There's not much ice left, Ellie said. God, you know what you're about. Can I hire you as my masseuse?"

The words hung in the air. He almost whimpered as she rubbed the depression above his shoulder blade. "We both know that would be a bad idea."

"Probably." He caressed her jaw. "Right now, I'm too tired to care."

"And I hear footsteps on the hardwood," she said, stepping back from him quickly and returning to the armchair. "That's probably best as nothing has changed since our last conversation on this point."

"Only you haven't grown any less beautiful," he said, holding her gaze as Ellie walked into the parlor.

"I have the peas and the pasta," Ellie said, extending them. "Is there anything more I can get you, Declan?"

"A masseuse?" he joked.

Katheen bit her lip, trying to muffle her laughter.

Ellie glanced between them. "I can look one up for you. Maybe there's one in Westport."

"He's kidding, Ellie." Kathleen crossed her arms. "Mostly."

"I'm going to take this upstairs and crash." He made himself lean down and kiss Ellie's cheek—but not Kath-

80

leen's, of course. "Thanks for this. You ladies have a good night."

With that, he left them and made his way upstairs, every step radiating agony through his bruised and sore body. He ate with an intensity that shocked him and then showered with the image of Kathleen's hands on him still fresh in his mind. When he stumbled to bed, she was his last thought.

He awoke from a fog to his brother jostling him awake. "What the hell?"

"Sorry, but Ellie was waiting up for me when I got home. She said she was really worried about you, which got me worrying even more than I already am." He cracked his neck. "She wanted me to check on you, and seeing your bruises I can see why. Jesus, Declan, you're a rainbow of pain."

"I'm training."

"Of course, Ellie doesn't know the real reason I'm worried about you as I haven't told her, and that's not something I like much."

He meant Sorcha, of course.

"You were wise not to tell her about that. The Yank and I are agreed. She's only here for a short time. It doesn't make sense to get together. We can fight the temptation." They were also doing it for Brady and Ellie, but he would say nothing about that, else Brady would feel guilty or argue it wasn't necessary.

"You and Kathleen agreed?" Brady pushed off his bed and paced a moment. "But that's not how it works. Sorcha—"

"I said I don't want to hear it, Brady." He pulled a pillow over his head.

His brother tugged on it, as he'd expected, and rather

than let him rip it apart and let loose hundreds of goose feathers, he didn't fight him. Easier on his stiff hands anyway. They glared at each other.

"But you could be happy. I want that for you more than anything," Brady said, pointing at him. "And it'd be with Kathleen, who's like Ellie's sister. We'd all be family. Why would you both fight against that?"

He wanted to bang his head against the headboard. He was going to have to say things better left unsaid. "And what happens when things end between us and she returns to Boston and her family? Would you have us both be tortured seeing each other for the rest of our lives as we meet again and again at holidays and birthdays and the like, seeing as she'll as good as be your sister-in-law?"

Brady paled. "But Sorcha—"

"First, Sorcha isn't infallible. Second, Kathleen doesn't know about Sorcha's claims. I think that's better all around, don't you?"

"But I want—"

"It doesn't matter what you want," Declan said, sitting up with a groan. "It matters what we want."

His twin let fly an impressive swear word before sitting heavily back on the edge of the bed. "I love you, Declan, so I'm going to say this much, even if it pisses you off. You should listen to Sorcha and go for Kathleen. She's perfect for you."

His words echoed Eoghan's all too eerily. "Leave it be, Brady, and don't be stirring up more trouble. If Ellie knew about Sorcha—"

"She'd have to tell Kathleen." He raised his hands in frustration. "Why do you think I haven't told my very own fiancée yet? She'll be honor bound to tell her. It's been my moral conundrum. I'm writhing in guilt."

"Then let me absolve you." He lay back and stuffed a pillow under his head. "Kathleen and I have talked about it, twice now, and we've decided. This is none of your affair."

"Do you want to go to your grave without a wife and a family?" Brady asked, his voice hoarse. "I remember what you used to dream about, Declan. You told me you were leaving boxing to have a family. You said you couldn't wait for our kids to race each other down the narrow roads on bikes or take a brave dip in the cold sea. I want that for all of us, dammit."

His mind churned up an image of two black-haired boys pedaling hard down the road, hunched over the handlebars, laughing madly. The quadrant of his heart that used to dream of such things throbbed painfully in his chest. The man who'd wanted those things had died a painful death, but he was, truly, dead. "Brady, I beg you. Leave this be."

His brother shook his head. "You need to put the past behind you. If you won't talk about this with me, will you at least talk to Liam?"

Finally he closed his eyes, unable to bear seeing the worried, sallow face of his twin. "Liam has left it be as well, for which I'm grateful. He respects a man's choices."

The bed dipped as Brady rose. Declan cracked an eye open, wishing he hadn't. Brady's face was full of sorrow. "All right. I can't force you. I can only pray something will make you—and Kathleen—change your minds. Good night, brother."

He wanted to call out to him, but what could he say? "Good night," was all there *was* to say, so he said it quietly as Brady let himself out.

When the scent of oranges surrounded him, he wasn't surprised to see Sorcha appear where his brother had been sitting. "She is beautiful, isn't she? It's too bad she won't turn ugly as you hope. She's only going to grow lovelier. Do you truly plan to fight her your entire life?"

The words seized his lungs and stole his breath. He couldn't imagine what it would take for him to hold out that long, and Eoghan's words about his internal battle affecting him as a man and a fighter rose unbidden in his mind.

Sorcha's green eyes glared at him before she disappeared.

They both knew he would give her no answer.

CHAPTER SIX

The bold sunrise was rising over the verdant hills when Kathleen arrived at her studio.

She took a moment to admire it, hoping to change her mood. The reds and oranges were almost molten in nature, something she could appreciate even though it was butt crack early. The emerging sun was burning off the dew clinging to the tall grasses in the surrounding pastures, dotted with puffy white sheep.

She needed that heat. Her body was chilled after a troubled sleep. She'd failed to turn off thoughts of Declan, his bruised body, and their attraction. She wasn't sure what was worse. Temptation or torture. They had both in spades right now, and she didn't like the situation one bit.

Pulling the heavy shed door open, she let herself inside and flicked on the lights, walking toward the perfectly organized tools on her worktable. The sight of the ship frame she'd welded together didn't lift her mood. While it showcased her progress, it didn't showcase her vision.

Her work lacked passion.

Just like her life.

God, she was in a rut. She knew what would add passion. Hello, Declan. But they'd agreed not to go there.

All her brothers always said you don't shit where you eat and getting it on with Declan would definitely be that and more. Thank God Ellie wasn't pushing her. If her friend asked her about Declan, she wouldn't be able to hide her emotional turmoil. Only, Ellie knew anyway... She was being a good friend, not saying anything.

She picked up a thin steel plate from her worktable and grabbed her pliers. She twisted it and twisted it until it looked like a crazy spiral of metal. That was how she felt inside.

When they'd agreed to fight the temptation of being together, she'd thought she was up for it. She was tough. She'd been trained by the best temptation trainers in the business—nuns at her neighborhood Catholic school—after all, and she'd fought temptation before. That last chocolate. That crazy expensive pair of shoes in the store window. She'd even stayed away from a few very tempting guys, knowing they were bad news.

None of that had prepared her for Declan.

She hadn't imagined how much energy they'd have to devote to their decision to stay apart. The cost had been clear on Declan's face. She'd concealed her own aches and bruises from pounding out her own frustration on the metal forming the frame for her pirate ship.

Temptation was getting the better of her. It was messing with her head. It was screwing with her art.

Usually the requisite parts came together easily in her hands, but since she'd started the project three weeks ago— right after her talk with Declan—she'd been all thumbs.

She'd never had this problem before.

Ellie knew she was struggling.

Kathleen knew she was struggling.

Even her brother Robbie knew she was struggling. He'd texted her a couple of days ago: *You're too quiet. What's wrong with you?*

She'd told him about everything but Declan. He hadn't pressed. Yet. But he probably knew she was twisted up about a guy. Her brothers never asked her about guys, preferring to pretend their little sister didn't date.

She touched the frame she'd built so far. She couldn't feel the pirate ship, crashing through the Irish sea. It wasn't *alive*. That was a problem.

She couldn't suck at this. She *wouldn't* suck.

But her piece's current suckitude wasn't reason enough to give in to the temptation and dive into Declan's hot, compelling arms.

Because after that, what would happen?

She'd found amusement in their banter. He'd told her twice now that she was beautiful. But those things only suggested she'd get attached to him, which would ultimately cause much more pain than she was currently feeling.

"Seeing as Declan is the first man to call you beautiful," she heard a woman say behind her, "don't you think you might reconsider the current way of things?"

Every nerve ending went on alert. She'd closed the shed door. How could someone be inside? And how did a stranger know exactly what Kathleen had been thinking? She turned around slowly and almost sagged to the floor as her knees gave out.

She knew that face from photos about the center. It was Sorcha Fitzgerald. "Oh. My. God."

The woman's white dressed flowed eerily, as if in a phantom wind, as she started toward her. Stumbling back onto the ground, Kathleen fought panic.

"I don't mean you any harm," the woman said in a gentle Irish lilt. "You'll recall Ellie telling you how I came to thank her for her donation and let her know how happy I was she and Brady had ended up together as they were meant."

She nodded, trying to clear her throat. When Ellie had told her about the encounter, she'd been shocked, but she knew Ellie. Her friend didn't lie. Kathleen had told herself, *It's Ireland, right? No biggie.* She'd even gotten a little warm and fuzzy upon learning about Sorcha's role in helping her friends.

Seeing Sorcha herself, however, was a completely different experience. Her heart was kicking madly in her chest and the dizziness made her head spin.

"I didn't expect to appear to you so early." The woman sat—*sat*—on Kathleen's worktable, her bare feet dangling. "Usually, I appear to the lady in question when all things are as they should be. It's the men who knew me in life. They're the ones I usually appear to and push and prod when necessary. But you and Declan are strong people, as strong as your metal. After last night, I concluded that you both are bound and determined to fight what's between you, even at great cost to you both. So here I am."

Kathleen scrambled off the floor and fumbled for her work chair. She yanked it under her, falling into it hard. "I'm watching your mouth move, but my brain is still exploding. Me and Declan? *You're here to help me and Declan?*" She was repeating herself. "I don't—"

"Understand?" Sorcha smiled softly. "Of course you do. You and Declan are meant for each other. Why else did you find him so irresistible the moment you met him? And he you? Your hearts recognized each other. It's your minds—hard as the rocks in the very walls that line our Irish roads—

that are getting in the way of what's meant. No offense meant in the saying, mind you."

Kathleen took a long breath, her hands gripping her knees. "This is a lot to take in."

"Is it?" Sorcha arched a fine brow. "You're already resisting what I'm saying to you." She tsked. "To think, thousands of people pay psychics in the hope of receiving such news. Let me be as clear as a summer sky. Dearest Kathleen, you and Declan are *soulmates*. You are the perfect partners for each other. You will make each other happier and more fulfilled than you could ever imagine."

She'd thought she and Axl were soulmates and had done a Rodin-like metal sculpture of their love. He'd written a song about it, one that had melted her heart. Later, it had all seemed like a lie. "I don't believe in soulmates."

"But you did," Sorcha said, moving off the table and walking along the skeletal frame of the pirate ship. "Before the man you loved broke your heart. Declan shared the same fate. We may love more than one person, true. But one thing is certain, Kathleen. Only a soulmate can bring you the perfect form of happiness and fulfillment on this earth. For you, that man is Declan."

She started to tremble. This was crazy. "You're a ghost, not God. And whatever you might say, I still have free will. I tell myself who I want to love. Not you."

"But you're already falling for him, aren't you?" Sorcha wound a lock of her long brown hair around her finger. "Otherwise, why didn't you sleep last night? I'm not taking your free will away, Kathleen. I'm only encouraging you and Declan to be open to what's in your own hearts. Can you honestly say you've done that?"

She held up a hand. "I don't—"

"Don't answer me now. You think on it. And if you

want a relatively unbiased and neutral reference for me, you can talk to Brady and Ellie, of course, but there's Kade Donovan, for one. I helped him and Megan. He'd tell you I mean no harm. So will Carrick, who I was married to, who is now happy with his beloved Angie. You see... I'm only here to help."

Kathleen laid her hands flat against her thighs. Arguing with a ghost wasn't for the faint of heart. "I believe that's what you think."

"Perhaps it would ease your mind if you understood why I'm intervening." Sorcha chuckled softly. "The reason is simple. All of Carrick's friends hold a special place in my heart, for they were always there for me and himself, never more so than after I died. I owe them a great debt. I want to see them all happily matched with their perfect partners before I move on."

Was she really having this conversation? Maybe she was going to wake up in her own bed, having dreamed this whole crazy thing up. "That's nice of you, I guess."

"I don't do this for myself, Kathleen." Sorcha walked over and stood before her, a wry smile lifting her mouth. "Declan, you see, is a boy I ran through these hills with. He might have teased me like the other boys, but he always had my back and made me laugh with his dry wit. He has suffered much from heartbreak. What Morag did to him was unspeakable, but it is time for him to put that in the past. It will probably anger you to hear it, but it is time for you to put your heartache and all the subsequent weeds of distrust aside as well. We'll speak again."

With that, she vanished.

Kathleen fell back against the chair, her body faint. Her heart raced like she'd run a sprint.

Good God! She'd seen a ghost. What would her

brothers say? Or Pop? She held her face in her hands, trying to bring the blood back into it.

Sorcha Fitzgerald had appeared to her so casually, like it was an everyday occurrence, and she'd told her Declan was her soulmate.

Holy. Ever-loving. Shit.

She stayed in her chair until her head stopped spinning. Her limbs were still buzzing, but her mind started to try and make sense of things.

One thing finally struck her. Sorcha had said she'd already appeared to Declan. He *knew* about all this. That asshole. Why hadn't he told her? It wasn't nice to let someone have a ghost appear to them like without warning.

He had some explaining to do!

She grabbed her car key and purse and left the shed, locking it behind her, and drove to Summercrest Manor. When she arrived, Liam emerged from the house in faded jeans and a T-shirt. "You're up early. Everything okay? Brady and Ellie aren't up yet."

"I'm here to see Declan," she said, her breath visible in the cold air.

"He's in the shower, getting ready for work." Liam's eyes narrowed. "The scent of oranges is all around you. Did you see Sorcha?"

Her head snapped back. "*You knew too?*"

His shoulder lifted. "I've always been able to smell her, but I haven't seen her yet. You look pale, Kathleen. I assume she told you about you and Declan."

This was unbelievable. "She did. Does everyone know—"

"Not everyone," he said, giving a chagrined smile. "Only me, Brady, Jamie, and a few others. Now you.

Sorcha's never appeared to any of the women so early to my knowledge."

She put a hand on her hip, tapping her foot on the ground. "I must be special."

"You seem pretty upset," Liam said, studying her face with that open gaze of his. Although they hadn't spent much one-on-one time together, she'd come to respect and trust his wisdom from their interactions at Summercrest and the pub.

"I am, dammit! Don't you think I have a right to be? A ghost just told me I should be with Declan."

That stillness he carried around him didn't waver in the face of her ire. "Is it that you believe her? Or do you think she's mistaken?"

Her heart rapped hard against her ribs as she ground out, "I think this whole thing is nuts. That's what I think. She balls out told me I can't be as happy with anyone else as I'd be with Declan. Who the hell is she to say that?"

"She's only trying to help," Liam said softly. "It's always your choice."

"She said that too." She took an aggrieved breath, knowing she was worked up. "I don't like being pushed around by a ghost."

"The pull is already there with Declan, though, isn't it?" He held up his hands like a white flag. "Hang on. I understand being upset by someone pushing you. But I think she's only intervening because she has a knowledge of things, from the other side. She's here to help us with our soulmates. Why does that make you so angry?"

"Because I don't like someone telling me Declan is my soulmate, that's what." She sucked in another breath. "That pisses me off."

"It pissed Declan off too." Liam inclined his head

toward the house. "You should go talk to him. I'm off to do some painting for the May Day celebration coming up next week. Good luck."

Good luck? She'd show them good luck. Stalking inside, she took the stairs two at a time and turned right at the top. She knew where his bedroom was since Ellie had given her a tour. His bedroom door was closed. She knocked on it briskly.

It swung open quickly to show him in nothing but a white towel wrapped around his waist. "What the— Is something wrong?"

She was struck mute by the sight of his glistening chest, all hard muscle, and a patchwork of bruises in yellows and purples. She raised her eyes back to his face. "I spoke to Sorcha."

He cursed. "That interfering— It doesn't matter."

"*Doesn't matter?*" She shoved into his room, closing the door behind her, and squared off with him. "You knew she was fixated on us being each other's soulmates, and you didn't see fit to tell me? I don't like surprises, Declan."

He ran a hand through his damp hair. "Why would I tell you? We've decided what we've decided. She's wrong about this."

"Damn right she's wrong." She put her hands on her hips. "How the hell is she supposed to know such things?"

"She's a busybody ghost, and I told her I don't agree with her opinions. I asked her to leave me the hell alone."

She stalked over to him. "I don't like this, Ace—"

"You think I do?" He stepped so close she could smell the strong pine soap he'd used. "Do you think I like all my friends thinking we're meant for each other? Or that I want a busybody ghost telling me how happy and fulfilled I'll be

93

with you? I'm doing my darndest every minute of the day to resist how much I want you."

Everything in her trembled. "I won't have a ghost tell me what's best for me."

"Neither will I." He lifted his hand and traced her cheek. "But know this, Kathleen—resisting you is worse than my bruises and sore muscles combined."

His touch was like a trail of fire across her skin. She let her fingers dance over the battered muscles of his upper chest. Their breathing was harsh to her ears. "That's pretty bad, Ace. If you must know, I didn't sleep well last night, and then I got pissed when Sorcha appeared to me this morning. I saw red as soon as my knees stopped knocking."

"Understandable." He gave a lopsided smile, his dimples flashing in the strong planes of his face. Even with the bruises, he was unbearably handsome. "You were pissed at me as well. Otherwise, you wouldn't have come over and barged into my room."

"You should have told me. But I guess I get why you didn't."

He laid his hand on her shoulder, rubbing the line of tension there, igniting a trail of fire. "If I had, it would have made it a thing. Sorcha tried to trap me with my own logic. If we're not meant for each other, then what would be the harm of enjoying some time together? She was canny in life, and she's just as canny as a ghost."

"I noticed that."

His touch reached the back of her bare neck, the sensation making her thoughts scatter. Why *weren't* they going for each other? She couldn't remember right now.

"You need to put petroleum jelly on your face so it won't crack."

He made a rude sound as her fingers traced the cut by

his eye. "Eoghan thinks word of how hard I'm training will travel through the county. It'll be good for my rep. I've been out of the game a while, you know."

"I have seven high-octane brothers. You tough guys drive me crazy."

He met her gaze head-on, his blue eyes filled with desire and something more. "You tough girls drive *me* crazy. So crazy, I can't seem to remember why I'm not supposed to kiss you."

Her pulse quickened as his fingers caressed her nape. God, she wanted his hands all over her.

She moved her head so their contact deepened. He shifted closer, putting his other hand on her waist. She let her hand spread over his pectoral muscle, the flesh hot as fire, and felt the answering response of his fast beating heart. Arousal pooled in her belly, low and liquid.

"Kissing isn't getting with someone, right?"

His hand tightened on the swell of her hip. "No... Kissing is nothing. A bare brushing of lips. Chaste as a saint. Nothing to worry about."

When his gaze lowered to her mouth, she found herself wetting her lips. The pull between them was magnetic, and she didn't want to fight it right now. His other hand cupped the back of her head, and he held her gaze.

"You're right," she whispered, nearly out of breath with desire. "Nothing to worry about."

When he lowered his head, she met him, mouth to mouth. She moaned at the contact—at the perfect pairing of their lips—and heard his answering groan. Her eyes closed as he brought her flush against him, banding his hand around her waist while keeping the other at the back of her head.

God, how she'd dreamed about kissing him again, and

this time there was a new tenderness along with a heat so powerful it destroyed her every sense. She wrapped her arms around him and caressed the line of his naked back as they tilted their heads for a better angle.

She let her lips move over his, tracing them with her tongue, discovering the faint taste of spearmint there. Their mouths opened unbidden, and the kiss turned carnal, his tongue tangling with hers, the pressure and agony of want calling up more dark moans and groans from deep within them.

"Declan," she breathed out as he broke the contact.

"You called me Declan."

"Yeah," she said before sucking on his bottom lip.

"Do it again," he ordered.

"Declan."

His mouth crushed hers in a wild kiss. Somewhere low, she started to pulse. She pressed into his body, the hard evidence of his desire resting against her belly. She uttered another agonized whimper as he gently bit down on her lower lip. A throaty rumble rose up between them when she gave him the same treatment.

"This is madness." His hands tightened on her hips, and then he pressed his forehead to hers, breaking the kiss.

His breath fanned on her mouth, and she knew she was panting too. Her body pulsed with the primal need to mate with him, and she knew he was experiencing the same sensation.

He finally moved her away from him and ran a shaking hand through his hair. "We agreed on a kiss. If we do more, we need to be agreeing to that as well, I think. God, that was — I can't tell you what it took to step back."

She pressed her hand to her throat, flushed with desire, trying not to look at the masculine beauty in front of her. "I know. Declan— I'm not often so conflicted, but you're right. We had reasons for not doing this. I just can't seem to hold on to them right now."

"You'd better go." He blew out a harsh breath. "So we can both breathe."

"And get our heads on straight."

"Kathleen... I can't say I've ever wanted anyone more than I want you."

Delight and desire rushed through her. He deserved the same honesty. "Me either." She wouldn't let herself wonder if it had anything to do with Sorcha being right. "I'll be going."

His face shuttered as she stepped toward the door. It felt like her heart was twisting within her chest. This could be their last kiss. Ever. That thought destroyed her.

"Goodbye, Kathleen," he said softly.

She stopped at the door and looked over her shoulder. He might as well have been made of marble, he was so still. "Bye, Ace."

His face slowly fell, which hurt to watch. Yeah, he knew it too. God!

When she closed the door, she knew she was closing it on the possibilities between them. She took a breath and started walking away. Caught in her thoughts, she didn't see Brady until she looked up. She froze. He stopped short as well, unshaven in a burgundy robe in the hallway. His gaze flew to Declan's room and then widened as he looked back at her.

She tried to make her mouth form a smile. "I stopped in early with a question. I was just leaving. Tell Ellie I'll call her later."

"Sure," he said, nearly stumbling over his bare feet as she passed him on her way to the stairs.

"Not a word, Brady," she heard Declan grind out in a harsh voice before a door slammed.

She flew down the stairs and out the front door of Summercrest Manor. When she yanked open her car door and flung herself inside, she finally realized she'd run out of her best friend's home without saying a word to her.

Not a proud moment. But Ellie would understand. She'd just kissed the hottest, most compelling man ever.

The scent of oranges surrounded her, and she choked.

Dammit, Sorcha!

She tapped her forehead against the steering wheel. *Somehow* she had to fight off the urge to do that again. God!

How was she going to manage that?

CHAPTER SEVEN

Bets' love life was in the dumps.

How in the hell had that happened?

Before they'd been hot, hot, hot. Now Donal trained and slept and trained some more. They weren't having sex like they used to, and that annoyed the hell out of her. Had boxing become his new mistress?

Since he'd started boxing training, she'd awoken alone every single morning, which made her grouchy as all get out. She hadn't expected Donal to roll out of bed to run four miles at five o'clock in the morning at the ripe age of sixty-three!

Sure, he used to rise at five o'clock before he'd retired a few months ago. A sheep farmer started his rounds early. But she'd thought he'd appreciated the change in his routine—staying up late with her and waking even later in the morning, mostly due to the fact that they couldn't keep their hands off each other.

Yes, he'd mentioned feeling a smidgeon of guilt from time to time, wrapped in nothing but a white bedsheet and sunlight, saying the robes of decadence didn't lie well on his shoulders.

But apparently bruises and sore muscles lay very well. He'd told her repeatedly as she'd offered to give him a massage with arnica cream that he wasn't feeling the training too badly. He was used to muscling four-hundred-pound sheep, wasn't he?

She wanted to scream.

Bets had wanted Donal to have a hobby. She hadn't wanted him to have an obsession.

Not that she could say anything, of course. This is what she'd said she wanted. She'd feared he would be too dependent on her in his retirement, and it seemed there was little danger of that happening.

Still, it was a bitter pill. Here she was alone in the morning again.

She sipped her tea and grimaced. It was downright tepid.

Much like her sex life.

Depressed, she cracked open her laptop, prepared to print off another crop of resumes and portfolios that had come into the center's email box, inquiring about a potential artist residency. After Ellie's donation, word of the center was spreading far and wide.

But the second email from the top was different from the rest, and it snapped Bets out of her stupor. Francine Pasquardo from San Francisco wanted to know if the center's classes were open to non-Irish people. She was a hobby artist who loved to travel, and she'd come across Angie's paintings at an online gallery show in the Netherlands. She'd love to take a painting class with the artist. While it would be possible for her to spend the three-month duration of the class in Ireland, presuming she could find a place to rent, she knew several of her friends would be there with bells on if something shorter were offered.

Bells on...

Bets took another sip of tea before she remembered it was cold, ideas spinning in her head.

They were going international. She could feel it. They'd talked about bringing in new artists and tourists with Kathleen's sculpture and Ellie's stained glass window. They hadn't talked about enrolling students from around the world. She started rocking in her chair in delight. Hell, she wanted to grab a boa and turn on Bon Jovi.

She knew just who she needed to talk to.

Picking up her phone, she called Linc.

"Do you know what time it is, Bets?" he barked, his voice sleep-roughened.

"Shit." It was barely three o'clock in the morning in Oklahoma, she realized as she glanced at the clock. "I got too excited and forgot to check the time. Go back to sleep."

She heard a rustling and then a giant yawn. "No, I'm up. Never have been one to fall back asleep after sudden awakenings. What's got you so excited? Because you wouldn't be calling me if it was Donal."

"If you knew how not funny that was at the moment, you wouldn't joke." She rushed on. "I got an email from a woman in San Francisco who wants to take one of Angie's painting classes. She mentioned her friends might also be interested if we had something shorter in duration than the three-month class. We have a whole new group to cater to, Linc. International students."

"But you have nowhere to put these people other than your two doll-sized cottages, Bets," he said with a sigh. "We need a hotel. I've been thinking about this."

"*A hotel?*" She opened and closed her mouth. "I hadn't—"

"Don't you remember me saying you were thinking too small?" He chuckled before yawning again. "Bets, the center just got a shit-ton of money. You've had artists emailing right and left about grabbing a residency. The Sorcha Fitzgerald Arts Center in Podunk, Ireland, is now on the map."

"Podunk, Ireland." She laughed. "That's a good one."

"Apt. Pretty soon, you're going to need a museum too, for all this art these resident artists are going to create."

A museum? She put her hand to her forehead. Yes, she supposed they would. Many arts centers required a resident to leave behind one or two artistic works. To think about having art like that a mere five minutes from her house... "That would be heaven."

"On that we might disagree, but it's going to be easier than the hotel—less overhead and management. I have some ideas on that too, ones I was planning to run by you and the board after I finish up the last of my own retirement business on this side of the pond."

She wasn't going to think about details right now. She was going to daydream a little. A museum. A hotel. "When are you coming back to Podunk, Ireland?"

"I was hoping to leave Podunk, Oklahoma, after all this boxing madness died down. Do you know they asked me to join in?"

"I thought they might. What did you say?"

"I said, 'Thanks but hell no.' The stone-throwing video Eoghan sent me terrified me so much I almost dropped my phone in my hot tub. The Irish like a little brutality, don't they?"

She'd heard about Eoghan throwing rocks at Declan in

the hopes the stories of his testosterone-laden training would spread across the county. Knowing Ireland, it would work. "I suppose. Throwing rocks at someone isn't what I'd called peace-loving."

"Not too hot on the boxing, eh?" He paused—way too long. "Doesn't it fall under your definition of a hobby?"

She scowled. "Of course it does."

Another pause, this one ripe with curiosity. "Anything you need to talk about, sugar?"

"Not on your life. Just get your ass back here. We have things to do."

"The planning permission is going to be a bitch," Linc said with a grunt. "The hotel will be the worst. I've invested in them before, and it's a painful process unless it comes with a casino."

She sputtered out a laugh at his long-suffering drawl. "The Irish like to gamble."

"I'm not kidding, Bets. I'm thinking you need the place to have a golf course too, but Jesus, it's going to be a slog. I'm not sure it's financially viable. Sometimes when you bring in a famous chef, you can draw visitors in that way too, but I don't think that's going to work in your neck of the woods."

Right. Podunk, Ireland. "A famous chef?" She sat back in her chair. "You're pulling my leg, cowboy."

"I am not. Bets, we need to think about what will bring both local and international interest. From what my research says, most tourists come to Ireland and drive from one place to the next, mostly along the ring of Kerry. People usually only stay in Dublin for three or four nights, and that's pushing it. That's a problem for us."

My God. Her heart was pumping faster at these ideas. "You really *have* been thinking about this, aren't you?"

"What the hell do you imagine I've been doing in this mostly retired stage?"

"Watching Eoghan's videos in your hot tub, apparently."

He snorted out a laugh. "Guilty. But I like me a good hot tub. Sugar, put your thinking cap on."

"Done," she said, miming the action.

Another snort. "You need to think about where you want to be in five or ten years with the center. If we're going to do it, Bets, we might as well do it well. We're striking Podunk, Ireland, from everyone's minds. Not to brag, but my daughter and the other artists are too good to be associated with anything less than excellent. I want the Sorcha Fitzgerald Arts Center and its museum to be one of the best in Europe, if not the world. What do you say to that?"

She had to take a breath, that's what. "From the moment you blew into town, you were a force of nature. We've missed you. Get your ass on your fancy private jet and come for dinner."

His soft chuckle made her miss him all the more. "I'll bring the wine—and a bottle of that bourbon you love so much. See you at dinnertime."

With that, he hung up.

She set her phone down with a smile. He would be there tonight. That was how Linc Buchanan lived, and she rather liked that about him.

She texted Ellie about coming for dinner with Brady and then decided to widen the invitation by having her bring Kathleen. When she called Donal to invite him, she got his voicemail. He was probably punching something.

She decided to punch something herself and headed to the kitchen to make bread for dinner.

Only Ellie texted she had night class—Bets had

forgotten what day it was—and Brady was working at the pub, another change Bets needed to get used to. So she asked Liam and Angie and Carrick. Angie declined, saying she was too pregnant to do much these days and was usually asleep by eight. Megan and Kade liked to put Ollie to bed early so she didn't reach out to them. Liam and Kathleen would do just fine, she thought, and to her delight, they confirmed they were indeed coming.

Hours later, the smell of baking bread was still present as Donal arrived with fresh bruises on his cheekbone. She was gentle when she gave him a kiss.

Donal didn't lengthen it. He grabbed her by the shoulders. "Your voicemail said you spoke to Linc just today. He's making it for dinner tonight? Isn't that a nearly seven-hour flight?"

She fought her disappointment about the kiss and walked over to the counter. "You know Linc." She tossed the salad as he helped himself to a whiskey. "He probably called his plane the minute he got off the phone with me. With the time change, he'll be here when the roast is ready. Liam is coming early to help."

That was probably a good thing since Donal didn't seem in the mood for any pre-dinner fun. She decided to churn some homemade butter with honey, the way Linc and Ellie had told her they served it back home.

When Liam arrived, she kept up a steady stream of talk. Donal didn't join them much, opting instead to read news on his phone since he hadn't caught any today while at the boxing club. She'd just shut off the oven when Linc and Kathleen arrived at the front door, a bottle in each hand.

"Linc told me he left Oklahoma right after you called," Kathleen said, laughing as she held out a bouquet of flowers. "That's Linc for you."

"I didn't have plans tonight," he said, giving an amused grin. "Plus, when Bets gives a summons, you listen. Right, Donal?"

"Right," Donal said, shaking Linc's hand after taking one of the bottles. "Good to see you."

"You look like someone took you to the woodshed too often," Linc replied, gesturing to the yellow bruise on his jaw.

"It builds character," Donal replied with a rueful smile.

The hell it did, Bets thought. "He's going for the Rocky look," she said, leaning in as Linc kissed her cheek.

Liam shook Linc's hand before taking the other bottle. "I saw a new bruise on Fergus' jaw when we met at the store today."

"He ran into my father's fist last night," Donal said with a laugh as they entered the parlor. "Those two are wiry fighters, age aside. What are we drinking?"

"Let's start with the wine," Linc said, putting his arm around Kathleen. "Although this one likes beer more, don't you?"

"I can drink French wine." She nudged Linc playfully. "I'll certainly drink the bourbon later."

"So will I," Bets said, eyeing what she knew to be a prized nearly thirty-thousand-dollar bottle. She'd enjoyed a similar bottle with him on their infamous trip to Paris.

She wondered if Donal remembered. When she looked over, hoping to meet his eye, he was grabbing wineglasses with Liam from the bureau.

Once they all had their drinks, she and Donal sat side by side on the gold settee, and she lifted her glass. "To the arts center and to good friends."

Everyone toasted. "*Slainte.*"

Bets took a moment to savor the wine. "That's nice."

"Good thing I traveled," Linc said, "because I sure wouldn't have stumbled into loving wine in Oklahoma. Everyone know why I flew back like my tail was on fire?"

"Besides Bets asking you?" Donal asked with a laugh.

"Besides that. Bets, you didn't say anything about our talk this morning?"

She shook her head. "I thought I'd wait."

Linc kicked out his feet. "Let me sum it up then."

He laid out their conversation, making Donal's brow raise like the second hand of a clock with each new revelation. "*A museum? A hotel?*" he managed to get out before Linc continued.

Liam shifted in excitement, literally on the edge of his seat. Kathleen only grinned, probably used to Linc and his big ideas after being Ellie's best friend for years.

"The hotel is a surprise although it probably shouldn't be." Donal blew out his breath at the end. "That's going to be a challenge—even with a golf course—but golf *would* be a fine draw. I'm not sure about people traveling for a museum, honestly. We're three hours from Dublin and a little more than that from the start of the ring of Kerry."

"That's in Killarney," Bets said when Kathleen tilted her head.

"We'd need a big draw, no doubt." Linc stroked his chin. "Ellie's finished window will be a start, but that's inside. Kathleen's pirate ship will be outside, as you know."

"Don't I ever?" Kathleen quipped. "I'm working on it nonstop."

"Of course you are," Linc said with a crisp nod. "You know, I got to thinking about other outdoor installations that bring people in from hundreds of miles around. Like the Jolly Green Giant statue in rural Minnesota standing at fifty-five feet tall."

"You're kidding me," Kathleen muttered, her face twisting. "Ellie would tell me to watch out. The sky is about to fall—"

"Then there's the giant Ball of Twine in rural Kansas—"

"There's such a thing? Twine?" Donal asked, laughing so heartily his wine sloshed.

"Americans have a weird sense of humor sometimes," Bets added, shooting him a look. "Especially ones from Oklahoma."

"What about the world's biggest lobster or frying pan installations in rural areas?" Linc asked, snorting with laughter. "People come from all around to see those beauties."

Kathleen swatted him playfully, Bets was glad to see. She might join in. Where was he going with this?

"God, nothing against those artists," Kathleen said, "but—"

"How about Elwood, the fifteen-foot giant gnome, in Ames, Iowa?" Linc fought off another of Kathleen's playful swats. "Before you send me to an early grave—with Bets as your accomplice—how about I mention the mythical horses standing at a nearly hundred feet outside Falkirk in Scotland?"

"*The Kelpies*? Okay, you have my attention," Kathleen said, crossing her arms.

"I'm sure Linc has a point here, but he's going about it in his usual roundabout way," Bets added dryly.

Donal gave a brief chortle. "I'm enjoying it."

"Me too," Liam said, chuckling. "It's like he's one of us already, storytelling in a roundabout way. I'm totally putting the giant gnome on my bucket list."

Bets rolled her eyes and gestured impatiently for Linc to keep talking.

"Let's talk turkey then. Consider the *Angel of the North* in Gateshead outside Newcastle in England. That metal sculpture is sixty-six feet tall and just over one hundred and seventy-five feet wide."

"That's Antony Gormley's baby," Kathleen said breathlessly, albeit with a raised brow. "Let *me* point out that it took four years to build and cost a whopping eight hundred thousand euros according to what I've read in my sculpture magazines."

"Eight hundred—" Donal whistled. *"For a sculpture?"*

Bets stared at Linc. What was he cooking up in that genius brain of his?

"For a sculpture," Linc kicked back. "The installation was locally led, meaning it started with... Wait for it. A local council. Much like you have here."

"I doubt that," Bets said dryly.

"Stay with me. They used local workers—everything from engineers to steel and ground workers."

"Don't forget the shipwrights," Kathleen added with a stern look. "Sculptors use them on bigtime frames for outdoor installations."

Linc gave a grin. "Indeed. The local council had this vison in an area losing manufacturing jobs and looking for redevelopment. They managed to raise the entire sum for the sculpture from a hodgepodge of groups. We're talking the Arts Council Lottery Fund, the EU, private sponsors, and some publicly funded organizations I won't mention."

"People gave all that money to build a sculpture?" Donal's brows slammed together. "I still can't imagine it. Why would they do that?"

"Attention. Tourism. And they didn't stop there. After that, they built the Baltic Centre for Contemporary Art, which they housed in an old mill."

She'd heard of that museum before. She hadn't realized it was in the same town as the famous *Angel of the North*. "No wonder you made a billion dollars on windows."

He smirked. "From there, the community built the Gateshead Millennium Bridge, a pedestrian and cycling structure, which has won some major awards. After that, they built Sage Gateshead, a famous music center. What you might want to know is that these projects bring in tourists and visitors alike, who spend £1.46 billion in the area each year."

Bets choked as Donal whistled again beside her.

"*How much?*" Liam asked, his eyes wide.

"You heard him," Kathleen said, tapping her thigh. "I agree it's a lot of money, but Linc, you didn't mention the local rumbles Gormley's sculpture caused in the beginning or the wider ongoing debate about public money going toward sculptures. I believe you've already had plenty of rumbles here in Caisleán."

"Plenty doesn't cover it," Bets said, the reminder making her snarl.

"But here you've had the reverse problem." Linc steepled his hands. "The council has been the one rumbling. The townspeople have supported you, with their own hard-earned money even. What if you could bring those two groups into balance? Have them both on your side?"

The thought was appealing, sure, but that wasn't likely to happen with her sister-in-law Mary Kincaid's pal Tom MacKenna as the head of the council. Bets rubbed the tense area at the back of her neck. "I don't want to deal with the council, Linc. Ever. I thought the whole purpose of becoming financially independent thanks to Ellie's donation was so we wouldn't have to deal with those bastards anymore."

Linc inclined his chin toward Donal. "You want to tell her?"

She swung her head around and pinned Donal with a look. "Tell me what."

"There's talk the council is considering stopping Kathleen's sculpture."

Kathleen inhaled sharply as Liam cursed.

Bets shot up off the settee, anger surging up. "On what basis, dammit?"

"They're still bandying that about, but they're talking about requiring us to have planning permission for the sculpture as it'll be outside and not in a shed," Donal said, his jaw clenching. "That's why I didn't tell you yet. I had this on someone's strictest confidence."

"But you told Linc?" Bets raged back.

"He has a strong head on his shoulders, and I needed someone to think through how we might counteract this move, should it come." Donal took her hand and squeezed it. "He showed how good he is at maneuvering the council after they closed the center a few months ago. He's also less emotional than you are, *mo ghrá*, and I don't say that to make you cross. God knows you have good reason to be."

She sat down hard on the settee. Her blood was boiling, yes, but her chest was aching too. She'd hoped the battle with the council was over. Then there was the way Donal had kept this from her. She didn't know what to do about that.

"You're sad now under the mad," Donal said, pulling her close to him. "I was too when I heard. Kathleen, I'm sorry you found out like this, but I'm telling you straight. It shouldn't stop you from continuing."

"Stop me?" Her eyes blazed, Bets was delighted to see. "I'd like to see them try. Hell, it makes me want to make it stand a hundred feet tall just to rub their faces in it. I remember what they tried to do to Ellie. I'll fight them to my last breath if I have to."

"Let's hope it doesn't get to that point," Linc said, patting her arm. "One thing I don't want is for us to revert to any talk of the Alamo around here."

Bets met his eyes, remembering the time months ago when she'd likened their fight with Tom and his minions to the Alamo. Linc had more than taken exception. He'd joined the fight and helped them win the battle. Now they seemed to have another one brewing.

"What about our new contact at the Arts Council in Dublin?" Bets asked. "Do you think she can help?"

Linc lifted a shoulder. "Locals don't like big brother coming in and telling them how it's going to be. That's why I think we might switch tactics here and try to get them on our side."

"*What?*" she shrieked.

"Hang on, Bets. Let me finish. I'm not saying we work on Tom or his wife, or your sister-in-law. There are other people on the council. Those are the ones we reach out to."

"But Tom leads with an iron fist," Liam said in exasperation. "That's a tough thing to break."

Linc's smile made Bets think of those movies about outlaws in the Old West. "I don't want to break it. I want to encourage that hand to unfurl."

Kathleen cursed, her expression fierce. She was a force to be reckoned with, Kathleen. It made Bets like her even more. "You're saying you want to put some goodies in that hand. God, I hate this shit. I just want to make my art."

"And yet your work is approved and paid for by public

bodies sometimes." Linc rubbed her arm. "Your work is in the public eye, Kathleen. Hell, if Ellie does stained glass windows for a church, she'll have to deal with religious figures and the like. Art ain't done in no vacuum, honey, certainly not good art. Seems you and Ellie—as well as this community—are along for the ride. But ride it we will. To victory."

Bets was already tired just thinking about another battle after the endless fights they'd had with Tom and company since she first started the center last August. Still, she said, "Where do you want to start?"

"I thought we might use the upcoming fights at the local boxing club." Linc waggled his brows. "That's always a good time to work people over, I've found. I hear Caisleán has a fighter in Declan McGrath."

"You have to be kidding." Bets raised her eyes to the ceiling. "A *boxing* match?"

"Men love to do business at sports matches, I've found," Linc said with a wink. "Something about the atmosphere makes them feel and act more like men. Most leave their Napoleonic complexes at the door."

"Exactly! We all walk around like the big cock in the yard," Donal said, grinning from ear to ear. "I'll talk to the others. Declan's first fight is in a month with Paul Keane—a tough fighter. We can reach out to Paul's manager and see if we can move the fight up. Declan will be ready. He's been training hard."

"Good," Linc said, rubbing his chin. "Be good to have another match shortly after that to keep the momentum going."

The two men shared a look before Donal nodded. "We'll want someone big for him to fight. I'll talk to the others."

"You should talk to Declan," Bets said, grimacing. "You're pimping him out, after all."

"Agreed." Kathleen ran her tongue over her teeth. "I'm sure Declan would love to hear that he's our tool for wheeling and dealing. Jeez. It's like I'm back in Southie. I think I'm going to need some of that bourbon now, Linc."

"Me too," Bets said, frowning at the idea of lobbying jerks while watching the male species bash each other blue. "Got any more bright ideas, cowboy?"

He simply leaned back and put his ankle on his knee, looking very pleased with himself. "Actually, yes. I'm going to teach the sheep farmers how to lasso. There's no reason they need to be chasing sheep like they do."

"That might work," Donal said, leaning forward. "God knows how many sheep I've chased, and not always successfully. The men will be eager to try it."

Kathleen groaned while Bets slapped a hand to her forehead.

They were in for it.

What was Linc going to think up next?

CHAPTER EIGHT

W hen she heard someone pounding at her door early the next morning, Kathleen's mind raced to Declan as she shot out of bed.

She had on the same shorts she'd worn last time, the ones he'd reached out to touch. Her skin sizzled. She thought about changing and brushing her hair—she probably had bed head. But it was his fault he was at her door early again. She tried to quell her pounding heart as she opened the front door.

It was Linc. "Oh, it's you." She winced. "Sorry, that came out wrong."

"Expecting someone else?" His silver brow winged up. "Not my daughter, it seems. Anything I should know about?"

"No." The last thing she needed was for Ellie's dad to question her about Declan. He was on her mind enough without having everyone constantly remind her of him.

Robbie's last text had been epic: *I smell a guy. You'd better fess up soon.*

Diversion usually worked with the male species.

"Didn't we just solve all the mysteries of the universe a few hours ago?"

"You'd hope so since it was close to three o'clock when we finally broke up." He laughed and ducked inside, closing the door behind him on the rain. "Donal was nice enough to put me up so I won't have to endure Bets' other dollhouse cottage. God, this place is as tiny as I remember it. Do your ankles hang off the bed?"

She looked down and wiggled one. The blood was finally coming back to them. "Yeah, that kinda sucks, but it's the spiders that are driving me nuts. Every time I turn around—"

"*Spiders?* Maybe the winter cold kept them away when I was here. Big?"

"One kind is big and hairy." She shuddered. "The other is delicate and white, and one of them was in my sock yesterday morning. Don't tell my brothers, but I might have screamed."

He shrugged out of his navy jacket and laid it carefully on a chair after checking it for vermin, she imagined. "I would have too. Speaking of your brothers, don't tell Ellie, but I got them all to agree to come to the wedding—on my plane. Your pop too. It's one of my wedding presents for Ellie."

Her mouth dropped open. "You're kidding! What did you do? Win an arm wrestling match?"

He inclined his head toward the kitchen. "You have coffee?"

"Yeah, I'm on my second cup. But first tell me how you got them to agree." She was still in shock as she poured him a cup and set it in the ancient microwave to reheat.

"I must be desperate for coffee if I'm taking it nuked." He made a face. "As for the O'Connors, I simply told them

Ellie would cry buckets if they didn't come and you might as well, although it was more likely you'd beat them over the head with a frying pan."

"I'd been contemplating that," she admitted, because having her family at Ellie's wedding was important, but she knew the O'Connor pride as much as she did the balance in their bank accounts.

He thanked her when she handed him the cup of coffee. "And yes, I asked who I needed to arm wrestle."

She started laughing. "Who volunteered? And how badly were you hurt?"

Linc took a sip of the coffee before heading to the fridge and pouring in some milk. "Tom volunteered, pulling my chain about how he's used to dealing with old people at the retirement center he works in. He only sprained my wrist."

"But he let you win." God, she loved those blockheads.

"Of course. They'd agreed to go if I beat him. This way everybody got what they wanted or preserved what was vital to them. Men will do anything to maintain their pride. Got any sugar?"

She yanked open a cupboard door that tended to stick, either from age or the damp. He remembered where the silverware was kept, she noted. After taking a spoonful, he stirred his cup thoughtfully as rain began to pound on the roof.

"All right, we've covered those topics." She leaned back against the counter. "Now tell me why I'm your first stop this morning and not your daughter."

He drank his coffee and nodded before saying, "I thought we were on a roll after last night. I wondered what you might think about increasing the size of your pirate ship. You did mention it a little last night."

She had. Something about rubbing their nemeses' faces in it. "Fifteen feet isn't enough for you?"

His mouth tipped up. "No, actually. Not for what I have in mind. Closer to fifty or seventy-five would be ideal."

She was sure the ground trembled under her feet. "Do you have any idea how much that would cost?"

"Not a problem," he said blandly. "Remember me talking about this last night? Plenty of groups and the like to hit up."

Right. Her head spun. "What about the time it would take to construct?"

"That, I think, *is* the problem." He tilted his head to the side, his blue eyes intent. "I know how much your family means to you. God knows how much they mean to my daughter. You only wanted to come for four months. What I'm asking is whether you'd consider staying for a few years —as long as a larger project would take."

She should have seen it coming, she supposed. But she hadn't. Her gut told her that a sculpture of the magnitude he was suggesting would take four years. Holy— "I'm going to need more coffee for this conversation."

"Good, because I didn't want to say, but I wouldn't feed this rewarmed drivel to a pig," he said, and then he laughed.

That was Linc for you. He'd pull the rug out from under you with one of his huge ideas and then try and make you laugh with something colloquial. Ellie was the same way. Kathleen made new coffee, and they went into the parlor. She watched as he tested a chair before gently easing into it.

"Your backside hurting you or something?" she drawled as much as she could manage. She'd never mastered the Southern accent any more than Ellie had managed the Boston one.

He patted the chair. "I might have cracked it the last time I sat in it. None of the furniture in this country seems fit for big men. But let's return to my idea... What do you think of it?"

She decided to pivot. "I know you're on the board for the arts center, but aren't you being a little heavy-handed, suggesting something like this?"

His brow knit, although a smile crossed his face. "Heavy-handed I might be, but I ran my plan by both Bets and Donal before I appeared on your doorstep this morning. I caught Donal before he left, seeing as I'm staying at his house. And Bets is usually an early riser. I texted her. She called me. She agreed in two minutes flat."

Two minutes was all it had taken to possibly change her life. Still, she tried to stay cool. "I should have been the first to hear about it."

His snort told her what he thought of that. "I got to thinking about all this when I was in bed last night. We need something tangible to sell to the council people, something that will be a tourist draw. The museum—which the board will support, I think—will take time. We need more artists to come through and donate pieces. Although we might reserve a wing of the museum to showcase a temporary show from time to time. Yes, that's it."

She pushed her coffee aside. "My God. You didn't retire. You changed careers."

He lifted a shoulder. "It seems a natural progression. Ellie's interest in the arts is one I've always shared with her. My whole career, I gave to the arts. Now I'm going to build the framework here in Caisleán with these great people whom I've come to respect and love. Plus, Ellie is here and, at some point, my grandbabies. Why the hell else wouldn't I make this my new home?"

They were all good points. "Linc, I came here on a four-month artist residency with the intention of returning home in early August before the beaches closed for swimming."

"Your pop doesn't want you to lose opportunities because of them," he said softly.

She set down her coffee. "You talked to my pop about this?"

"I didn't, which I'd hope you would know." When he leaned forward, his chair gave a terrible creak, which had him easing gently back again. "He brought it up to me in the O'Connor kitchen after he ran out for Dunks coffee and Southie Scramblers, the morning after I beat your brother at arm wrestling."

The mention of the breakfast sandwich loaded with eggs, bacon, sausage, onions, peppers, and cheese shouldn't have made her homesick, but it did, as much as knowing that her pop had told Linc something he'd never told her. The O'Connor men were terrible at expressing their feelings.

"I'm sorry. That was unfair. What did he say?"

He gave a soft smile. "He said Ellie had found her way and her happiness here in Ireland. He wanted the same for you. You know how much he loves the old neighborhood, but he thinks you've gone as far as you can there. You know everyone, he said, and that has its limits. He wanted me to give you this. He thought it would help you understand."

Linc reached into his pants pocket and pulled out something on a chain. Her emotions scattered as she beheld the simple silver Claddagh ring her father had given her mother.

"My pop worked extra shifts at the salvage yard to buy that for my mom," she said, taking it. "They were sixteen when he asked her to go steady with him. They married at eighteen and the rest is history."

"Your pop loves you—like I love my Ellie. He and I understand each other, and while we've had different lives, we want the same thing for both of you girls. Happiness. Family. A man who'll love you like you deserve. Your pop thinks you'll find all that here *in magical Ireland,* as he called it. To do that, you need to stay longer. He said he 'felt' it while he was in church one morning lighting a candle for you. His words."

The smell of oranges wrapped around her, making her sit up straighter in her chair. Goose bumps broke out over her skin as she swept her gaze through the room. Surely Sorcha wasn't involved... Pop went to church faithfully and had what he called "moments of deep knowing." Said it was probably the Irish in him. Sometimes he thought it was their mother, helping from heaven. Kathleen had liked to believe their mother still helped them. It was a comfort. But this felt different.

"You going to faint?" Linc asked, taking her hand and patting it in brisk taps. "I didn't think that's how you were going to react, but what the hell do I know."

"I'm not going to faint." Her head was fuzzy, though, even though she didn't see that infernal ghost. She was so not going to ask Sorcha if she'd been involved.

He rose and put a steady hand on her shoulder. "I'll leave you to kick it around. How does a few days sound? We'd like to start using it on the councilmen we hope to influence at the upcoming fights."

She had to laugh, although she wasn't sure it was funny. "That's so like you, Linc. Deadlines and whatnot."

"I might talk slow but I'm not one to dawdle." He leaned down and kissed her cheek. "See you later, sugar."

"Sometimes you're so sweet, I'd swear you'd make a person's teeth fall out."

He gave a hearty laugh. "Or give 'em cavities. Funny thing about sweets though, and something to remember... People don't mind the prospect of their teeth falling out when the goodies are so delicious along the way. I must remember to tell that to Bets. Have a good one, honey."

A good one, huh? She picked up her coffee and kicked her feet up on the table, her eyes on her mother's necklace, as he let himself out.

"He's good craic, isn't he?" Sorcha said, appearing in the chair he'd vacated.

Kathleen jumped and almost fell backward, but she managed to catch the end of the table. "Stop doing that!"

"You sound as vexed as Declan." She chuckled, completely unrepentant. "Your pop seems to know the way the winds are blowing, doesn't he?"

She glared at the ghost. Oh, what the hell? "Did you—?"

"Your father has his own way of knowing things, doesn't he?"

She nodded slowly. But in the past, they'd been smaller things—when her brothers were up to "no good" on a Friday night, when the Patriots were going to win the Super Bowl, and when he'd sworn he'd known which lucky number to buy for his lottery ticket only to win a couple hundred dollars. This was like a wallop to the head. He'd sent her mother's ring and told her to stay in *magical* Ireland.

"When are you going to accept what's in front of you? I mean, I probably shouldn't have looked, but the kiss you and Declan shared yesterday could have started a fire in the woodstove. I know kisses. The ones you shared didn't speak of a mere attraction."

She crossed her trembling arms. "No?"

"Those, my dear Kathleen, are the kind of kisses that are only possible between two people meant for each other." She gave a saucy wink, her green eyes alight. "Soulmates. Everything is conspiring to keep you in Ireland longer. Linc's visit suggests it. Perhaps you should... What did he call it? Kick it around?"

With that, she vanished. Like she'd never been sitting beside Kathleen and pecking at her.

Kathleen gave in to the urge to give a healthy screech. One good thing about being in the middle of Ireland was that she had no neighbors. Boy, did it feel good. She did it again a couple of more times. Her heart rate steadied, and she took a deep breath.

The sun came out even though it was still raining, and it shone on the necklace, light dancing off the silver onto the ceiling. She cocked her ear as the faint notes of an Irish ballad played on the flute and violin whispered on the wind that shook the windows.

Where was the music coming from?

More gooseflesh rippled over her arms. Her parents and grandparents always talked about the magic of Ireland. They'd always claimed magic still lived inside all the O'Connors from their Irish blood. There were reminders of it all over her tough Irish neighborhood, many of them kitschy. Signs with dancing leprechauns and fairies. Bumper stickers with *Luck of the Irish* or *Kiss Me I'm Irish*. T-shirts that said everything from *Don't Piss Off The Fairies* to *Póg Mo Thóin*. Welcome mats like the one at the home she'd grown up in, which had simply said, *Fáilte*.

And, yes, Claddagh rings to give your girl when you wanted to go steady or get married.

She kissed the ring before slipping the necklace over her

head and adjusting the symbol to rest over her heart, where her mother had told her it belonged.

The silver felt warm against her skin, which seemed impossible since she'd only just put it there.

Growing up, even though she was a Boston girl born and bred, tough and pragmatic, she'd believed in magic. When Danny had told her that fairies watched over his pub, she'd bought it. All of them had wanted to believe in something, she guessed, coming up in the kind of rough place that was Southie, where little if any magic was found.

She closed her eyes as she gripped that ring. Her very foundation rocked with the realization that she didn't want to stop believing in magic. She needed it. It had helped her become the woman she was. It had fueled the artist she was still becoming.

Why would she turn down the chance to create a pirate ship that could top out at fifty or seventy-five feet? She had come to Ireland to make her mark. A sculpture of the stature they were discussing would launch her well beyond her current five-year plan.

"I guess I'm going into the catapult then," she said softly into the silence.

Opening her eyes, she gazed down at the ring. Her pop had tucked it into his sock drawer after her mom had died. Although he'd given her other treasured belongings from her mother—a plate she'd bought at Niagara Falls on their honeymoon and an afghan knitted by Kathleen's great grandmother—he'd never parted with this ring.

Until now.

Her pop *knew* something. She believed that. He'd sent the ring with the message he'd conveyed through Linc.

The scent of oranges surrounded her again, and she frowned.

"I was just getting to a good place with all this, Sorcha. Dammit, girl, you could live in Southie, you're so in my face."

Laughter was her response, and yes, it still freaked her out a little.

"I preferred the Irish music on the wind better." Listen to the crazy coming out of her mouth.

Except it *wasn't* crazy and neither was she.

And Sorcha had been dead-on about her kiss with Declan. It hadn't been the garden-variety kind.

Kathleen imagined the rest of her interactions with Declan would be anything but ordinary too. It had been like that from the moment she'd seen him.

She held the ring as she thought about what it would mean to stay.

Fighting the current was stupid, especially when the current was flowing in one direction. She'd best stop trying to paddle the other way.

What would Declan do if she told him she'd changed her mind?

CHAPTER NINE

W hen Declan arrived at the boxing club after work, his eager trainers were waiting for him...only none of them were dressed for training. No one's hands and wrists were wrapped. No one was wearing the club's green robes over athletic shorts.

Dammit.

The only thing that had gotten him through the endless chatter and orders at the butcher shop after that earth-shattering kiss with Kathleen yesterday was the prospect of hard training. Even that hadn't been enough to banish her from his mind, and the anxious looks his brother had darted at him on his short stop at Summercrest hadn't helped.

"Did you codgers finally agree you're too old for this?" he asked, walking over to his locker.

"We need a moment, Declan," Eoghan said, holding up a finger. "Donal, you should tell him."

The large man led the group of volunteer trainers from where they'd been standing beside the boxing ring. "Tell me what?"

"We've changed the timetable for your first fight."

Donal rested against the dented metal locker beside him. "Cormac got Paul Keane's manager to agree to move it up by two weeks."

That would put his first bout on the third Friday in May. He glanced at his father, who gave him an encouraging smile, and then back at Donal. "Why the urgency?"

"You're ready," Donal continued. "You've been training hard, and there's nothing like a real match."

"You still haven't told me why, and since it's me who's going to be fighting, I'd like to know."

Donal nodded. "We want to be chatting up some people of interest a bit earlier, is all."

Their bluster smelled of old fish. Something else was afoot. "Speak plainly."

"A fight is a good place for chatting with people you'd like to influence on certain things," Eoghan said, smoothing the gray wisps of hair on his head. "There's a plan in the works regarding the arts center."

"It's not something you need to be concerned about," Donal was quick to assure him. "You only need to fight."

"You don't even have to win," his father said, slapping him on the back. "Just do your best."

He narrowed his eyes at that. "Thanks, Dad. You're all acting odd. What does this have to do with the arts center? Are there problems again?"

Did this new batch of trouble have anything to do with Kathleen? Every new artist had gone through hurdles owing to Tom MacKenna and Mary Kincaid and their lot. He'd helped as much as he could when they'd closed the center a few months ago. He wished he could ask these men for details, but if he did, it would only prompt them to raise their gray brows in a knowing way, something he didn't want or need.

"We're hoping to head them off," Donal said, his tone emphatic. "Linc has some ideas, ones I agree with. All we need is for you to fight."

"I don't like hearing there might be trouble again," he said. "Maybe Cormac can arrange for me to fight Tom MacKenna. I'd love to knock him out for the trouble he's caused."

"As if that bastard would fight fair," Seamus said with a snarl, flexing, his arms heavy with muscle from years of hefting slabs of meat. "He's more inclined to plot in the shadows."

"We could challenge him," Fergus said, holding up his fists. "Tell him Eoghan and I would give him a handicap by fighting him at our age."

"We'd lay him flat," Eoghan said, his usually affable face contorted with a scowl. "But there's a plan afoot to box him into a corner thanks to Lincoln Buchanan. Saints preserve us! He's a man to have on your side."

They all made a sound of assent, one that had him wondering again at the details. He would chat Ellie up later when he went home. "He's back from America?"

"As of last night," Donal said, nodding. "Full of ideas as usual. He's a gift to this town, he surely is. He'll be staying at my house until he can find a better house. But sad news, boys. He doesn't want to box."

"That's a right pity," Eoghan said, hanging his head. "He'd be a fierce opponent."

"He said he's too old to want to be hit in the face," Donal said with a grin. "I told him it might improve his looks."

They all laughed at that. There was no denying the lot of them looked like a bunch of bruised jackals.

"We should start the training." Eoghan opened Declan's

locker and gestured to the equipment inside. "We'll be working you harder than ever. I hope you're ready for it."

Harder than ever? He prayed it would stop all thoughts of Kathleen's luscious body pressed against him, their mouths tangled in a kiss he'd remember until he was in the ground, God help him. "Do your worst."

They surely did. Brutal rounds of chin-ups, push-ups, sit-ups, along with calf-screaming sets of jumping rope. They'd all agreed to fight him for two minutes apiece save Eoghan and Fergus, who critiqued his every move in the ring.

Donal got in one of his meaty right hooks, but Declan managed to pin Seamus to the ropes, and to rush his father after his dad led him on a merry chase around the ring. He was improving.

When Eoghan called an end—being the senior trainer of sorts—he forced himself off to the showers and welcomed the sluice of torrentially cold water along his battered, bruised muscles. It was only when he laid his head against the shower's concrete wall that he saw Kathleen in his mind, beautiful and bold. God, would it ever end, the wanting of her?

"It's time to stop fighting it," a familiar voice said softly.

He didn't have the strength to lift his head. "It's a low move to appear to a man when he's naked in the shower."

Sorcha snorted. "I'm not interested in your naked parts, Declan McGrath, and I'm a mite offended you would even suggest it. That's not why I'm here."

"I'm too tired to fight you, Sorcha," he said, his voice near hoarse to his own ears. "Say your piece and then leave me be, for the love of God."

There was silence for a long moment, and he wondered if she'd left him. He wasn't sure how he felt about it.

Then she said, "Kathleen will be staying for years in Ireland," and destroyed his peace.

He gripped the shower knob before wrenching off the water. His heart leapt in his chest. She was staying? What would that mean?

He needed clothes for this conversation. The towel he used was across the room, and he decided to forgo modesty and strode to it. Wrapping it around his waist, he finally turned to face her. True to her word, she had her back to him.

"Talk."

Her white dress whirled as she spun around, and a smile danced on her lips. "When two people are meant to be, events conspire to bring them together. I am not the only agent interested in seeing you and Kathleen together. That you should know, and that you will surely see more of soon."

"Speak plainly, Sorcha." He raked the wet from his hair with an impatient hand. "I'm too tired to walk a rambling road this eve. You might as well be related to Liam, for you both sound like Yoda to me."

"We cannot help our wisdom or our words." She gave a light chuckle. "As I was saying, the road will ramble, and walk it you will, but plain I will speak since you ask me. Linc Buchanan has a grand vision for the center that holds my name, and Bets, Donal, and the others are in agreement. He has asked Kathleen to enlarge her vision and her sculpture, which would entail her staying for years to complete it. She has agreed for a number of reasons, which she will share with you when she's ready. You have the chance to explore what's between you..."

He shifted his weight as the impact of what she'd said rolled over him. *They had a chance...*

God, it would be so good to be with her.

"Four months of temptation you may have been able to fight, Declan McGrath, but not years." She walked toward him, her dress billowing along with her hair. "Kathleen is of the same mind. She's decided to stop fighting, as you will discover when you next meet. I appeared to you so you may fashion your reply in advance and not mess up your words. Speak from your heart, Declan."

He glared at her. "Last I looked, people understood me just fine."

"You think I don't know you? You said and did what was expected with Morag. With Kathleen, you're learning a new way. You need to learn a new way of communicating along with it—one that is brighter and bolder, because that is how you feel."

He took his time considering her, his thoughts as worn as his muscles. She was right. With Morag he had done what was common. Expected. A man found a woman he thought he could have a family with. One from the area. They married. They settled down. They had children.

With Kathleen, nothing had gone as expected. In fact, he never knew what would happen next. His heart and body were pushing him toward something he couldn't wrap his head around—something bigger than he'd ever experienced. Since the first moment he'd met Kathleen O'Connor, he'd felt more alive, like he'd been asleep all those years.

The newness was exciting, and yes, it also made him feel raw and vulnerable. That part he hadn't liked.

Sorcha lifted a hand to trace his cheek, but her touch only passed through. "The entire course of your life will be set by what you do next. She's waiting at her cottage for you. She wanted me to tell you. Good luck, Declan."

She disappeared, leaving him alone with the only sound

being the drip of water from his shower. He sank heavily onto a worn wooden bench and put his head in his hands. This decision would affect his entire life, and he wasn't ready to make it.

He wasn't sure he would ever be ready. What if he got it wrong again? He would be hurt. But so would others. Kathleen herself. Brady. Ellie even.

The drip of water grew louder in his ears. He looked at the puddle gathering, and in the water, saw Kathleen's form, the siren call in her brown eyes, the allure of her slender body. He could hear her laughter, as if carried on the wind.

Sorcha was right. He might fight the temptation for four months, although their kiss had more than chipped away at his resolve. There was no way he could fight her constant presence here for years. Certainly not if she'd stopped fighting the temptation herself.

He had to say yes. He *wanted* to say yes. And yes and yes again.

The atrophied pieces of his heart pulsed painfully with life. Of all the hurts he'd had with boxing, from the bruises and the battered, knotted muscles, this pain in his chest was the worst. It stole his breath and brought a hot burn to his eyes.

Morag had shown him the folly of loving, the brutal pain of betrayal.

Could he trust himself and his heart to another?

When Kathleen's image remained in the puddle, her bright eyes shining at him, he knew it was a sign. He could and would trust her.

There was no other way.

CHAPTER TEN

Meeting Declan at the door in nothing but a short nightgown seemed nutso, no matter how late it was getting, so she was still dressed...dressed and feeling like an idiot. What if he didn't come? Not a happy thought.

She told herself she was still dressed because the cottage was cold from the endless rain today. To comfort herself, she'd chosen her favorite pair of worn jeans that had frayed hems from walking barefoot on the Cape—along with the signed Tom Brady jersey her brothers had given her one Christmas.

She'd already celebrated her news about staying with Ellie, who had squealed loudly enough to make her ears ring. They'd hugged and jumped up and down like little kids. Then she'd made her friend laugh by saying she was going to wait until evening to tell Linc since he'd given her a timetable.

Ellie had asked her to come over for dinner, but she'd begged off, saying she needed to start reworking her design with the new dimensions. Most things could be easily enlarged, but the new scale would allow her to make certain embellishments that wouldn't have been possible previously.

Once home, she'd called Linc to confirm that she would go for the seventy-five-foot height, and he'd chuckled before telling her, "You're going to make one hell of a splash with this sucker, sugar. It's going to look fabulous, rising above those hills beside the Sorcha Fitzgerald Arts Center."

She could already see it in her mind, and her energy was charged with excitement and a little trepidation. Only natural, she told herself. "I'm going to need to hire a crew so you'd better put your money where your mouth is."

Her reply had sent him into fits of laughter. "We've got you covered."

Shortly thereafter, Bets had walked down from her cottage to tell Kathleen how delighted she was by the change in plans. Linc had texted her, of course. As the setting sun turned a brilliant red over the emerald hills outside her cottage, they'd enjoyed a celebratory whiskey from the bottle Bets had brought in a gift bag. They'd shaken their heads over Linc and his big ideas, but in the end, they'd agreed they wouldn't want him any other way.

Kathleen's impulse had been to find Declan after he got off work, but she'd resisted it, knowing he had training. To interrupt it would be rude. She would want him to respect her time and work, wouldn't she? So she did what she'd never have imagined doing.

She called Sorcha, wondering if the woman would come, and sure as hell, she had, appearing in her tiny cottage after Bets had left. The woman had assured her she'd deliver her message—and then vanished into thin air.

Her brothers and father still didn't know about her decision, and she'd given plenty of thought to how to tell them. Her pop was clearly on board, and she imagined her brothers would be too, in the end. But it wasn't a conversation she wanted to rush into. They would have questions, and right now, she didn't need to take on any more tough guys.

Declan was plenty.

Only he didn't look so tough when he finally knocked on her door shortly after ten. He looked exhausted standing in the meager light from the rising full moon overhead.

"You're using Sorcha to deliver messages now?" he asked with a dry note to his usually steady voice.

In the shadows, she couldn't see his face or tell what he was thinking. "You're here, aren't you? Declan—"

"Is it true?" he asked, his hand wrapping around her arm and pulling her against him.

She was half-in and half-out of the cottage, she realized, as she gazed into his serious face. This time she didn't need to ask what he meant. The hoarseness of his voice told her all. "Yes, I'm staying."

His other arm gripped her so she was locked against him. His gaze seemed to rake over her face. "And you want this?"

She pressed closer. "Yeah, God help us. You in, Ace?"

His mouth tipped up at the right, the first break in the granite angles of his face. "I'm for it. Kathleen, I can't seem to want anything but you. If I come in now..."

Her belly liquified with pure lust. "I want you to come in."

"But you called me Ace just now." He locked gazes with her, his blue eyes molten. "Ask me inside, and when you do, say my name."

135

God, that was hot. Desire coursed through her. "Declan, please come inside. Now."

He came inside and kicked the door closed, his hands banding around her waist. "I like it when you use my name. Kathleen, I'm not going to be able to go slow the first time."

An agonized laugh spurted out. "Who's asking you to? I should be the one asking you about your bruises. Do *I* need to go slow?"

"I'll die if you do."

"Okay, then."

She pulled his head down to her own. The meeting of their mouths was like their first kiss—and the second—all-consuming. Flames rushed over them, wrapping them in the brutal desire they had for each other. She moaned as his hands lifted her, their mouths dueling, and then wrapped her legs around his waist.

He grunted and walked briskly into the bedroom by the front door, laying her on the bed. She kissed him deeply as they started pulling at each other's clothing. A seam ripped, making her laugh again, and his delicious smile made her toes curl with pleasure. Then he took off her bra and fastened his mouth on her breast, making her cry out, her back arching. His hand pulled her jeans down to her knees and then pressed between them, making her come. Just. Like. That.

He pulled off the rest of their clothes until their searing flesh met again. She was still pulsing as he laid her back and opened her legs.

"God, I need a condom," he said, turning away.

She grabbed his arm. "I'm on the pill, if you're clean."

"I'm clean," he muttered, closing his eyes, his face an agony of desire. "Jesus."

She knew what he was struggling with, the brutal urge

to mate, to join, to be taken. She rose up until she was sitting and pressed her open hands on his chest, knowing any other touch would destroy him.

"Come into me," she whispered, lying back again, taking his hands with her, bringing him into position over her. "Now, Declan."

When he met her gaze again, he was feverish with want. He pressed against her and then found his mark, thrusting into her in one restrained move that stole her breath with its power. Her belly tightened again, and she knew the urgent call of another orgasm was rising within her. She lifted her hips to him, urging him on, and he finally let go of his control. He withdrew and then thrust back in, the beautiful, agonizing stroke making her cry out.

He froze.

"Oh, God, don't stop," she panted. "Please don't stop."

He propped himself onto his elbows, wedging an arm under her hips. "I don't want to hurt you."

She grabbed his rock-hard butt in her hands. "You won't. Give us what we both need."

As she tightened around him, he finally heeded her, thrusting first deep and then shallowly until neither of them could control the wild rhythm of their straining bodies. The razor-sharp claws of passion had her gripping him hard as he thrust into her. Fast, deep, hard—perfect. She knew she was going to come, could feel the tide rising, and she locked her legs around him and made him come with her.

She broke into a million pieces, every cell in her pulsing. He reared back, and on his next thrust, he cried out.

She lay back heavily on the bed as the pleasure swept through her every cell, making her skin tingle from it. "Oh, God," she managed, the electricity stronger than she'd ever had to bear.

This was no soft glow of pleasure—this was the agonizing conclusion of being tossed onto the beach after riding through a hurricane.

"You all right?" he uttered between loud, urgent breaths, his head on the pillow beside her.

She found her hand—it lay on his back—and stroked him briefly, her nerve endings still buzzing from the avalanche of release. "Getting there. You?"

"I might be able to move in ten years." He gave a quick laugh. "Good God."

"Yeah, that's my consensus." Nothing had ever been as powerful as this. "It was like turning my blowtorch on full throttle. God, I swear if I smell oranges right now, I might get violent."

"No one likes a know-it-all, do they?" Another laugh rumbled from his chest. "I'm as wrecked as I've ever been. Jesus, Kathleen. Has it ever been like this for you?"

"No. You?"

"Not ever," he said, inhaling deeply, "and I thought nothing could surpass the time I got with a very experienced Portuguese girl who knew more than I did as a lad of eighteen. Is that improper to say right now?"

This time she laughed and gripped him in a quicksilver hug. "It's honest, and I like honest. So your best sex was exotic vacation sex. Funny how I talked about wishing I could meet you on vacation."

He pressed onto his elbows and looked into her face, his blue eyes as brilliant as ocean waves lit by the midday sun. "You did at that, but we didn't meet on vacation, and what happened here made that seem almost tepid in comparison. How does that sit with you?"

She traced his sweaty hair falling over his forehead.

"Are we talking now? Because if we are, I must demand a water break."

"You're a lightweight then," he said, the makings of a rare full grin on his face. "You need more training."

Her heart expanded like metal from heat. She liked him like this, sexy, funny, daring. "A lightweight? Say that again and see what happens."

"Lightweight," he spit out with a laugh.

She exerted pressure to push him to the side and he let her, rolling with it. His eyes fired blowtorch blue as she climbed on top of him. "You leave me no choice. I'm going to have to show you what happens when you call me names."

"So long as you call me Declan while you're doing it, I won't mind."

"I can handle that. Declan. Let's see about my training."

Her mouth discovered him, something she'd been imagining all day while she waited for him to come to her, hoping he would. His breath caught and then came out in a ragged exhale. His groans delighted her as her teeth found sensitive places on his body. She was careful with the bruised parts this time. There was plenty to feast on, and feast she did. He had his eyes closed and his hands fisted at his sides when she finally lowered herself onto him and took him inside her.

The feel of him was delicious, and she arched back, pressing their hips together in one fluid line of passion. His hands rose to grip her hips, and they began another urgent rhythm, less wild but no less powerful. When she came, he followed, and she lay on his chest, his hand stroking her back in an easy caress. Inside her, the soft glow of her orgasm began to spread. Her heart seemed to catch fire until all she was, all she could imagine being, was a warm, beating heart.

The smell of oranges came to her then. But with his arms around her, she found she didn't mind.

Indeed, she was downright thankful, although she didn't plan to tell Sorcha. Yet.

CHAPTER ELEVEN

Declan lay facedown in pure bliss.

He hadn't known he could feel this good. That anything could feel this good. His life was filled with contrasts. In boxing, he felt only invigorating torture. Here, in her arms, sweeping ecstasy. No middle ground for Declan McGrath, it seemed. No one who knew him would be surprised.

Kathleen's hands were now working his shoulders, digging into the sore muscles. He'd never been a man who understood or sought out pampering, but if this was how things were going to be between them, he was ready to fight off his every fear about relationships. "I could get used to this. Your hands might as well have been touched by the fairies."

Her gusty laughter made him smile. "I like that. Imagine how much better my sculpture will be for it."

He craned his neck to look back at her, and what a sight she was, straddling his back in her glorious nudity. He never wanted to see her clothed again. "Tell me more about the new plan for your ship."

"I like you wanting to know." Her thumbs found sore tissue in his trapezius and dug in, making him groan. "I'm revising it to stand seventy-five feet tall."

"How much is that in meters?" She arched back for her phone, the sight of her strong yet slender body making him start to sweat again. God she was lovely. Beautiful. Bright. "Maybe I'm tired or maybe I'm just sated, but I'm wondering why we ever fought this."

"It's nearly twenty-three meters," she said, fitting herself back onto him. "And we're tired and sated because of fabulous sex. We haven't talked about the soulmate part."

"Twenty-three meters is giant," he responded, "and you're right. We haven't talked about the soulmate part. Do you want to?"

Her fingers rubbed his trapezius, but this time he fought the groan. There were in serious territory now. Then again, they'd already gone there during the sex. Only it had felt so good, the falling and surrendering, he hadn't known how serious it was until afterward, when they'd lain beside each other and gazed into each other's eyes. Hers had been filled with light and a new softness had been on her face. She'd looked young and fresh and more beautiful than any woman he'd ever met. She might have grabbed his heart and held it, then and there.

"We'll need some guidelines, Ace."

"Declan," he corrected.

"Declan." She found a line of bone and muscle, easing her fingers into it in a way that had his eyes closing. "We clearly are going to want to keep having sex."

"Absolutely."

"I don't want us to be with other people."

He pushed up onto his hands and rolled her off him so he could face her. "I don't want anyone else, *mo chroí*."

A rare flash of vulnerability streaked across her face, making her look years younger. He understood. They'd both been betrayed that way, in the most intimate way a person could be.

"Good. I'd like to go out sometimes, although I know you're training hard. Also, I like the Gaelic."

He would have to remember that. "My first fight has been moved up," he said, taking her hand, "but we'll find time for each other. In the bedroom and out of it."

She nodded crisply, and it struck him how practical she was trying to be. Calling him Ace fit the part, he supposed. He drew her closer and caressed her cheek. "Let's talk about Sorcha. I plan on making up my own mind about the way things are between us. I won't be telling anyone I fell for you because a ghost told me to."

"God, neither will I!" she said with a snort, putting an open hand on his chest, a touch he was starting to recognize as a natural one for her—and one he already craved. "She's right about our connection being unusual, but you do realize what she means when she says we're soulmates, right?"

His brow knit. He thought of Sorcha telling him about this new language he was to navigate. Here they were. "The happily ever after stuff."

She made a face before laughing, but he noticed she wouldn't meet his eyes right then. "Let's not kid ourselves, Ace—Declan. I'm not Cinderella and you're not Prince Charming. We're just two people with a strong attraction to each other who happen to like each other. I figure we'll find out if there's more as time goes on. We have years, after all. You good with that?"

"You don't plan to rush me. I like that."

"*I* don't like to be rushed." She climbed onto his lap.

"Except in a few things. This seems to be one of them. I'd like you to stay the night—if you're game. That's rare for me since my breakup with my ex."

After their night together, he couldn't imagine being anywhere else. "The thought of leaving you isn't something I want in my thick skull."

Her fingers traced the back of his neck in a sensual massage as a smile broke across her face. "What time do you have to start training in the morning?"

He grimaced. "Five. The whole crew meets up for a run."

"God, that's early!" She wrapped her legs around him. "It's one now, and I should let you go to sleep, but I can't seem to stop myself from having you again."

What man wanted to sleep when a woman like her was naked before him? An eejit, that's who. "Say that once more, if you please, and with my name this time," he said, holding her big brown eyes.

She framed his face, her palms warm on his cheeks. "I can't seem to stop myself from having you again, Declan."

He adjusted himself and slid into her, their gazes locked. "All I want is to be inside you and feel you around me. Hear you cry out my name."

"Then you'd better get to it," she said with a grin before their mouths met in a slow, deep kiss that led to him calling her name as well. With Gaelic for good measure. Because she liked it.

Fitting her against him afterward, he asked, "When you asked me to stay earlier... You said that was a rarity for you. Will you tell me why?"

She sighed in the dark. "My brothers always said they kept their distance from a girl by leaving after sex. I thought it might work for me. If you don't think about what comes after... If you make sure there *isn't* an after..."

He let that information sink in. "I did the same. After Morag."

"So we're in a season of firsts, huh?" Snuggling into him, she yawned. "But if you snore, I'm kicking you out and making you sleep in the other bedroom."

"Is the bed as small as this one?" he asked, curling up against her as best he could so his legs wouldn't hang off. But they did. He wouldn't complain.

"It's about the same, I think. I'm surprised we didn't break the bed, honestly."

Her rough chuckle caught him by surprise. "I thought I heard the frame crack earlier, but I was too occupied to care."

"Terrific. I can just see myself telling Bets I needed to order a new bed because we broke it having sex. Actually, she'd probably think that was awesome."

He'd prefer not to think about his mother's friend finding out he'd broken her bed during sex. Seeing the Lucky Charms dance to Bon Jovi with their boas was bad enough. He didn't want to talk about broken beds over tea or at the butcher counter. For that story would truly travel. "Go to sleep. I'll try not to wake you when I leave."

"Then you'd better kiss me goodbye now," she said, laying her hand over the arm he'd wrapped around her.

He pressed a soft kiss to the side of her neck and heard her sigh again. She might be tough in some ways, but he was starting to realize she was downright romantic too. He needed to be careful with her. He already knew she would be careful with him.

When he awoke to his alarm, she mumbled as he untangled himself. He kissed her again and grabbed his clothes from the floor using his phone's torch to guide him. He closed the squeaky door, wincing at the sound, then dressed quickly and headed out the back door.

The full moon was resting on the rolling hills like a giant golden scoop of ice cream, he thought, in the cool indigo night. He caught sight of a cluster of white daisies illuminated in the grass.

He hadn't left Kathleen a note. He didn't have any pen or paper, and with the newness of everything, he wouldn't have known what to say anyway. Something inside him was changing—her too. He'd seen it when he'd caught a flash of that young, vulnerable look on her face.

They would walk a new road together after this indigo Irish night. What would come? he wondered.

He walked over to the daisies and picked a cluster of them, fighting off his own nerves. She deserved flowers at the very least, even wild ones from the garden. He left them on the dining room table before he could reconsider his actions. When he let himself back outside, he jumped at the sight of Sorcha standing in her white dress with the full moon behind her.

"And she says you aren't Prince Charming," Sorcha said softly. "You always did have a good heart, Declan McGrath. I am proud to call you friend."

She vanished as quickly as she'd come, and he took a moment in the garden to steady his heart. The quiet around him was only punctuated by the early cry of a hungry lamb and the mournful call of the curlew looking for its mate.

His mate was inside that tiny cottage behind him, he realized, and he felt surprisingly bereft as he left her and walked to his car. Discipline had him leaving, else he endanger his boxing debut and his stake in the butcher shop.

As he drove back to Summercrest, he couldn't help but notice the world around him looked brighter. Morning blues and greens blazed in the surrounding countryside. The shadows didn't seem as strong as before. His blood was racing with excitement, both for the fight awaiting him and for the woman he'd left behind.

Declan McGrath had come back fully alive.

CHAPTER TWELVE

The scent of oranges was still present in the cottage when Kathleen awoke to find the white daisies Declan had left scattered on the dining room table.

She made sure Sorcha wasn't around before she lifted them to her cheek. God, she was going to have a total girl moment. But it was pretty sweet of him, and so unexpected. She needed to think of something to do for him next time. Maybe tomorrow morning.

She hugged herself, the wild possibilities racing through her. She was getting screwy, but she didn't mind at all. In fact, it felt awesome. She was going to do some great work today.

She went to make coffee, and the orange smell receded over the pungent notes of roast beans and caramel. Several minutes later, she was sipping her coffee when she heard a car brake hard in front of her cottage. Declan? Her skin tingled. No, he'd be at work, wouldn't he?

When she reached the door and opened it, Ellie stood there. No makeup. Unbrushed hair.

"Declan didn't come home last night. Did you—?" She blinked knowingly, almost coquettishly.

Kathleen raised her cup of coffee and grinned. "Yep! It seemed stupid to keep fighting it now that I'm staying longer. He agreed."

Longer was the word she'd decided to stick with for now. *Forever* seemed premature.

Ellie rushed her and wrapped her in a giant hug. "I knew it! You're lit up like a stained glass window. *Morning After Goddess*, I'd call it. This is awesome!"

"Come have some coffee." She gave her best friend a final squeeze. "I'm really glad you came, babe. Last night was colossal for me."

Ellie pulled out another rickety chair at the small table in the parlor and plopped down. "I know! Brady kept listening for Declan's car last night, and we finally concluded he *had* to be with you. I checked my phone, but you hadn't texted me. Brady finally heard him come home while it was still dark—"

"Training," Kathleen filled in.

"But he left almost immediately after showering. You hadn't texted. Brady actually checked my phone to see. It was so cute. So we went back to sleep. When I got up the second time, I had to dash over here to see how you were doing."

"Thanks, Mom. Let me get you that coffee."

Ellie jumped up and strode into the kitchen with her. "You plan on filling me in, yes?"

As she poured the coffee, she found herself grinning the whole time. "It's what best friends do. Let me start at the beginning."

"Yes, please."

When she was finished, Ellie slumped in her chair.

"Goodness! I mean I've known you a while, but you really do commit all the way once you decide something. I love that about you. I'm glad Declan is equally committed. You both deserve it."

She liked it too actually, everything from their agreement to be exclusive to their deep dive into intimacy. Asking him to stay the night had been big for her, but she knew this was no fling. "Whatever Sorcha might think or say, we're still making up our own minds, but I have to admit... It's *really* good so far, and we're only just getting started."

Ellie made a sizzling sound. "That's so hot! I'm so happy for y'all. I think Brady is too, but he's still a little worried about Declan. Brother and all."

"I know. I have them. I'm going to wait to tell mine about us until we're further along. Robbie already suspects something guy-related is going on. He told me I was too quiet."

"I won't say a word," Ellie said, miming zipping her lips. "I've told all of them every piece of news has to come from you directly. You know how sneaky they can be."

She laughed and then sobered. "Pop seemed to have a sense about how things would be for me here. Don't freak out when I show you this."

She pulled out the necklace with her mom's ring on it and preceded to tell Ellie the rest of the story. By the time she finished, her friend was practically splayed in her chair, sweet tears in her eyes.

"Goodness! There really are a lot of forces helping you and Declan come together. Is that weird or wonderful?"

"A little of both, I think," she said dryly as the scent of oranges wrapped around her again. "Do you smell that?"

She asked out of curiosity because she was still trying to glean Sorcha's ways.

"What?" her friend asked blankly. "The damp? It's everywhere."

"Right," she answered, having her answer. Even though Sorcha had appeared once to Ellie, her friend didn't seem aware of her presence. "You see your dad yet?"

"He said he'd pop by when he could get away from the boxing mania and Bets' stack of resumes and portfolios from interested artists." Ellie rubbed her hands together. "Did you know he's staying with Donal? We offered. He said he feared the dungeon, but I think he was more worried about seeing Brady in his bathrobe."

"Already seen it. It wasn't too bad. You know, the other night at Bets' house, I heard there were a lot of new artists interested in joining the center. Be fun to see who."

"I know! They're going to short-list them for us to look over, in case we know anyone. I can't wait to see who we're going to select next."

Kathleen would be here for the next artists to grace Caislean, she realized. Now she had a stake in helping them choose someone new. "I wonder if we'll have someone with a new rep like us or someone well established with an international reputation."

"How about one of each?" Ellie asked, her eyes bright with excitement. "But think of how awesome it would be to learn from someone who's already made it big."

"After your window and my installation, we're going to be in a new class." She planted her elbows on the table, indulging in a moment of daydreaming. "We've been talking about it, wishing for it, and working damn hard for it. We're finally on the cusp, babe."

"It feels great, doesn't it?" Ellie asked, reaching for her hand. "Thanks for being on the ride with me."

She squeezed it tightly. "I wouldn't want to do it with anyone else. Can I show you my new design for the larger pirate ship?"

"You have it ready?" She laughed. "Of course you do. When you move ahead—"

"I move ahead."

And that was exactly what she did for the next week.

She met with Linc and Bets about her new design. They told her to move ahead on the down low, so she ordered more supplies to make her design model—she'd need one for a project this size—while internally debating the kind of help she'd need.

Declan gave her some helpful insights on hiring locals as she massaged his sore shoulders with the new peppermint-scented arnica cream she'd picked up at the pharmacy for him. She'd seen it on the shelf and immediately thought of him. When she'd bought it, she'd decided it was official—she was acting like his girlfriend.

"Liam can help you," Declan said as he shifted his shoulder under her hands. "He has good contacts in the county. Maybe he can even pitch in. He's done some welding, and he's the one who put together your shed."

She was going to need a bigger workspace, but that was a ways off. "I'll talk to him."

"The other locals will want someone they know to explain why they should join an arts center project and not keep welding at a factory." Declan groaned as she hit a tender spot. "Most people have full-time jobs with pensions."

"It's the same in the States, minus the pension," she

said, reaching for more arnica cream. "For that helpful insight, I'm going to give you a little present. Turn over."

"With pleasure." He had a sexy smile on his handsome face as he did as she'd asked.

He had sexy scruff on his face, having given up shaving for a few days since it left him with more time to stay with her in the early mornings. He'd taken to showering at her place and then heading directly to training from her cottage. Showering at the boxing club would only raise questions, ones he said he'd prefer to hold off.

She got it. She hadn't told her pop or her brothers about them yet.

Only... She was a couple of days away from suggesting he use the top drawer in the second bedroom for his things, a monumental move for her. She reasoned it was practical. They hadn't spent a night apart.

She refocused on his muscles. Her hands knew the planes of his body well after the nights they'd shared, and she started to massage the powerful muscles of his chest. She told herself it wasn't weird that they were inseparable when he wasn't working or training. They were too hot for each other.

But as she laid her hands on his chest and met his eyes, she knew there was more to it. Her breath didn't just catch. Her heart expanded at the sight of those blowtorch-blue eyes. He might arouse her more than anyone, but he also made her happy.

It wasn't like he was working at it. He was just being himself. He left daisies some mornings or a quick handwritten note. He'd said steaks didn't count as gifts, what with his job, but he brought her the best cuts of the day sometimes. When he showed up after his training and wrapped his arms around her, holding her securely, he asked about her day and *listened*.

Then she'd make him a cup of tea, or they'd drink a whiskey with her feet propped in his lap, and he'd tell her about *his* day. Sometimes he had a funny story from the butcher shop, like how he'd come back from the meat cooler and discovered that Jamie had stuck a tennis ball in the mouth of a large salmon. Other times, he had a good one about his training buddies, like how Fergus had put mayonnaise in Eoghan's old boxing gloves, prompting the man chase him around with a water hose in retribution.

More often than she expected, he made her laugh, which only had her falling for him. It felt as easy and joyous as sliding down a warm spring slide on the playground.

She was totally screwy over him, and she knew it. The *L* word kept trying to pop into her mind. So far, she'd tucked it away. Time enough for that.

"Come back here," he called softly, laying his hands over hers against his heart. "You're so beautiful."

She was mush when he said that.

"Sometimes I stop breathing, looking at you."

Mush. Complete mush.

Aware her pulse was speeding up, she went for a snarky comment. "You clearly don't stop breathing for too long or you'd turn blue."

"Why would I risk death when I've only just found you?"

They loved to tease each other, so she'd expected laughter or a witty comeback. His tone was serious, though. His eyes steady. Her pulse skipped, and sure as hell, she smelled oranges. Did he?

She didn't have the courage to ask, and that annoyed her.

"Good thing you're a smart man." She let herself take another plunge, one she'd been chewing over for a few days. "I'm going to be at the Brazen Donkey tomorrow night with Ellie and some of your friends. Can you cut your training early and join us?"

They hadn't had an official date yet. Few save Ellie and Brady—and Liam, of course—knew that they were together. She'd thought a group night might be the way to get the message out. People could see them together. Make inferences.

He sat up and pulled her more squarely onto his lap. She crossed her wrists around his neck as he studied her quietly. Yes, he knew what she was suggesting, and he was thinking it through.

"I can meet you and the rest tomorrow night, *mo chroí*," he said, his voice a rough rumble of baritone delight.

The Gaelic endearment almost had her grinning in relief. They were so doing this. "Super. It'll be fun."

He kissed her softly before whispering, "Will you let me buy you a drink?"

Did he remember how she'd asked him that the day she'd first arrived? "I will, yes."

His fingers slowly traced her jaw, the caress causing her belly to tighten with need. "Will you sit on my lap if one of our friends needs a chair?"

That *would* be one hell of a declaration. Her heart raced with the knowledge of what he was telling her. "Of course."

His mouth curved, his dimples flashing. He gently gripped the necklace she never took off, fingering the ring he'd asked about days ago. She'd told him it was her mother's without going into the story. "You know the Claddagh ring doesn't only mean true love. That's one part, represented by the heart. The hands holding the heart mean friendship."

She knew the symbolism. Her parents had told her as much. But she wanted to hear the words from him.

"And the crown over the heart?" she asked, everything within her still as he held the ring between his thumb and forefinger before raising his gaze to hers.

"That's for loyalty."

She could feel the message in the timbre of his voice. Having been betrayed, she knew the importance of loyalty in addition to love and friendship. "My pop believes all three are needed for a happy marriage, which is why he gave my mom the ring when he asked her to go steady." He'd known he wanted to marry her, even then, he'd always said.

"Were they happy?" Declan asked.

"Yes." She took a breath and took another plunge. "I believe it's because they got the formula right. It's one I believe in."

He slowly lowered the ring until it rested over her heart. "It's early yet, but I figure we're making good progress at all three."

God, the openness between them tonight was going to slay her. "I'm glad you think so. I agree with you."

He kissed her again, the merest brush of lips. "It's like training. You measure benchmarks as you go."

"Benchmarks, huh? That's something my brothers would say, but you're right. How's this for a benchmark?"

She leaned in and rested her cheek against his, wrapping her body around him. His hands encircled her, one embracing her around the middle of the back while the other pressed her low at the waist. She could feel his arousal wedged between them, but he didn't move away from the tenderness of the moment.

Something she'd learned about Declan was he was surprisingly tender. Maybe that wasn't the word he'd use. He was a physical man, after all, and physical acts of affection seemed to be second nature to him. A few of her brothers were like that. They were the toughest guys around, but they were also the huggers, the ones who'd wrap an arm around you as you talked or watched TV. Their affection—when they trusted you—seemed to be infinite.

"I like this," she whispered, feeling her way through the newness of him and what lay between them.

He kissed the side of her neck, making her eyes close in sheer bliss. "So do I. Let me show you how much."

He already knew how to inflame her senses slowly, and he took his time, using his hands to urge her slowly to her peak. She crested over it easily, the ride smooth and luxurious. When he didn't join her, she knew what he had planned next. This time, he gripped her nape and kissed her, sucking her bottom lip until she opened her mouth and let him in. Their tongues dueled, and the pressure of his hands at her waist increased as he rocked against her.

Her system flew into the urgent need to mate, and she shifted to tell him so. He broke the kiss and stared into her eyes before fitting her on his lap so he could slide inside her. They both groaned as he began to move. She bowed back to take more of him, and he held her suspended against him as he thrust and thrust and thrust until they both cried out, holding each other tightly.

She floated on a cozy sea as the scent of oranges enveloped her, and this time, she whispered, "Do you smell the oranges?"

He laid a warm and heavy hand on her side, tucking her closer, as he replied, "Yes, but I'm not ready to tell her she's all the way in the right yet."

She didn't have to ask who he meant. Sorcha never seemed to be far away. With his arms around her, she realized she was close to giving the ghost credit where credit was due. They might very well be the soulmates Sorcha had claimed.

The realization wasn't as scary as she'd imagined it would be.

CHAPTER THIRTEEN

L inc had already doubled their money.

Bets was sure her mouth gaped like a Ballina salmon at the grinning man who sat sprawled in one of the chairs around the table at the arts center's first official board meeting. They'd decided to hold it at the large table in the kitchen.

Linc had asked to kick the meeting off with some good news.

Talk about good news.

"Let me get this straight," Bets said after checking out the shocked faces of her other board members—Donal, Eoghan, Nicola, and Carrick and Jamie Fitzgerald. "You took the one million euros your daughter donated and turned it into two million euros. In two months!"

He shrugged his big shoulders. "Actually, I only invested five hundred thousand after you and I talked about it briefly, Bets, and you added me to the bank account since I'm the treasurer and financial advisor. Remember? You had some green mask on your face because you were getting ready for a date with Donal."

He was a mad lunatic, as the Irish said. "I remember you mentioning it in passing when you suggested we open an investment account for the center after Ellie's donation. Where did you find the time?"

"Some people meditate in the mornings. I spend thirty minutes of mine playing the markets."

"Jesus, Mary, Joseph," Eoghan said in a thin voice. A cut near his eye attested that he was in the thick of boxing training with the others. "I can't imagine such a thing."

"Me either," Donal said, shaking his equally bruised head, "but good job. My God, Linc, how much do you plan to make for us by the end of the year?"

"Fifteen hopefully," Linc said, cracking his knuckles. "Plenty to cover Kathleen's new design and then some, although we'll still go after funding. Oh, and plenty of money to cover the art room, lessons, and field trips you were thinking of for the kids, Jamie."

"I don't know what to say," Jamie breathed out. "My students screamed at the top of their lungs when I told them you'd asked me to be on the board so we could find a way to involve them in the arts. This is more than anyone expected, I think."

"Damn right," Bets said, blowing out a breath. Well, that took care of the other item on her agenda. Holy hell.

More exclamations ran through the room, the kind that involved a good number of saints and sinners, catch phrases only the Irish could deliver with aplomb.

Bets gripped her knees, trying to stop her mind from spinning like a Tilt-A-Whirl. "When you talked about investing part of Ellie's donation, I didn't realize we were talking about these kinds of numbers. It's a lot of money to manage." Her belly quivered. Had she gotten in over her head?

"That's why you've got me working for you on the endowment, Bets," Linc kicked back. "We're going to need big money to pursue loans or grants to build things like a museum or pay for other big installations at the center. Everyone okay with that?"

Eoghan raised his bony hand. "I'm fine with it and more. Only I'd like to propose we hire Linc to teach investing at our beautiful center so we can all become as rich as he is. Surely it's an art."

"You can also come teach at my school anytime, Linc," Jamie said, his eyes wide. "Maybe if they start learning as early as they are, they can become as successful as you."

"And I thought his lassoing classes were groundbreaking," Carrick said, rubbing his forehead.

She'd heard about the lassoing classes around town. They'd been so successful catching the sheep, the hardware store had sold out of rope. "Go figure," Bets added.

Linc's boisterous laugh rumbled out. "Markets and lassoing are pretty similar, actually. I wouldn't go so far to say either is an art form, but there is a *certain* art to making money and reeling it in. I'm happy to help y'all, of course. Only I wouldn't have a clue how to teach."

Lord help her. If they offered that class, they would have people from around the world signing up. And they still didn't have a place for them to stay. "We're getting off track," Bets said, staring at the agenda she'd prepared.

None of the six bullet points she'd listed seemed big enough now. She decided to be dramatic and threw it over her shoulder. Donal spurted out a laugh along with the others.

"Talk, cowboy," she said, waving at Linc. "I know you have more in that crazy head of yours."

"You're in a growth spurt," he said, his blue eyes

gleaming with delight. "You now have nearly two million euros to the center's name, and that's public info once we put it up on the new website. That kind of dough will attract attention. Bets already has a whole bunch of artists sending in their portfolios and resumes, asking about a residency. I went through all the applications last night."

So had Bets, seeing that they'd agreed to talk about them today. "I'd planned to present my top ten for everyone to consider. What did you think?"

"I like Harrison the painter to start," Linc said. "He's had some major shows in Europe."

"He's on my list too," Bets confirmed.

"Angie likes his work," Carrick said after glancing at his notes. "About the man, she's heard mixed things."

"He might be a dick is what you're saying," Linc said, nodding, "which could be trouble. You want someone who's going to do incredible work here, sure, but you also want them to love what they do like crazy and sing that from the rafters. I'm going to propose something out of the ordinary."

Eoghan patted his hair down. "I find I'm liking this talk very much. It's more excitement than we've had in Caisleán in an age."

Bets had to laugh. "Shoot, Linc."

"I think we go after one of the most talented and *nicest* artists in the world." He pulled a piece of paper out of his suede jacket and folded it like a paper airplane before flying it across the table toward Bets.

"Cute," she said dryly as she caught it.

"We land her—or someone like her—we open up the center to the *crème de la crème* of the art world. We can still bring in newbies and rising artists. My Ellie and others have benefited from that model, after all. Truth be told, we'll get more donors if we have some artists who are already top tier. More private funding. More prized pieces in the museum we're planning."

Bets unfolded the paper and read the brief bio. Accompanying it was a picture of a woman in her mid-thirties with brown hair, an open smile, and warm green eyes. "Sophie Giombetti. She's a glass artist."

"Sophie is also the daughter of a couple of world-renowned artists, which is one of the reasons she skyrocketed to fame at twenty-one after a series of glass installations in New York and Europe's finest capitals."

He tossed Bets another paper. Sophie was standing under giant colorful ribbons of glass in a large modern room, overhead lights raining color from the glass over her entire body. "Wow! It's like Candyland or something."

The others exclaimed as she passed the papers around.

"Well, candy is about right," Linc said. "She's known for being a sweetheart, and having run into her over the years, I can attest it's the honest truth. She's also known for baking museum or gallery staff chocolate chip cookies to say thank you for making sure everything comes off with a bang."

"That sounds in line with our community," Jamie said as others nodded.

Bets wasn't sure grateful cookie baking was going to sell her. "I'd want to meet her."

"Of course!" Linc opened his hands. "I thought you might like to go to Saint-Paul de Vence with me and meet her in person. She's working there right now."

"Where's that?" Nicola asked.

"France," Jamie answered.

Linc gave them one of his shit-eating grins. "Good man. Provence specifically. It's a big art town not too far from Cannes, where the big film festival is held. I also happen to know Sophie has a highly talented six-year-old girl and is looking for a nice, quiet community as a change of pace. I thought Ireland might work for her."

"Her daughter would be more than welcome in our school," Jamie added before Bets could say anything.

"How do you know her?" Donal asked.

"I first met her when I was on the board of the Metropolitan Museum and then later at a few shows in Europe. The art world is small, so it's not uncommon to run into the same people. Sometimes that's not a good thing, but in this case it was. Sophie never chatted me up about money or buying her work. We talked about how the art world is filled with sharks and later about being single parents."

Did he like the woman? Bets wondered. He'd said she was in her thirties, but it wasn't unusual for a man to form an interest in a younger woman. "I can visit her with you whenever you think plausible."

"I thought Eoghan might be a good addition to our visit," Linc said, turning toward him. "You're a great ambassador for Caisleán, and your new love for art has incredible charm."

Eoghan flushed crimson but he brazened it out by puffing up like a rooster and saying, "And I've bigger muscles now from our boxing training. She won't be able to resist me."

"Good." He drilled the table with a finger to punctuate the point. "Then it's settled."

Settled, her foot. "How are we going to handle the new space we'd need in the center?" Bets asked.

"I know Angie and Megan are eager to have another artist share this space," Carrick volunteered.

"We'll need a space for the kids as well," Jamie said with swift nod, "once we fashion a plan."

Space was at a premium as it was. "And aren't we going

to need a large space for the glass firing for Sophie if she agrees? That'll require more of an initial investment," Bets said, thinking of the new Excel template Liam had helped her draw up when she'd begged for help on one of their movie nights.

"Sure," Linc said. "I'm no expert, but where there's fire or a kiln, it's usually a bigger, more complicated setup. With fire code crap and the like. Kathleen is going to need more space. I wondered if we don't have Sophie work in the shed. Outside is better for the fire marshal or whatever you call it here."

"I'll handle that with the locals." Donal nodded. "They didn't have a clue what they were dealing with when we put in the pottery kilns, but presented with the right papers, we got it done. Glass blowing would be a nice addition, I think. But I like the idea of more artists."

"What *are* the main types of art, by the way?" Nicola asked. "Technically speaking."

Bets gestured to Linc. "Take it away, cowboy."

"Painting, sculpture, and architecture," he said. "We have the first two in spades. I was wondering if we might seek out the architecture part in the person who could design the museum and its grounds. Of course, we'll need to buy some more land around the center for it."

"I'm happy to sell more of my fields for the museum if there isn't a conflict of interest, being on the board," Carrick said. "What about you, Bets?"

Bets bit the inside of her cheek. "You devil, Linc. That's a clever idea. I hadn't thought of that. And yes, of course, I'd 'sell' some land to help the center expand."

Linc made everything seem so easy, and man, did she like that. She'd been racking her brain on how she could entice an architect on that scale to come to remote

Caisleán in the wilds of Ireland. They weren't a dime a dozen.

Donal nudged her. "He's got ideas up his sleeve like playing cards. We'll need a lot of planning permission, you know. I'm wondering if politicking at the fights will be enough."

"But if we land a very famous architect to design the museum, would they say no?" Linc cracked his knuckles.

"Tom MacKenna and his like would," Jamie said. "God help us."

"I've been wondering if we don't ask a few of them to be nonvoting trustees for the arts center," Linc said, shooting Bets a look. "I know it won't be popular given the trouble they've caused, but we need them on our side."

The mere thought made her blood boil.

"I like the nonvoting part," Carrick said with a frown. "Those weasels have done nothing but cause trouble. I wouldn't like to invite them to the pub for a drink, if you know what I mean. They could cause more problems if they're directly associated with the center."

"We control their role." Linc tapped his thumbs on the table. "Most people don't want more work for themselves anyway. They just crave recognition."

"Sounds like he already knows a lot of Irishmen in politics, doesn't he?" Donal said with a grin.

"It's the same everywhere," Linc continued. "We'll butter them up and help them see how prestigious it is to be on the board of trustees. We'll put their names and photos on the website. Tell them they're getting in on the ground floor before trustees are expected to donate a hefty sum to be associated with our dear center."

"*Donate*?" Eoghan sputtered. "And how much would that be for?"

Linc's shoulders shook with laughter. "When I was on the Metropolitan's board, it was ten million dollars to secure your seat and then annual donations in the millions. Obscene when you think about it."

Eoghan crossed himself as a few people's shocked gasps filled the room.

"I can see everyone's wheels turning," Linc said. "Remember, that's one of the world's top museums. Some more local and less prestigious museums only have an entry check of a quarter of a million."

Donal gaped. "That's still a lot of money."

"It's what they do," Bets said, having done her research. "People pay hefty sums to be associated with the art world." She'd just never expected to be among such company. Holy ever-loving Christ.

"You think people will be paying *us* for the privilege to be on our board?" Eoghan asked with a gasp. "You might as well be telling me we can turn water into whiskey."

"People are going to pay." Linc waggled his brows. "Trust me. In fact, before long, they'll be lobbying for spots on the board. Bets will have more luncheons and dinners than she'll know what to do with. Although to be honest, I think we should reserve a few seats for people who have incredible vision or gifts, but not the money. Like a Nobel Peace Prize winner who loves art, for example."

"A Nobel Peace Prize winner?" Jamie whispered in awe.

Bets understood. She felt a little faint herself. From the beginning, she'd hoped the arts center would expand her horizons, bringing in new people from different walks of life, all united by their love of art. This was more than she'd ever dreamed. "We'll draw straws for who'll accompany me on these meetings, of course," she replied.

"Count me out!" Carrick answered, holding up his hands. "The sheep take up enough of my time. The rest I want to spend with my family."

"I'll go..." Eoghan gave a clever wink. "If I'm still walking among you."

"None of that talk, Dad," Donal said, but his mouth broke into a grin. "We'll have to get you taught up in elegant table manners. The bar variety won't suit those fancy white tablecloth places."

"I can make the sacrifice," Eoghan said with a sigh, making them laugh.

"What else?" Bets asked.

Donal raised his hand before saying, "In advance of Declan's big fight, Linc and I can approach members of the council who might be open to coming over to our side. We'll start conspiring, as the Irish are wont to do, in the pub."

"I'm happy to come and talk about how much this would mean to the children in the village," Jamie said with a knowing look.

"Do whatever you have to do to move things forward with those blockheads," Bets said, glad she wouldn't have to be at those meetings. "If you need anything on that score from me, you know where to find me. Mr. Treasurer—"

Linc drawled, "Yes, Madam President."

She liked the new title, she had to admit. Donal was vice-president, and Nicola had agreed to be the secretary since her notetaking abilities were strong.

"Do you have any other business you want to mention?" she asked with starch in her voice.

"I'd like to propose we hire Madame President an assistant so she won't get cross trying to print out resumes and portfolios and other sundry items like meeting agendas.

Liam might have mentioned your battle with a jammed printer..."

She supposed the story had been too good for her son to keep to himself. "I wasn't thinking when I stuck my letter opener in there, trying to wedge it open for me to yank the wad of stuck paper. It shorted out the whole printer. And then it started to smoke."

Donal started laughing along with the others. "How did I not know about this?"

Usually he knew all her stories. But she and Donal hadn't seen each other much lately, what with him being at the boxing club training or learning to lasso or hanging out at the pub or at his house with Linc, who was still staying with him. But she couldn't say that to him in front of everyone else.

Indeed, she wasn't sure how to say it to him at all.

She forced a bright smile over her clogged throat. "You were at boxing training at the time. I wished you were there to give that darn machine a right hook or something. I almost got electrocuted."

"And that would have been a damn shame," Linc drawled, "especially if it had fried your hair. I got shocked by an electric fence trying to see some horses one time, and my hair stood up straight for a week."

The laughter continued, and she made herself join in. She wouldn't say that she'd cried a little when it happened. She'd wondered if the electrical current had kicked up some hurt in her heart from how things were with her and Donal.

"I call this meeting to a good conclusion," she said, standing up. "I just so happened to make chocolate chip cookies as a thank you for coming like this Sophie Giombetti Linc is so big on. And Jamie brought us some drinks.

Thanks for coming, everyone. It's going to be an interesting few weeks."

People milled around the arts center's kitchen, chatting while they enjoyed the refreshments. Linc came up beside her, munching on a cookie.

"We're going to need a proper meeting space," she told him.

He handed her a spare cookie in his other hand. "I'm only giving this to you because you look like you need some comfort food. You okay, sugar? Something tells me that printer dustup bothered you more than you let on."

Was he fishing? He had to know Donal was spending more time with him right now than he was with her. How could he not when he was sleeping in Donal's guest room? "Getting shocked isn't the kind of fun anyone likes."

"You sure that's all it was?" His blue eyes scanned her face.

She took a giant bite of cookie and shook her head. With her mouth full, she wouldn't have to say anything. She couldn't.

"All right..." he drawled after a moment. "How about I tell you more about Saint-Paul de Vence?"

She looked over her shoulder and caught Donal talking to Carrick and Jamie. In the past, he would have been by her side, talking with their friends. She felt a pang that shook her whole being. "Yes, please tell me all about it."

As he did, she realized the arts center wasn't just her life's purpose.

It had become a distraction from her personal troubles.

CHAPTER FOURTEEN

Declan was about to declare to the entire village that he and Kathleen were a couple.

As he strode across the parking lot of the Brazen Donkey, he could have sworn the stained glass donkey in Ellie's window was smirking at him.

Seeing Sorcha had opened up his senses to strange and otherworldly things, God help him. He couldn't wait for that to stop.

As if his thoughts had summoned her, she materialized before his eyes as he reached for the brass door handle to the pub, making him jump a mile. "Jesus, Sorcha!"

"You know you'll miss me," she said with a wry smile. "Keep your wits about you, Declan McGrath. Your evening is going to look nothing like you were expecting."

Then she was gone.

Terrific! More twists in the road...

He almost turned around and went home to tend to his aching muscles from another hard training session, but he'd promised Kathleen. Besides, he had a powerful yearning to see her, one that never left him.

The moment he entered the pub, his eyes found her. He nearly gaped. She was behind the bar next to his brother, pulling a Guinness, looking competent, compelling, and completely in her element.

Forget that she stood out like a grey heron on an Irish beach in her attire of black leather pants and jacket with rough silver jewelry dancing at her ears and wrapped around her slim neck, a look his male parts found absolutely combustible.

People called out greetings to him, which he absently returned as he hung his jacket on the coatrack by the door. Kathleen's gaze was upon him the moment he looked over, and he couldn't help but smile. She looked particularly beautiful with the mellow light from the bar fixtures washing over her face. He inclined his chin in the way of a greeting as someone thumped him on the back.

"Isn't it a grand sight?" Seamus gripped his shoulder enthusiastically, the same way he'd always done at the butcher shop. "That Kathleen O'Connor looks like she belongs behind the bar. How was the training today? I had an errand in Castlebar."

"Donal treated me well enough, although I caught him in the jaw," he replied. "He was bitching about how much it hurt to shave these days when I left him in the showers."

"Find me after tonight's festivities." Seamus grabbed him by both shoulders and shook him with as much enthusiasm as he greeted spring lambs for Easter. "We have big news about your second fight. Cormac is beside himself. The single prize will more than cover you buying the butcher shop."

The man strode off before Declan could press him for information, leaving him with a pulse jumping with excitement. *More than cover it?* Buying a shop in their small town wasn't like buying a house. Nowhere near it. Still, he expected it would require a big sum—more than could be brought in from a fight with Paul Keane, say. He started to go after him, but his brother called out his name. He swung around.

"Do you see this?" Brady asked with a lopsided grin, pointing to Kathleen as she worked beside him.

How could he not have noticed? "Brother, are you putting Kathleen to work?"

His brother swung a companionable arm around Kathleen's shoulders as she finished pulling a beer and handing it to Carrick, who was sitting at the bar with the rest of their friends.

"Ellie bet me that Kathleen could pull a pint as good as me," his brother answered, "and then Cormac got his betting book out. Dad let out a cheer at the idea, and everyone went mad. You're just in time to judge."

"It's a grand contest, for sure," Declan's father called out from behind him.

Turning, he caught sight of his dad at the table where Seamus now sat with their close friends, including Bets and the Lucky Charms and Ellie's father, Linc. In the corner, Cormac sat at a small table with his black betting book out, a sly smile on his face.

Donal came in through the front door and shot Declan a glance, the kind fighters give each other, before heading over to join them. Yeah, his jaw must still hurt like hell. Well, it was sparring, after all.

Cormac called out another invitation for betting. Tattered bills were spread out on the table by denomination. From the looks of it, a lot of money was going to be made by someone tonight. He wasn't sure who he should root for—his twin brother or the woman whom he had more than fallen for.

"I'd say you're in trouble, Brady." Declan strode to the end of the bar. "Kathleen does look more than competent. You'd better watch yourself."

"You're right there, Declan," Kathleen said, flashing him a wicked grin. "I've been pulling beers since I could reach the tap. Not that my brothers or pop let me serve at that tender age, of course."

"We did the same with our dad, Kathleen," Declan managed, grateful to learn something new about her. There was so much about her he had yet to learn, and every day presented him with a new chance. He only wished he wasn't training so hard, because they never seemed to have enough time together.

But he did know many things already. He knew the tenor of her laughs—the gusty one when she was being a little irreverent, the light one when she was laughing at herself, and lastly, the hearty rumble when she was amused by nothing in particular. He loved them all, but he favored the gusty one, since it was the one she used most with him.

"Those were good days when Dad let us behind the bar," Brady said, wiping down the mahogany top with his ever-handy bar towel, exactly as their dad used to when he was in charge.

He'd always told them they should have pride in what they did, and both of them had taken that lesson to heart. Declan kept his butcher counter clean like that as well as his boxing equipment. The little things mattered. They made the bigger things possible.

"You can have my chair since you'll be judging this impending showdown," Liam said as he vacated his seat beside Ellie.

Eoghan and his cousin gave a dramatic squeak before Eoghan said, "I'm not sure close relations should be judging an event such as this. We need someone independent, and with plenty of beer drinking experience."

"True enough," Declan said, glad to be out of it.

"We'd be the perfect judges, of course," Fergus added. "I'm in me eighty-eighth year, and I had my first pint when I was eight. After Paddy O'Malley's funeral dinner, God rest him. I still remember the frothy head touching my lips. I finally understood why they called Guinness 'mother's milk.' I thought I'd died and gone to heaven like good ol' Paddy himself."

"That's eight decades of experience." Kathleen leaned on the bar with her elbows. "You should definitely be a judge, Fergus."

"You'll need a younger man as well," Carrick Fitzgerald threw out from his position at a nearby table. He had one hand on his very pregnant wife. "I volunteer myself."

"Have at it. Another drink might help you stop worrying about me giving birth," Angie said, rolling her eyes. "He has sheep lambing right and left—"

"He's not married to a sheep," Liam said practically.

"Sheep aren't stupid," Donal called out, "but I don't think they fret about birthing."

"You should know," Bets said, rolling her eyes. "The world over, men seem to think they know what childbirth is like. Holding someone's hand and saying 'Push' just doesn't cut it."

The rest of the Lucky Charms nodded and agreed enthusiastically, joined by Angie's sister, Megan.

Declan shot Brady a look. Childbirth talk in a pub? Their father would have turned up the music and poured another round, only he didn't interfere since retiring. No, when he turned his gaze to their father, their dad was downing his whiskey with a disgruntled look on his face. Declan almost laughed.

"Who will you be betting on, Declan McGrath?" Cormac called out. "Your brother, the man you shared a womb with, or the beautiful Yank?"

How was he to go against his brother or his woman? Inspiration struck. "I'm placing a fifty on my brother here as well as the Yank."

Kathleen gave a sweeping bow in his direction while Brady downright grinned. Murmurs rippled through the crowd. It was an unusual bet, and everyone knew it. He glanced at Kathleen. How was that for announcing his feelings?

"Only a stupid man would bet against a beautiful woman," he added, "even if the man *is* his brother."

"*Especially* if the man is his brother," Carrick called out. "I would bet on Angie before Jamie here."

"Nice save." Liam looked over his shoulder before shifting on his feet and grinning at Declan. "Must be the boxing training." His gaze turned shrewd. "Plus, you haven't been at Summercrest much lately, and you'll be thanking me for not saying a word about it right now."

He nudged his friend's shoulder like they were boys. "Thank you."

Another round of betting followed his bold declaration, and he caught Kathleen's appraising look. He knew the many variations of light in those brown eyes of hers. They were as startling and bright as diamonds after his bet. He shot her a smile, his heart pulsing in his chest.

"All right, let's start this contest," Cormac called out, closing his book. "You'll have to settle on who's judging."

Donal volunteered Bets as she'd been a bartender back

in the States, but Bets declared she was having none of that madness. Having said as much, she promptly took over the arrangements and organized what she called a *proper* beer contest.

People who wished to judge were ordered to put their names in Eoghan's houndstooth tam hat, and he drew out of it five judges with his usual showmanship. Minutes later, the chosen judges were sitting in the bar's dark wood chairs, their backs to the bar as Kathleen and Brady pulled pints.

Declan eyed the people presiding over the contest. Fergus had said good luck was with him, being that his name was the first to be pulled. Kade Donovan was sitting beside him in his usual quiet way. Seamus had also won a spot, along with Bets herself, who got roped in, and Lisa Ann.

Ellie pulled paper from the notebook she kept in her purse for the scoring. Liam found each of the judges a writing implement. Declan—being a good brother—brought over the pints after tagging them with a secret symbol to keep the pourer's identity anonymous for the judges.

Declan fixed his eyes on Kathleen as he talked to his friends. She was busy pulling pints alongside his brother, her brow knit with concentration. By God, she was as serious as they came. His father had been right. Brady had better watch himself.

A blind test had never been done in the Brazen Donkey, and as the judges drank and wrote notes and drank some more, Eoghan called out, "Maybe we need to have the winner go up against Gavin to see who's the best pull in Caisleán after this."

Brady grinned, but his father grimaced like he'd tasted foul fisherman's stew during Lent. "I'm not in charge anymore, Eoghan. Besides, I'd rather not go up against my own boy, should he win. I'll be wanting my Sunday dinners to stay peaceful. This contest will be the last."

Declan wandered over to his father after that. "You all right, Dad?"

"It's hard to remember sometimes I'm not in charge anymore," he replied, pulling a face.

"You need only ask me," his mother said, poking her husband with a knitting needle for emphasis.

That was Declan's cue to head back to the bar, where his friends had returned to their spot to watch the judging. Kathleen, still behind the bar, stepped in front of him with a challenge in her eyes.

"Hiya," he simply said, losing track of everything around him. She took up his whole world when she looked at him.

"Hi back," she responded, her mouth twitching. "Fancy a pull?"

He had to bite his lip to hold back his laughter. He knew just what kind of pull she meant, and wasn't she clever to use the Irish way of giving a phrase a double meaning?

"I would, yes," he managed, muffling his laughter with a cough.

"I'll give it my all," she said, leaning on the bar top, her neck a long line of grace and smoldering beauty. "Don't you worry."

She was going to kill him on the spot. He couldn't wait to get his hands on her.

"Isn't she lovely?" Jamie said to him, nudging his arm. "I'd say the fairies have managed to bring us the nicest and prettiest Yanks in all of America." His nose crinkled. "Wait a moment. Do you smell oranges?"

"Watch the contest," Declan ground out, although he

smiled sweetly at Kathleen when she placed his beer in front of him. As expected, it was absolutely delicious, and he had to pull his gaze from her in order to keep his cool, especially with Jamie at his side, clearly disturbed by the smell of mischief that meant Sorcha.

Never let it be said that some judges didn't milk the competition for all it was worth. Fergus claimed he needed another tasting round to be sure. Seamus agreed and Kade joined in, then Bets looked at Lisa Ann, and they both signaled another round as well.

After serving the judges their second round, Brady and Kathleen filled a couple of glasses for themselves, and Brady hoisted his up. "To a wonderful Yank and pretty damn good bartender. You have a job if you want one, the judges' findings notwithstanding."

She clinked her beer against his brother's. "Thanks, Brady. It would break my brother's heart if I worked in another pub besides our family's, but given how happy you've made my best friend here, I might make an exception. Of course, I'm not going to have much time since I'm here to build a kick-ass sculpture people from miles around will come and see."

She hadn't mentioned all the precious time she was spending with him, of course, or her best friend. Come to think of it, they hadn't much declared they were a couple to the village yet. Well, there'd be time for that later tonight.

"My loss, but the village's gain," Brady replied with a grin.

"My gain too," Ellie said, lifting her glass. "So many people are happy you're here, Kathleen."

That was Declan's cue to raise the beer she'd pulled for him. "*Slainte*," he said, and with his gaze holding hers, he added, "I don't believe I've tasted better."

Ellie choked on her beer while Liam let out a chortle before muffling it. Brady's eyes widened, but he reached across the bar top and patted Ellie's arm, murmuring encouragement as her choking turned to laughter.

Kathleen's mouth widened into a full, breathtaking grin. "Good to hear, Declan. Good to hear."

"I smell oranges again," Jamie whispered, eyes wide.

This time Liam whispered back, "Oh, drink your beer, man."

"The judges have finished their scoring," Cormac shouted, making all conversation cease. "Jamie, being the certified math expert around here, come help me, boy."

Liam had to slap their ghost-averse friend on the back to bring him around. He rose with a rueful shake of his dark head.

"Poor man," Liam told him close to his ear. "Carrick told me Jamie fainted dead away when he saw Sorcha back when she was helping him with Angie."

"Fainted?" Declan asked. "She probably enjoyed that, but it's not very kind, is it? He's been afraid of ghosts since he was a boy."

"He used to race past any haunted houses or church-yards we'd pass," Liam said with a nod. "He's still leery of visiting us at Summercrest even though I told him I cleaned it energetically."

Declan still had no idea what that meant, but he trusted Liam. If he did something, it wasn't just for show—it had a purpose. "Jamie is looking pretty green. I'm going to make sure he can handle the math with the light-headedness. Be right back."

When he reached Cormac and Jamie, the bookie wiped his brow. "I called Jamie over to make the scoring seem complicated."

"Maybe we shouldn't say," Jamie whispered, shielding the sheet from view.

Declan grabbed the paper from his hands and read the results—Kathleen had swept the contest and won outright. His brother hadn't earned a single point. He stopped his brows from shooting into his hairline, aware people were watching.

"Don't give the scores, for God's sake," he whispered back. "Just say the Yank won."

"It's a right surprise, isn't it?" Cormac asked in a harsh voice. "Maybe it's the woman's touch. Delicate hands and all."

"I don't care what the reason is." Declan put on his game face. "Just announce the winner. I'll burn the scores later."

"Good idea," Jamie said, shoving the individual judges' sheets at him.

He jammed them into the pockets of his leather jacket. Imagine. His brother had just taken over the pub, and he'd been handily beaten—by an American, no less. Declan's Yank. He hoped Brady wouldn't take it to heart, but he knew him well enough that he might. He had a soft heart, his brother. "Get on with it, Cormac."

"Ladies and gentlemen, if you please," Cormac said in a booming voice before removing his betting book and slapping it against his thigh. "The results are in, and fine results they are, depending on who you bet on. Please join me in congratulating the winner. Kathleen O'Connor!"

Ellie let out a wild hoot, punctuated by a yawp from Kathleen herself. They high-fived, grinning from ear to ear. Declan watched as the shock rolled over Brady's face before he stuck a smile on it. He grabbed Kathleen in a hug, congratulating her.

"He's a good man, your brother," Jamie said beside him.

He was at that. He sought out his father's face and saw the same forced smile he always plastered on after a surprise, or at a funeral.

People clustered around Cormac to settle up from the betting. Declan went behind the bar and over to his brother, whom he grabbed in a half hug.

"If you had to lose, better it be to a beautiful woman and your intended's best friend," Declan said, shaking his brother to help him past the shock.

"You're right, I'm sure," Brady said with a sigh. "Kathleen, darling, I'm throwing out my beer. Do you mind pulling *me* one from your own hands? I'd like to see what I've been missing."

His brother could teach anyone how to lose gracefully. Only, Declan didn't plan to lose.

Everyone who heard the request laughed, and Kathleen hugged Brady again before pulling him the drink he'd requested. While his brother drank, Declan grabbed Kathleen's hand and pulled her from behind the bar.

"I believe you've done enough work for tonight," he said, aware that plenty of people were watching. "Take your congratulations, and then come and sit with me."

Eoghan appeared, his face flush with excitement. "Some are saying it's a sad day for the village, with our own pub owner being beaten by a Yank. I say it only shows how much magic the Yanks are bringing in with them. Come, dear Kathleen. I have some money to spend. I bet on you, you see."

He gave a devilish wink as he grabbed her other hand. She glanced between the two of them. Age would always win out, to Declan's mind.

"Go on," Declan said with a smile. "He'll keep you in good company."

She squeezed his hand before releasing it. "Keep my chair warm."

He nodded and watched as she went off, Linc Buchanan grabbing her in a hug and saying something to make her laugh in that gusty way of hers.

"Cormac!" Seamus called to the bookie as he sidled up to Declan with a glass of whiskey. "Come tell Declan what magic you conjured for his second fight. It'll be a few weeks after the first, on the second Friday in June. Cormac here brought out all the stops when he heard how important this fight was to the village and the future of the arts center. Confidentially, of course. It's going to bring people in from far and wide, let me tell you."

Cormac's face was red, likely from the heat in the pub due to the crush of people who'd surrounded him, asking for their bets to be settled. He'd managed it with impressive speed, but then again, he had nearly a lifetime of practice.

"Oh, it'll be a grand fight, Declan McGrath. You are going to fall to your knees and weep when you hear the competitor. I'd put out word in the third-level midweight boxing circles you were back and ready to fight, and do you know who called me out of the blue?"

He could hear his heart beat in his ears. "That big, eh? Who reached out?"

The man's wrinkled face broke out into a wide grin, showcasing his gold tooth. "It's a man you've faced before, time and time again. Some would even call him your nemesis."

His nerves prickled. There was only one man he would call by that name—the very man who'd ruined his life.

Declan made himself utter the vile name. "Jimmy Slavin."

"Of course it is!" Cormac said. "His manager said he was thrilled to hear you were back to fighting. We agreed there was no one better matched against you, the same way it's been since you were boys, and even though you've been out of the circuit for years, your trainers thought you could hold your own against him, especially with the rumors surrounding him. He never made it out of the third-level because of them."

"What rumors?" he asked, although he'd heard the whispers and they hadn't been a surprise. Jimmy didn't have what it took to be in the champion circuit. Declan used to think he'd have a shot at it, and maybe he would have if he'd continued with boxing.

"Well, it's rumors, mind you. He might drink more than he should and run with some fast women. Then there's the talk of drug use. Some say those things have made him meaner. But he's still a worthy opponent, Declan. We wouldn't set up the fight otherwise."

Jimmy and him. Fighting. His heart was pounding. God, Sorcha had been right. This was the last thing he'd expected to face tonight. And yet...

"I'll be ready. Don't worry."

This was his chance to pay Jimmy back for every misery. In the beginning, he'd wanted nothing more than to avoid Jimmy, but now...he thought maybe he could win.

"Of course, of course!" Cormac gesticulated widely with his short arms. "After all, Jimmy was your first and last fight—with you winning the first and him winning the last. Oh, it's a grudge match for the ages, and we're going to sell more tickets than we have seats for. With the prize money I negotiated, should you win, you could buy the butcher shop and then some."

"That's good news." Declan cracked his neck. The money seemed small in comparison to him beating Jimmy right now. His anger over Morag had made him reckless in their last bout. Not this time. He would be relentless, and they would see which of them lay on the floor at the end, blood and sweat dripping from his very body.

He would not lose. He wouldn't allow it. His every focus had to be on putting Jimmy on the floor until he couldn't rise before the final count.

"Jimmy's manager told me that he's never been as eager to fight anyone as you," Cormac said, knocking him in the arm.

Every putrid cell of rage inside him broke through the confines where Declan had buried it. "Not as eager as me. Excuse me. I have more training to see to tonight."

With anger raging through his blood, he turned and walked out of the pub.

CHAPTER FIFTEEN

Declan had up and left.

Kathleen sat back in her chair, her whiskey untouched. She'd been raised with seven brothers, so she wasn't a stranger to erratic male behavior. But she was super pissed he'd gone home without saying a word to her.

What the hell was the matter with him?

You just didn't up and walk out like that.

He'd known what tonight meant to both of them. Hell, he'd agreed to come. Of course, she hadn't planned on the impromptu beer contest. That had certainly shifted the focus off their informal date. She would own that. But still...

News of the fighter he'd be facing was on every person's lips in the pub. Already people were making bets after Cormac's dramatic telling of how he'd finalized the arrangements for the fight late this afternoon. With a Jimmy Slavin, she'd heard. Liam had called him a mean and dirty bastard.

People were buzzing with the news at the tables around her, saying Declan would have his hands full but would no doubt make Caisleán proud.

When a few people exclaimed about Declan disappearing, wanting to talk to him about the fight, Seamus puffed up and said Declan was probably so eager to fight his old nemesis that he'd immediately gone off to the boxing club.

"Should we join him, boys?" he'd all but bellowed, and Donal and Eoghan and Declan's father had left with him to do just that. They'd taken the whiskey bottle on their table with them.

"There's something screwy about this," Kathleen muttered to Ellie.

"Agreed," she said. "Let's go talk to Brady."

They headed to the bar, Kathleen leading the way, and as soon as she reached it, she called out, "Hey, Brady! What do you think about Declan fighting this Jimmy guy?"

"What?" he asked, pausing in his polishing of a pint glass.

Like her brother, Danny, Brady seemed to hate finger-prints on his glassware. "Declan fighting this Jimmy guy?"

He gripped the glass and looked away. "He and Jimmy have a long history between them. Declan's last fight— Never mind. He'll do fine. Excuse me. I need to see about refills."

"Was that weird?" she asked Ellie quietly.

Her friend pulled a face. "Brady doesn't usually look like someone bashed his head in when he's behind the bar."

"And Liam doesn't usually call people mean and dirty bastards." No, he was the peaceful type, inclined to like most everyone.

"Agreed. He's usually all about being positive." Ellie pulled her into a hug. "Don't worry. I'll ask Brady later. What are you going to do about Declan? I know him leaving upset you. This was supposed to be a big night for you two."

"Yeah. I'm having a hard time giving him a pass here."

This kind of thing used to happen with Axl, who used

to run off if the mood took him to write a song, or so he'd say. She still thought it was rude. She'd never left *him* when she'd gotten an idea for a new metal sculpture.

"Me too," Ellie said. "Do you want to leave?"

She wasn't going to let a guy ruin her time. "Not on your life. I'm going to hang with my BFF and drink some more whiskey."

"Can an old man join you?" Linc drawled, draping his big arms around them in a hug.

"Please!" Kathleen and Ellie made room so he could stand in the middle of them.

"I heard you wowed them at the board meeting," Ellie said, giving him a searching look. "Daddy, I thought you were retiring. Not becoming the new developer for the Sorcha Fitzgerald Arts Center."

He set his whiskey on the bar top. "What can I say? I have a skill set that will make things easier. Did you hear about my idea to go after Sophie Giombetti?"

"Yes, and I love it!" Kathleen said, knocking her whiskey against the one he'd set down. "Her work is brilliant, and I've heard she's so nice."

"She is..." Linc said with a wink. "About as nice as y'all."

"I can't wait until people come and beg me to make a sculpture for them." Kathleen hugged herself. She would think positive thoughts and not how she wanted to rage a little about Declan.

"I don't plan on begging Sophie." Linc rolled his eyes. "The case speaks for itself."

"Whatever, Daddy," Ellie said with a laugh.

"After your installations, you both should be able to write your ticket," Linc said, lifting his glass. "I'm only doing what I can to showcase your work more."

Kathleen glanced at Ellie for her reaction, but her friend seemed unbothered. She and her father had found new ground. In the past, Ellie had taken his support poorly, thinking it would prevent her from achieving success on her own merit, but he'd backed down, and she'd bucked up, and it was wonderful to see.

"Cheers to that," Ellie said, and Kathleen repeated it.

They toasted again, and Kathleen thought this particular whiskey was all the sweeter for the moment they were celebrating. She almost forgot about Declan. Almost.

"I hear you and Bets are going to be taking another trip together to see Sophie," Kathleen said, nudging him in the side.

"Don't you start with that kind of ribbing," Linc said. "Lord, if I'd known the teasing our dinner in Paris would cause. Eoghan's coming, in case you didn't hear."

"I heard." She smiled. "He's beside himself. It's so cute. He's never left Ireland before."

"They're going to love Saint-Paul de Vence," Ellie said with a sigh. "I told Eoghan the entire village is magic and that the roses and jasmine should be starting to flower, perfuming the air."

"It's going to be one hell of a trip." Linc stood up as Brady's mother slid behind the bar. "Oh, no," he said with no small measure of amusement. "Seeing that woman next to Brady only means one thing. The Lucky Charms are about ready to start dancing."

"Let's join them," Ellie exclaimed as "Born To Be My Baby" started to play. "I love this song."

Linc put a hand on Kathleen's arm as Ellie rushed off to where the women were congregating. "You sure you're okay? You look like you've got something else on your mind."

She made herself smile. He couldn't know about her and Declan, could he? If he did, he would probably take Declan to the woodshed for up and leaving her. "Of course, Papa Linc. How could I not? I mean, I'm about to dance to Bon Jovi in an Irish pub in Ireland. Do you mind videoing it so I can send a clip to my brothers?"

She could well imagine their tortured response. The fun thought punched through her pique.

"I'd prefer to be shot and stuffed by a local taxidermy than video you dancing like that," Linc groaned, but he took her phone when she handed it to him. "You're going to owe me, O'Connor. Especially if your pop finds out I took this video of you two strutting your stuff."

Laughing, she took her place between Ellie and Bets as the guitars purred and the song began to rock. She let her eyes close and danced out her frustration. Ellie bumped her hip, making her look over at her friend, who was grinning. They put their hands on each other's shoulders and started to sway like they would have back at O'Connor's on a Friday night. Man, it took her back and made her miss home.

She'd told her family about the expanded project—and timeline—on their Sunday call. Pop had been thrilled for her—they all had—but she'd caught the telltale gleam in their eyes. She'd thought about telling them about Declan but that had seemed premature. Tonight had proven that.

He'd blown it. All the way.

She was honest enough to admit that it raised a measure of mistrust in her. Since it also reminded her of Axl, it was never a good thing for a girl to think she might be repeating toxic relationship patterns.

She ended up staying at the pub late with Brady, Ellie, Liam, and Jamie, the latter of whom she was coming to know better. The other Fitzgerald brother could be quiet, but he had a dry wit and the kind of sweetness that probably made him a good teacher. In fact, they were the last ones left in the parking lot when Sorcha appeared out of nowhere.

"Oh, Jesus!" Jamie cried, clutching his chest. "Not again."

Kathleen couldn't sum it up better.

Sorcha cocked her hip and laughed boldly, her white dress illuminated by the waning full moon. Never say the ghost didn't enjoy a touch of drama.

"I waited until the others left so I'd have you to myself. Both of you. Jamie Fitzgerald, you're as green as the first time I appeared to you. Your day is coming, man! Be ready for me by the time the autumn tide begins to swell."

"Don't torture me with such threats," the man said, standing his ground. "I can take care of things myself, Sorcha Fitzgerald. I don't want your help."

"Still you will have it, my dear," Sorcha said, her brown hair blowing despite the lack of wind.

"You can't tell her anything," Kathleen muttered.

"You should be nicer to me, Sorcha," he shot back, "seeing as I'm going to help the children of Caisleán find a way to enjoy your center. Maybe some will even become artists like Kathleen herself."

Sorcha arched a delicate brow before saying, "It's happy I am, what you're about. But in the love department, you're in desperate need of help. If you could have handled it, Jamie Fitzgerald, you'd be married by now. I'll see you soon, Jamie boy. Now go! I need to speak with the Yank."

A lock of curly brown hair had fallen onto Jamie's forehead, making the whites of his eyes appear even bigger. "I'll be letting the Yank give me leave, Sorcha. It's not that I don't trust you—we were kin—but I won't leave a woman alone with you unless she bids me."

Kathleen pursed her lips. Jamie had gallantry. "I'll be fine, Jamie. She likes to jerk my chain, but as she's finding, I can jerk back."

The ghost chuckled darkly. "She and I understand each other well."

He crossed himself. "Kathleen, you'll find me if you need me. Good luck."

She waited until he was gone. When she turned back to Sorcha, she raised her brow. "*Really?* Is this how you get your kicks in the afterlife?"

"If you mean *craic*, yes, I do enjoy moments such as these." She walked to Kathleen, the white nimbus of light around her growing brighter. "You think you had a setback tonight."

This damn ghost was downright telepathic. "Setback? In my neighborhood, we'd say he fucked up."

Sorcha's laugh was so rich it startled a bird into flying off. "I like you, Yank. That's exactly the way of it. Only... I'm here to tell you that sometimes we don't see the truth of things. Declan fighting Jimmy Slavin and taking himself off without a word to anyone, yourself included, is much like an arrow being pulled backward. The motion might seem contrary—until the force of the revolution is applied to sending the arrow sailing even farther ahead. Straight to its mark."

Not the arrow analogy! She'd heard musicians talk like that, and it had always seemed like a bunch of bullshit to cover up bad behavior. "We'll see. Can I go now? Or were you hoping I might faint?"

"Faint? That would be the day. Declan will need your understanding because there is much force driving that arrow back. I hope you remember that when you see him later tonight."

Her laugh was bitter, and didn't she know it? "I don't plan on seeing him later."

If he thought he could waltz in and get lucky, he had another thing coming.

"That's the kind of thinking I'm telling you won't be of help here—to you or to him." Sorcha sighed heavily. "I wish I had learned that before I died. It would have saved me many an unhappy night. I could have been ensconced in Carrick's arms as opposed to angry enough that I spilled cold potato leek soup on him for forgetting to call me about missing dinner. Learn from my mistakes, Kathleen O'Connor, if you will. Never go to bed angry—when there's love. Of course, he should apologize when he does you wrong. But where there's true love, there's regret in hurting another."

Her green eyes beat into Kathleen, who felt a growing feeling of disquiet. The thing was, whatever had prompted it, she wasn't ready to let Declan's behavior go yet.

He'd hurt her.

The first time someone did that in a relationship was the most potent. She could still remember the first time Axl had done it. She'd cried in the bathroom at the club where he'd left her without even paying their tab. Why had she let that go? She should have seen it for what it was—a red flag. She'd been stupid to ignore that kind of crap, telling herself it was all in the course of real relationships and "true love." What bullshit.

"No witty reply, Kathleen?" Sorcha smiled sadly when she said nothing. "I'll see you soon, nonetheless."

After she vanished, Kathleen stood there for a moment

longer, taking a few cleansing breaths to calm herself. Man, she was worked up.

Overhead, the indigo sky was filled with a million diamonds, and she tried to draw the beauty into herself. A blazing star fell from the sky, its brightness fading into nothing.

The sight of it only saddened her, as if something beautiful had winked out, vanishing from the universe.

She realized that was how she felt, as if her excitement and growing feelings for Declan had free-falled tonight. All day she'd been excited to see him, imagining their shoulders brushing as they laughed and talked with friends. Or what it would be like to sit on his lap as he'd suggested.

Then he'd up and left.

Sure, this Jimmy thing had thrown him for a loop, but did that matter? Axl had always insisted he had perfectly good reasons for treating her like shit too. After their breakup, she'd promised herself that she wouldn't play second fiddle to anything ever again.

When she finally drove home, she rolled the window down. Back in Boston, she'd still be fighting traffic and angry drivers at this hour, which would have been a welcome distraction. Not here. Only the sound of some forlorn animal ruptured the night as she made her way along the narrow road with the rolling hills, some shadowed, some bright with brilliant moonlight, reminiscent of Sorcha's dress.

At her cottage, the full force of her sadness wrapped around her like a hand-me-down coat, the kind that couldn't keep the chill out. Her heart was cold, a thought that only made her sadder.

She fixed herself tea and was just about to text her brother to comfort herself when she heard the crunch of tires on the gravel drive outside her cottage. She knew that sound and who it belonged to. She went over her choices.

She could pretend she was asleep, but the light was on, so it might not work.

She could ignore the knock on the door when it came, and sure enough it did, the hard rap insistent in the quiet night.

Or she could answer it and let him see how his actions had affected her. How he reacted would be telling. It would help her decide whether she'd made a mistake with him. If so, better to know now so she could call it.

Straightening her spine, she chose that last option and hoped the ice around her heart would melt from the fire she had to gather to face him.

His face was all harsh angles in the moonlight when she opened the door.

"I'm sorry," he said softly, nothing more.

A tightness gathered in her middle. She could barely take a breath. Was she going to accept this, only two simple words of contrition?

"You hurt me," she managed to get out. "That's hard to admit."

He swallowed thickly. "You're brave to tell me, but I already knew. How could I not when I know you? My only excuse is how much I was thrown off guard by the fighter Cormac found to face me. The news took over my mind to the exclusion of all else."

She'd heard this before. "Can you tell me it won't happen again?"

He laid his hand on the frame of the open door where they stood. "I want to tell you it won't, down to my bones. I have history with this fighter, Kathleen. It's powerful history. Ground I haven't covered in a long time. I feel like

I'm stuck in a bog right now, the muck gripping my feet, threatening to take me under. I'm fighting it with all my strength, *mo chroí*, and I'll continue to fight. I only beg you to have patience."

His voice was grave and a touch hoarse, and she discovered something she hadn't known earlier—that compassion could melt the ice and warm her heart again.

"I will promise that I'll do my best to ensure it won't," he continued. "That might not be enough for you, and if so, I'll understand."

His blue eyes lifted and met her gaze then, and in them, she saw both an entreaty and fear.

So he knew they were at a precipice.

That he was filled up to his ears with regret was obvious, but she made herself press him. "Do you want to call it?"

He cleared his throat. "No! God, no! How we've been, together, has been as beautiful and powerful as a sunrise over the sea. I don't say words like that lightly. He stole something from me, Jimmy did, and I desperately want it back. This fight... It means everything to me. It's a fight for my very self. But at the boxing club tonight, when I was shadowboxing Jimmy—hitting the bag and imagining it was him—I feared I wasn't whole enough to continue to be with you as I'd been. As you deserve."

That made tears burn her eyes. Axl had never said anything like this when he'd apologized. She could feel the remaining cold shattering inside her like ice in spring sunlight. "Oh, Declan. Don't be stupid."

His snort had him rubbing the tip of his nose. "Is that stupid?"

"Yeah, stupid. So you have an old foe to fight who's got you doubting yourself and making you forget everything else. You'll be riding that wave until you fight him, but you'll still be you, the Declan I know, if you want to be. The question is, do you want to be? Because I like that Declan an awful lot. Not the one who up and left tonight. In fact, I've fallen for that other guy."

She hadn't imagined telling him how much she cared like this, but maybe it was fitting. Tough guys didn't like Hallmark cards. Those sentiments were too banal for her and Declan.

After a moment, his mouth tipped up on the right, and a dimple appeared in his bruised cheek. "I might be stupid in some things, but I know myself. I've fallen for you as well. If you'll forgive me, I'll show you how much that Declan missed having you by his side tonight as he watched you beat his brother in a beer contest in front of the whole village."

She fought the smile twitching her lips. "You owe me a night out."

He stood from where he'd been leaning and traced her jawline. "I owe you more than that. Am I forgiven? Because I hurt you. More than you could ever know, I'm sorry for it."

Taking a few steps closer, she laid her face against his chest. His shirt was coated in sweat, as if he had raced over, not bothering to shower. "You're forgiven. Come inside."

He wrapped his arms around her, cradling her nape in one of them. "In a minute. My granny used to say to never let ill will pass over a threshold lest it bring bad luck to the house. I would never want that for you or for us."

Wasn't that like what Sorcha had told her earlier? That ghost really did know too much for anyone's good.

Kathleen let him caress her hurts away as a gentle Irish wind blew around them. His tense muscles relaxed the longer he held her, while hers softened in response. When she heard the steady beat of his heart, she lifted her head and cupped his jaw.

"Now come inside and make love with me."

Something flickered in his eyes, relief and longing, before he nodded.

There were no words as they undressed each other, using their hands and mouths to further heal and assure and arouse. The passion finally sparked between them, as if awoken from being banked earlier when he'd left and her heart had grown cold from his absence.

The fire this time was of the cleansing variety—the kind that burned away any impediment to growth and harvest, the kind that brought forth unimaginable bounty.

When they lay in each other's arms at last, she took his face firmly between her hands and kissed him softly, communicating everything she felt in her kiss.

He cupped her neck to hold her there and accepted every offering she gave. In turn, he laid his mouth over hers when she broke the contact and shared with her his own deeply felt emotions.

When their eyes finally met again, the blues of his weren't of the blowtorch variety—they put her in mind of a tranquil, open sea, a place she could happily find peace in. She smiled and watched as his mouth formed a beautiful smile as well.

Then they wrapped themselves around each other—a place where, Kathleen was coming to believe, they both belonged.

CHAPTER SIXTEEN

Declan knew he had to show Kathleen how much she meant to him as much as he had to train for his upcoming fights.

The day after their disastrous pub date, he took her on a challenging hike on the Nephin Wilderness Mountain Trail. Midway up the eight-kilometer trail, she'd punched him gently in the shoulder as they started to ascend a tough section with a fifty-degree ascent through rough-hewn rocks. "You're using this as training, aren't you?"

He watched the pulse pound in her neck and gave in to the urge to pull her close and kiss it. "You said you'd like to go on a hike and have whipped ice cream after, like Ellie recommended. It so happens this trail is good for my boxing regimen. I wanted to spend time with you this weekend and not be in the gym all day. Are you angry?"

She pushed him back and stared at him. "No, because I wanted to spend time with you too. I know your first fight is coming up. This is practical. Still, sometime, I'd like a real date where I can wear a skirt."

He'd never seen her in a skirt, he realized, and he

stepped back to appraise the long legs he loved wrapped in simple yoga leggings, now covered with spots of mud from the boggy patches on the hike. "So would I. How about next Friday? We'll go somewhere really special."

She agreed, thank God.

The next week passed in a blur of training and his sweet Kathleen, and before he knew it, the day had arrived. When he knocked on her door before their date, he felt both nervous and excited, as if he hadn't shown up at this very door every day for the past weeks. She answered it in the deep purple skirt she'd chosen for their evening out. It skimmed her knees, and she'd paired it with knee-high black boots, showing no leg, he was sad to see. He made her laugh by telling her so. But she looked gorgeous and sexy, with her eyes painted with silver and navy and her lashes thick and curled with that black stuff women favored.

He took her to Westport for a fancy dinner at a place Brady and Ellie adored, where they'd had fancy Irish food— something of an irony to him—with potato leek patties along with a salad served with black pudding and rashers, which wasn't bad, followed by batter-dipped cod served with curry sauce and cabbage relish, which he didn't see the purpose of. Even the peas had been fancy, smothered in some sour cream and chives sauce, which Kathleen had agreed was weird but admitted to loving.

Afterward he held her hand as they strolled through the busy and packed streets, ending up at Matt Molloy's Pub for a pint and some music.

She knew of the Irish band The Chieftains, God love her, and she'd been delighted to learn Matt was a member, a fact he advertised with the Grammy awards displayed prominently in the pub. Her love for Irish music was stronger than his own, to his mind, but perhaps that was a

Boston thing. After all, how many reels, hornpipes, and jigs could a person stand?

Kathleen clapped and did her best to sing along with the band playing, missing words but making up for it with enthusiasm. She even took pictures to send to her brothers, but he noted that he wasn't in any of them. They hadn't spoken much about her family, and truth be told, he hadn't told her much about his own family yet. She knew Brady, of course, but he had yet to introduce her to his parents as his woman.

They were still making their way in these early steps.

Her bright smile made it all worthwhile, and by the time they left, he'd decided to buy her one of the band's CDs as a memento and arrange for Matt himself to sign it. He thought it would be a nice present to give her when the mood called.

On the hour-long ride back to Caisleán, he took another plunge. "Care to spend the night at my place?"

He knew it would be a big step for both of them. She'd never spent the night at Summercrest Manor by joint agreement. They had more privacy at her cottage, and it kept things separate from his brother and her best friend.

"My bed is bigger, and so is my shower," he added. "Plus, it has more hot water. No immersion heater." They both hated having to wait fifteen to twenty minutes to take a longer shower and savor each other.

For a moment, the only sound in the car was the rock music on the radio. Then she said, "Are you making breakfast, or do I have to sneak out the window after we have sex?"

She got a good squeeze for that on her cute little knees peeking above her boots. "You thinking I'd kick you out? I might be thick in some things, but I'm not going to miss the opportunity to spend all night with you in nothing but one of my T-shirts. It's my second most favorite way of viewing you."

"What's the first?" Her voice had turned sultry.

"Completely naked, what else? Sometimes it's the image I bring to my mind when I'm so tired after my training that I can barely see straight. It helps me get to your cottage—and to you."

She snorted. "Let me make sure I understand you. My naked body helps you see straight? I'm going to have to write that down."

He laughed. "Come on. You know how much I love your body. And yes, I'll make you breakfast. But honestly, you'd be better off if Brady or Liam cooked for us. I usually try to time my visits to the kitchen for when I can smell cooking in my room." Not that he was home for breakfast much these days. He was always at training.

"You're just like a couple of my brothers. I swear, they get out of cooking and cleaning by perfect timing, and they're proud of it."

"It's an art." He slowed his speed since she hadn't answered. "Does that make me an artist?"

Her gusty laugh had his heart turning in his chest. "In your dreams, Ace."

He could handle that nickname sparingly, he supposed. "So are you coming home with me, or am I going home to yours?" He trailed a finger over her hand before clasping it.

She tapped her newly painted nail against the dashboard, the line of red flashing in the dark car. "We'll try out your bed. And shower. Only I reserve the right to climb out the window. After."

There they were again. Talking about what to do after spending time together in the quiet, indigo Irish nights.

He knew she was mostly teasing, but it bothered him. They might be finding their way, but they were still as shy as horses in some areas.

"I'll make sure to knot the bedsheets myself if you feel you must lower yourself from the second story," he added, releasing her hand to shift gears as he turned toward Summercrest.

"I might take you up on that, just to see you do it," Kathleen said, chuckling. "I'm going to have the walk of shame in the morning in these clothes. Maybe I can borrow something from Ellie."

He didn't like that phrase coming from her lips. There was no shame between them. "I can stop by your place if you want to pick up a bag. You can even have a drawer if you fancy it. Since you've given me one."

That had been quite a moment. Fraught with tension, with as few words as possible, she'd pulled open the empty drawer and gestured to it before walking out of the room, leaving him to stand there and stare at it with slack hands. She hadn't seen his smile in the end.

He looked over to see how she was taking his invitation to share his space. Her brow was raised. Yes, trust was as hard won with her as it was with him, but each victory was like winning a championship match. She was no pushover in love.

Love!

His hands tightened on the wheel. God! He couldn't believe it had happened so quickly, but there was no denying that's what it was. Wasn't he making arrangements to bring her into his life?

"I'll take the drawer, but if you touch my underwear, you're a dead man."

Her feisty humor always helped him settle in moments

of intense emotion. He wondered if she knew. "What do you mean? I touch it all the time."

"No, you take it off or play with the edges when it's on my body. When I fold it and put it away, it's different. You don't mess with that."

And she said men were thick? "You're a mad lunatic, aren't you?"

Her throaty chuckle filled the car. "And you're a real romantic."

For her, he seemed to be. Wasn't he picking up daisies off the road and arranging for an autographed Chieftains CD? "I took you on a date where you wore a skirt. That's what you asked for. Some would say that's romantic. What can I do next? Sing you a ballad? Pack a picnic basket?"

He would do it too and likely enjoy it. He enjoyed everything they did together. The lengths he'd go to for this woman.

She kicked her feet out as he turned onto the road to Summercrest. "Honestly... I've had a song written for me and someone has also packed me a picnic. My feeling is that those kinds of gestures don't amount to shit without any sentiment behind them."

Was it any wonder she was perfect for him? "That's one I'll need to write down."

They both laughed, and when he pulled to a stop in front of the well-lit house, he locked his jaw as Sorcha appeared in the car's headlights.

"Shall I run her over?" he asked teasingly.

"You'd only run through her and into your house. I suppose we better get it over with and see what she wants."

Kathleen exited and he followed.

"How was your date tonight, you two?" Sorcha preened.

Declan glared at her. "You're a right bother, do you know that? Go haunt someone else."

"I only wanted to tell you how good you look together," she said, her smile as wide as a rainbow. "This time you're spending together will reap good fruit. Enjoy it!"

She vanished.

"Typical," Kathleen muttered. "Delivers a cryptic comment and then disappears."

He shook his head. "I never knew her to be such a busy-body when she was alive."

"Death becomes her," Kathleen joked and then laughed out loud. "Have you seen the old classic with Meryl Streep?" Her expression brightened further. "Hey, do you want to watch a movie? We've never done that."

He took her hand as they walked to the front door. "What's a movie? I've been working so much I've never heard of them."

"Funny, Ace!"

He was aware it was the second time she'd used that name in a short timeframe. She always did it when she wanted distance. He knew she was more guarded with him since he'd left her at the bar the other night. She hadn't fully let that hurt go yet. "It's Declan."

"Right."

Her voice was rich with irony. He decided to tease her into relaxing. "And I most definitely am not watching a movie about a ghost."

"It's not totally a ghost movie, but if you have your heart set on one, we could watch the chick flick ghost romance with Patrick Swayze and Demi Moore."

Chick flicks and ghosts? "No way in hell."

She laughed and nudged him with her body. At the door, he let her precede him inside. He realized she was nervous as she clutched his hand. She probably had another "Ace" in her.

"Hi, Liam!" Ellie called when they entered the house. "We're in the parlor."

Kathleen put her finger to her lips and let go of his hand to tiptoe to the doorway, where she pressed herself against the wall. He stayed where he was, watching in amusement. She obviously planned to scare her friend.

"Liam?" Brady's heavy footsteps sounded, and then he was stepping into the entry hall.

"Boo!" Kathleen shouted.

His brother let down every McGrath for seven generations by squealing like the fatted hog. Exactly as he'd done when someone had scared him as a child.

"Jesus fucking—" Brady pressed a hand to his chest as Declan and Kathleen burst out laughing.

"That was terrible," Ellie said, appearing in the doorway, fighting laughter.

"I was hoping it would be you, babe," Kathleen said, snorting with laughter, "but I'll take Brady. Oh, that was fun!"

"*Fun?*" Brady gave a proper scowl. "If that's fun, I'll have to watch out for you. Or maybe *you* should watch out for me, Kathleen O'Connor."

She shook her hands in the air. "I'm so scared."

Ellie hugged Brady, chuckling softly. "You guys stopping in for something?"

Kathleen's laughter took off again, so strong she was wiping tears. "Wild sex. Got a problem with that?"

Dear God. She'd overridden her nerves with boldness. That was his Yank. This time he snorted. But he couldn't deny that he *was* wondering how long they'd need to chat with the couple before heading up to his bedroom.

Brady's brows shot to his hairline, but Ellie gave in to a fit of giggles before saying, "Not a one. This is going to be great. It's like double dating."

"It is not," Kathleen said, putting an arm around her friend's shoulders as they walked toward the kitchen. "Got any snacks? I'm still hungry. I couldn't touch that cabbage relish."

"Yuck!" Ellie said, resting her head against Kathleen's arm. "I have just the thing. I found an easy brownie recipe with four ingredients, and I rocked it. You want ice cream?"

"Do I want ice cream? When have you ever known me to pass that up?"

They continued to banter as they headed for the kitchen, looking absolutely adorable to Declan's mind. He turned to his brother, who had his brows back in place and no longer resembled an owl from their mother's macrame days. "You can tell how strong their bond is, can't you?"

Brady turned to gaze after them, a lopsided smile on his face. "Like sisters. So... You're staying here for a while? Or all night?"

There was a question in there—one he ignored. "I hadn't written down our itinerary. I only thought it was time to have her stay here. With me."

"Good. About time, to my mind."

The sound of Liam's motorcycle interrupted anything else Brady might have added, thank God. Declan never let anyone rush him. Not Sorcha. Not even his brother.

"Our pirate is back from his hot date," Brady remarked, waggling his brows.

"That's nothing out of the ordinary."

Liam never brought a woman home. When asked, he said that was for serious relationships. Declan thought he more than had the right of it. Right now, Yoda was only having fun. Plus, it kept expectations in check, which he was very upfront about, Declan knew.

When Liam blew in the front door with a grand slam, Brady grimaced. "Be careful with Ellie's window, man."

"That window will live to see someone's great-great-grandchildren, it's so well anchored," Liam said, shaking out of his coat after dropping his motorcycle helmet by the coatrack. "Nice to see you in your own home, Declan McGrath. You've been missed. Kathleen with you?"

"She is," Declan said, smiling as he answered Yoda. "*You* missed her scaring the life out of Brady. Now she and Ellie are having brownies."

Liam smacked his lips together. "I had one earlier. They're mighty good. You should try one. You've been training pretty hard. You worried about facing Jimmy Slavin again?"

Declan crossed his arms over his chest as Liam reached them, ruffling his blond tangle of hair after wearing the helmet. He had an assessing look in his green eyes. Yoda, it seemed, couldn't help himself.

"I've been out of fighting for a time, yes, but I'm training hard and will be ready. For Jimmy *and* for Paul."

He should probably focus on his fight with Paul Keane. That match was the first, after all, but he was obsessed with facing Jimmy in the ring again. He'd even watched some of Jimmy's recent fights on YouTube in between customers at the butcher shop. The changes in form as well as function were obvious. Jimmy dropped his left arm more as a fight went on, and his right hook didn't snap a man's back so hard spittle flew from his mouth. But his footwork was still good, if a little slower, and he knew how to time a punch.

He had the experience Declan lacked.

"Dad said the talk is Jimmy isn't the same," Brady said, shooting him an encouraging smile.

He made himself nod. "I can see it in the film I've watched of his recent fights. I'll be ready for him."

Of course, some nights when he lay awake, he wondered what lengths Jimmy would go to this time to beat him. Last time, right after they'd tapped gloves, Jimmy told him that he'd fucked Morag. Declan hadn't questioned it. One look at her, sitting in the front row with a defiant look on her face, had convinced him it was true.

Those thoughts tortured him. He didn't fear Kathleen would be a mark, but Jimmy would think of something if he wanted. Declan would have to keep his guard up.

"That's not what I meant and you know it," Liam said, holding his gaze steady.

Brady was now looking between them like they were volleying at Wimbledon. His beloved brother had never guessed who Morag had cheated with, and because he was Brady, he'd only been there with a whiskey and a kind ear. He hadn't made any demands or asked for details. None of his friends had.

From the way Liam was looking at him, though, he figured Yoda had guessed like the others and said nothing before this.

"Don't do the Yoda thing on me, Liam," Declan stated back. "I'm having a grand night. I'd rather not talk about that eejit."

"Fine, but if you want to talk about it, I'm here." Liam slapped him on the shoulder. "I'm off for brownies. You'd better join us, or I can't promise there will be any left."

With that, he left, and Declan stared after him.

"What's Liam talking about?" Brady asked, grabbing his arm and planting himself in front of him.

He ground his teeth. "Nothing. Old history. You know how long Jimmy and I go back. You were at our first fight... and the last."

Brady's brow knit. "Liam's more canny than that. He only gets like Yoda, as you say, when he knows something is below the surface. You holding out on your brother about something with Jimmy?"

Dredging up old business would only weaken him as a man and a fighter, just like Eoghan had predicted. Shadow-boxing Jimmy was one thing. Throwing open the box of destruction Jimmy had gifted him, one tied to Morag, would only amplify his already volatile emotions. He needed to keep them contained. Fighting with a volcano of emotion inside you was a good way to lose.

"It's my own business and nothing for you to worry about," Declan said, taking him by the shoulder. "Come along. Let's grab the brownies before they disappear."

Brady didn't let him past. "You know you can talk to me too, right?"

"When do I talk to anyone?" Some things a man didn't talk about. "Don't pull that worried face. You know me."

"I do, and you've been wound tight, tight as ever. Dad says the same. He's worried you're burning the candle at both ends."

"I haven't fought in five years." He sighed, knowing he'd need to give his brother more. "It will be in front of the whole village, first with Paul and then with Jimmy, and you know how far he and I go back. Further, the outcome is important to the arts center, which is beloved to my future sister-in-law and Kathleen and our friends. Then there's Kathleen herself and all. Surely you can understand why I would be wound up."

210

Brady's mouth tipped to the right. "You've fallen pretty hard for her, haven't you? Sorcha—"

"Don't bring her into it," Declan said as he heard the ghost's sudden laughter in the entry hall, making his hairs raise. "Dammit, I hate it when she does that."

"Sorcha always was good for a bit of *craic*," Brady said, looking around for her before shaking his head. "Anyway, I'm glad you two are together. I might be biased, but Kathleen is grand to the core."

"I don't need a character reference. Now can we go and have some brownies?" Jesus, he was begging for brownies. But it was better than undergoing Brady's continued inquisition.

"I'll race you," his brother said, streaking ahead like he'd done since they could first toddle on two legs.

Declan strolled slowly, taking his time. When he reached the kitchen doorway, he leaned against it to give himself a moment.

Kathleen had chocolate in the corner of her mouth, close to her sexy mole, and she and Ellie were laughing as Liam pretended to hide the brownies under the table from Brady.

She was surrounded by people he cared about and looked as though she belonged there. Much like she'd looked when she'd pulled beers behind the bar at the Brazen Donkey.

The knowledge that she fit in all the places that mattered to him made his heart swell like a melon in his chest.

He didn't mind that they ended up in the parlor, demolishing brownies and watching *The Matrix*. Better that than the ghost chick flick she'd mentioned. Who in the world would find something like that romantic?

Now *The Matrix* was another thing, and when she leaned against him, soft and warm and smelling of chocolate, he bent closer to whisper, "You know. I think you look like Trinity."

She narrowed her eyes to slits. "Believe me, I've heard it before. It's the hair—and my black coat. My brothers love asking me if I've seen Neo lately. But they're a bunch of morons."

"They sound like a good group."

"They're the best." Her face was radiant, he thought, but then a shadow seemed to fall upon her features.

"You miss them badly, don't you?"

Her shoulder lifted and she turned her attention back to the kung fu fighting on screen. "Yeah, of course. Wouldn't you miss everyone here?"

He wasn't a man to dwell on his emotions but looking at his brother and one of his best friends sprawled on the old furniture, he had to admit he would. He nodded. She didn't say much after that, but as the movie played, he thought about her family. To his surprise, he found himself wanting to meet them.

When good had prevailed and Neo had saved Trinity, they all broke up and went their separate ways after a round of hugs started by the women. Closing the door to his bedroom, Declan watched Kathleen sink onto his bed and start unlacing her boots.

"Bare bones decor," she said with a smirk. "Exactly what I was expecting, except your bed is bigger than mine, as promised. You're such a guy. My brothers are the same way. I swear they'd run if I threw a colorful throw or ruffled pillow at them. But that's why I love them. WYSIWYG. What you see is what you get. Like me."

Her mention of her family changed the look on her face

again, making it soft and sad. He didn't like it. "Have you thought about going home to visit them? Do you have the money for it? I'd like to give you some from the purse for my first fight, if I win."

Being a newbie again, he'd have to win his fights to make money, unlike an established boxer—like he'd once been. Back then, his manager and the opponent's manager would negotiate purses for the loser and the winner, with the winner making more, as was fair.

He wanted to win his first fight even more now.

She glanced up, her fingers arrested on the laces. "That's... You don't need to do that. You're saving up to buy the butcher shop. I have a stipend for my artist residency, and I imagine I'll have a lot more money coming in once the new statue is approved."

That wasn't what he'd meant, and she knew it. "Still, I'd like to help. You miss them. You should go visit."

"It might only make me miss them more." She started yanking at the laces. "We all need some time to get used to this new way of things."

"Have you told them about us?" he decided to ask, trying to look casual by leaning against the door.

"Ah... No. I'm staying in the moment, Ace, as we agreed, and making up my own opinions."

Ace again. His diaphragm tightened. He wanted to knock down the distance he heard in her voice, but he wasn't sure how. "Probably a good thing, and yet, you're staying here tonight. At my house. Soon the village will know about us. Which means my parents will know too. They'll want to have you over for Sunday dinner at some point."

Her eyes narrowed and she peeled off her boot, which

thudded to the floor in the silence. "How about we cross one bridge at a time, Ace?"

He couldn't make himself nod. Not when she'd called him that, putting up a wall again. "We're getting close to that bridge, I'm thinking."

She gave her attention to removing her other boot, but it was a slow process to his mind. "Do we have to talk about this right now?"

His breath seemed to burst from his chest. "Yes. I can't seem to help myself with you calling me 'Ace' four times tonight."

Earlier he'd been thinking about love. Didn't she understand what she meant to him?

"Old habits die hard, Declan." She lifted her knees and wrapped her arms around them, looking young and vulnerable.

"Don't I know it." He'd been the one to introduce this mistrust. He needed to be the one to fix it. "I haven't had anyone spend the night with me—since Morag. I haven't given anyone a drawer since then either. These are big steps for me too. I want to continue making them. With you." And he sure as hell was going to give her money from his first purse when he won, because that was what he wanted. What she used it on was up to her.

Her mouth parted and she was still for a long moment before saying, "Noted. And...thanks for saying that. That means a lot, honestly. I know this is big for you. It's big for me too."

"Hence your joke about knotting bedsheets and leaving by the window?" His throat had a sliver in it. "*Mo chroí*, I love the teasing between us, but I never want you to feel like you have to think about leaving me like that." Or ever, he thought to himself.

"Consider all thoughts of knotted bedsheets gone from my head." Her entire soul was in her eyes. "Declan... We haven't spent a night apart since we've started. I want you to know, I might joke—it's my way—but I know we're close to that bridge. Okay?"

She wasn't much better with this new language than he was, he realized. His heart pressed against its confines, wanting more. He breathed through the tension like he did when boxing, and it shifted. He made himself say, "Okay," because he knew their talk had reached an end for the night.

But he still had another way to speak to her.

He crossed to her, kneeling at the foot of the bed. He took her hand loosely as she gazed at him with wide, searching eyes. When she leaned in to kiss him, he thought he heard them both sigh in wonder at that first touch.

That night, in his bed, as the wind traced the panes of glass, they reached a new level of intimacy. There was love as their eyes held, and there were promises as their arms held each other.

After their cries washed through the room, she laid her head against his chest. He stroked her back and let his mind imagine a time in which the moonlit scene outside his window might instead be the city lights from her bustling neighborhood in Boston. In that imagined future, he had just met her family, and they'd accepted him.

He was amazed to discover how much he looked forward to crossing that bridge.

CHAPTER SEVENTEEN

Mary Kincaid had the audacity to apply to be her assistant.

Bets carved the damp soil under her roses to unearth another thistle. Spring brought budding roses and her other nemeses: thistle and nettle. They stung even through her gardening gloves.

Much like her sister-in-law.

With their prize roses starting to flourish, both Bets' and Mary's mind would be on the annual rose competition in August. Mary had obviously just been poking at her when she sent in her pathetic one-page resume of charity and county events. Bottom line: she wanted to get into her head.

Last year, they suspected Mary—or her thug-like son, Owen—had let Donal's sheep out of his pasture by tampering with his gate. Those fluffy white idiots had thundered up her drive and eaten her prize roses, hurting her chances for the rose competition.

What did that bitch have in mind this year?

Because this resume suggested Mary had her cauldron out again.

Bets had the urge to ask her for an interview just to call her on her shit.

"You digging for treasure, sugar?" she heard a familiar drawl call out.

She didn't bother to turn around as she worked the thistle's roots with her spade. "I wish. Donal told me the two of you had scored another win with your pub drinks."

He'd texted her that actually. Texted! And begged off coming over to her place, saying he was wrecked from boxing practice and the meeting at the pub. Another sign things were not going well between them. She was trying to be positive. He was helping the arts center. Only those texts had made her tear up.

"We did at that," Linc drawled.

"That's two other council members who would like to be trustees, and all this before the first boxing match. Not bad, cowboy."

He dropped to his knees and had his hands on the thistle before she could warn him. He howled. "What the —? *Jesus*! My hand is on fire. Take me to the hospital. My hand is going to fall off."

Bruce and her three boys had always been terrible about pain. If men were the ones giving birth, they'd never shut up about it. But thistles did hurt like a bitch. "It won't fall off. Come on. I have some salve inside. Jesus, Linc. Haven't you come across a thistle before?"

"I didn't look," he accused, cradling his swelling hand. "You were weeding, dammit! I was trying to help."

She tossed her spade aside and rose. "In Ireland, we don't have to worry about snakes while gardening, but some of our weeds leave a nasty mark."

"I'm never weeding again," he muttered as they walked briskly to the house.

She needed to get his mind off his swelling appendage. *Oh, don't make that joke, O'Hanlon.*

"You want to hear something funny? Mary Kincaid applied to be my assistant. I'm thinking about interviewing her and asking things like *How do you handle failure?* and *What do you do when people don't like you?* Linc, that bitch is trying to mess with my head. It's no accident it's rose season again."

Of course, that was small Irish potatoes compared with Mary's aims. She still wanted to take the arts center down or get control of it for herself.

He blew on his hand like he was trying to put the fire out. "Your rose competition is legendary, I hear. I can't wait to see this fight. I gander the boxing match won't be anywhere near as intense as you tangling with Mary over tea roses. Jesus, this hurts like a—"

"Tea roses?" She let him inside the kitchen and walked to the drawer with the salve. "What do you know about roses?"

"Women like them," he said, trying for a smile but failing.

"Give me your hand," she said, dipping her hand into the salve. "It's going to hurt for three days from my experience. Good thing you aren't boxing. You couldn't wear gloves."

"Donal and the rest of those loons never stop training," Linc said, wincing as she gently covered his rash in sweeping movements. "If politicking with the council members weren't so important, I don't think he'd ever leave the boxing club."

Sore subject, that. "Don't I know it?"

"I swear, I can't imagine wanting anyone to hit me at this age. I got into some dustups when I was a teenager.

Mostly over girls. But I like not having to exercise like I'm twenty. Because I'm not."

"Donal was in sheep, which involves a lot of running and physical labor. He didn't ride a desk like you. But you're right. He's not twenty anymore."

She still hadn't mustered the courage to ask Donal about the distance in their relationship. They weren't having sex. He was usually at the club training or out now for politicking drinks with Linc. Things were weird between them, and she knew it.

Linc thanked her as she capped the jar, then tilted his head to study her. "Your face is as dark as those skies outside, portending rain. Something on your mind?"

"Tons." She dropped the jar in the drawer and put the kettle on before remembering Linc hated tea. "Coffee?"

"Whiskey," he said, cracking his neck. "You Irish would say it would help my hand, right?"

"Probably, but let's stick to coffee for the moment." She found the coffee grounds in the cupboard and dumped a good measure in the French press. "Biscuit?"

"Jesus, Bets, this isn't a garden party. You know, I can interview Mary Kincaid with you if you want to mess with her back. Might be fun to ask her rude questions—"

"I'm loving this idea," Bets replied, all the while knowing it would be a stupid move. Still, it was fun to pretend.

"That's not why your face is dark," he continued. "This is about Donal, isn't it? I'm a current houseguest so I know he's been home every night after training hard all day at the boxing club. When I asked him if he was tired of me, he said he was happy for the company. Seemed odd, that."

It was more than odd. It confirmed her worst fears.

Donal was avoiding her and using Linc as a buffer. "Leave it alone, cowboy."

"As your friend, I can't do that." He dragged out a chair with his foot and sat down, cradling his hand.

The kettle whistled. She wished she could unleash her own inner cry like that. "I'm not without compassion."

He snorted. "Look, I was married—three times. I can read between the lines. You're not feeling as wanted or appreciated. However, I might point out that Donal's training has nothing to do with you and everything to do with him finding his purpose in retirement and being a man. I think that's why he likes me being around. I'm in the same boat, so to speak."

She threw her hands up. "When does that ever stop? This being a man thing."

"Damned if I know." He blew on his hand. "I'm feeling my way through the same mess of retirement garbage but dealing with it differently. I'm helping you build a museum and hopefully a hell of a lot more here. Kathleen and Ellie seem to think I've started a whole new career, in fact."

She started laughing despite herself. "I could have told you that."

"Good. Then no more talk about me retiring. The added bonus of my new endeavor—I like that word—is I'm helping Ellie, my pride and joy, and this community that's embraced me wholeheartedly. Your sweet self included."

"I also knew that, and thank you. I don't think I could do what we're planning without you."

"It's a big effort. No doubt. Only... You're realizing there's more to life than work. You're feeling a bit left out, is all. Sugar, Donal and the boys haven't even taken me up on my invitation for another lasso lesson. That's how busy they are."

He was full of shit. "Well, I feel so much better now."

"Lord, Bets. Talk to Donal. He loves you. He'll adjust. Only you're going to have to adjust too."

Adjust, huh? To what? Not having her so-called beau around? Not having him want her anymore? That was so not what she wanted to hear. Pressing her lips together, she poured the boiled water over the grounds and pressed down hard.

"I can't wait to find you a woman so we can have this conversation with you in the hot seat."

"That will be the day," he said in a John Wayne accent.

Her laughter trailed off. She finally decided to ask the question that had been plaguing her. "You interested in this Sophie Giombetti?" she baldly asked as she poured two cups of coffee and brought them over.

"Cradle robbing? God, no!"

His outrage couldn't be faked. Good. She spooned in some sugar and stirred, cocking a brow. "I could see if Mary Kincaid is still interested in you."

His glare said it all as he tried the coffee. "Funny. As for Sophie, I think we visit her after the first fight. I want a little more assurance of the council members' support. We have two of them. I'd like more."

"And Tom might talk them out of being on our side," Bets said, her mouth twisting.

"Yes, and I need a little longer to prepare my pitch on lodging for Sophie and her daughter. Your doll-size cottages aren't going to cut it with the bigwigs."

She added more sugar to her coffee. "Ideas?"

"I told Donal I think we should ask for planning permission to bring in a few luxury manufactured homes and set them up. Even prefabbed, the options I've found fit the bill. We have enough money in the kitty to do it. I imagine the land should be cheap to acquire. Donal has some places in mind that will make people gasp in awe."

"Artists would want a nice view. I don't blame them. I like the idea too. It never crossed my mind before because we didn't have the funds. The added bonus is that a new house won't have the damp. Once it gets in, there's no getting it out."

His face scrunched up. "So I'm finding, the longer I live here. I'm thinking I might get one for myself too, so I have somewhere to hang my hat. I can't keep staying with Donal—"

"All right," she said, cutting him off. "Draw up a budget." She didn't want to think about what happened when he and Linc weren't doing their version of *The Odd Couple*. If Donal still didn't come around, that would mean...

"Already done," Linc answered, grabbing a biscuit from the tin on the table.

"Maybe *you* should be my assistant," she quipped, a smile tugging at her mouth.

He leaned forward and winked. "Don't tell anyone, but I kinda am."

She was mighty glad for it. "I still think it would be fun to poke at Mary, but I know it would only stir up trouble."

"I agree on letting sleeping dogs lie mostly." Linc crunched on his biscuit. "But we can daydream about it. Only not too long. That smacks of bitterness, and bitterness keeps you from flying, like the good ol' Tim McGraw says in one of his songs."

"You quoting country music to me?" She took a biscuit for herself. "You're a long way from Oklahoma, cowboy."

"Not in my heart," he said, lifting his coffee and taking a sip.

Her own heart warmed. She felt like that, being an American in Ireland, even after all these years. "Some roots grow deep, huh?"

"Like that damned thistle." He eyed his hand a moment. "By the way, I have a few architect candidates to run by you for the museum."

"We can't prefab that too?" she joked.

He shuddered. "God, that *would* be a statement. If I were a tony art person, I would spin it as 'a deconstruction or anti-establishment statement.'"

He said it in a tony accent, and they both snorted.

"Are we cynical?" Bets asked.

"Hell, yeah. That's why we're sitting in your kitchen having coffee. We see things the same way."

They rather did, didn't they? "I'm really glad you came to Ireland, Linc Buchanan."

Their eyes held for a moment. She felt herself start to smile as a big grin broke out across his face.

"So am I, Bets O'Hanlon. Thanks for keeping me out of retirement hell."

"You're welcome. Now tell me about those architects."

Her mind was spinning by the time he finished. Never let anyone say that moss grew between his toes. And he said this was only the beginning. She liked the sound of that. Before her days had been planned. Pretty boring. She was glad that had changed.

"You know what?" She decided to find the whiskey to celebrate and poured them each a finger. "I can't wait to present you with my candidates for your woman."

Sorcha hadn't moved on the case yet. Bets fashioned it wasn't the time yet. But it would be.

"Candidates, eh?" He kicked out his feet and downed his whiskey. "That will be the day."

She laughed again at his John Wayne accent but sobered quickly as the scent of oranges filled the air around them.

"You baking something with oranges, Bets?" Linc asked, sniffing the air.

He'd never smelled the oranges before. Bets only smiled.

Linc's soulmate might show up sooner than he thought.

CHAPTER EIGHTEEN

Declan's first fight was tonight.

Kathleen was like a cat on hot bricks as she pounded on metal in her shed, hoping to dissipate the tension inside her. She didn't want it to show when she was in the audience tonight. The thought of watching someone hit him made her stomach turn, but she would get through it and support him.

God knew, Declan was nervous enough for both of them, although he'd tried not to show it this past week. But how could he not be? He hadn't had a match in five years.

His kiss this morning had told her how much he needed her. If he'd held her a little longer than usual, neither of them had said. He hadn't trained this morning, saving his reserves for the fight, so they'd stayed in bed together until late morning, making love and talking. Anything to keep his mind off Paul Keane and fighting in front of the village for the first time since his big loss.

When they finally got out of bed, she made coffee and showed him a video Robbie had sent her. Ever since he'd entered the police academy, years ago now, he'd started sending everyone in the family videos of "stupid criminals" caught in the act. Her brothers loved them, and she had to admit, some of them were pretty funny. This one had been particularly epic—a bystander had witnessed a man trying to steal a car, ineptly, and called the cops. While he was waiting for them, he'd gotten a video of the would-be thief. The man had shocked himself repeatedly while trying to hot-wire the old Honda, yelling in fits, his body jerking from the current as he kept trying. Total moron.

Declan had laughed so hard he'd clutched his gorgeous abs. Then he'd done a search for stupid Irish criminal videos, suspecting they existed. Sure enough, Ireland had them. Kathleen pointed out to Declan every criminal was a guy. He'd snorted, saying women were the smarter sex, which had made her laugh as she poured cream in his coffee.

After watching a few more videos in her front parlor, she'd sent a gem to Robbie. It had been of a drunk Irishman dressed as a leprechaun on St. Patrick's Day in Dublin. He'd stolen a horse from the parade and taken off singing "Wild Rover" for three blocks before being arrested. Kathleen's favorite part was of him hiccupping on camera while telling the officers that the fairies had made him do it. Robbie had sent back four crazy laughing faces, which was a slew of emojis for him.

After she and Declan had wiped their eyes from laughing so hard, she'd kissed him on the cheek and said, "You've been inducted into the stupid criminal video club."

"I can't wait for more of them," he'd replied in a tender tone, caressing her cheek and gazing into her eyes—something that always made her get all mushy inside.

While she hadn't told her brother the video was from Declan, she planned to mention it soon...but first she'd need to tell them about him. She wanted to share her family with him, she was coming to realize. This would help them like him. Axl hadn't cared for the video tradition, and her brothers would remember that. The O'Connors were a weird lot, but they liked people who shared their sick sense of humor. Declan fit the bill. She couldn't wait for them to hear his butcher jokes.

She dropped her hammer, letting her hand rest. The repeated strokes made her fingers buzz. God, she was in deep with Declan. Her stomach turned into a ball of nerves again. She went back to working on the design model for her pirate ship and let her thoughts wander to the larger design.

She would need a strong frame to hold her ship up with the Irish wind being so tempestuous. She'd decided to use COR-TEN steel as much for its durability and weather resistance as the copper addition that would give her sculpture a beautiful patina as it aged. She surveyed the frame for the ship's bow and brought up her schematic for the larger design in her head. She was going to need an engineer to check the land around the museum to make sure the ground wasn't too damp underneath.

No doubt about it, she'd need a good team to bring this together. Eoghan had told her he had a friend who'd worked for a local American steel company, who also had other welder friends. She couldn't interview them before they got planning permission, but it made her feel better to know Eoghan and Liam were both looking out for her interests. They knew the local scene.

"Hiya," she heard a male voice behind her. "I heard all the pounding and had to come and see what it was about. Everyone in the village has heard about your sculpture. You must be the artist."

She turned and studied the younger man in front of her. He was in his early to mid-thirties with sallow skin and a leached thinness she ascribed to someone who used drugs. Her gut immediately went on alert.

Robbie had urged her to always listen to her instincts, even when she didn't know why—he'd seen the worth of gut reactions a million times as a police officer. She drew herself up to make herself project as someone taller, something she'd learned in the self-defense classes her brother had given her.

"Yes, I'm the artist," she said casually. "But because of all my tools and the like, we don't allow visitors in here."

She pointed to the Danger Arc Welding sign prominently displayed inside the shed. He'd obviously ignored the one on the outside.

His eyes narrowed and he shifted on his feet before he came toward her. "You're not welding now."

She didn't step back. To do so would give him the edge he was hoping for. Intimidation. Little did he know she was used to confronting bigger and scarier men in her old neighborhood. "Actually, I'm going to have to insist. It's a rule for a reason. Besides, I was also wrapping up and getting ready to leave." She wasn't but she was going to move him along.

"You're a rude one, aren't you?" he commented, walking closer to her. "Yanks usually are. They think they own the world."

His nastiness only raised her concern. "Your opinion, of course. Like I said, I'm heading out now."

He walked over to her worktable, ignoring her. "Is this your design?"

Dammit. She liked to unroll her larger design and look at it while she worked on the model. It helped her visualize the bigger sculpture in her head. But she didn't want him to see it. She walked over to the fully rendered design and rolled it up crisply and returned it to the architectural tube she'd bought.

"Yes," she replied, tucking it into her satchel and lifting it over her shoulder. Then she grabbed her phone but kept it in her hand. "I'll see you out—"

"I like pirates." He gave a leering grin. "The ladies seem to like them too."

Creep! That was it.

She walked to the door of the shed. "Let's go."

His mouth thinned, anger pinching his lips. "You're not very friendly."

He had no idea just how nice she was being. "I need to be somewhere. There's the fight—"

"Yeah, I plan to be there." He strolled some more through her workshop. "Plenty of time until it starts. Maybe we can even sit together."

Not on your life. "You really need to leave."

He only smiled, and that insolence had her going still. He wasn't only annoying. He was dangerous.

"Always in a rush, you Yanks. Lot of fine steel in here. You should really lock it up. The travelers like to steal, you know. And the tinkers. They're sometimes the same and sometimes different."

Had he just threatened her? She put herself on the outside of the shed door and took stock of the situation. Ellie had explained those terms when she'd heard them used in passing at the pub. "Travelers" was the Irish word for Gypsy—or the Romany people, as was more common these days. The tinkers were nomadic tinsmiths back in the day, many of them of Romany decent. They weren't considered settled people like most Irish.

Her takeaway. Every country had its ethnic and cultural

distinctions. Still, she knew the farmers talked about tinkers coming around and breaking into their sheds, looking for scrap metal. They'd put a lock on her shed for that purpose.

She hadn't expected a problem, but this weasel seemed to be threatening her and her steel. More of Robbie's self-defense instructions came to mind.

"I'm sorry, but I didn't get your name." She smiled as she lifted her phone and aimed it at him. "I like to take photos of people so I can remember their names and faces."

He darted toward her. She was glad she was out of the shed. This way she was in plain sight of the center. Classes were going on. Someone would see her or hear her shout if it came to that. She hoped he wouldn't get physical. Otherwise, she was going to knee him in the nuts and take off.

"You shouldn't take photos of people without their permission," he snarled. "Give me your phone."

When he reached for her arm, she lifted her chin and evaded him. "You don't want to do that. There are other artists inside who can see and hear me. My advice to you is to head on out, Ace. Quit while you're behind."

"I want you to delete that photo," he said flatly, his entire body poised to spring.

No way that was happening. "Take off. Now."

He took a menacing step toward her, so close she could smell the foul odor of stale cigarettes and onions on his breath. She didn't step back, meeting his eyes. The worst thing you could do with a bully was run or back down, Robbie had always said.

"Kathleen! Hey!"

Ellie's voice was welcome, but she didn't want her coming any closer. She didn't take her eyes off dip wad.

"Better go, Ace," she told him again.

He strode off in angry strides, his fists clenched. She walked after him, all the way to the parking lot.

"Was that guy bothering you?" Ellie asked, breathing hard next to her. "Sorcha appeared out of nowhere and told me to find you."

God love Sorcha. Sometimes her nosiness was a blessing. "In a minute, babe."

Dip wad caught her staring at him as he opened his car door—an ugly red Berlingo faded from age and weather.

As he drove away, she lifted her phone, zeroed in, and took a picture of his license plate like her brother had taught her. Who knew whether she would need it? Man, he was creepy.

"What happened?" Ellie asked, rubbing her back. "Who was that?"

She became aware of how tense her muscles were. "You don't know him, huh?"

"No." She put her arm around Kathleen. "You okay?"

She probably would feel the nerves in a minute. She always did after a tense confrontation. "I've had worse in Southie. Come on. Let's see if anyone knows who this jackass is."

Angie had her painting class going on the first floor. It was the closest classroom, and she knew neither the teacher nor the students would mind the interruption. When she opened the door, Angie muscled out of her chair, which she was using more the closer she came to term.

"What's the matter?" she asked, putting a hand on her large belly.

"I had a jerk come into the shed on the pretense of seeing my work. The whole thing was weird." She pulled out her phone and brought up his picture. "Know this guy?"

Angie's eyes widened. "*This guy* came into your shed?"

"Yeah. And he wouldn't leave."

She blew out a breath. "Oh, hell. That's Mary Kincaid's son."

Ellie swore like a Boston native. Kathleen nodded slowly. Now she understood why he'd shown up out of the blue.

"Well, shit," she said. "I guess we'd better find Bets and tell her the whole story."

Mary Kincaid was intent on causing more trouble. Right before Declan's first fight too, which the men planned on using as an opportunity to press their agenda for the arts center.

That couldn't be a coincidence.

CHAPTER NINETEEN

The weathered clock in the club told him how much time he had until his first fight.

Three hours.

Too damn long.

His stomach muscles were too tense as he tapped the speed bag, warming up. They still had the club to themselves, and he would use every minute until Paul Keane and his crew arrived before heading to the locker room. He needed his body to fall into a rhythm if he was going to win tonight. He knew that.

He modulated his breathing with his punches and slowed everything down, trying not to look at the rows of worn metal chairs arranged around the boxing ring for the people who'd bought tickets. The fight was sold out. A hundred people were coming to watch.

He was going to be sick.

No, he wasn't. That would only make his dad and the others start clucking like hens. He drank the last of his orange juice and chewed on the last of his candy bar. Then he swallowed his nerves and kept punching, searching for that calm place inside him.

An image of Kathleen rose in his mind, of her smiling at him in her favorite Patriots sweatshirt and those little shorts. She'd told him only this morning that her brothers had told her she was a lucky charm for fighters because her initials were KO—knock out.

He couldn't wait to find her after the fight and kiss her senseless. She was so supportive, his Kathleen.

She'd even shown him those "stupid criminal" videos earlier to help distract him. After this morning, he was really looking forward to meeting her brothers. How could you not like someone who sent around "stupid criminal" videos? They were great *craic*. He'd already shared a few with his friends, and they'd distracted him with some happy texting.

Then there was that tender look Kathleen had given him when she'd declared he was now part of the "stupid criminal" video club—the one she shared with her family. Whenever he thought about that look, it helped ease the unrelenting tension in his chest. It made him feel like they'd started crossing that bridge they'd talked about.

His fists seemed to soften in his gloves. He tapped the bag more easily as peace rippled through his chest.

Was it any wonder he was in love with her?

He frowned as someone's phone rang shrilly, like an alarm. Since most of the people he knew only used their phones for emergencies, he knew something was wrong.

Donal perked up, then rushed to his phone and picked up the call as everyone fell silent. His mouth went flat as he muttered and hung up.

Declan paused in hitting the speed bag. "What's wrong?"

Donal's bruised jaw was one hard line. "Hell of a time for this, but that might be intentional. Bets called to say Mary Kincaid's son showed up at Kathleen's shed. He made some threats."

His heart in his throat, Declan strode over to the older man with the others, his shoes slapping on the concrete floor. Owen Kincaid had always been a bully, the sort who would pick a fight and then hide in his mother's skirts afterward and plead innocence. He was a gutless coward. But still dangerous. "Is she all right?"

"She's a tough one and says she's fine," Donal said, holding his gaze. "Owen only shot his mouth off, thank God."

Declan slumped in relief. They all knew Owen had put his hands on women before, although none of them had ever named him. The villagers still knew the culprit. "Where is she?"

"At Bets' place. I'm headed there to discuss things. Declan, you focus on the fight. We'll take care of this."

The answer came from his gut: *no.*

She'd be upset. There was no way in hell he was staying here. "I'm coming with you. I need to make sure she's okay."

They looked at him, their faces lined with concern.

"There's time," he added.

He hadn't officially told any of them how important she was to him. He supposed that's what he was doing now.

"We'll make it." He let out a tense breath. "Delay the fight if you must."

His father patted his back. "Yes, there's time. I'll stay and take care of Paul Keane and his manager when they arrive. Someone should be here to welcome them and show them their locker room."

"I'll stay with you," Seamus said after they all nodded as

one. "Declan, you run along and check on Kathleen. Then you hustle back here. Your head will need to be emptied out after this, but you should see for yourself that she's all right."

He nodded. "I'm off then."

"That she-devil, Mary, and her devil son, Owen." Eoghan put his hand on his forehead. "They're up to no good, threatening dear Kathleen. And on the day of your fight."

"They're a pack of cowards," Seamus said.

"I want to punch them," Eoghan ground out in a tone Declan had never heard him use.

"Me too, but it won't solve anything," Declan's father said harshly.

Everyone around these parts knew Gavin McGrath was the most affable of men—and most of the time it was true. But he could be roused to a righteous anger when a wrong was committed, especially against someone he cared about or a woman.

He looked around at the lot of them, then asked, "Is anyone wondering if I plan to stop by the hole Owen's living in and beat him to a pulp?"

"Wouldn't blame you," his father said, "knowing you're after the Yank. You love her. You haven't said as such, but I know my son."

He paused for a moment. So everyone had known his heart. He wondered if Kathleen did too. "I do, at that. Dad, I don't want Mary and her poison to touch her. Or Owen. He's a bad man."

"If there's one thing as sure as rain in Ireland it's that Mary and her minions will continue to do their evil," his father said. "But we stand ready to respond to it."

"She won't go down without a fight," Donal said. "She must have heard about our politicking with council members and our hopes for the fight. Hard to contain such talk in this town. She and her like are worthy adversaries, but those are the most enjoyable to defeat. I'm off. Dad, are you coming?"

Eoghan nodded, and they all started for the front door. Seamus busied himself with aggressively rearranging chairs already straight.

"I'll be right behind you," Declan called.

His father put a hand on his arm, his eyes gleaming with emotion. "I'm glad you love the Yank. She's good for you."

His throat filled. His emotions were running high, way too high before a fight. "I'm good for her as well. Only, we're taking our time."

"Good to take your time, but take the advice of a man who's been married forty some years... Don't take too much time for things after things are understood. It only pisses a woman off. You understand me?"

"I understand. Thanks for taking care of things over here, Dad."

He took the roads a little faster than he should, but he'd known them since he was a boy. When he arrived at Bets' house, Kathleen was waiting outside, her arms crossed. She immediately charged toward him past the other cars in the driveway.

"I tried to call you to tell you I was fine, but your phone was off," she said the moment he'd left the car. "Donal got here a few minutes ago and told us you were coming. Go back and focus on your fight."

When she stopped in front of him, he gripped her arms and then pulled her against his body. "How can you think I wouldn't come to you after what happened? I have half a mind to visit Owen and give him a beating for what he did today."

"That's a great idea." She pushed back and stared at him with a small smile. "Let me visualize it for a moment. A right hook to his creepy mouth and a hard kick to the nuts..." Her eyes brightened with humor. "Okay, I'm done. Declan, he isn't worth it. Plus, you need to save it for Paul tonight. Owen was majorly icky, but I took care of it. And Sorcha appeared to Ellie to send her out to the shed—"

"I'll have to thank her for that," Declan said, sniffing the air for oranges and finding none. "She knows his true nature. We all do. Kathleen, I don't want you alone in the shed anymore."

She rolled her eyes, pissing him off. "That's ridiculous. Owen was just trying to cause trouble—and right before the fight. His mother must be some piece of work. Please go focus on the fight. It's less than two hours away. I don't want you to worry about this—"

"Not worry?" He took her face in his hands. "Dammit, woman, how could I not? *I love you.* For fuck's sake, Kathleen, don't tell me my business."

She poked him in the chest. "Excuse me?" she said with wide eyes. "Did you just say, 'I love you'?"

"Yes!" He kissed her once, twice. "I thought it was about time you heard it."

Grabbing his neck, she pulled him down for another kiss. This one had urgency and longing. Then she pushed away and stepped back, her hands on her hips. "I love you too. Now go and get ready for your fight, dammit."

She strode off, but he'd seen the glow in her eyes. He rubbed his chest as he watched her stalk inside. She loved him. She might as well have hit him with a board. He'd known it, but hearing it... His head went light.

Seamus was wrong. He'd need more than his head emptied. She'd filled his chest up too. Only...

238

He didn't want to empty out her love. He would let it fill his entire being so he could win tonight's fight.

But first he would handle other matters. As he drove back to the boxing club, he called Liam. "Kathleen wouldn't let me go inside."

"And I didn't want to interrupt you," Liam answered. "She had things needing saying. Declan, I can't control Owen's actions, but I am sorry it happened. We've discussed adding a better lock to the shed and some cameras. We'll look out for her, especially now that we know to be vigilant."

The tension in his chest receded some. "I'm going to ask Kathleen to stay at Summercrest after the fight tonight." He'd been too caught up in the moment to think of it.

"That's good. A word to the wise... Tell her you want her with you. Don't make this about her safety. Her sense of toughness will rebel."

Yoda always knew. "You're right. Thanks. I'll see you later."

When he entered the club, Paul and his manager were already there. He strode over and shook hands with the other boxer as someone from one of the county newspapers took their photo. Paul's grip was firm, his eyes assessing. Declan held his gaze as they sized each other up.

"Been a while, McGrath," Paul said as they released the lengthy clasp. "I thought you were only punching beef in the meat locker these days."

"Cows aren't proper opponents." He set his weight. "Men are better."

Paul's mouth lifted up on the side. "Word has it your trainers have you catching stones. That's more for building a rock wall, I'd be thinking."

The posturing was like cold water on a hot day. "The

stones are for a fair more than for walls. It helps a man take a wallop in the hands, you see." He held up his battered fists. "I'll see you in the ring."

He headed off to his locker room, hearing steps behind him. Inside, he turned and smiled at his father. "I've missed that."

"You're still good at it." His dad blew out a breath. "Just a whisper of violence in your words, son. You must get that from your mother. Sometimes her very way of saying things makes my balls shrivel."

Frowning, Declan stalked the length of the small concrete room painted a deep green. "I hate the waiting before the fight. We used to play cards."

His father dug into his pocket and pulled out a deck. Giving him a crooked smile, he said, "I brought them in case."

He knew his father wouldn't ask him about Kathleen. He would hear what had happened from the others. They all wanted him to focus. *He* wanted to focus.

They grabbed two chairs and used the athletic table for a few hands of Twenty-five. When Eoghan entered, he exclaimed, "Deal me in the next game."

"Kathleen still all right?" Declan asked as the man joined in.

"She's in a fine temper, but yes, she's well." Eoghan nudged him in the side. "Concentrate on the fight. That's what she wants."

He nodded. Word must have been spread not to visit him in the locker room because no one else joined them. His father and Eoghan left a few times to check on things or bring him more water to drink, but he was never left alone, and cards were always being played. He'd long since lost track of who was winning overall.

When someone knocked on the door—hard—he knew it was time. The locker room wasn't equipped with a clock on purpose. His belly tightened and he took a deep breath as he laid his cards aside and stood up. The green boxing club robe he wore was about as thin as his skin. His flesh would be tested today. No amount of sparring could ever compete with a real fight.

"You're going to do grand," Eoghan said, lifting his hands and punching them gently. "Let's put on your gloves."

When the door cracked open, Declan saw someone crooking a finger toward Eoghan. He frowned as the older man hustled out. He didn't know why he knew, but he felt certain that finger meant trouble.

Eoghan reentered the room no more than a minute later, his mouth awash in wrinkles from his severe frown.

"What is it?" he asked.

"You'd best be knowing it before you walk out there," he said, shaking his head woefully. "Jimmy Slavin has come to watch you fight."

He stopped breathing.

"He's sitting next to Owen Kincaid, I'm told, who strode in bold as brass and introduced himself to Jimmy. They're looking downright chummy."

His father swore as Declan's breath left him. "Did Owen do anything to Kathleen?"

Eoghan grabbed Declan's face and looked him in the eye. "She's being looked after."

"Declan, I'm going to find my seat now and watch your girl," his father said, hugging him briefly. "Have a good fight, son."

He was glad to see his father go. Knowing everyone was

taking care of her helped. He just hated that he couldn't be the one to do it.

"Now listen," Eoghan continued, his tone as tough as ever. "You aren't to look at them when you go out there. Hear me? You look at Paul. He's the only one you need to be concerned with tonight."

Since he understood, he nodded. He would have to wait until after the fight to stare down Jimmy. And Owen.

Still, he would have liked to look for Kathleen in the crowd. Indeed, he'd hoped to find her before the fight and let her love fill him again.

His stomach went topside. He was sure he was going to puke, but the sensation passed when he breathed shallowly. Had he been this nervous before past fights? He didn't remember. He jogged in place and shadowboxed the air, focusing on the splintery crack in the concrete in the corner. Focus. He needed it.

When the door opened again, Donal was standing in the frame. "It's time."

The man gripped his shoulder as he left the locker room, Eoghan in tow. They'd agreed Donal would join him in the ring with Eoghan popping up if needed between rounds. Donal's hands were the steadiest to seal cuts from the fight and staunch the blood.

The murmur of the crowd was like a hive of bees in his ears as he stepped out into the main hall. Every chair was filled, and people clung to outer walls like ivy. Cormac and his trainers had outdone themselves by building up the event so they could work the crowd for the arts center. Tonight wasn't just about winning the bout and the purse— the stakes were higher. His stomach flipped again.

More cameras lifted as local reporters caught sight of him. He ignored them, striding toward the ring. When he reached it, Eoghan stopped him with a hand. In plain view of the crowd, he lifted a large gray stone out of his pocket. The smile that flashed across his weathered face was filled with mischief as he tucked it into the right pocket of Declan's green robe, to a chorus of laughs from the crowds. A right showman, Eoghan.

"Remember your training," was all he said to him.

He could feel the weight of that rock as he stepped into the ring and found his chair. While Donal massaged his shoulders, Declan looked across the ring to the man sitting across from him, knocking his gloves together. The muscles of Paul's face seemed pulled over the bones. Their eyes locked, that timeless look fighters exchanged before they started bashing each other.

Declan tapped his feet on the wood of the ring. He knew every inch of it. He had home advantage. He'd best use it.

"Get away from here," Eoghan called out, his tone no-nonsense.

Declan turned his head. Jimmy stood holding the ropes, his mouth pitched into a smile filled with malice—the same kind of look he'd had when he'd told Declan he'd slept with Morag. His heart rapped hard against his ribs.

"Be quiet, old man," Jimmy spat. "I'm only wishing my old friend here some good luck. It's his first fight in years. Makes a man's belly turn in fear, that."

He forced himself to smile over the rock-hard tension in his gut. "Not all men. Good to see you, Jimmy. I'm looking forward to our fight. Be ready for me." He lifted the stone Eoghan had given him and extended it. "Here. You might need this."

Jimmy's eyes flashed, but he didn't take the stone. "Tricks don't win fights."

"No?" Declan shot back. "I thought you were the king of tricks."

"Enough of this!" Donal stepped in front of him and leaned over the ropes. "Find your seat, Jimmy. Or I'll be helping you to it myself."

"You're surrounded by old men, Declan," Jimmy shot back. "Easier to win that way in sparring, I expect. Good luck."

Eoghan uttered a Gaelic curse word Declan hadn't heard since he was a boy.

Declan watched as Jimmy took a chair next to Owen. The younger man was laughing. Laughing! After what he'd done to Kathleen. Declan wanted to tear him apart.

He searched for her in the crowd. He had to despite Eoghan's advice. She was sitting in the center front row, wearing her Patriots sweatshirt. Their eyes met, but she didn't smile. She was worried. He knew it.

"Give me the stone, Declan."

After he did, Donal lowered to his haunches in front of him and waved it under his nose. "You remember how tough you are tonight. Forget Jimmy. He's not the one you're fighting tonight."

He turned back to Paul. The other fighter had been watching every moment. He'd fought Jimmy as well. He knew their history, of a sort, and he'd use it against him if Declan allowed it.

He cracked his neck and tried to focus. Donal was right —this match was against Paul, and he'd do best to remember it.

The referee began announcing the fight. He rose when his name was called and joined Paul in the center. They tapped gloves as was customary as the man gave them instructions. Three judges were weighing the fight. They would go ten rounds with a minute rest in between bouts, rules Declan had known for years, but he nodded all the same.

Paul leaned in at the end. "Jimmy still getting to you?" he said with a laugh. "You fought like shite the last time you faced him. Must be hard to be reminded of it."

Declan stalked back to his corner and took his seat. He knew what Paul was doing, but even so, it shook him. His mind kept summoning the image of Jimmy standing over him in victory. He shook himself. He was losing his focus before they'd even begun. He bit his lip, willing the pain to bring back his concentration, then shoved his mouth guard in and gripped his knees.

When the bell rang, he sprang up and took his stance, his right foot slightly behind the other, gloves up. He and Paul prowled around each other before Paul shot forward and took a swing with his right. Declan ducked it, but his adversary's left fist pummeled him in the gut. The blow reverberated through him. Paul always could hit hard with a sweep. Jesus. He took a few steps back, but Paul had him off his timing already. He got in another punch at Declan's waist before Declan drove a right hook into his jaw. Paul dropped back and then circled him a few times before landing a few more punches.

The bell rang. Declan detoured to his corner.

Donal gave him some water while saying, "He knows your timing is off. Don't let him take the offensive. Go at him. Make him move."

The bell rang. Declan moved with purpose and landed a blow on Paul's jaw before the man hit him dead center in the stomach, stealing his breath. His pause gave Paul an opening, and he landed four more blows on his abs before the bell rang.

His body was throbbing, and he was having trouble breathing as he sat down. Donal helped him to water, which he didn't want but drank anyway. "He knows you're frustrated and he's using it. This time, let him come to you. Make *him* frustrated."

When the bell rang, he nodded. Facing Paul, he stayed out of reach this time. They circled each other, Paul darting forward, testing Declan's retreats until Declan held his ground and landed a hard blow to the man's jaw. Paul's head shot back, and Declan stepped in, landing more blows on his stomach and kidneys until the bell rang.

Back in the corner, the water was a cold rain down his throat. Donal mopped his face with a towel. "Good. Keep making him come to you. Widen your stance a little. Lift your gloves when he approaches. He won't have the opening he wants. Block him with your gloves and elbows and then give him a left hook."

The bell sounded, signaling the end of the break. He kept back, making Paul pursue him. But when Paul finally drew close, he managed to grab Declan by the head and smash him with his right fist.

Declan staggered back. Hit the ropes. Paul landed more blows on his body. He tried to block them, but his gloves glanced off. He was pinned against the ropes. More blows. He fought to stay up.

When the bell rang, he had to focus on heading to the chair. Everything seemed to tilt. Donal didn't give him water first. He mopped his face. The towel was bloody when he set it aside. When Declan looked across the ring, he was pleased to see Paul's mouth was cut.

"You're hanging in there. By God, you are. He's a canny bastard, he is. You go at him, and you hit him. No more evading. You land your blows, Declan McGrath."

When the bell rang, he moved swiftly. He hit Paul in the face with a right. Then a left. Then another right. The man staggered back—Declan closed in. Landed another right to his kidneys. Then Paul latched around him, holding him so he couldn't punch. Declan pushed him away, but Paul's right came up and hit him under the jaw. His head snapped back and he fell.

His head pounded.

Sweat stung his eyes.

He heard the count of the referee. *One. Two. Three...*

The crowd was shouting, the screams and calls reverberating in his ears.

Get up.

Kathleen's voice.

He pulled himself up slowly. The referee fell back. Paul advanced. He got in a few more body shots before the bell rang.

Declan shuffled to his seat. His mouth hurt as he drank. Donal was saying something, but it took him a moment to process it. "Get in there. Close in on him. Don't let him set the tone."

His head bobbed. "Got it," he managed.

The bell rang too soon. Paul seemed to be waiting for him. He couldn't block the right hook. The blow slammed into his jaw, followed by a solid hook to the body. Jesus, his ribs. He stepped back. Paul followed, raining more body blows. They were toe-to-toe now.

Declan got in a few jabs. Paul kept coming, holding him in place and moving him around, punching him. Declan wobbled back, his feet dancing on the wood like it was fresh poured concrete. Paul landed another right hook in his jaw, followed by a body shot that took him down.

Declan couldn't get up. The floor was cool.

One. Two. Three. Four...

He squeezed his eyes shut to staunch the burn. He was not beaten. He planted his hands on the ground and pulled himself up again.

Paul was waiting, his eyes intent—the eyes of someone about to go in for the kill. Declan bent at the waist, breathing hard. Paul started playing with him, holding his glove out, nudging him. He knew he had the upper hand.

Declan got in a few more blows, but his hits had no power. He was tiring and they both knew it.

The bell rang.

The short distance to his chair was like walking through the sea at high tide.

"God, man!" Donal mopped his face gently and helped him to water.

He coughed, tasting blood. "I won't go down."

"I know that." Donal gripped his shoulder as he dabbed Declan's eye. "You keep getting up. Only hit him when you have an opening. Save your strength for a solid punch. He thinks he has you. That will make him cocky. Find your mark."

He couldn't nod. The bell rang.

His legs felt like rubber. He took his stance.

Paul landed another right hook. Declan's head whipped back. A second punch shook his kidneys. He hit the ground. Pressed his hands into the floor and pushed himself up.

The referee kept Paul from hitting him as he rose. Respect was evident on the man's face. Seven rounds.

He could make it to ten. He had to make it.

Paul rained more body blows when he came at him. Declan gripped him with his body and landed a few hard blows to his kidneys.

Still, Paul pushed back and circled him. His ears buzzed from the crowd. The bell rang.

Water. Donal was saying something. Then he was back up, gloves up, staring at Paul. Eyes blurring. *Everything burning.*

Paul put his glove out, taunting him. Declan shifted to the left and then lunged. He caught Paul's jaw with a left and landed a body blow with his right.

Paul's fist snapped his head back.

He was falling backwards into the ropes. They bit into his back. Paul was on him, raining body blows. He held on, pushing against the ropes to move the man back. Had to move him back.

He leveraged him right. Paul wobbled. Declan hit him in the side and followed up with another to the face. He went down but rose quickly. His eyes flattened. He was pissed. Good. Declan smiled and tasted blood.

The bell rang. The distance to his chair didn't seem as far.

"Jesus, Mary, and Joseph," Donal said, tending to him. "You keep at him."

"His right arm is dropping," Eoghan said, sticking his head in. "Look for it, my boy."

He washed his mouth out with water, but the metallic taste stayed after he spat. The bell sounded tired to his ears. Like him. He rose again. This time Paul didn't charge out of his chair. Declan smiled again. He wasn't the only one who was tired.

They circled and landed a few hits—Paul a jab to his belly, Declan another shot to the face. He didn't feel the blows anymore. He angled back and looked for the drop in Paul's right.

There it was.

He waited until Paul moved toward him and harnessed his strength into a hard blow to his side. Moving in, he rained down more body blows, but Paul gripped his neck and pushed him back. Punched him hard in the face.

He fell. Everything throbbed. He wanted to lie there. He clenched his eyes shut and pressed his gloves into the wood. His body straightened slowly. Paul started for him. The bell rang.

"Last round," Donal said when he sat down. "Take it to him. He's tired. His punches don't have the power they did. You stay up until the final bell, Declan McGrath."

When he rose this time, he pushed his feet into the floor. Called up the last of his strength. Paul shuffled forward, his arms hanging lower, and they circled each other.

Declan looked for an opening. Paul's right dipped. He flew at him, his punch hitting him square in the middle. Seconds later, Paul knocked his head back with an undercut.

He staggered. Hit the ropes. Paul was on him. Punches rained down on him. Declan tried to grab his arms. *Stop him.*

Paul kept coming.

The bell rang, and the referee pulled them apart. He looked to the judges. They conferred, heads close together, then handed the referee a paper. He opened it and nodded before raising Paul's arm in victory.

He stood there, his vision wavering. Paul's arm couldn't be up. He couldn't have won. But the man was grinning, his mouth bleeding. His manager hugged him and put his robe around him.

Hands touched Declan. A whisper of cool cloth surrounded him. His robe.

"You made it ten rounds in your first fight in five years," Donal said, taking his arm. "You did good."

Good? He'd lost.

Jimmy had watched. Kathleen had watched. The whole village.

He crossed to congratulate Paul. The man barely glanced at him.

The press was firing off questions. "Did you ever worry the judges would declare Declan McGrath the winner?"

"No," Paul replied. "The better fighter won today. They knew it."

Teeth gritted, Declan walked off to the corner. Eoghan laid his hands on his arms and tipped his face to the right and left before saying, "You stayed right in there until the end. You be proud of yourself."

"Any fighter can stay up," Jimmy called out from where he stood beside the ropes.

Beside Owen Kincaid.

"Only a real man takes the prize, McGrath." Jimmy's sudden laughter rang in his ears.

He meant Morag…

Declan's stomach heaved. He bore down the gore, but then he saw Kathleen marching toward him, her face composed, as if Owen was nothing to her. God, she was tough. His brother and Ellie were with her.

Jimmy stood watching.

Then Owen lifted a hand and waved. "Hi, Kathleen. Good to see you again."

That *bastard.*

She stopped short and gave a tough-as-nails shrug as if he wasn't worth her time.

Declan's every protective instinct rose up, but before he could move toward Owen, Eoghan stepped forward and pointed at the man. "Get off with yourself before something happens, Owen. Something you deserve."

Jimmy leaned against the ropes and crossed his arms. Watching. If he knew how much Kathleen meant to Declan, he would do something to her. Kathleen wouldn't be open to any kind of overtures from Jimmy, but he could *hurt* her. For God's sake, he'd been sitting with Owen, who'd spent his afternoon trying to terrorize her. Who was trying to do more of the same now.

The image he'd had in his mind all day of taking Kathleen in his arms after the fight died inside him. He couldn't let those bastards see them together.

He had to keep her safe.

Before she could take another step toward the ring, he made himself turn his back on her.

"I'm headed to the showers," he told Eoghan. "Clear everyone out of here."

He walked off without a backward glance.

CHAPTER TWENTY

He'd turned his back on her and walked away before she could reach him.

What the hell?

"Where does he think he's going?" she hissed to her best friend.

"Owen? God, I don't care. I just want him gone."

"Not him. *Declan.*" But she kept an eye on Owen as he wandered through the crowd with that other jerk. She couldn't believe his gall, waving at her like they were chummy. Total creep.

But Declan leaving like that? She knew he'd seen her.

Ellie took her arm. "He's probably got a concussion and isn't thinking right. I mean, he just kept getting hit. It was awful. It couldn't have been easy to lose." She twisted her mouth to the side. "I can't believe the judges didn't award his effort. Maybe he didn't see you."

"I want to believe that." He had taken punch after punch and kept getting back up. She couldn't imagine what that had taken out of him. But this didn't feel right...

It *hurt.* She'd wanted to go to him after the fight.

"I couldn't watch after the first few punches," Ellie said. "I had my eyes closed the whole time. But I could still hear the sound."

The hard *thwack-thwack-thwack* of punches landing on Declan's body had made her cringe. Kathleen had never liked boxing, but she loved men who seemed to enjoy it. Her older brothers had never allowed her to watch their fights, thinking her too young, but one time she'd snuck in to watch Robbie fight. She'd come home crying.

Tonight hadn't been any better. She hadn't cried as Declan had taken punch after punch, but she'd felt each blow as if it had landed on her. His beautiful face had swelled and bled. Sweat had dripped. When he'd hit the floor the first time, she'd dug her fingernails into her hands to keep from making a sound or jumping up to help him.

God.

God.

She never wanted to watch him box ever again. He'd gotten up every time like a warrior, the kind of man you can't keep down. She'd always liked men like that. She was an idiot.

Also...

Fights put him in a terrible mood. She didn't like that either.

She watched his robe ripple as he walked into a side door and disappeared. Losing had to suck, especially hard on his male ego, but why hadn't he looked for her afterwards? They were a couple, for Pete's sake. She'd been about to give her version of moral support. *Good job, babe. You took hit after hit and stayed with him. You did incredible for being out of the ring five years.*

She wanted to march in there after him.

"The only reason I'm not jumping on him right now is

that he left this very gym to check on me after Owen came to the shed."

Maybe Eoghan had told him to go to the locker room, sensing violence.

"You okay?" Liam asked, appearing beside her. "Don't worry about Owen. We've all got out eyes on you."

"You're safe," Brady told her as he stepped forward and put his arm around Ellie.

They thought she feared Owen? She wasn't stupid. He was creepy. But she wasn't going to let him mess with her. "He doesn't concern me."

"Good, but we're all still going to mind ourselves," Liam said, his mouth grim. "Owen and Jimmy were thick as thieves tonight. That's a sight to scare a ghost out of graveyard."

"No one imagined Jimmy would come so far to watch a fight," Brady said harshly. "It threw Declan off, which was exactly what he intended."

"Wait. That was Jimmy Slavin?"

"Yes, that's Declan's boxing rival going way back," Liam said.

Okay, that pacified her some.

Kathleen looked over her shoulder again and found Jimmy in the crowd. He and Owen had stopped to talk to someone she didn't recognize. Their eyes met, and she felt a momentary pang of alarm. She knew men with eyes like that. They were always looking for ways to stir up trouble. No wonder he and Owen got along.

"How bad is the blood between Declan and Jimmy?" she asked.

"Black blood, you might say," Brady said as Ellie shivered next to him. "The kind that doesn't wash off. You have to scrape at it for days, but it still sticks to you."

The Irish really had a way with words. "Lovely."

"No matter." Liam gave her a friendly smile. "Kathleen, I was to ask if you'd be amenable to a sleepover at Summercrest. It was Declan's idea, but he's got other things on his mind just now."

More help to talk her off the edge. "I appreciate the invite."

Ellie hugged her gently. "Come on. We'll wait for him at the pub."

"It's going to be a mad crush," Brady said, eyeing the milling crowd around them. "I'd better be opening the doors soon or they'll batter them down. A good fight makes people thirsty."

Usually she was game, but tonight she was feeling raw. "I've had a day. I'm going to call it a night."

"Me too," Ellie said in sweet solidarity. "We'll go to Summercrest and make brownies. Declan shouldn't be too long, right?"

Liam grimaced. "They'll want him to go to the pub. Let me see if I can find out what's going on. Be right back."

He melted away, following after Declan.

When they reached the outer edges of the crowd, Liam returned to them. "Declan is refusing to see anyone. Donal's guarding the door to keep people away. Sounds like he's taken this one hard. The men are worried."

That wrecked her. "Liam, is there anything we can do for him?" she asked.

His expression uncharacteristically somber, he said, "He'll shake this off and come home."

Brady shared a look with him before nodding. "Take the women back to Summercrest, Liam. My dad and the others will see to Declan."

Kathleen darted another look at the door Declan had

disappeared through and watched as Donal waved off some local reporters. It made her feel helpless, but there was nothing more she could do here. "All right. Let's go."

When they arrived at Summercrest, Liam insisted on barbecuing in the backyard and capitalizing on the good weather. Neither she nor Ellie had an appetite, but they went along with it. Declan would be hungry, wouldn't he?

Liam grilled cheeseburgers while she and Ellie baked the brownies in the kitchen. They set the picnic table behind the house and brought out candles and wine. She and Ellie managed to choke down some food at Liam's nudging.

Afterward, they settled into the patio furniture Ellie had bought and stretched their legs out, wineglasses cradled in their hands. They spoke about art and travel and tried to fill the time while worry formed a hard ball in Kathleen's stomach.

She kept looking at her watch as the hours passed. When was Declan going come back? He had to be exhausted. Was he still at the pub? She'd decided not to text him or call him. He had enough on his plate.

When Brady arrived home, she knew something was wrong. He squinted as if trying to see into the darker part of the backyard. "Declan's not here yet? It's nearly two in the morning. I had to shove out the last of my customers."

"He didn't come to the pub?" Ellie asked, tensing beside her.

"No. Dad said he was so bruised he could barely sit up. I'm going inside to call him."

Liam stirred from his chair and went inside with him.

Kathleen dug out her phone. No messages. No missed calls. She was sick to her stomach now. And a little pissed.

Didn't he know she would be waiting for him? Dammit. "He hasn't reached out."

"He has to be upset," Ellie said softly, gently stroking her arm. "I can't imagine how hurt his body must feel. He'll be here."

But where was he right now?

Brady and Liam came back outside.

"He didn't pick up," Brady said, pulling a chair close to Ellie and taking her hand. "We both called. Kathleen, has he—"

"No." She blew out a breath. "I've heard nothing."

Ellie slid out of her chair, and Brady gathered her to him, hugging her tightly before settling her head against his chest. "After his last fight, he barely said anything for three months. I don't want that to happen again."

"Morag called off the wedding after he lost to Jimmy," Liam said, pouring Brady a glass of wine. "That was different."

"Should we go looking for him?" she said.

Brady shook his head. "He'll come home when he's ready. He probably needed some time to himself."

Three o'clock came. Everyone was exhausted, their yawns punctuating the silence more than conversation now.

Where the hell was he? He wouldn't have gotten into a car accident. No. Caisleán was a small village. If something like that had happened, they would have already heard. She crossed her arms over her chest, a chill touching her.

"We should get some rest." Liam rose and stretched. "He'll come home when he comes home. We can tell him we waited up. I'll even text him again."

"I will too," Ellie said, unwinding from Brady's lap and following Liam inside.

"He's not coming home tonight, is he?" Kathleen asked before getting out of her chair.

"I don't think so. No." He paused, giving her a sidelong look. "He's not with another woman, if that's what you're thinking."

She stammered, "I didn't think that. Not for a minute."

Even though Axl had cheated, her mind hadn't gone there. Not even for a second. She *trusted* Declan. Wasn't that an odd win on a horrible night?

"Good," he said, pulling himself out of the chair with a grimace. "You should sleep in his room."

Nerves rippled through her stomach. "I should go home."

He should have come home. To her. That's what people in a relationship did. Was she pathetic if she stayed?

He took her hands. "I know this looks bad, but— Please stay."

She hugged him. "You're a good brother, Brady. I know. I have seven of them."

Ellie was waiting for them just inside the door, and she hugged Kathleen fiercely before she and Brady headed upstairs. She didn't follow them. There was no way she could sleep. She dug out her phone again. No message from him. She finally gave in and sent a short one: *We're all a little worried, Ace. I'm at your place. Where are you?*

She waited to see if he would answer, and when he didn't, she shoved her phone back into her pocket. Liam had the kettle boiling from the sound of it. She walked that way and hugged the kitchen doorway. "Can I have a cup of whatever you're making?"

"Tea with whiskey." He pulled out another mug. "Good for the wee hours of night."

She pushed her way into the kitchen. "Are you staying up with me, Liam?"

"You look like you need a friend." He extended a tea box to her, and she chose chamomile because it was supposed to be calming, right? "I don't imagine you feel very comfortable right now. How about you take a few deep breaths?"

Her first attempt brought in a mere puff of air to her lungs. "God! I hate this. Liam, I know he was upset, but when I was coming over to him, I'd swear he purposefully turned his back on me."

Liam opened a cabinet and brought out a half-empty bottle of Redbreast. "You have to honor what you believe, but I've known him a long time. I don't think he'd do that. He cares about you. He wanted you to be here. He called me after he left Bets, making sure you were okay. He told me that he wanted you to stay here tonight. His last thought before the fight was about you."

"He told me he loved me today." Her hand shook as she reached for the coffee mug Liam offered her. "And I said it back."

"Then you have nothing to worry about, do you?" He pulled out a chair at the kitchen table for her. "He's battered right now, Kathleen—body, mind, and spirit. I can't know what that kind of beating feels like, but it looked to be a bad one. That wouldn't be easy for any man, least of all Declan. Most Irishmen are very proud."

She took her seat and set her mug down before she spilled it. She knew all about men and their pride. But dammit. This felt different. "You don't strike me as proud."

He rubbed his pirate earring. "I work on it. It can make you think crazy things as a man. I just want to be happy and find my purpose."

It was nearing four in the morning. They might as well talk about deep things. "Do you know what yours is? I figure mine is to create art and be with my family and friends."

He sipped his tea and sat back in his chair. "I think I'm coming closer to it. I love art. I've been doing some sculpting with clay lately, and it feels really good. I fell in love with throwing on the wheel in Bali."

"Oh, Liam. Bali? Really?"

"It's a cliché for a reason." He laughed, his sandy blond hair catching the muted kitchen light. "Made you smile for the first time all night. That's something."

"No kidding." She remembered to breathe. "Tell me about Bali."

He told her about his holiday love affair with the potter who'd taught him ceramics and then showed her some of his recent work.

"This is really good, Liam." She pointed to the tall clay buildings he'd built, glazed in soft creams and golds with slate gray for the roofs. "This doesn't look like Ireland."

"No. But I keep seeing those buildings in my head when I meditate. And I hear 'La Vie en Rose' playing. I feel like it's Paris."

"*Paris?*" She looked closer. "Yeah, I can see that. On my bucket list. Ellie loves it."

"I've also had this urge to start learning French." He sipped his tea again. "Can't say I know why yet, but it's a step. When you know you have a step to take, you take it. But you know that already. You're in Ireland, after all."

She played with her mug handle. She *was* here, and even more surprising, she was in love. "Yes, life is weird sometimes."

"Or wonderful." He took a deep breath of his own. "It's

all in how you look at things. Me, I try and be positive. That's why I'm not worried about you and Declan."

"You're not?" She must be tired to ask. "Seriously? It's almost five, and he hasn't come back yet. Or even texted me. Nothing. That's not what a boyfriend does."

His green eyes darkened. "All right. Since you asked, I'll tell you really why I'm not worried."

She went still on the inside. Suddenly she was scared to hear his take. She wished she could rewind the conversation.

"You went pale again. You needn't. I'm not worried because of Sorcha. If she says you're meant, you're meant."

Her diaphragm clenched. Not this again. "She's not infallible."

"No, because you and Declan get to choose." He smiled. "I trust you'll both choose well. If you choose love, then everything that threatens it is like background noise. It's like you Americans say about the cream rising to the top. You toss out the whey and move on."

"Toss out the whey." She put her hand to her forehead. "Okay, I'm totally fried. No wonder they call you Yoda."

He laughed. "Drink your tea. It will revive you."

She was falling asleep in her chair when he reached out and touched her arm. "Why don't you go to sleep?"

When she reached Declan's room, she almost started crying when she smelled him on the sheets. Where was he? She texted him again: *No loss is worth you staying away like this. Come home.*

When she woke, she was groggy. He wasn't in bed next to her. She checked her phone. It was almost nine. There'd been no word from Declan. Nothing. He should have called.

He should have let her be there for him.

She didn't want to wait anymore. Her clothes were wrinkled and dirty. She wanted a shower. She needed to brush her teeth.

She left Ellie a note on the kitchen counter and slipped out. The tears came as she drove home, blurring her vision. She'd gone and done it. She was totally screwy over a guy again, and sure enough, it had made her miserable.

"Sorcha!" she yelled, suddenly angry. "You'd better be right, girl."

The spirit didn't appear, which only made her tears fall harder. She scrubbed at them the whole way back. When she reached her cottage, she realized she was hoping Declan would be there, asleep in her bed.

Only he wasn't.

After she let herself inside, she kicked the door closed.

Okay, he'd lost a match, but he was being completely inconsiderate. She was so done with this. Why in the hell would she want to be with a man like that?

Sorcha materialized before her.

She jumped and cried out. "Jesus! You scared the shit out of me."

"If you hadn't been so mad, you might have smelled oranges." Her dress didn't flutter like usual, nor was there a smile on her face.

"I *am* mad." She heard how hard her tone was. "Getting madder by the second."

She nodded. "Mad is fine. Losing faith isn't. Declan won't make this next part easy for you. He's going to be one of the most stubborn men you've come up against. The question is, will you trust your heart and his when his words don't match his feelings?"

Pain gathered at the back of her head. "I'm tired. I'm

pissed. And I'm done being the nice guy here. He can't say he loves me and then not even text me."

Sorcha's mouth twisted. "You will have to decide if you're willing to look deeper and trust both of your feelings. It's always been your choice, Kathleen. Choose wisely."

She wanted to rail—at a ghost. "You should talk to Declan then. Not me. I'm the one who stayed at his place all night waiting."

"Women wait on men in Ireland." She wiped her brow. "I did. My mother did. My grandmother did. We might be eejits for it, but we loved and were well loved in return. When we weren't dumping cold soup on them for being late."

"I need to make soup then. I'd dump it on him right now for sure."

She chuckled, and with it, her white dress fluttered. "It has its satisfaction. Declan might not be easy to love, but you love him all the same. Can you accept who he is and still love him? That is what you must wrestle with. Because he did tell you he loved you only yesterday. He left the boxing club to check on your well-being. You might remember that when things don't add up."

Terrific. She sounded like Liam. "Soup it is. You have a recipe you can give me?"

Sorcha's dress stilled along with the rest of her. "One last thing, Kathleen. Watch out for Owen."

Their eyes met and held.

"Take care, sister."

Kathleen sat down in the nearest chair after the ghost vanished. Sorcha's final warning rolled over her. She didn't scare easily. But she rose and locked the door.

Then she went into the kitchen and pulled out a big pot.

CHAPTER TWENTY-ONE

U sually the mist hovering over the Irish hills brought Declan an ounce of peace.

Not this morning.

Staying away from Summercrest and bunking at Jamie's last night was one of the hardest decisions he'd ever made. Now he would go to the cold sea to soak his stiff body like he used to after past matches.

Leaving the club, his muscles had been rubbery. Hours later, after he'd lain awake all night covered in ice packs and arnica cream, he couldn't even bend his fingers as he dressed slowly. Everything hurt. His slip-on shoes scraped on the hardwood floor as he let himself out of the spare room.

He heard rustling, and then Jamie cracked open his door and emerged, tying his blue robe. "You're walking worse than a hunchback. Where are you going?"

"Home. I mostly have my head back on straight." He'd needed time to clear his mind and sort out his misery and humiliation over losing in front of the entire village. His wild emotions. His rage at Jimmy and Owen. His heartache for having to turn his back on Kathleen. And, worst of all, his fear that he wouldn't be able to protect her.

"Do you now?" Jamie scratched his curly brown head. "If it were me, I'd still want to take Owen to task for what he'd done to Kathleen."

He sighed heavily and leaned against the hallway wall. "I talked myself down from going after Owen. I'm glad Eoghan had the sense to put you in front of the door of my locker room just in case. You always were a good influence on all of us. Last night, I saw the teacher side of you too. You were a calm presence until my worst urgings left me."

Jamie managed a smile. "I can understand if you still want to give Owen a good punch in the mouth for what he did. But somehow I've always known violence comes from violence. We've known him since he was a boy. He was a bully in school. Meeting him on his level would only make things worse, especially as you are not his target."

"Right," was all he said.

That was why he'd gone willingly to the locker room, after all. To protect Kathleen.

Now he had to make sure she didn't become Jimmy's target too. It had been the right move for him to walk away from Kathleen last night.

Jimmy had seen him go ten rounds with a good fighter. He'd pull out all the stops to keep from losing their upcoming fight. If he knew Kathleen and Declan were together, he would target *her*—and given his apparent friendship with Owen, he had the perfect way to do so. Using Owen to get to Kathleen, and thus Declan, was exactly the kind of thing Jimmy would do. He liked to burrow into a person like a wasp into wood and wreak havoc on their foundation.

So did Owen. Declan couldn't get rid of that insolent

wave he'd given Kathleen and the way he'd called out to her. Going to the shed had been bold, and it hadn't ended there. He'd keep bothering Kathleen, and if Jimmy egged him on, he was likely to do something much worse.

That scared him, down to the bone.

"Do you want me to drive you home?" Jamie asked. "I can't imagine what you feel like after that fight. I've watched many of your fights, but that was one of the best."

He scoffed, which made his mouth throb. "The best? It's not your way to lie, even a white one."

His friend shook his head. "Your head isn't on straight if you can't see the courage and toughness you exhibited last night. Your head is as thick as Carrick's sometimes, as is your temperament. I'm tempted to call Sorcha to take you to task and beat some sense into you, but you've been beaten enough, I think."

He couldn't lift his arms to gesture to the bruises raining his very skin. "You're mostly afraid to call her because she scares the hell out of you."

"There's that too," his friend leaned forward and whispered, "but don't tell her, it's oddly comforting knowing she's looking out for us. I mean, what she did with Carrick is a miracle. You might be the same way after Morag. The Yank is pretty great."

His heart swelled in his chest. He couldn't wait to put his arms around her. "She is that and more. Thanks for putting me up, Jamie."

"A friend is always welcome. You know that."

Declan could barely incline his chin but he did anyway. "Go back to sleep. I'm off to the sea."

"She'll see to your woes."

God, they were Irish. He bid his friend goodbye and limped to his car and drove slowly to the sea.

The sun was a giant mass of orange in the sky when he arrived. No one was on the beach save a few egrets and seagulls. After undressing, he waded out into the freezing waters, hissing between his teeth at the stinging sensation. Then he stopped, feeling the saltwater on his cuts, and instead felt his body go numb.

Like his heart.

He'd just told Kathleen he loved her. Now he would have to tell her they needed to keep their relationship private until after his fight with Jimmy.

Declan would use Owen's threat to convince her of this wisdom. She wouldn't like it. But she might understand his worry that Owen would be more likely to target her again if he knew about their relationship. After all, it was obvious Owen had come to Kathleen's shed at his mother's bidding. He'd done it to get information, sure, but the timing was no mistake. They'd wanted to cause trouble before the fight to disrupt the elbow-rubbing that Declan and the others had planned.

Those closest to Declan already knew that he was with Kathleen, but they didn't talk out of turn. They'd also watch out for her. He trusted them.

He would tell her he couldn't concentrate on the fight, having to worry about her. Yes, that was it.

"You're banking on an awful lot, Declan McGrath," said the spirit he'd been thinking of, suddenly beside him in the water.

"Jesus!" he exclaimed, scattering a seagull. "I'm naked here."

"And you're underwater. I can't see anything." But she didn't laugh like usual.

"How is she?"

"You've stayed out all night with no word. Oh, you men

vex us like no other species. How do you think she is? She's ready to pour cold soup on you."

Carrick had told him tales about Sorcha doing that, and of course, he'd seen his own mother do it to his father when she was especially cross with him. "You must have suggested it. She's not that Irish."

"You hurt her," she said as the sea lapped at them.

He shoved aside a sliver of gold and green moss that brushed his bruised chest. "I know. I did it to protect her."

"Of course you did." She trailed her hand through the water, only it didn't part for her. "You know what would be wise? Tell her everything that lies between you and Jimmy."

She asked too much. "Men don't speak of failure or being made a fool. They certainly don't speak their fears aloud. That puts them on the wind."

"Which means they might come back to you." She sighed. "My grandfather used to say you should never say your fears or hurts out loud because the fairies or ghosts might hear and torment you. Carrick believed it too, or near enough."

"Men understand each other."

She gave a rude snort. "I grew up believing those pishogues too, Declan, and me a woman. We have our pride too. Except, here I am—a ghost—and all I want to do is help you."

He sighted a gray seal cutting through the water with two adolescent white-as-snow pups swimming at her side. They didn't startle. No, they swam around him and Sorcha in a circle. His breath caught. He'd never been this close. He'd always tried as a boy, but they were too fast and would soon disappear into the sea. Happy sounds met his ears, and then a small pup surfaced before him in the water, his expressive black eyes almost smiling as his head emerged.

"I wonder why these seals defy good sense. They have reason to fear us, but they do not. Maybe they trust they can handle what comes because they are surrounded by others who will support them. Kathleen can handle herself, even more so if she knows the truth of things. So can you. Reflect on that, my friend. I'll be talking to you soon."

The seals swam around him as if he were the center of their world, hooting and crying. Another nudged him gently under the water before rising out of the frothy black waves and taking off for the golden orb rising slowly in the orange and red-streaked horizon.

He waded out of the water slowly, as much in respect for the mossy rocks under him as his bare feet. When he reached the shore, he sat on one of the ancient rocks on the beach and hung his head.

She wanted to pour soup over him.

He couldn't blame her.

He should have texted her, but he'd avoided it and provided himself with plenty of excuses for why. His hands had hurt so badly he couldn't close them, least of all hold his phone. He'd left it in his gym bag and not touched it. Even now, he was afraid to turn it back on and see the volume of messages from those he knew.

When he reached his car, he pulled his phone out of his bag and set it on the hood. The sea had numbed his hands, but it still hurt to clench anything, even the steering wheel. He had a slew of messages, as many as there'd been after he and Morag called off the wedding. God!

He checked Kathleen's messages first. He blew out a breath as he read them. She'd been worried. She'd wanted him to come home. His heart longed for her. He would find her and apologize the moment he left the sea.

He decided to read the other messages, too, and leave

his emotions about those with the tide. He had calls and texts from Brady and Liam, wondering where he was, telling him to come home. Guilt wrapped around him at that. A slew of others had reached out about the fight, too, congratulating him for his effort. That pissed him off. What was there to congratulate? He'd lost.

Finally, there was a text from a number he didn't recognize. The preview made him clammy so he opened it.

You looked old in the ring tonight. Good thing you have three weeks to get ready for me. I'm going to make Paul seem like an angel. Watch yourself, McGrath.

That chilled his already numb body. The fucking bastard. Declan would never text a threat to another fighter. Never. In doing so, Jimmy had only confirmed his worst fears.

He drove in view of the sea as far as he could, the window down to cool his battered face. When he reached the fork to Caisleán, he headed to his place first, but her car wasn't in the driveway, so he kept going. When he reached her cottage, his heart rate spiked. She was there.

The door opened before he reached it. A frown marred her beautiful mouth, but it was the wariness in her eyes that made him ache. He stopped a few meters from the door.

"I was so upset I needed to get my head on straight." He could admit that at least. "I'm sorry I didn't call. I should have."

She drew in a harsh breath. "I appreciate the apology, Ace, but I'd rather you didn't do anything you need to apologize for. Where were you?"

They were back to Ace. He was sorry for it. He'd done this.

"I was at Jamie's." He took another step closer. "Eoghan was worried I might go after Owen, so he put him to watch me after I went to the locker room."

She only crossed her arms. "Being pissed at Owen isn't enough. I was pissed at him too."

Shit. He shifted on his feet. "Dammit, I lost the fight. I went home with Jamie because he knew I didn't want to talk. He gave me space to stew and cool."

Her brown eyes flattened. "And you didn't think *I* would? Or your own brother? Or Liam or Ellie? Dammit, I'm trying not to— I can't imagine how hard it was to lose the fight, but you went ten rounds. After not fighting for five years. Declan, that's incredible. I'm not saying losing doesn't suck. But you have nothing to feel sorry about. Nothing!"

He tapped his head. "I know it here, but that's not what I feel. I lost in front of the whole village. And you."

"Like I care!" Her anger made her shake.

"A man wants to be a winner in the eyes of the woman he loves."

She was working up to a boiling fit, judging by the red staining her cheeks. "Don't be stupid. It's not about that. I love you, dammit."

His bruised mouth split when he smiled. "A man has his pride."

She gave the impression of a fire-breathing dragon. "I'm trying to understand. I really am. But you should have come home. You should have known I wouldn't think any less of you."

"I knew you wouldn't." He took a step toward her. "But it stung my pride all the same. Worse, I lost in front of Jimmy, and what does he do? He sends me a text after the fight about me getting old."

"Fuck that." She stormed out and stood before him.

"And fuck him too. Look, Ace. I can't possibly know your entire history with this guy, but considering he cozied up with Owen at the fight, he's obviously a real champ."

"That's what I'm saying—"

"Screw them both. You'll fight Jimmy. You might win. You might not. But you'll give your all. Except here's the thing..."

She pressed her hand to the bottom of her nose as if she were fighting off potent emotion. He could feel it too, swirling around them like the black water he'd just left.

"Tell me."

When she lifted her eyes, there was a wetness there she hadn't been able to conquer. "The thing is... I might have gotten it wrong, but I thought you turned your back on me when I came to see you after the fight."

Tension filled his chest. "I'm sorry you thought that. Kathleen, you aren't going to want to hear this, but I did that so Owen wouldn't know there was something between us—"

"What?" she cried.

"Hear me out. Owen came to the shed and threatened you yesterday. He did it because he wanted to find out what Donal and the others have been up to—and possibly to cause trouble before the fight. I don't think he knows about us yet."

She tapped her foot impatiently. "He didn't say anything about you. I admit he's creepy—"

"Have you thought about what Owen might he do if he *did* know how special you are to me?" He met her shocked gaze head-on. "My next fight is still important to Donal and the others' efforts to influence the council members—"

"For heaven's sake—"

"Dammit! Listen to me. He might tell Jimmy, and—"

He was getting swept away, and he knew it. "I want you to look at a text he sent me, okay? Owen is dangerous, but I can assure you Jimmy is worse. You have to trust me on that. Together, they'd be a nightmare."

She worried her lip for a moment before holding out her hand. "Show me the text."

He could feel her eyes on his back as she watched him limp back to the car. His stiff hands didn't fumble any less when he tried to open the car door.

"Oh, for God's sake. Tell me where your phone is, and I'll get it. It hurts to watch you."

He told her where to find his phone and then leaned against the car while she retrieved it. Her mouth hardened as she read the message, he was relieved to see. "This could be considered harassment," she said, her mouth grim.

"It's out of line, but we're boxers."

"Fine, I see your point. I saw Jimmy with my own eyes, and yeah, he turned my stomach. But don't you think you're being a little overprotective?"

He shook his head.

"Of course you don't. We're a pair, aren't we? I like you because you're tough and protective—to a point. But that doesn't absolve you from not coming home or finding me. We're in a relationship. We're supposed to support each other. I wanted to be there for you last night, and you shut me out!"

So they were at the cliff again, the sea crashing against the rocks of their relationship. He would steer them away. "I know. I'll be in a better place after the next fight."

"And what about the next fight? And the fight after that?"

He saw what he wanted suddenly with the clarity of Waterford crystal.

When he'd agreed to start fighting again, there hadn't been anything else going on in his life. He'd seen it as a chance to make the money he needed, and yes, redeem his reputation.

But then Kathleen had come along. Before his life had felt empty, purposeless. There'd been plenty of room for training, for fighting.

She'd changed all that. He wanted to come home to her and wake up with her. He wanted to be able to hold her without his hands hurting from the swelling after another punishing fight.

"I won't be fighting anymore. After Jimmy, it's done."

"What about the money for the butcher shop? Will you have it?"

"I'll find another way to get it if I must." He would not utter the words, *if I don't beat Jimmy*.

She only shook her head. "You can't train and fight like this unless something is driving you."

Before it had been the money for the butcher shop, but in the end, he had to admit this was a chance to vindicate himself. With Jimmy. With the town. "Kathleen, I don't want to continue like I am, stealing a few hours with you."

Wariness came into her eyes. "I don't like it either, but—"

He cupped her arms softly. "Look at me. After this next fight—which the arts center needs, might I remind you—I'm done. I will never fight in another professional match. Yes, I will probably hang out some at the boxing club, but it won't be like now. I only want to be with you and—"

The clarity was so strong it had rainbow prisms. He took a breath.

"I want you—and a family. Dammit, I want to get married. And live with you for the rest of my days."

Her mouth parted and her arm tensed under his hand. "Don't say things you don't mean."

"I mean every word." He gripped her more tightly. "I'm not a man to say much, certainly not idle chitchat. When I said I love you, I meant it. I mean everything I'm saying now."

She pulled back. "I want to believe you. Declan, if you want to do this, you have to share your heart with me."

The words were like frigid water. She pulled the chain she wore around her neck and held it out. The silver Claddagh ring sparkled in the morning sunlight.

"I want a partner in life. Not a man who won't tell me how he's feeling and trust me with it. Do you think I don't know how scary that is?" She pressed the ring to her heart. "I'd have preferred to go down a dark alley in Southie without my pepper spray than tell you how screwy I am over you. But we have to trust each other all the way, even when it's messy, or this won't work."

He extended his hand to her and then let it fall. "That's not easy for me. A man doesn't like to talk about being a failure or a fool."

She uttered a frustrated cry. "I know all this. I have seven of the toughest guys for brothers. But Declan... You aren't a failure or a fool, although you're as stubborn as they come. When you get negative about yourself, I'm going to tell you're being stupid and slap you upside the head. Tell you to snap out of it. I'd want you to do the same for me. God, are you really serious about getting married?"

She stormed a few paces away, muttering to herself.

"Do you want me to get on my knee right now and ask you?"

"God, no!" She put her hands to her hips. "All right,

let's circle back. You want three weeks of us hiding our relationship."

Hearing it that way made him wince. "To protect you," he added softly.

"I can't choke out those words, but I'll be on guard, don't you worry."

He would worry. He loved her. There was no getting around it. "Thank you."

"Three weeks!" She let out an aggravated sound in the quiet around them. "You train. I'll work. We won't tell anyone we're together."

He was glad his knees didn't give out in relief. "Until after the fight. Then I plan to shout it from the rooftops."

"I'll buy the megaphone," she said tartly.

He almost smiled. "You're a good woman, Kathleen O'Connor."

She stalked back to the open door and then swung around. "God! Is it any wonder I want to pour cold soup on you? Overprotective, aggravating—"

"Tell me you love me," he called as she continued to mumble under her breath.

"I love you." She glared at him. "But like I said, that makes me pretty screwy."

She slammed the door in his face.

He blew out a breath. She would be safe from Jimmy and Owen. As for the rest of what she wanted... He probably needed to talk to Yoda about all this sharing. In all honesty, he'd rather she dumped soup over his head. Except she'd almost cried when she'd told him what she wanted.

More than anything, that made him want to lay his heart at her feet.

CHAPTER TWENTY-TWO

B ets couldn't wait to leave.

And it wasn't just over her excitement to visit France again and wine and dine a world-famous artist.

No, she wanted to get out of her house. She and Donal were bungling around this morning, trying to pretend nothing was wrong after he'd arrived early to assure her Kathleen's shed was secure.

The big stink in the air wasn't just that he hadn't spent the night again. He hadn't kissed her on the mouth when he'd arrived. Her cheek still felt stained with his tepid kiss.

"I installed the GoPro and new locks," Donal said, taking the list she'd scratched up this morning to keep herself busy and not running for the woods. "Didn't want you worried while you were gone."

She took the list back and scratched it off, not wanting to look at him. "Great. Thanks." God, this was awkward.

He cleared his throat, equally uncomfortable—as he should be. "Kathleen blustered about it being overkill, but she looked relieved."

"No one should ever have to be afraid at the arts center."

He shifted his feet again, and the floor squeaked. "Bets."

She dug her pencil into her paper. "What?"

"I can visit Owen and give him a sound talking to. I know we agreed we wouldn't, but if it will make you feel better, I'll do it."

The only thing that would make her feel better was being close to him like they used to be.

They needed to talk about it, but she didn't know how, and she was too embarrassed to talk about it to anyone else. Something was slipping away between them, and it didn't matter how hard she tried to catch it and hold on to it. It kept moving further out of reach.

He sat down suddenly on the edge of a chair at her kitchen table, his green eyes narrowed. He cleared his throat again.

"Do you want some rose lemonade?" She shot up and over to the fridge and pulled out the pitcher. "I made it with fresh petals from the garden."

"Sure." He nodded, a quick glance in her direction before he looked away. "You must have been up early."

That sentence was loaded. He hadn't been there like he used to be, and they both knew it. She wasn't sleeping well, feeling lonely and more than a little sorry for herself. Every morning at dawn, she was out the door in her garden, weeding, pruning, and then grinding and grinding rose petals to make rose lemonade. Anything to keep herself occupied.

Anything to keep her from the truth.

He didn't kiss her anymore. He didn't seem to want her anymore. She'd known this would happen. *This* was one of the big reasons why she hadn't wanted to get married, because she'd feared the physical connection would fizzle out. And here they were, not married, and it had still happened.

She felt uncertain and undesirable. Oh, hell. Her throat went scratchy from holding back the words she feared saying.

Maybe it was better she was leaving for a few days. Maybe...

God, she didn't know.

She poured herself a glass of lemonade after remembering what she was about. When she came back to the table, she realized she hadn't poured Donal any.

He shrugged and coughed briefly. "No bother. You have a lot on your mind this morning. I'll let you finish your packing. I told Linc and my dad to take care of you. Have fun in France."

When he rose, he kissed her cheek. *Again.* Yeah, they were in big trouble.

"You sure you don't want to come?" Maybe it would help...

He stilled for a moment, which made her rub the space above her bruised heart. "No, I'll keep working toward our goal here. Declan will need some rebuilding after the fight, and there are a couple more councilmen we should approach. Word is quietly spreading about the new opportunities, which might be why Mary got wind of it and sent Owen to spy for her. Bets, if you land this artist—"

"It will be a big feather in our cap." Then she realized it might also bring in more trouble. Not something she wanted to think about.

"Call me when you know." His mouth lifted slightly, without his usual good humor.

She watched him stride to the back door. The words caught again. But she couldn't let him go like this. "Donal."

His back muscles tightened. He turned around slowly, his eyes guarded. "Don't, Bets. I don't have answers for you."

She swallowed thickly as he quietly let himself out.

The lemonade was sour to the taste. She set it aside and went to finish her packing. When she finished, she brought her carry-on outside and sat at her garden table. The house was too quiet and filled with thoughts she'd rather leave at the doorstep.

Dammit, she was going to France today. To meet a world-renowned artist, the kind she'd dreamed about working with someday. That was what she needed to concentrate on.

When Linc drove up with his Range Rover, Eoghan waved from the passenger seat and called out the open window, "Grand day for a journey, isn't it? Not a cloud in the sky."

When Linc exited the car, she made herself smile. "Ready, cowboy?"

"I'm always ready." He reached out and gently lifted her chin, studying her. "Don't take this wrong, but you look terrible. What happened?"

She shook her head and put on a brave face. "Nothing. Let me put my glass inside and lock the house up."

"You and Donal get into it finally? He said he was coming over after installing the new safeguards for Kathleen's shed to make you feel better."

"No, we didn't, and I don't want to talk about it. I just want to focus on convincing Sophie to come to Ireland and have a good time while we're doing it."

"All right, sugar." He took hold of her carry-on. "Let's get a move on then."

His private plane was exactly as she'd remembered it,

all sleek cream leather stocked with champagne and bourbon and anything else you could imagine wanting.

Eoghan's reaction to the luxury brought a smile to her lips at last. He cooed like a turtledove as he stroked the leather. "It's the most beautiful thing these eyes have ever beheld. Linc Buchanan, if I die today, this will be a fine place to breathe my last."

Linc snorted. "Don't expire, Eoghan. I'd have to get a new plane. Can't abide the thought of someone dying here. Now... What would you like to drink?"

"You have drink too?" He gave a dramatic sigh. "It's better than any pub, and you know how I love the pub. Whiskey, of course."

"Bourbon like our last time, Bets?" Linc asked with a cheeky wink.

God, what a trip that had been. She made a face at him for good measure, determined to get into the swing of things. "On the rocks, cowboy." She stopped short of ordering a double.

Linc introduced them to the blond flight attendant and then gave her their orders.

Eoghan smiled like a schoolboy and sagged back in his seat. "You live a grand life, Linc."

"It's better with friends like you." Linc kicked out his feet. "Time to buckle up. We're taking off soon. Won't be long before we're in Nice."

That certainly was true. By the time they landed, Bets had herself in hand and had gone over her pitch three more times. Man, she was so ready!

When they deplaned, Eoghan raised his arms to the sky. "To think, I've only been a few short hours away from a place with this much sun. It's glorious. My bones feel as if I'm sitting inside a wood stove."

Bets breathed in the heat. The contrast to Ireland with all its rain, damp, and cold couldn't be greater and she loved every bit of it. She was going to do good here. She could feel it.

After they finished with Customs, Linc led them to the silver Range Rover waiting for them. "We're about twenty minutes from Saint-Paul de Vence. Let me text Sophie we're on our way."

The road was windy and cut through mountains lined with dense green trees and gray stone peaks—the lower Alps, Linc said.

"I read that this town has been a magnet for famous artists for a long time," Bets said from the back seat, trying for conversation.

"Yep. Picasso. Matisse. Hell, Marc Chagall is buried there. It was also a huge draw for French actors like Yves Montand and the like. We'll visit Saint-Paul de Vence tomorrow if you're game. Sophie lives in a villa in the valley."

A villa? That was where they were staying tonight? He'd said Sophie had invited them to bunk at her house. Nerves surged. How could they compete with a villa?

When they arrived at the compound, Eoghan gave a squeak after Linc called through the box and was admitted. Bets could have squeaked herself. The villa was two stories of golden stone with a dozen gleaming windows. A fountain of two nude figures embracing was set in the middle of the circular gravel driveway. But it was the endless roses in the formal garden to the right that stole her breath.

"It's paradise, it is," Eoghan said with awe as he exited the car and wandered away.

Linc was no doubt used to places like this, but Bets had only seen them on *Lifestyles of the Rich and Famous* a million years ago. She shot Linc a look. "Yeah, housing is definitely going to be an issue."

He winked again, calming her nerves with that one action. "Let me do the talking."

She opened the car door and pressed her hand to her heart as she inhaled the most luscious scent imaginable. Roses, and something else. She looked around. White blossoms trailed from the garden walls. Jasmine. Purple flowers flowed over another stone wall like a brilliant carpet. Tall cypress trees swayed in a gentle warm breeze.

Bets couldn't imagine ever wanting to leave this place.

"Linc!"

She turned her head as a woman came running down the steps. Her straight brown hair was pulled back in a ponytail, and Bets caught a flash of green eyes over a beaming smile.

Linc opened his arms and she rushed in, hugging him with a familiarity Bets hadn't expected. She headed in their direction, Eoghan's footsteps sounding on the gravel behind her.

"You've been working on your tan," Linc teased.

"*Please.*" The brown-haired woman rolled her eyes and shot Bets a smile. "You step out of your house and get a tan here. You must be Betsy O'Hanlon. I'm Sophie. Linc has told me so much about you. I love what you're doing in Caisleán."

"She loves a woman of vision," another woman said in what Bets could only call a sultry accent, French to her ears. She appeared at the edge of the garden in a stunning blue sheath. "We both do. Hello, Linc."

"Hello, Brigitte," Linc drawled. "Ain't this a surprise."

Bets tried not to stare as the woman walked over. She'd never seen someone prowl like a feline before. The woman's hands were dripping with rings—diamonds and sapphires and a yellow stone Bets imagined was a yellow diamond. Her perfume reached them before she did, floral with a hint of musk. Everything about her bespoke of money and elegance and confidence, from her dress to her coiffed white-blond hair. Then Bets realized she wasn't wearing a bra. Well...

"Mother arrived this morning out of the blue," Sophie said, making a face.

This was Sophie's famous painter mother? God, some people had all the luck.

"She swore it was to see Greta," Sophie drew out almost sarcastically, "but I know better."

"I had to meet the woman who'd lured Linc to the wilds of Ireland, didn't I?"

Of course, she didn't look in Bets' direction once, but the way her eyes slid over Linc... Whew! Brigitte wanted to lap him up like a cat did milk. Had *they* been lovers? If not, Brigitte still had Linc on her bucket list.

Bets didn't think Sorcha would approve. She knew *she* didn't. Something told her this woman was a lot like Linc's three ex-wives.

Brigitte turned her cheek like she was a flower in the sun, and Linc kissed it obediently with an amused grin. "Those wilds have a lot to recommend them," he said, glancing toward Bets with a gleam in his eye. "Including this woman of vision, as you said, and the oldest artist at the center. Eoghan, come meet Sophie and Brigitte."

He greeted them with a flush of his weathered cheeks and a firm handshake, God love him. "It's a pleasure to meet such beautiful women and renowned artists."

"What kind of artist are you, Eoghan?" Sophie asked.

"I've fallen in love with clay and stained glass," he said,

"and at the age of ninety-three, I'm only just beginning. With the sunlight here, the stained glass must be amazing."

"It is," Sophie said, smiling. "Mother, imagine working as an artist until ninety-three."

Her rose-painted mouth twisted. "A nightmare, for sure."

Bets didn't know what to make of that. Sophie only chuckled. "Mother is having a creative crisis. She's riddled with doubts over whether to use oil or acrylic in her upcoming showing in Milan. She just needs some new inspiration, like we all do from time to time."

"Which is why Ireland might be the perfect place for you, Sophie," Linc said, taking her arm. "Where's Greta?"

"She's watching us from behind the fountain. Pretend you don't see her. She likes that."

Bets glanced over and caught a curly blond head before it disappeared. "She's six, right? One of my boys was shy at that age, and he hid in trees."

"She likes the sound of water," Sophie said.

"Which is why I think you should encourage her to take up watercolor, darling," Brigitte said. "She has an untapped gift, I think. Her drawing is already well beyond what yours was at the same age."

Sophie's mouth thinned. "Greta gets to choose what she wants to do. You know that, Mother."

"Linc, she hides my gifts for my own grandchild." Brigitte took Linc's other arm as they walked to the front of the villa. "What do you think of that?"

Bets thought the woman was being clingy, that's what.

"I only know Ellie started drawing on my windows, and now she's a world-class stained glass artist. You know my idea of parenting, Brigitte. Build them a nest but let them fly. Then again, I always thought kids were smarter than adults."

Sophie laughed and laid her cheek against Linc's shoulder. "That's why I love you. Oh, I'm so glad you're here. I can't wait to hear more about Ireland."

Bets was encouraged by her eagerness. Brigitte was another story. She decided to keep her lips zipped for the time being. Way too many undercurrents here, and since she didn't like Sophie's mother—God, was she running her soft-pink fingernail down Linc's arm?—she didn't want to converse with her.

Not that Brigitte would want to talk to Bets anyway. No, all she had eyes for was Linc. Bets had the urge to shoo her away from him like she would a sheep. Apparently, she was protective of Linc. He was her friend, after all.

"Come," Sophie said. "I want to introduce you to my treasure, Sandrine. Linc's met her, so he knows she's the one that keeps everything working in my life and has since I was a baby."

"Hiring her was the only thing I did right as a mother," Brigitte said dramatically.

Linc chuckled. "She reminds me of Lupe. Best thing I ever did, finding her for Ellie."

Bets couldn't even imagine having someone to help with raising kids. Think of the other things she could have done! Another way in which this world was totally foreign to her.

"Eoghan, do you swim?" Sophie asked, turning back to look at him.

"I've swum in the Irish sea since I was a boy," he replied as they all entered the house, which was instantly cooler. "Jesus, Mary, and Joseph," he said with a whistle. "It's like a museum."

Bets looked around and tried not to gawk. The floors

were in light gray marble while the walls were a cool white stone. Paintings hung on every wall, the colors bold, the brushstrokes sweeping. Bets wondered if any were Brigitte's. There was a twelve-light crystal chandelier overhead, which shot prisms throughout the open space from the second-floor windows surrounding a wide circular staircase.

"You have a beautiful home," she managed to get out.

"Thank you." Sophie gestured to the room. "It's my grandparents'. They thought I'd like it here after I got divorced."

"Oh, Sophie," Brigitte said, tsking. "You aren't to bore them with that."

Sophie's mouth thinned. "Only stating facts, Mother. Sandrine, come and meet our guests."

Bets heard what she really meant. *Come save me.* She sympathized.

The woman who appeared on the top of the stairs was as beautiful as Brigitte, Bets thought, although older, perhaps in her early eighties, although it was hard to tell. Her posture was impeccable as she walked down the stairs. The light touched on elegant cheekbones, which set off a face that bore only a few lines. Her hair was white and rich, falling to her neck. The blue shirt dress she wore matched her eyes. She smiled warmly. Bets liked her immediately.

The younger woman made the introductions.

Eoghan sputtered and flushed red when he took Sandrine's hand and held it. "May I say... I haven't beheld a more beautiful woman in some years. It's as though the fairies have blessed me."

"Fairies, huh?" Sandrine had a slight accent, which Bets thought sounded French. "Greta likes fairies. Don't you, love? Will you come out and meet our guests, sweetheart? You remember Mr. Buchanan, of course."

Bets looked around casually but didn't see the little girl. She must have crept in quietly enough for the door not to creak.

"It's been a couple of years," Linc said, drawing something out of his pocket. "So long that I wasn't sure whether Greta might still like to play with jacks, but I brought a set just in case."

Greta's head appeared above the back of a blue leather couch, only her hair and her big eyes visible. "I still like them."

"I'll put it on the table here," Linc said, strolling over to a buffet carved with flowers and cherubs. "When you're ready for them."

"I'm ready now. Thank you, Mr. Buchanan." She edged along the couch, her brown eyes taking in everything. She wore a white eyelet top and yellow shorts, and her pink sandals were bedecked with flowers.

Bets smiled at her and gave a slight wave. The girl's mouth tipped up on the right. A victory.

Greta touched the silver case. "They painted stars on this. I like that. Jacks look like stars."

Bets had never thought about that, but she could see it. "When I was growing up in Baltimore in the States, we used to play jacks at the waterfront. You had to make sure the ball didn't bounce into the bay."

"I'm going to play with them by the pool." She picked up the case and took off for a side door.

"You let her be alone too much," Brigitte commented.

"You didn't let me be alone enough, Mother," Sophie shot back. "My house. My rules. You can always fly back to Malaga."

Brigitte touched the tiny curls by her ears like she was in some English melodrama. "I bet your Ellie doesn't talk to you like that, Linc."

"She surely does, Brigitte, and most times, I deserve it. Right, Bets?"

She sputtered, "Yeah, usually."

He sent her another wink. Was he trying to assure her he wasn't falling for Brigitte's nonsense?

He clapped his hands. "How about you show us where we're all bedding down and then tell me where I can pour myself a drink?"

"Come with me," Sandrine said, gesturing to the stairs. "Each of you have a bottle of rosé chilling in your room."

She had to be kidding. Only Bets knew she wasn't. Holy hell. She was in a French version of *Downton Abbey*.

"You got someone to grab the luggage?" Linc asked.

"Of course." Sophie laughed. "Would I ask Sandrine to haul up the bags? Please make yourselves at home. We'll be having dinner early since I thought you might be tired. Feel free to use the pool or the hot tub. We also have a sauna, but I find it too hot right now with the weather warming up."

God, what a problem to have! Bets wished she had known to bring a swimsuit.

"I didn't know you'd have a pool," Eoghan said. "I'm afraid I didn't pack for it."

Sophie leaned in conspiratorially. "You're in France, Eoghan. We have nude beaches everywhere. You don't need to worry about wearing a swimsuit."

He gave another squeak and blushed again. Bets imagined she was red too. No swimsuit...

Sandrine was fighting a smile. Brigitte had resting bitch face.

"Buck naked, eh?" Linc drawled. "What about Greta?"

"She won't come out when others are in the pool," Sophie said. "And her bedroom faces front. You're in the clear."

"Good to know. Been a while since I went skinny-dipping. What about you, Bets?"

She gave him the fisheye, her cheeks growing warmer. Last thing she needed was to think about going skinny-dipping, especially with Linc. Her body didn't look the way it had at twenty, when she'd snuck into the bay without any clothes on.

"I might find some inspiration again, seeing you nude, Linc," Brigitte said, looking him over. "It's been a while, and while I can paint from memory, a live model is always best."

"I'd be happy to pose for you, Brigitte. When they serve ice cream cones in hell," he added with a chuckle. "You know how I feel about nudes. I like looking at them, not being in them."

So they *had* been lovers. She banished the frown starting on her face. Well, who could blame him? Brigitte was a gorgeous world-renowned artist, and she lived the high life, if Malaga was any indication. She was a far cry from anyone he was likely to meet in Ireland. Herself included. Hmm... Maybe she didn't like France so much. Not when women walked around looking like this.

She suddenly felt drab in her simple black pants and pink top. Linc had told her to dress casual. Sophie was casual, he'd said. He wasn't wrong about that, but Brigitte was something else, and she found herself wishing she'd worn a dress. Oh, don't be ridiculous, she thought. She could never compete with a woman like Brigitte.

Then she caught herself. What in the hell was wrong with her, thinking like *that*?

As they followed Sandrine up the stairs, she couldn't

help but poke at Linc. "Your thing with your old flame isn't going to be a problem, is it?"

He held her back as Sandrine and Eoghan walked down the wide hall, chatting pleasantly, and entered the first doorway. "That was ages ago, and Sophie knows her mother. Brigitte is used to being admired. All her life, she's been wanted as a woman or an artist. When the cards don't fall that way, she's like a porcupine in a bouncy house."

"A porcupine— Linc Buchanan, your brain... Oh, never mind. Forget I said anything."

"You sure? You seem flustered."

"That woman would drive a saint to distraction." *Good save, O'Hanlon.* "Are we really going to wait until dinnertime to talk about the arts center?"

He stared at her for one more beat before glancing at his watch. "It's about five now. You that restless? Bets, you really should talk to Donal."

She shook her head and started walking after Sandrine and Eoghan. "Not on your life."

"You sure you don't want to go skinny-dipping?" he called after her.

Surely he was teasing! She couldn't reach her room fast enough.

And what a room... Sandrine showed her everything in detail as she tried not to gape. The ceilings were fifteen feet at least, lined with carved plaster. White billowing curtains overlooked a giant swimming pool, the one she wasn't going to skinny-dip in. Her king-size bed was a white four-poster lined with wooden ivy and flowers that looked fit for some old French queen. The fireplace was wider than her Mini Cooper, made of carved white marble with green veins.

When she sat on the bed, she almost purred. God! Had she ever been on a bed this soft? She glanced at the bottle of rosé in a silver ice bucket. She poured herself a glass and took a sip. Nearly swooned. Jesus, this place was unreal.

But her thoughts kept veering back toward the bed and her current problems with Donal. She let out a frustrated cry and left the room, taking her glass with her. She would check out the gardens. The roses specifically. There might be a new variety for her to consider for the annual rose competition. She wanted to beat Mary Kincaid's ass every year until one of them died.

When she reached the roses, she thought about Donal and about the roses he'd given her to show her how he felt. Love's Magic, for one. She brushed a few tears away. Things hadn't been the same between them since she'd told him she didn't want to marry him or move in with him. He'd said he was okay with it, but maybe he wasn't.

Was that why he was pulling away?

"Ireland looks pretty from the photos I saw on the internet," a young voice said softly. "Have you ever seen a fairy?"

Bets scanned the garden and found the pink sandals peeking out from behind a rose bush. "The fairies are too small for humans to see, but the Irish like to say that you can hear them singing in their fairy forts."

"Mama says we might go live in Ireland for a while. Linc likes it, and he's particular. He also doesn't mess around, Mama says. Do you like it?"

She stayed where she was, waiting to see if Greta would come out. "I do. The people are nice, and it's really beautiful. The light is incredible, or so the artists tell me all the time. There's always a rainbow, sometimes more than one in a day."

"I like rainbows," the little girl responded. "The entire spectrum of visible light. But when you try and touch them, nothing is there. Mama says you started the arts center. What's it like?"

The sun was hot on her head, but she didn't want to move into the shade. "We've only been going about a year now, but we have painting, ceramics, stained glass, and metal sculpture. We're hoping for more artists to come and share their art."

"Mama does glass, you know." The pink sandals disappeared, and suddenly Greta was standing in full view, touching a flower. "She can make anything. Last week, she made me a necklace with tiny jasmine flowers. It's hard to make flowers that tiny, you know."

"You're a lucky girl. Maybe you can show me your necklace later?"

Greta walked over, fingering her eyelet shirt, and came to stand next to Bets. She unfurled her hand. "Here. I like to hold it sometimes. You can't crush them like real flower petals."

The workmanship was exquisite and delicate. Every flower bespoke of love and an attention to detail. "I've never seen a necklace like that. It's incredible."

"Art is always incredible when you do it from your heart." She tucked the necklace back into her hand. "What kind of art do you do?"

Nothing like that, she almost said. "Well, I started painting, and I do some knitting."

She never seemed to keep going with anything though. She got excited about trying new things, but her interests always seemed to change. She thought of Donal. Was their excitement gone? She loved him, but it didn't feel the same anymore. Was that how he felt too?

The only things she still liked to do were grow roses,

beat Mary Kincaid, and run the arts center. What did that say about her?

"One of my true passions is the arts center. It's been like my baby from the first."

"You take care of things." Greta raised her knowing eyes. "Do you like Linc?"

She stepped back in surprise, her heart rapping in her chest. "Why would you ask that?"

The little girl shrugged. "You watch him like you like him."

Bets jolted before bunching her hands into fists at her sides.

"He's a nice man." Greta pulled a few jacks out of her other pocket, which flashed in the sunlight. "He remembered I like jacks. My grandma likes him too, but he doesn't think much of her. Mama says Grandma likes to be difficult. She thinks it makes her art better. We don't know why. The truest beauty is created out of simplicity."

Bets needed to take a deep breath. This little girl was throwing her one curveball after another. "You remind me of one of my sons."

"What's his name?"

"Liam." She needed to get over her embarrassment and talk to Liam. Stat. He'd helped her with Donal before. Maybe he could help her sort out her feelings about him...and Linc.

"Greta!" Sophie was walking down the front steps of the villa toward them. "Sandrine has a snack for you."

"Thanks for talking with me," Greta said, flashing her a small smile. "Lots of adults don't like kids."

She ran to her mother, who leaned down and kissed her cheek before whispering something in her ear. Greta laughed and ran inside.

Bets finally took that deep breath she so desperately needed.

Sophie started down the steps, coming toward her with a smile. "She likes you, and she doesn't take to a lot of people. I was like her when I was a kid. I'd hide or find a corner and read a book. Only I had talent, which my parents took to mean they were even bigger gods in the art world. My father's American, you know, and we spent most of our time in New York before they divorced."

She waited for the woman to continue. There was emotion in Sophie's voice, the kind Bets understood needed to claw its way out.

"I'm divorced too, although my mother hates me to talk about it. She sees it as failure. I see it as growth. My ex and I realized we weren't good for each other. He's a quiet, sensitive musician, the polar opposite of my loud, dramatic parents. It took four years with him for me to realize I was working out other issues."

That she could relate to. "It seems like we're always working out some issue, doesn't it?" She sure had some humdingers herself.

"I suppose, but I think I've turned a corner. I can tell my mother I'm going to Ireland and not cave in three days later after she's browbeat me nonstop about what a bad decision it would be for me and Greta. Artistically."

She really needed to step out of the sun. She had to be light-headed. "I'm sorry. I didn't hear you right. Did you say you're coming to Ireland?"

Sophie laughed gaily, plucking a pink rose and twirling it in her hand. "I wanted to find you right away and tell you. You weren't in your room. I'm so excited to come to Ireland, Bets. I meant what I said. I think you're doing something incredible there. I want to be a part of it. Besides,

Greta likes you. So does Linc. That's more than enough for me."

"I really need to get in the shade." She wiped the sweat on her brow. "Just like that? I had a whole pitch I'd planned to give you over dinner."

Sophie plucked another rose and tucked it behind her ear. "I know when something feels right—and I've learned to trust those feelings. Besides, this way, we can have more fun before you leave tomorrow afternoon. I'd love to show you the village and a few of my favorite shops. After we get through dinner tonight. My mother is probably going to put on a hell of a show. She's never forgotten that Linc ended things between them. So... How long have you and Linc been together? Ellie must be thrilled."

Bets locked her trembling knees. "You think we're together?"

"Oh, don't be coy." She grinned. "I understand wanting to be professional, but I feel like we're going to be fast friends. You two *really* look at each other, and a couple of times, I swear it was like you were reading each other's minds. He's wonderful, isn't he? A man of contrasts. Irreverent yet respectful. Smart yet unassuming. Easygoing and yet driven. There's no one quite like Linc."

God, the woman's description had her smiling despite herself. From the moment she'd met him, he'd surprised and delighted her, sealing their friendship by taking her to Paris that first night. "No, there's not," she managed.

"When he called me, I knew my life was about to change. He's like that. He blows in and everything shifts."

Yes, everything had. She thought back to the incredible wind the night Ellie had first arrived in Ireland. That was also the night Donal had told her that he was retiring and wanted to move in together and get married. She hadn't wanted those things. She'd wanted to keep things as they were. He'd walked out. She'd thought they were through.

Linc had shown up on the tail end of that storm.

An *anfa*, the Irish called them—the kind of storm that changed lives. Hers had changed. She hadn't fully realized how much until this very moment. Her heartbeat was pounding in her ears suddenly.

"Are you all right?" Sophie touched her arm. Her brow was knit with concern. "The heat can get to you when you're not used to it. Let's grab you some water. You can sit down."

She didn't need to sit down. She was having a nervous breakdown or something.

"Hey!" Sophie took her arm gently, and the wineglass she'd forgotten about tumbled out of her hand.

"Oh, God, I'm so sorry," she said, feeling like she'd tumbled along with it. Down a rabbit hole.

"Don't worry about it," she said gently. "Come with me now."

Sophie picked up the glass for her, and they headed for the door. The moment they stepped inside, Linc sighted them and rushed over. "What's wrong?"

"I think the heat's gotten to her. Some Perrier should do the trick."

A glass of water wouldn't solve anything.

Strong hands helped her into a soft chair in the living room. Then they reached up to frame her face. The heat from them made her gasp.

"You're red as a lobster." His brows slammed together. "You aren't going to faint on me, are you?"

His handsome face took up her whole world. The strong jawline. The light blue eyes. The full mouth.

She felt shock rip through her. Holy shit. Greta was

right...and so was Sophie. She didn't know when it had happened, but she was in love with Linc.

"I need space."

He dropped his hands and stepped back.

Bets O'Hanlon, you've done it but good.

She was *in love* with Linc. She put a hand to her head, struggling with the sudden revelation.

All the signs had been there. Why else would she be so interested in who he'd been involved with? So happy to see him? So eager to hear what he'd say or plan next?

Donal must know.

Oh, God! *Donal.*

Linc's soft touch on her arm seemed to burrow deep into her bones. She jolted again.

"Don't you dare faint on me, Bets," he said in a rumble. "Once you cool down, you'll feel more like yourself."

He was a moron. No, she wouldn't.

She was in love with two men.

CHAPTER TWENTY-THREE

Linc Buchanan had delivered again.

"Say it one more time," Kathleen told him over the speaker phone as she and Ellie stood in the Summercrest kitchen eating pizza. They were doing everything they could to make things feel normal after Owen's appearance at her shed a couple days ago.

Kathleen had been glad for the new locks and cameras, she had to admit, especially since Declan had insisted so adamantly that Owen might still be a threat.

"Sophie Giombetti is on board," he said, plenty of victory in his voice.

"Woo-hoo!" Ellie held up her hand for a high five. "I can't believe it!"

"I can," Kathleen said, giving it a happy smack. "Papa Buchanan could talk a lobster into walking on land."

"Easier to catch that way," he drawled.

"The center is on the map now for sure," Ellie said. "Once word gets out, we're going to have A-list artists clamoring for a spot here. Bets must be thrilled."

"She is," Linc said. "Made her a little light-headed. I thought she was going to faint."

Kathleen topped up their glasses with the potent orange drink everyone loved in Ireland—MiWadi—which tasted like a cross between Orange Crush and Tang. Crazy good with pepperoni pizza. "I might have fainted too. I have a serious artist crush on Sophie Giombetti."

"Me too! Oh, Daddy, this is the best news ever."

"Sure is. Now we have a little more bait to lure the locals into cooperating. I might also have a line on someone to design the museum. Sophie suggested one of her friends, who was already on my list. I'm going to send Bets and Eoghan back with the plane and fly to Oslo to meet this guy. He's finishing up a project there."

"Bets isn't going with you?" Ellie asked.

"She's better off at home right now, I think. I can have her meet him later. We need to have the locals on board officially before we can make a formal offer anyway, although we made great progress at Declan's fight the other night. Two more informally agreed to back the center, with hints that they want to be on the board, of course."

"That's more great news!" Ellie nudged her and she nudged her back.

She *was* glad something positive had come of it, and of course, it put her closer to being able to start on her larger installation.

Only...

Declan was still walking like an old man and working through things. Like a typical guy, he wasn't sharing much of his feelings about losing the fight or getting ready for the next one with Jimmy—or his worry about Owen. He'd asked her to stay over at Summercrest the last couple of nights, both wanting to be with her and to keep her closer.

She wasn't going to let anyone make her cower. Still, there was no denying she was on alert when she was by herself, both at the cottage and in the shed. Her friends were always quick to offer their company, but she couldn't be with them constantly; there were moments when she had to be alone.

"Who's the architect?" Kathleen asked, happy to hear more news about the future of the arts center. "You just said some guy. I know better than to think you'd try to corral just anyone."

He chuckled. "Wait for it. Thomas Sarkesian."

"You're kidding!" Kathleen all but shouted.

"No. Way." Ellie put a hand to her forehead. "He designed—"

"One of your favorite museums in Vienna," Linc filled in, his tone gleeful. "Yeah, I had to be a little cool when Sophie first mentioned his name. She called him and set up a dinner between us in two minutes flat. Things are moving fast."

Ellie slumped against Kathleen's side. "God, I'm almost faint with excitement. Daddy, if you pull this off—"

"You guys have to secure planning permission," Kathleen said, her own blood buzzing. "Fast."

"After the next fight, we should have enough votes. Donal thinks we should make a formal presentation then. We'll be ready."

"You're always ready, Daddy." Ellie blew him a loud kiss. "Have fun in Saint-Paul de Vence—and Oslo."

"You want anything?"

"Some lavender sachets," she said. "It will offset the damp smell."

"I'm beginning to hate the damp," Kathleen muttered. She'd killed another massive spider in her cottage this morning. "Bring home a bottle of champagne. We need to celebrate."

"I'll bring a case. Oh, one last thing, Kathleen..."

"Yes, Papa Linc?" she tried to drawl, prompting Ellie to wince.

"Sugar, you are so not meant to drawl, but you *do* deserve to get paid a lot more for your larger installation. Bets and I talked about it and kicked around some figures. She's going to talk to you about it when she gets back. You might do some thinking yourself."

Her heart rapped in her chest. "But we don't have planning permission yet."

"True, but I'd like to have a budget ready to present to the council after Declan's fight, presuming things continue to go well for us, which they will. This is done all the time, sugar, with the understanding that the terms hinge on official approval."

"He's right," Ellie said, bouncing on her heels and grinning at her. "The new modern museum in Washington, D.C. made conditional offers to key artists before submitting their budget for approval—"

"They also needed money," Linc said in a wry tone. "In our case, we already have the money. Still, we plan to show the council a couple artists and their thoughts. We already have yours, Kathleen, and Sophie is drawing up an early design, which we've agreed she can change later, to show the council. We've discussed some terms with her as well. If I can get Thomas to agree, I'll be including him in the proposal as well, design pending, of course. It's the full enchilada, girls."

Thank God she was sitting down. Her brain kept sending shock waves through her at the thought that she was going to be included in a proposal with Sophie Giombetti and Thomas Sarkesian. "I'll talk to Bets."

"Good. Then I'll let you go. You girls have fun."

When the call ended, she and Ellie hugged each other and then gave a giant yawp.

"OMG!" her best friend cried.

"What you said." She touched her temple. "I can't feel my face. It's buzzing."

"Of course it is! Hey, do you want to look up what other metal sculptors have been paid for something like your piece?"

"Hell, yeah!" She watched as Ellie raced over and grabbed her tablet off the kitchen counter. "I want to be ready when Bets gets back."

They spent the rest of the night preparing, so when Bets texted her the following day to arrange a meeting, she was indeed ready.

When she arrived at Bets' front door, Kathleen fidgeted with the skirt she'd decided to wear. Jeans had seemed too casual. She had her proposal in one of Ellie's nice leather satchels. Still, she could feel the sweat at her back.

As she knocked, she told herself to keep cool. In researching artist commissions for projects of this scale, she and Ellie had also come across cautionary advice: sometimes plans fell through. A museum didn't get built, which meant a proposed artist didn't get commissioned in the end. Of course, many artists simply took their designs elsewhere —to another museum or city project. In the end, the art was commissioned, and the artists were paid.

Her takeaway: *don't count your chickens before they hatch.*

When Bets opened the door, Kathleen noted the fatigue on her face despite her warm smile.

"I hear you had one hell of a trip," she said as Bets showed her into her parlor.

"The understatement of the century." She gestured to the pitcher of lemonade and, when Kathleen nodded, poured them each a glass. "Do you want to just dive in or talk first?"

"I'd love to ask you about your trip, but I have to admit I'm a little nervous. Maybe we can just start." Kathleen took a hasty sip before setting the glass aside. Her hands weren't steady.

Bets leaned forward after they sat down. "Totally understandable. What's easiest? Linc said I might just cut to the chase and lead with our thinking and then see how you feel about it. Unless you'd like to start."

Kathleen folded her hands as she considered things. Her gut told her that she should kick things off. She was the artist. She and Ellie had made a list of ten installations of the same scope and the artists' commissions for each. The only problem they'd had in the end was her *newbie* status. She wasn't Antony Gormley—even if she was going to build a giant outdoor installation. Plus, they had to consider the cost for the materials. Her ship was going to be expensive. She and Ellie had agreed on a number to start with. God, she hoped it wasn't crazy.

"I have a proposal based on some research." She took a deep breath and reached into her satchel, taking out the simple one-pager she'd prepared and handing it to Bets. "For a four-year project with only my commission, I was thinking fifty thousand a year."

Bets bit her lip before covering her mouth with her hand. Kathleen's palms began to sweat.

"That figure isn't going to work, I'm afraid."

Her stomach dropped. "Okay."

Bets tossed the paper onto the couch and laughed. "Linc thought you might come in low. Kathleen, we'd like to offer you eighty thousand a year—"

"Oh, my God," she whispered, her mouth going dry.

"With bonuses for on-time completion, which we expect you'll pull off given your work ethic. For a total of four hundred thousand euros."

Her brain wouldn't fire. *Oh. My. God!* "You're kidding me. Okay. That would be great. Would it be weird if I hugged you?"

"Be weirder if you didn't," Bets said, her eyes sparkling. "This is one of my best moments since opening the center."

"Then we are so hugging."

She jumped out of her chair and rushed the petite woman, who started laughing.

"I've never seen that many zeroes. Oh my God! I mean. I have to call my family—and Ellie."

Declan flashed into her mind. She wanted to get in her car and tell him. Right now.

"If this is part of the job, I love it." Bets was grinning when she pulled back. "I mean, Sophie Giombetti just agreed to come here too, and Linc and the others think we're closer to planning permission than ever before. Hence this bigger proposal. It's like a roller coaster. Only, we won't celebrate until it's official."

She sat down and gripped her knees. "Right. I keep telling myself that. Only, God, I'm so happy. The council just has to give their permission. They'd be crazy not to."

"Mad as hatters," Bets said, her exuberance dipping as well. "You probably have a few people you want to share the news with. Confidentially, of course."

"Only Ellie and a couple of friends and my family." She thought again about Declan—she couldn't wait to tell him.

"My pop is going to want to light a candle. Hell, all my brothers will."

"That's a nice thought." Bets blew out a breath and laughed. "Thanks for agreeing to stay and take your design to the next level."

After she left Bets, she called her father, who picked up straightaway. Sure enough, he said he was heading to the church to light a candle right away. Gripping her mother's ring, she sent love to her in heaven. Her mom would be smiling down at her, she knew, and damn if tears didn't fill her eyes at the thought. Then she texted all her brothers. They blew up her phone after that, and she loved every minute of it.

When the fervor died down, she checked the time. Declan would have just closed the butcher shop and gone to train. She texted him: *Meeting with Bets went awesome. Can't wait to tell you about it. See you after training.*

He'd walked in on her and Ellie researching, and she'd told him all about it. His endearing smile had warmed her heart and she'd cherished his words. "We have to keep you in Ireland, after all, don't we? I couldn't do without you."

Yeah, she was coming to realize she didn't want to do without him either.

After that, she raced over to Ellie's. Although they'd told her she didn't need to knock—no one did in Ireland— she still didn't feel comfortable just walking in.

Liam answered the door, looking as dashing as ever. "You're glowing."

"I'm walking on a cloud," she said and proceeded to tell him her news.

"Congratulations!" He closed the door after she'd danced inside. "Let's find Ellie and have a drink."

When she told her friend how the negotiations went, she screamed and grabbed her in a bear hug.

"It's even more than we thought! You're hot shit now, babe."

Kathleen started laughing. "I feel like hot shit. I mean, whew! That's a lot of money for an artist. God, it's crazy. Knowing this is in my hand and yet not having the planning permission yet."

"We're going to get it." Ellie hugged her again. "My dad and Bets and tons of others are doing everything they can to make it happen. Oh, babe, I'm so happy for you. You deserve it!"

She lifted her hand to her forehead. "I'm, like...the happiest I've ever been. But maybe we should chill. The ink isn't dry, so to speak."

"Having people see your worth and reward you for your vision is always something to celebrate." Liam handed her and Ellie a whiskey before grabbing his own.

"I agree!" Ellie said. "You have a negotiated offer you could take anywhere now. Not that you're going anywhere because you're meant to stay here in Ireland."

The thought of taking her design somewhere else depressed her. She wanted to stay in Ireland. She was starting to see a life here. Declan included. "All right, then, we're celebrating the offer. *Sláinte.*"

"*Sláinte,*" her friends cried out happily.

The party got going from there. Ellie put on one of their favorite playlists and they danced in the hallway, the kitchen, and then out the back. Liam volunteered to make burgers on the grill to celebrate.

When Declan appeared in the garden, freshly dressed and showered, she jolted in surprise. "You're here!"

He gave her a rueful look. "Of course I am. I got your text. It went well, I take it."

Since he was nearly shouting, Ellie darted over and turned the music down. "Tell him!"

Her mouth curved as she walked over to him. He'd left training early. For her. "I got offered a crazy sum of money today for my sculpture. Pending approval by the council."

"That's grand, Kathleen." His mouth tipped up to the right, his dimple appearing. "Congratulations. You deserve it."

She leaned in to kiss him before pulling back and meeting his eyes. They hadn't kissed in front of anyone in the house before. He tugged her to him moments later—an answer to her unasked question—stealing her breath. She fell into the kiss and tangled her hands in his damp hair. When he released her mouth, she caressed his still-bruised face.

"Hope that didn't hurt." They'd been careful of his bruises.

"Not at all. Mind if I join your party?"

She nodded crisply. "I'm glad you came home, Declan."

"Me too, *mo chroí*."

There was a giant pressure in her chest as Ellie got them drinks for another toast. When they cheered each other, she could feel herself falling into his eyes. Even though he looked dead on his feet, he joined them on the patio set, sitting as close to her as he could. She could smell him, the rich scent of sweat and man. Heady stuff for her happy brain.

When Brady came home from the pub, they were still outside talking, laughing, and dancing. Declan hadn't moved from her side, even though she'd caught him disguising a yawn or two. Whenever she looked at him, he was smiling at her.

When Brady pulled Ellie against him to "I Don't Want To Miss A Thing" by Aerosmith, Declan stood and stepped in front of her.

"Will you dance with me?" His blue eyes were bright with love.

She stepped into him and laid her head on his chest, swaying softly, and his arms came around her and cradled her close. She could feel the steady beat of his heart. She wrapped her arms around him and fell into the moment.

When he pressed a kiss to her neck, she gave him more room. He nuzzled her softly, his breath hot against her flesh. Desire pooled in her belly and rushed through her. She pressed her forehead into his chest. He caressed her back, running his hands from the top of her spine to the base, igniting fires everywhere he touched.

"I love you," he whispered.

"I love you too," she said, her voice raw with longing. "Declan, I'm so glad you were here to celebrate with us tonight."

It felt like a new anchor in their foundation. Soon his fight would be over and they could simply go about being together. She couldn't wait for that moment.

She caressed the back of his neck. He took her hand, and they left without saying good night to anyone. Which she imagined was okay. Their friends would understand.

In his room, he undressed her quickly. "I can't wait. I'm on fire for you."

"Ditto." She tugged his shirt off and gasped at the tapestry of bruises covering his chest and torso. "*Declan.*"

"The bruises always color worse days after a fight."

He didn't need to remind her of how bad that fight had

been. But still, she hated to see evidence that he was hurting...

He lifted her chin. "Hey! It looks worse than it is."

She wanted to call bullshit, but she knew he was only trying to assure her.

"Eyes on me, Kathleen. Now let me love you."

She nodded. All she wanted to do was fill herself with his beautiful face. With him. "Yes, make love with me."

She had him sit on the edge of the bed—the best position not to hurt his bruised body—and lowered herself over him. The feel of him inside her had them both groaning.

"I love you," she whispered again as she touched his tense face.

His blue eyes flashed with emotion, and then he was kissing her as she rode him—gently at first, and then her urgency took over. Bowing back, she moved swiftly against him, his hands holding her at the hips as they crested into each other. Her orgasm slammed over her, making her cry out. He stilled, coming inside her, pumping into her as he groaned deep in his throat.

Somehow they managed to crawl to the top of the bed. When he pulled her to lie against his side, she went slowly. "I don't want to hurt you."

"The only thing that could hurt me tonight is if I didn't hold you."

Her heart burst in her chest, and she kissed him softly, slowly. "I can't wait until this damn fight is over."

He wouldn't be bruised anymore. And they would be together for everyone to see.

"I wish I had my money now to help you buy the butcher shop. That would save your body, which I happen to love."

He froze next to her. "No, *mo chroí.*"

His reaction made her settle onto her side so she could see his face. His jaw was as tense as his voice. "You're upset. Are you saying you wouldn't take my help if I could give it to you?"

"This is a moot point, since you don't have it."

Something still niggled at her. "But what if I did?"

He gave a crisp shake of his head. "I couldn't take it. That's your money."

"And yet you offered to give me some for a ticket home—"

"Which I couldn't do since I lost my first fight, which is all the more reason I need to win the one coming up."

Suddenly the room was filled with tension. She hated it. "This is why I would give you the money. I don't like seeing you like this, so driven and bruised from head to toe."

"I can take it. I need to do this, Kathleen. The village is counting on the fight. Everything is set up. Every ticket has been sold. They need it for the arts center. They need it to help secure permission for your sculpture, or don't you remember?"

How could she forget? "I still wish it were otherwise."

"I don't," he said harshly. "I can't walk away from a fight with Jimmy, Kathleen. Not with our history."

Stupid men, she thought, but she kept her mouth shut. Her offer of support had become a point of contention.

His eyes flashed then. "Are you doubting I can win?"

She wished she'd never said anything. "No, of course not. I just hate seeing you like this."

He was silent a moment before he leaned over and kissed her cheek. "All right. Let's go to sleep. I hope I don't wake you. I'm going to get up a little earlier and head to the club."

"Earlier than five?" she asked, startled.

When he nodded, she bit the inside of her cheek. He was back to being the driven man she didn't completely understand, the one who'd stayed out all night after his fight rather than coming home, the one who felt distant and unreachable. She turned on her side, away from him, trying to hide the surprising tears in her eyes.

"It's only a little longer, *mo chroí*."

She found no comfort in his assurances.

CHAPTER TWENTY-FOUR

Fighting had the power to drive a man to madness.

Especially when he was facing his greatest opponent for the highest of stakes. His relationship with Kathleen. Her sculpture and the arts center. His ownership of the butcher shop. The pride of the village. The vindication of his past humiliation.

As he paced in the locker room before the bout, Declan reflected that he couldn't wait for it to be over.

In the lead-up to the fight, a distance had been growing between him and Kathleen, the roots planted the night she'd started a hypothetical conversation about giving him money not to fight. He'd punched out his anger at how poorly the conversation had gone more than once. He'd even sent her a few "stupid criminal" videos to lighten her mood.

But it hadn't worked. She'd been hurt by his refusal, and it was the kind of hurt that wasn't dissipating with time.

The whole thing was as imaginary as the fairy world—she didn't have the hypothetical money, so she could no more offer it than he could accept it—and yet, it had caused her to be more guarded with him. She'd called him Ace a few times and slept at her cottage for a few nights, citing the need to be ready to start the upcoming installation once planning approval was given. Suggesting *he* needed to conserve his energy for the upcoming fight. When he'd protested, she'd insisted.

He knew better than to accept her words at face value. Wariness had crept between them. This morning he'd presented her with red roses and the autographed Chieftains CD he'd finally received, wanting some time with her before the fight today, and even though she'd grinned and carried on about it, he'd sensed her holding back. She'd been supportive going into the match, of course, and they'd made love with an urgency that had felt soul deep. But he knew her heart, and it had closed some of its shutters to him.

He had ground to make up, and make it up he would—after this fight.

"I'm about ready to find those stones and start throwing them at you," Eoghan said, rising from his chair in the corner. "You need to focus, my boy. I saw Jimmy earlier. He's as cocky as ever. You'll need your wits about you to beat him."

He knocked his gloves together. "I'm ready."

I've been ready for five years. He closed his eyes and imagined knocking Jimmy out again. That image had kept him going these last weeks.

Donal let himself into the locker room. "How are you holding up?"

"I'm grand." Declan met his gaze head-on. "How's your politicking?"

"Tom MacKenna's here with Orla and Mary Kincaid

this time, and Owen is trailing behind them. But don't worry none. Linc and I have everything in hand."

Both men were finally back in Caisleán. It had surprised and unsettled Declan that one of his major boxing trainers had decided to have an extended family visit right before the fight. As for Linc, he'd been off meeting with potential artists, according to Ellie, likely to aid their upcoming proposal to the council members, one they hoped to present tomorrow.

"How does Tom look?" Eoghan asked.

Donal gave a dark chuckle. "He's grim as a goblin, Dad."

"Good." Eoghan nodded. "That means he knows we're making inroads. Go. Make some more. I have the young buck."

Sometimes he hated when Eoghan called him that.

"*Go gcuire dia an t-ádh ort*, Declan," Donal said and let himself out.

He'd take all the luck he could get. He paced some more and drank his final allotment of water before the fight. His heartbeat ticked like Eoghan's ancient timepiece, wrapped around his bony wrist. He was going to go crazy.

"Tell me about your new girl, Eoghan," he said, desperate for the distraction. "The one you took a fancy to in France."

The older man's face turned up like wattage on a light-bulb. He lowered back into his chair as if settling in for a long talk. "A fine way of passing these moments, I'd be thinking. Her name is Sandrine, and she works for Sophie Giombetti, the artist we're hoping to bring here. We've talked every night on the phone."

Declan angled a chair across from the man and sat down, planting his hands on his knees. "Has she agreed to be your girl yet?"

Eoghan got a gooey smile on his face. "She has and is eager to join me here in Ireland. Declan, my boy, I'm in love. I swear these passions have been deeply buried for decades, since my poor wife passed away. It's a marvel to feel this way again. But you know that for yourself. Isn't love wonderful?"

"It is at that," he said, his mind filling up with an image of Kathleen, her brown eyes alight with tenderness. "Love looks good on you, Eoghan. Tell me more."

For a while, he put away all thoughts of what was awaiting him outside the green locker room. Except his father opened the door not long afterward, sheet white. Declan immediately stood.

"What is it, Dad?"

He closed the door slowly and pressed his fingers to his forehead. "Son, we debated over telling you something fierce, but the crowd is buzzing with— There's no easy way to say it."

His stomach dropped to the floor.

"Owen Kincaid is telling anyone who will listen that Morag slept with Jimmy before your last fight." His father gripped the back of his neck. "Declan, I suspected something odd but not with Jimmy himself—"

"Believe it then from my own mouth," he ground out, anger searing his very skin. So he'd been right to fear Owen and Jimmy—only he'd been their target this time and their weapon had been disgrace. "Goddammit! He won't rest until I'm humiliated before the entire village publicly."

Kathleen would hear now. Everyone he knew. He couldn't take it, them knowing what a fool he'd been. Being laid out like gossip, it would be sifted over like old belongings.

He started toward the door, but Eoghan moved over to

stand beside his father to block him. "No, my boy. It's a cowardly way to throw off your balance but going off half-cocked as a mad lunatic before the fight isn't the way. Save it for the ring."

Turning around, he gripped the chair he'd vacated. Then he lifted it up off the ground. He was close to heaving it against the wall before reason prevailed. He set it back down. He'd known Jimmy would pull something dirty, but somehow he hadn't expected this. More fool he.

He sucked in a breath, telling himself to be grateful Kathleen had been safe from them. That had to be a comfort in this moment.

"Let's wrap your hands and put your gloves on," Eoghan said, coming toward him, his wrinkled face lined with pity. "We don't want you hurting your hands before the fight, now do we?"

He wanted to bury his head in his hands. How was he supposed to hold his head up after this? No man wanted his family and friends to know that his fiancée had slept with another man, least of all his most bitter rival. "Dad. Is Kathleen out there?"

Eoghan paused in reaching for his gloves. They shared a look before his father nodded. "She is to be sure, son. Of course she'd be here, cheering you on. Now, she'll understand—"

"What?" he demanded. "That Jimmy made a fool out of me? He's disgraced me in front of the entire village. The woman I love. You don't know what I'm feeling. What I've felt since Jimmy whispered that news to me moments before our last fight began."

Eoghan made a very Irish sound and crossed himself. "The devil will surely be waiting for him in hell for such a thing."

"Declan, he's a small man," his father told him, crossing and laying both of his hands on his shoulders. "People know who you are. They respect you. Don't you forget that, Declan McGrath. I'll be leaving you to prepare yourself. Knock Jimmy Slavin's head off, will you?"

He swallowed thickly and nodded, watching as his father let himself out.

Declan eyed the door. On the other side was a world of people who knew his deepest and darkest secret, the one he'd never wanted to be spoken. Jimmy had ruined that. He was going to pay.

Eoghan got him ready in silence. The ticking of the older man's timepiece seemed to blare in Declan's ears, so loud he wanted to throw open the door and rush out.

Not to escape. No. Only to be alone. He tapped his foot on the concrete floor to a different beat to cover up the sound of the clock.

"I'll give you some time to yourself now, I'm thinking," Eoghan said, rising. "I'll only be outside if you need anything."

Alone in the silence at last, he could lower his head into his gloves.

Everyone knew. He didn't know how he would hold his head up.

He had to win this fight and hope it would buffer his pride.

When Eoghan finally came for him, he stood and tapped his gloves together. He lifted the hood of his green robe to cover his head, pretending he was invisible. No one could see him. No one could think anything of him.

He didn't look at anyone as he followed Eoghan to the ring. Donal was waiting for him in the corner, a grim set to his jaw. Eoghan gripped his shoulder. Just like last time, he slipped a stone into his pocket. "Imagine Jimmy's a stone. Catch him and throw him aside."

After Donal helped him remove his robe, Declan took out the stone and laid it on the ring floor, for all to see. A murmur went through the crowd.

"Good move," Eoghan said, patting his shoulder. "I'd say Jimmy Slavin is spoiling for a fight, don't you? I believe he's going to have one. Isn't he?"

Declan nodded, loosening up, keeping his eyes down. The announcer started to introduce the two fighters, saying how they'd been facing each other since they were eleven years old.

He wasn't a boy anymore. Neither was Jimmy.

The crowd started cheering. He imagined it was for him. Moments later, there was a chorus of boos. That would be for Jimmy.

He tuned out the crowd and went inside himself. When Donal nudged him to the center of the ring, he walked over. Now he would lift his gaze and look Jimmy straight in the eyes. Let him know he was more than ready for him.

The referee started droning on, but Declan tuned him out as well.

Jimmy's thin lips sported a cocky grin. He hadn't put in his mouthpiece as was customary.

"Everyone knows I'm the bigger man now," Jimmy said as the referee talked about having a good clean fight. "Get ready for me to wipe the floor with you."

He touched gloves with Jimmy when the referee finished. That Jimmy didn't touch back with good sports-manship, only cockiness laced with dark intent, didn't surprise him. He'd never change.

He returned to his corner again. Donal shouted encouragement to him. He touched his gloves together, focusing on nothing else. Cracked his neck.

The bell rang.

He came out with his gloves up and went for Jimmy. He got in a left and a right before Jimmy danced back.

He wanted to play, did he? Draw out the humiliation?

Declan was having none of it.

Jimmy circled him. Stopped. Snarled. Took his stance and bobbed from the waist. Dashed off some punches in the air. More delays.

Declan went in with a quick jab and followed through with a punishing right. He punched at Jimmy's body repeatedly, his muscles already burning with sweat.

He drove drive him back into the corner, right where he wanted him.

When Jimmy's back hit the ropes, Declan went for the uppercut. It landed hard, enough so that he felt the reverberation through his hands.

Jimmy tried to block him as he followed through with more body punches.

Declan shoved him back. He hit him with another hard right and then went in with another punishing uppercut, knocking him senseless.

Jimmy was falling.

Declan kept punching until the man was down on the floor. The referee stepped between them, and Declan gave him space.

He heard the count. *One. Two. Three...*

Declan watched his nemesis lying on the floor, his heart pumping as the count continued. Jimmy wasn't getting up.

The referee called the fight and raised his arm.

It was over.

It was over.

His mouthguard contained his shout of victory. He'd won. He'd beaten him in the first round. He could hear the crowd screaming in the background.

Jimmy didn't look at him as his manager helped him to his feet, but Declan refused to let him walk off without any acknowledgment.

He went over to Jimmy and touched his glove. The man didn't even lift his head.

"We are done, you and I," Declan said, knowing this was his last fight. His future awaited him, with Kathleen.

Jimmy finally raised his battered face and managed a sneer. "Next time, McGrath—"

"There is no next time. This is it. You will never darken my road again."

Jimmy's brows rose briefly—both of them knew the Irish phrase, always uttered with the utmost seriousness. Declan shook his head and walked off.

The crowd noise blew in like an old steam locomotive, making his ears ring. Donal was hugging him. Then Eoghan.

Where was Kathleen? She was the one he wanted.

More people swarmed the ring. His father gave him a bear hug. Seamus, a firm grip on his shoulder.

"The shop is yours now, my boy!"

Yes, the prize money. He had his future set. He could even give Kathleen a ticket to Boston to see her family, if she'd accept it. Maybe she'd want him to come along.

Where was she?

Someone clapped him on the back. "God, what a fight." Brady was beside him, hugging him and jabbering about victory like a magpie.

Other friends joined in. Carrick. Kade. Jamie. Liam. Cormac. Fergus.

In fact, he couldn't see past the crowd gathered around him. Where was she? He needed to find Kathleen.

Pushing his way to the edge of the crowd, he scanned the packed space and finally found her at the edge of the front row, next to Ellie. Their eyes met.

She didn't look right. Her face was pale. Why wasn't she cheering?

Then he remembered the humiliation Jimmy had dealt him before this very fight. Did she think less of him because of what Morag had done?

He lifted his glove to her, but she shook her head and looked away. Leaned in to whisper something to Ellie. His breath froze in his lungs as he watched them get up and start to leave.

She was turning away from him because of what she'd heard.

His heart wrenched in his chest, stealing his breath. God, he hadn't imagined the hurt of it.

He rested his gloves on the ropes for support. Now his knees were weak, his lifeforce running out of him like blood.

"They're probably going home," Brady said, appearing at his side. "It's a mad crush here. Drink some water, Declan."

He didn't want water. He wanted Kathleen to look at him the way she used to. With love and joy and everything he'd ever wanted.

He took the bottle because Brady gently shoved it at him. The fight hadn't been long, but somehow it had lasted for decades, this thing with him and Jimmy. "I need to go after her."

He couldn't let her go like this. If he did, it would be the same as letting Jimmy win the fight.

Brady put his arm around his shoulder. "Take a moment. The whole village is with you. You brought a lot of pride to Caisleán tonight. Also, Linc thinks they have the support they need. They plan to call for a vote tomorrow on Kathleen's sculpture and the museum."

He was glad for her, but it hurt that he didn't know if he would be by her side to celebrate that victory. "That's good. That's everything."

Brady set his hands on the ropes. "Why did you never tell me?"

He didn't have to ask what his brother meant. "Knowing me as you do since we shared a womb, are you really surprised?"

"I suppose not, brother." He put his arm around him again. "Come on. We're all for the pub to celebrate your victory."

All feelings of victory had drained out of him. "I need to go and talk to Kathleen."

"I know you do, but Ellie has her." His brother's words suggested he knew something was wrong. "The village needs this. *You* need this. Come for twenty minutes. Please."

The villagers were gathering around the ring, cheering his name. He wasn't going to be getting out anytime soon. Maybe it would even boost his spirits for his talk with Kathleen. He nodded. "Twenty minutes at the pub."

Of course, the celebration ran longer than twenty minutes. He only had one whiskey, and that was to toast his trainers, those tireless men who'd risen at five o'clock every morning and stayed late into the night, pushing him.

Before he made a break for it, he put the stone in

Eoghan's pocket, saying he'd forgotten something at the boxing club—which he hadn't. The older man smiled at him and handed it back. "Keep it. Tell your children the story."

Children. His chest grew tight. He wanted to have a family with Kathleen. Did she still want that?

He left the bar with a heavy heart, fearing the future he'd imagined was lost. He had to find Kathleen. She wasn't at Summercrest. Neither was Ellie. He detoured to her cottage. The light was on and two cars were in the driveway.

As he left the car, Kathleen emerged from the house. "I plan to save my friend the discomfort of hearing what I have to say to her future brother-in-law."

The whip of fear lanced his skin.

"Let me—"

"No, I'm talking." Her voice was a near shout in the silence around them. "You didn't trust me to tell me something as important as this. You didn't say anything. Not one word! But that's not the worst part."

"Dammit, I didn't tell *anyone* about Jimmy and Morag."

"That isn't the point," she said in a hard tone. "No wonder you got all weird about the idea of me giving you money so you wouldn't have to fight Jimmy. *Nothing* would have stopped you from this fight. This was a grudge match. Straight down the line."

"Hang on—"

"You proved beyond a shadow of a doubt that you cared more about beating Jimmy for what he did to you with Morag than you do about us. Declan, you're still stuck in the past, and that's not where I want to be. Maybe that's the real reason you wanted to keep our relationship a secret from everyone."

"That is not why!" he said, striding closer.

"You weren't ready to commit," she continued in a hurt tone. "Despite what you said about marriage."

He sucked in a breath at the blow. "That's unfair. I love you and want to marry you. On that, I am resolute. My fear of Owen and Jimmy wasn't a fantasy. Dammit, didn't both of them come after me this very night and ruin my reputation? The only silver lining is that he didn't go for you like he did Morag, *mo chroí*."

Shock covered her pale face. "Wait! You thought that *asshole* could seduce me?"

When he saw the tears in her eyes, he gripped her arms. "No, of course not. You would never do that— Never!"

She pulled her arms away and lifted her chin. "That's something then."

He touched her face, feeling the raw pain between them. "Tonight, after the fight, I thought you'd stepped back from me because you thought me a fool. Jimmy made me look like a fool and a lesser man once, and now everyone knows my shame."

Her hand went to her forehead, which made him lower his hand. She was silent, gathering herself. "Oh, Declan. It hurts, hearing you'd ever believe that of me. Or yourself. Only a lesser man seduces someone's fiancée to win a fight, and Morag was either a real bitch or fool to participate."

His head throbbed like he had a fever. He had never thought of their actions in that vein. "Maybe I should have told you, but it was hard for me to even think about it. You can't know how hard, feeling humiliated as I did. Better to bury it deep inside me. What you bury stays buried, the Irish say."

This time her gentle hands cupped his jaw. "Declan, their actions don't reflect on you. Not to me or anyone else who cares about you. Screw anyone who thinks otherwise.

You lift your head up everywhere you go. You have nothing to feel humiliated about, okay?"

He kissed her palm, but she dropped her hands and stepped away. His heart thudded in his chest. "Then why are you stepping back now?"

She rubbed at her nose, which was running with feeling. "You have your ideas about how things should be, and you decide them without talking to me. You kept something important from me. And you know Axl cheated on me. Declan, I told you before. I don't want to be with someone like that."

"But that's done now. The fight is over. I'm *never* facing Jimmy or taking the ring professionally again. I can give you that ticket to Boston I promised you—"

"Those are things, Declan. Things! I don't want that. I want you to share yourself with me—how you think, how you feel—even when it's hard."

He took a deep inhale and nodded. "I'll try, Kathleen. I promise you."

She rubbed her eyes this time. "I don't know how I can trust you again. I need more than that."

"Then I'll give it to you." He took her hand and kissed it. "Tell me what I can do to make you trust me again."

"I don't know." She pulled away again, her brown eyes wet. "I really don't, Ace."

She might as well have tapped a chisel to his heart and watched it shatter. He hung his hands at his sides at the use of that name. She wanted distance, and the chasm opened wider between them.

She started to walk back to the cottage, gravel crunching like eggshells under her shoes. He took a step after her and said the only truth he knew might reach her.

"I love you, Kathleen."

She turned and gripped the necklace around her throat. "It's not enough."

When she closed the door on him, he stayed out there in the darkness.

He would have to figure out what would be enough because he couldn't lose her like this.

CHAPTER TWENTY-FIVE

They had planning permission!
Just. Like. That.

For Kathleen's grandiose sculpture *and* for the new museum—with Sophie Giombetti's installation as well. Hot dog!

Bets sunk into one of her squeaky parlor chairs and stared at the two men who'd made it possible—the two men she was in love with, God help her.

"I still can't believe it." She put her hand to her forehead and hoped blood would flow back in.

"They were all wound up after the fight," Linc said, grinning from ear to ear, "and eager to hear our proposal. Money always talks, Bets, and the potential tourism revenue we could rake in with the statue alone had everyone's mouths watering—"

"Except Tom," Donal added.

"By the time I got to the museum and its benefits to the community, they were all in. Tom Sarkesian's portfolio was mere icing on the cake."

"Linc has figures in his pocket like some men have

handkerchiefs." Donal nudged the other man companionably. "Tom didn't know what hit him. He had no witty arguments at hand."

"We have some financing to nail down," Linc said, "but it's a sure thing with the kind of artists who are interested in joining us. Sophie's ready to put out a press release once I call her. Expect to be called for interviews, Madame President. This is a big coup."

She patted her hair. "Interviews!"

"Next up, I'm going to work on the proposal for a hotel," Linc continued, not taking a breath. "That will be done with a different cast of characters and money, separate from the arts center, of course. There's no reason not to move on it soon. We'll have the two built at the same time. Open at the same time. Makes sense."

"Even an eejit could see that." Donal gave a short laugh. "We'll need to add a few people's names and faces to our list of nonvoting members."

"I'll get right on that," she said as he dug out a list from his jacket and handed it to her.

He grinned at her. "My dear Bets, you have your center, the one you always hoped for."

Donal had called her *my dear*. Not *mo ghrá*. She met his green eyes. Her throat caught. He'd come back from Dublin different. Although he'd arrived right before the fight, they had yet to be alone. She made herself smile. "Thank you, Donal. Thank you both."

Linc jingled the change in his pocket, interrupting the ensuing silence. He was different as well. Like Donal, he'd returned right before the fight, finished for now with his wheeling and dealing. They hadn't been alone either.

The whole thing felt weird.

Being in love with two men made her the Queen of Weird.

"Well, if you don't object," Linc drawled slowly, "I'll be driving over to find Ellie and Kathleen to share the news. Then I'll give Sophie and Tom a jingle..."

"I'll call Angie and Megan... There are so many people to tell. It's such great news."

So why didn't she want to shout from the rooftops? Right. Because somehow she knew the other shoe was about to drop.

"I'll be letting you get to that then." Linc nodded like a turtle crossing the road, the action rich with what was unspoken. "I'll be seeing y'all."

Was he leaving again? She watched him walk out of her parlor. Taking a breath, she looked at Donal. He was waiting quietly, patiently. She could see love in his eyes, but it was banked.

She sighed. "Isn't it strange that no one is jumping up and down and suggesting we all have a bourbon?"

He sighed too and sat in the squeaky chair across from her. On the edge. As if he didn't plan to stay. "I think you know why."

Her throat hurt along with her heart. "Donal, I—"

"No, let me start." He swallowed thickly. "I've finally got my courage to say things. I wasn't honest with you about being happy with keeping things the way they are. I did want to live together. Hell, I wanted to get married."

She caught the past tense, and her heart tore at the hurt between them. "I'm sorry."

"You have nothing to be sorry for. Hell, I shouldn't have said otherwise. It wasn't fair of me to hope you'd change your mind, Bets. I'm the one who needs to apologize."

Tears burned her eyes. So he was going to do this. She had to meet him partway. "It's understandable. Hoping for that. I would have done the same in your place. It doesn't mean I love you less." She couldn't make herself use the past tense just yet.

"I know that." He rose and gestured to the golden couch. "Shall we sit?"

They'd sat together on that couch more times than she could count. She knew in her heart this would be the last time. Nodding, she joined him, with him still resting on the edge. But he took her hand, which made the first tears fall.

"We helped each other open up to what was inside ourselves," he began slowly. "I'll always be grateful for that. The truth is you had a lot inside you that was banked. So did I, it seems."

He paused a moment and smiled ruefully. She tried to smile back.

"Bets, I know you're in love with Linc."

She gasped and pressed her other hand to her mouth. "I didn't mean for it to happen!"

"I know that too." His eyes were overbright. "I also know Linc didn't plan on falling in love with you either."

Her breath stopped. "We haven't—"

"Of course you haven't." He squeezed her hand. "You're both good people, and ones I count as friends. If I were on the outside looking in, I'd say he's a good man to fall for. We talked about it last night, he and I. After the fight. As I knew he'd be moving out today."

She shot to her feet. "*You did what?*"

He shrugged. "There was whiskey and frankness was in the air. I told him you were in love with both of us and as confused as I'd ever seen you in the last thirty-odd years."

Her legs trembled, and she sat down again before they gave out. "I don't know what to say. Part of me is angry at myself. The other part is a little ashamed. I don't know how I got this crazy. It's not like me."

His wide smile was the old Donal all over again. "Maybe it's having more choices in life. I've been thinking a lot about that. Our little village has stayed the same until now, but the arts center has ushered in so many changes. Might be retirement too. Suddenly, it feels like there are so many new possibilities to explore."

She was the one who gripped his hand this time. "It does, doesn't it? It's a little scary."

"We'll stick to the good stuff right now. Bets, do you know this is the first time I could stay in Dublin and see my girls without having to rush back to handle my sheep? I played tourist. I went to museums I'd never visited. I saw the Harry Clarke stained glass. I ate at new restaurants with fancy tablecloths and food termed fusion. I haven't done anything like that since I was a young man. And I loved every minute."

A couple more tears slipped down her cheeks. "Donal, I'm so glad."

"I figure we both have more to explore. I still need to figure out what I want to do with myself and the rest of my life." He wiped the tip of his nose, which had started to run. "It's hard to say, but Bets, I think you not wanting to live with me and marry me might have been the best thing that's ever happened to me. Do you understand? You were right about falling into old patterns. I was doing it all over again, going that way."

"Oh, Donal."

She laid her head against his shoulder and cried a little. He stroked her back until she settled. His eyes were shining when she lifted her head.

"You know, all my dad talks about these days is the

wonder of life. He's so grateful he has the time to explore things. Hell, he's even in love again."

She'd seen it before her very eyes in Saint-Paul de Vence, him and Sandrine walking together in the garden holding hands, and it was beautiful. "He might teach us all a thing or two about these so-called twilight years."

"Indeed. Bets, I don't want to squander my time either. I'm thinking about traveling some. I can go now, knowing your arts center is safe and in good hands."

He meant Linc. "Donal, I don't know what to do."

"Give yourself some time, Bets." He kissed her cheek. "You'll figure it out."

"God, I hope so." She reached for a tissue and blew her nose. "I detest being a mess. And I detest being in love with two men."

"Consider my suit withdrawn, if it makes things easier." He wiped her tears, his green eyes steady on her face. "Bets, I think we've run our course."

She found her voice. "Me too."

His smile was soft before he nodded and shifted away from her. "Now... Linc won't mind me telling you this, but he doesn't think he's a good bet for a relationship with three ex-wives. He isn't going to press his suit. So you need to decide what you want, Bets."

She lifted her hands to the ceiling. "I cannot believe you're talking about this."

He rolled his eyes. "I love you both and consider you friends. It's what a friend would do. Since that's settled, I'm going to head over to my dad's house to pick him up. I told him we'd go visit his girlfriend in France once we squared everything away with the council. He wants me to meet her. I thought we'd stay awhile."

Her heart couldn't be any fuller in her chest. "You're the best of men, Donal O'Dwyer."

He smiled, but she saw his throat move with emotion. "Enjoy this time, Bets O'Hanlon, and take care of your roses. I plan to be present when you beat Mary Kincaid at the August fair."

She thought of the roses he'd given her. She hoped she would win with one of them. "Have a grand time in France."

"I plan to." He nodded and walked out.

She closed her eyes and listened to the sound of his boots on her floorboards—a sound she'd always loved. More tears fell. Her heart seemed to sigh at last. Somehow, there was peace. She didn't know where things were going, but she knew everything was going to be all right.

CHAPTER TWENTY-SIX

Her sculpture was officially a go.

Kathleen focused on celebrating that news—with Linc, who brought the good tidings, and Ellie. They had a bourbon in the kitchen, although the whole celebration was muted. That pissed her off. Just because she'd cried most of the night over Declan didn't mean they shouldn't be yelling like crazy.

"Go ahead and hire your welders," Linc said after downing his bourbon. "I've asked Donal and a few others and looked into various surveyors. One name stands out, and it's been associated with big projects. Hotels and museums. I want to meet with them and get things going. You're welcome to come."

"Consider me there." Focusing on business worked for her. "And just reminding you—I'll need a bigger work space ASAP, especially with Sophie coming and taking over my current shed."

"My girl's going to need a warehouse," Ellie said, bouncing in place and doing her part to raise the energy. "And Sophie's going to need—"

"I've already got her list." Linc laughed. "About more artist space... The board wants to construct a few of the larger sheds—including one for the kids—away from the arts center. Keep it less cluttered-looking. You okay with that?"

She nodded. "We want the focal point to be on the arts center, the sculpture, and the museum."

"We do at that," Linc said, grabbing Ellie close. "You'd best start thinking about doing a window for the museum. A big one!"

Ellie hugged him tightly. "After I finish the one in the arts center. I'm almost done."

"And I've got four years to go." Kathleen laughed, but it died fast.

When Ellie's face pinched with concern, she forced a smile that probably convinced no one. She had four more years in the same town as Declan. This was exactly what she'd feared—stuck in the same small town with her ex, who happened to be her best friend's future brother-in-law.

It would be hard for a while.

"All right then," Linc said. "I'm off."

Ellie laid her head against his shoulder. "Where to this time?"

"Munich. Sophie wants me to meet another artist. Hans Shumaker."

Ellie squealed.

"Jesus, Ellie." But Kathleen's heart blipped too. He was a post-modern painter who was on track to be as renowned as Dali, Picasso, and Monet, some said. His giant canvases were famous for their sweeping brushstrokes and utter simplicity. He'd be a big fish.

"But it's Hans Shumaker! He's one of the biggest artists in the world."

Linc snorted. "Do you know that when you put that

into a Google search, people like Justin Bieber and Ed Sheeran come up? I swear, sometimes I don't know what the world is coming to."

"Is Bets going with you?" Kathleen asked. "If she's gone, who's going to help me hire people?"

"I'm headed off on my lonesome," he said, clearing his throat. "You tell her what you need, and if she needs my help, have her email me."

Ellie rounded on him. "What's up with you and Bets?"

"Not a thing, sugar." He tapped her on the nose, which made her frown. "Nothing to worry your pretty little head about."

"I hate it when you talk to me like that. I'm not blind, Daddy. I was afraid you had a thing for her. Of all the—"

Kathleen raised her brow and studied him. His poker face wasn't completely intact. Was that a flush on his cheeks?

"Come on, Ellie." He hugged her again. "I have three ex-wives. I've sworn off relationships. Bets is too smart to be tied up with the likes of me."

"And she's *also* with Donal," Ellie reminded him.

He went absolutely still, his blue eyes turning icy. "You questioning my character? I wouldn't."

Kathleen nudged Ellie, trying to diffuse the sudden tension. "Come on. You know your daddy. He's rambunctious, but he isn't a jerk."

"Thank you," Linc said, kissing her cheek. "If you ever need adopting, I'd be proud to call you a Buchanan."

She laughed. "Thank you. Now, Ellie, tell your father you're sorry for flying off the handle."

Ellie crossed her arms over her chest. "Fine. I'm sorry. But since I went through the experience of your three ex-wives—my mother included—I can say I agree with your estimation. You, sir, are not marriage material."

His throat moved, and Kathleen knew the words had hurt him, but his mouth tipped up into a charming smile. "I'll ask you to remind me of that if I ever go crazy enough to consider that august establishment again. Don't get into too much trouble while I'm gone."

"Would we do that?" Ellie asked, linking arms with Kathleen. "Seems everything is on track now. What could possibly go wrong?"

———

That call came at dawn, jarring Kathleen awake. She lunged for the phone, fearing the worst.

"Kathleen," Bets said, "someone broke into the shed and took a sledgehammer to your things. Carrick found the damage at the center when he was out checking his sheep."

Her stomach went queasy. "This is because of the votes."

"Yes, dammit. They also broke a couple of windows at the arts center. The only good news is we have video of the crime from the GoPros. Carrick called the police. I'm meeting them at the arts center. Kathleen, it was Owen Kincaid."

She shivered. Of course it was. It was a bitter irony that Declan had put distance between them because he'd feared what Owen might do under Jimmy's influence—apparently he had plenty of hate of his own to drive him, just as it had done before. It struck her that Mary Kincaid's son was also Bets' nephew. That couldn't rest easy with her. "I'll meet you there."

"I called Liam. He's coming to pick you up."

She knew she was being assigned an escort. "I'm fine going alone."

"Owen came into your shed before. Let's just be smart about things until the police find him. I'll feel better. In a million years, I never imagined this. I'll see you soon."

After Kathleen hung up, she dressed quickly. She made a quick check of the cottage and the surrounding property. She didn't think Owen would be around, but she wanted to make sure. Her heart rate calmed after her search, and she went inside to grab a cup of coffee. When she heard the sound of wheels crunching on gravel, she went to the front door and was surprised to see two cars. Liam was in one.

Declan was in the other. She wasn't surprised, really. This was everything he'd feared. He stared at her through the window, his entire face in warrior mode.

Her heart started tripping like a jackhammer again. An insane urge to cry and rage surged up within her. She wrapped her arms around herself as Liam exited the car.

"He wouldn't listen to me when I said I was picking you up." Liam held his hands up. "You don't have to drive with him. He only wants to make sure you're safe. Until the police pick up Owen."

She knew police procedure in the States because of her brother. She imagined it was the same in Ireland. "Is a warrant out? Are they looking for him?"

"Looking for him, yes." Liam walked closer until he was a foot away. "Not sure about him being openly accused yet. The police around here... Never mind. Honestly, I'd rather Declan stay close. I don't want him going after Owen. Declan's first question was about whether you were there when it happened."

She hadn't thought that far yet. She supposed she could

have been. Chilling thought, that. "Fine. You keep an eye on him. I'm driving my own car. You can both follow me."

When they arrived, the arts center was lined with cars and police vehicles. Shattered glass covered the ground. Rage in the form of dangerous shards, she thought.

Ellie rushed over to her, followed by Brady, who hung back while they hugged. She imagined Liam and Declan were behind her somewhere.

"It's awful!" her best friend cried. "I can't believe anyone would do this."

"Thank God you hadn't completed your window." If she had, Owen would have broken it for sure.

"That's what Brady said." Ellie wiped her eyes. "We're going to have to install a serious security system. I don't know why we didn't before."

"Because this kind of thing doesn't happen here," Brady said, putting an arm around her.

Bets came running over. "Kathleen. The Garda would like to take your statement about the time Owen came and made threats."

Robbie always said motive and preparation helped seal a criminal's guilt, along with the evidence. "Happy to."

She accompanied Bets and met the officer in charge, who wanted to interview her in the arts center's kitchen. He was in his thirties and hadn't taken the time to brush his curly brown hair, she noticed. He took out a small black leather notepad and a pen and started asking questions. She answered them crisply and as factually as possible. Robbie would have been proud.

Of course, he was also going to be pissed—all of her brothers would be, actually, but she didn't need to think about that now.

When the officer was finished with her, she left the

kitchen and stopped short. Declan was waiting for her with his back against the wall. Her insides turned to mush. "I hope you're not here to say I told you so."

His brows slammed together. "No, I only wanted you to know we have your back. That you are safe. It had to shake you. It sure as hell did me."

"I'm fine." She tried to calm her racing heart. "Declan, I'm not your responsibility anymore."

"That doesn't stop me from worrying about you." He raked a hand through his hair. "Or loving you, for that matter. I'm only looking out for you until I figure out how to get you to trust me again."

Her heart tore at his confirmation that he still wanted to try. "You're only making this worse."

She left him in her wake and went outside. Angie and Megan were out there fuming with Ellie, and other people from the village enfolded them in outrage and concern. Everyone wanted to help, but they couldn't clean up the arts center yet. The Garda were still handling the scene.

She wasn't even allowed to see the damage done to her work. Truthfully, though, she wasn't sure she could take it right now.

It started to rain. The drops were heavy with a touch of cold. Sea rain, they called it. She grew chilled as she stood, aware Declan was watching her from the periphery like the warrior he was.

When she heard it would take maybe a week before the Garda reopened the crime scene, she made her decision. Turning to Ellie, she leaned in to whisper, "I'm going home for a while."

"I'll come with you," her best friend said, taking her hand.

"Are you sure? Brady—"

"Will be fine. He'll understand us not wanting to be around while this is going on. It'll be good to go back to the old neighborhood and see your family. You need some time to heal."

Kathleen looked back at the shattered arts center and tried to imagine her pirate ship rising up into the sky. Right now, she couldn't see it. Her heart was too heavy. She would go home and regroup. Her eyes found Declan again, milling in the crowd.

She had to get herself back on track to do what she'd come here for.

CHAPTER TWENTY-SEVEN

K athleen was gone.

"What did you just say?" he asked Brady as his heart roared to life.

His brother finished adding grounds to the coffee pot. "Even with the police arresting Owen last night, I think it's better they're—"

"Brady, what are you talking about?"

"Kathleen and Ellie left early to take a plane to Boston this morning. With the arts center being closed—"

"I'm going after her."

He still needed to prove she could trust him, but the more time it took, the more distance grew between them. Now she had an ocean between them. He wasn't going to allow it.

His brother's footsteps sounded behind him as he strode out of the kitchen. "Declan, I think you should give her some time."

"I can't afford more time, Brady. I have to get her back." It had been two days since their fight. He couldn't wait longer.

"*Liam!*" Brady's yell filled the entire house.

Declan swung around. "Was that necessary?"

"You need Yoda." His face was grave. "Stop being so prideful and thinking you have to do everything on your own."

Those words echoed Kathleen's, which seemed like a sign, so he stayed put.

Liam jogged into view, dressed in his simple white meditation pants and a T-shirt that said *Don't Be Trapped, Free Your Mind*. "What is it? I heard your bellow all the way down in the dungeon."

"I'm going after Kathleen," Declan said without preamble.

"Good." He smiled warmly. "I hoped you would."

"He needs help, and I can't be the one to do it." Brady grimaced. "I want to, but Ellie is really upset about all this..."

He wasn't going to come between his brother and the woman he loved. Declan pointed to the door. "Go to the pub. You have no knowledge of this."

"How will you find her in Boston?" his brother asked with another agonizing scrunch of his face. "Ellie will never forgive me if I give you the address. I'd leave it lying around for you to find, but she'd never believe it was unintentional."

He remembered the name of their family bar—it was her last name, after all—and he also knew the first name of her eldest brother, the one who looked out for her. That was the one he'd find. How many Robbie O'Connors could there be on the Boston police force? "Don't worry about me. Get on with you."

Brady hugged him. "I'm rooting for you, brother. Remember Sorcha. *Dia duit.*"

After his brother left, Declan turned to Yoda and cut to

the crux of the matter. "Liam, Kathleen doesn't believe love is enough anymore. I need to regain her trust."

Liam walked over to the stairs and sat on the last step. "Because you didn't tell her about Jimmy and Morag."

"You know I didn't tell anyone." Declan sat down beside him. "She said that wasn't the issue. She said I put the past before her. Before us."

Yoda waited.

Declan gritted his teeth.

"What do you think?" Liam finally asked.

"That I fucked it all up, just like she said." He set his elbows on his knees and lowered his head into his hands. "She doesn't want to be with someone who won't tell her things."

Liam patted him on the back and stood. "Then you'll have to figure out how to convince her you will. You have the whole plane ride to Boston to think about it."

"That's it? That's all I get from Yoda?"

"Only you can share your heart, Declan." He smiled. "But I can give you a drive to the airport. Come on."

"Now?" The butcher shop was closed today, but he'd have to call Seamus and tell him that he was taking a brief holiday. Declan had planned to present the check to him to buy the butcher shop, but he could do it after he returned. Rising to his feet, he said, "Okay, yes, now."

"Nothing like the present when it comes to making a different choice and forging your future."

"You really should do something with all that...wisdom. But don't you have someplace to be?"

"Nothing I can't postpone, especially with my mother shutting herself off in her proverbial cave right now."

He had no idea what that meant. "I need to buy a ticket."

"Then go buy it." Liam started walking toward the dungeon. "I'll finish meditating and then grab your suitcase. What a remarkable twist to my day. I love surprises."

Declan could only stare after his friend. Surprises? Yes, leaving for Boston today was that and more. He went to buy a ticket. There was an early afternoon flight on Aer Lingus that would put him into Boston midafternoon. Even with the three-hour drive to Dublin, he could make it.

When they arrived at the airport, Liam took his shoulder in a friendly clasp. "It's time to share your full self with someone, Declan. That's what a true relationship is all about. Wouldn't you want her to tell you everything?"

He realized he did.

"Think about what she's said she wants. If you love her, you'll give it to her. Because I can promise you, she'll do the same for you. That's what you do when you love someone."

He wanted to snarl in frustration. "Liam, you've known me your whole life. I'm not a talker."

His friend laughed. "No, you've always been a man of secrets. If not, you would have told your closest friends about Jimmy and Morag. Might be time to change that. When you're trying to figure out what to say to her—how to show her you've changed—put a hand on your heart. I also tucked a journal into your carry-on. I thought you might want to write something down. Good luck, my friend."

Luck. He should have packed a leprechaun in his suitcase.

When he got on the plane—in a middle seat, no less—he looked at the movies being shown and then sat back and considered his dilemma.

Kathleen didn't want secrets, and Liam had told him he was a man of secrets. He hadn't seen it like that. To his mind, he'd only kept things to himself.

He snuck a look around at the two people he was squashed between, but both women were watching some chick flick. God, they probably wanted men who'd share things too.

Well, if that's what she was looking for...

He almost grimaced as he put his hand over his heart. It felt weird, but if Yoda thought it would help, he'd try it. He would do anything to have Kathleen back.

Falling back on his boxing training, he started breathing deeply and cleared his mind. Secrets. Sharing. An idea filtered through the mess of his thoughts, discomfiting as hell. He dug out the journal Liam had snuck into his bag—God bless, Yoda—and he started writing.

Secrets, huh? Well... He could do that.

When he finished writing, he sank back in the chair. Nothing could be as hard as that.

He'd been wrong.

Finding police officer Robbie O'Connor—that's what the Yanks said—was like trying to find a needle in a haystack. From the search on his phone, which he conducted in a corner booth in the airport bar, he discovered there were over two thousand officers in Boston and an endless number of what the Yanks called precincts. He got a hostile response when he called the first three asking for a Robbie O'Connor. He feared it was futile, but he kept making calls.

He could simply head to their family bar, of course, but he suspected he wouldn't be welcome. They were protective and might close ranks. He also didn't want to involve

Ellie. That wouldn't be fair to her. Besides, he knew there was a chance Kathleen would shut the door in his face.

He couldn't let that happen. He had one shot at this.

Everything she'd told him about Robbie O'Connor said he was the guy to approach. It sent the biggest message. He was the oldest brother, the one everyone looked up to, the one who took care of everyone. He had to speak to him. He had to convince him to let him talk to Kathleen. Maybe he could even get the man on his side.

On the sixth precinct, he learned there *was* an Officer Robbie O'Connor. When the woman asked if he wanted to be put through, Declan declined. No, he would take a cab there and meet him on his own turf.

The cab ride was death-defying. He'd had to convince the driver he wasn't turning himself in for a crime and only dropping in from Ireland to surprise an old friend. Suspicious people, these Yanks.

And Jesus, did they have filthy mouths! People shouted out at other drivers and yelled obscenities. Even a couple of old ladies, he was shocked to witness. The traffic crawled so slow he could have gone faster on one of his friend Kade's ponies. He'd never been to Boston, but the city was gritty, edgy. Like Kathleen.

God, he missed her.

When the cab finally dropped him off at the precinct, he had to draw himself up. A couple of the policemen smoking outside stared him down like he was planning on robbing them. The sight of guns in their belts was a little shocking. The Garda didn't equip themselves like that where he came from. These men seemed more deadly for it, even more so because they were decked out in dark blue uniforms with black ties.

He made himself smile. "Is Officer Robbie O'Connor around? I'm a friend of his sister from Ireland."

The youngest of the group sauntered over, his right hand fingering a black baton at his side. "We heard some Irish guy was calling around other precincts looking for Robbie. What's your name?"

He hadn't expected the interrogation to start this early. Damn if Kathleen's accent wasn't a touch nicer than this man's. "Declan McGrath."

The two other officers joined the first, circling him. "What's Robbie's sister's name?" the young one asked.

"Kathleen, and her best friend, Ellie Buchanan, is marrying my brother, Brady McGrath."

The oldest of the group tilted his head to the side. "What's the name of your brother's pub?"

He jolted. He hadn't said his brother had a pub. "The Brazen Donkey."

The man nodded sharply. "Okay, you can come see Robbie. We had to make sure you weren't some insane Irishman here on some vendetta. Robbie's put some bad people away with ties to Ireland."

He hadn't thought about that. But yes, he'd heard such stories. "Thank you."

"Sure thing," the man said in that same accent. "You want some coffee? It tastes like shit, but it's better than the crap my girlfriend makes."

His head was spinning. These were Kathleen's people. Some things were making better sense. "I don't mind drinking shite myself. Keeps a man honest."

That made the older cop he'd been talking to laugh. "I'll have to tell that one to my old lady. Come on. We'll take you to Robbie."

They checked his carry-on at the door with more efficiency than airport security. He was a little surprised by that. Once inside, there were officers everywhere, mixed in with regular people—some angry, some crying, some handcuffed. He tried not to stare.

His guides grabbed him a coffee on the way down the hall, and they passed a lot of people pushing paper in small offices.

When the older officer stopped in one doorway, he ducked his head in while the other two kept an eye on him. "Hey, Robbie! Your Irish guy checks out. He's not a terrorist, and he's a regular riot. Says drinking 'shite' coffee keeps a man honest."

A tall, well-muscled man appeared in the doorway. Declan saw the resemblance to Kathleen immediately in the eyes and the nose. "Then we're the most honest bunch of assholes in the whole of Massachusetts, aren't we? So... Who the hell are you?"

The younger police guy said, "He knows Kathleen and Ellie and—"

"I'm Brady's brother, Declan." He lifted his chin, knowing he needed to meet him man to man. "Is there someplace we can talk?"

His brow rose, but he smiled. Thinly. "Sure thing, Ace."

The nickname had him stilling. He never wanted to hear it again.

"Come on in and teak a seat, Declan. Then you can tell me what kind of trouble you're in."

Declan rolled his carry-on inside and sat down in the ugly brown chair in front of a battered gray desk. "I'm not in any kind of trouble."

Robbie sat behind the desk and kicked back. "You're in a police station. You look like you just got off the plane. You have bruises all over your face."

Yeah, he'd noticed people staring at him weirdly. "Can you believe no one asked why?"

He laughed. "Yeah, I can. Trust me. You're in some kind of trouble. You're the asshole who broke my sister's heart, right? She hasn't said anything, but I know her. She didn't just come home because some asshole vandalized the arts center. I could break you into a million pieces for hurting her," Robbie finished conversationally.

His chest filled with tension, but he nodded. "I would deserve it. Robbie, I'm here to make it right. That's why I wanted to talk to you. Kathleen says you're the oldest, the one everyone looks up to."

Robbie put his hands on the top of his desk and leaned forward. "So you figured you'd persuade me to help you with my sister. Boy, this had better be good, or I'll give you a personal police escort straight back to Logan Airport."

As a boxer, he knew plenty of men who radiated toughness and menace. Kathleen's brother all but rolled in it. He decided the tack he would take. "How do you feel about sharing your deepest, darkest secrets, Robbie?"

He scoffed. "I fucking hate it," he said, sounding very much like Mark Wahlberg.

Declan almost smiled. "What about sharing your emotions?"

"I fucking hate that too." His eyes narrowed. "What was this secret you kept from my sister?"

He was too smart by half. "I didn't tell her—or anyone, not even my twin brother—that the boxer I fought a few days ago had slept with my fiancée before our wedding nearly five years ago."

"Jesus fucking Christ. Now that's an asshole."

He grew hopeful. "He's been called a lot of bad words and deserves every one."

"Yeah." Her brother fingered the edge of a black notepad on his desk, the kind Declan had seen police use to take interview notes. But he didn't open it and start writing, thank God. "So you didn't tell anyone. I get it. I wouldn't have either. Don't tell Kathleen I said this, but women want us to be all tough and strong, and then they expect us to wear our hearts on our sleeves when we're with them. Some of the girls I've been with want me to tell them how I feel when I'm processing a murder site. Like I want to relive that or share it with them. Hell, the whole thing makes a man feel like he's on a teeter-totter in the romance department."

Damn, but he really liked Robbie O'Connor. "I think I have a way to show Kathleen how I can give her more of what she wants in a relationship. In a marriage."

Robbie tapped his notepad against the desk. "You want to marry my sister, huh?"

"If she'll have me, yes." He leaned forward and looked the man straight in the eye. "I'll talk to whomever I need to in your family for permission, your dad included, but first, I need to talk to your sister, I'll be thinking."

Robbie laughed darkly. "You'd be thinking right. Damn you talk funny, but I dig it. All right, so you want another shot at my baby sister. I'm thinking a public place—in case she wants to storm out or cry for help. A place where all her brothers can look out for her."

All seven, he recalled. "That sounds more than fair. I didn't want to just show up at your family's pub or ask Ellie where she was staying."

"I'm glad you didn't put Ellie in that position. She's like a sister to us. If you'd made her cry too, we'd have to kill you for sure and throw you into the bay."

Declan cleared his throat as the image rolled through his mind. It wasn't hard to imagine.

Robbie stood, cracking his neck. "I'm just kidding. Mostly."

Yeah, mostly. "You probably have a slew of ideas from your 'stupid criminal' videos on how not to dispose of the body, right? I was thinking they were amusing before, but..."

Robbie's shoulders started shaking. "So she showed them to you. You come up with the drunk leprechaun video she sent me?"

"That's right. Don't judge us Irish by his example."

He punched him in the shoulder none too lightly. "Ace, I might be starting to like you. Come on. You can sit in one of the interrogation rooms until I arrange everything with my brothers. Everyone's getting off work about now."

Inside the interrogation room, he concluded Kathleen's brother was having the time of his life trying to intimidate him. He stared at the bare walls and the two-way mirror and wondered if Robbie was observing him. In a few days, Declan hoped he'd be in a position to see all this as a bit of good *craic*.

When Robbie finally opened the door, he lifted his chin. "Let's go, tough guy. Everyone's meeting up at O'Connor's. You have one chance. Here's the rules."

He raised his brow. "There are rules?"

The man made a rude sound before saying, "One, you don't touch her. Two, if she walks away, you don't follow. Three, if you blow it, you never talk sweet to her ever again."

That was going to be hard. They would be in the same village while she worked on her sculpture. He'd feared the agony and longing of wanting her before. This would be interminable. But it was fair, and he knew it. "Done."

"And last thing... My brothers Billie and Danny insisted on this one."

He wasn't a fearful man, but he knew this one was going to be mad.

"You make her cry, they're going to knock out your teeth and rip your limbs off. Break some bones." Robbie grinned like a jackal. "You ready to go or what?"

He nodded.

He didn't plan to fail.

CHAPTER TWENTY-EIGHT

H er brothers were acting weird.

Kathleen wondered if there was a full moon. Or maybe Billie was hooking up with his ex again and didn't want her to know.

Not that she could get on her high horse. She hadn't even told them about Declan yet. The arts center news had them upset enough.

Robbie had asked police questions. The rest of her brothers had offered to head to Ireland and rough Owen Kincaid up. Pop had wrapped her in one of her mother's crochet blankets as if it wasn't a whopping eighty degrees outside.

Then they gave Ellie the same treatment, which had made her friend cry a little. She was one of them, after all.

Her brothers had watched them like hawks and made run after run to their favorite take-out places. She'd drunk so much Dunks coffee she could slosh. She'd had a lobster roll, of course, and she and Ellie had split the quart of clam chowder. Food. It was what the O'Connors used to scuttle away troubles. She was okay with that. It was home.

If she missed the quiet countryside or the lilting cadence of the people she'd come to care about, she didn't say.

She hadn't imagined missing Ireland so much.

She'd *known* she'd miss Declan, of course, but she'd just have to get over that.

"Kathleen!" Danny yelled. "I told you girls to sit in that back booth."

She exchanged another glance with Ellie. "We're fine at the bar, Danny." She hated being by the kitchen door. It was a good way to get run over when the servers burst from the kitchen with orders.

"We always sit at the bar," Ellie whispered. "What's gotten into your brothers anyway? It's not like Billie to ask us to cancel our plans."

They'd planned on having dinner at one of their favorite seafood places on Cape Ann, but he'd asked them to come to the pub for dinner instead. "I don't know. Maybe they've really missed us. I mean, they all showed up tonight. Usually a few of them have dates. It's weird."

Billie appeared beside their seats at the bar. "Go to the booth, will you? Please, for the love of Christ, just this once, listen to your brothers."

She glared at him. "Why?"

"Kathleen Mary O'Connor, get your scrawny backside over to that booth." Billie pulled her gently from the seat.

"Hey!"

"Hey nothing." He picked her up and carried her over, her feet dangling, as people started laughing.

She thought about kicking him, but that wouldn't be nice. "I'm just going to walk back to the bar the second you put me down."

He snorted. "I'm beginning to have pity for the man—I swear, I'm gonna tell Robbie you're acting like a baby."

"Am not!" She pushed at him when he deposited her onto the booth's wooden bench. "You're the ones acting nutters."

"Nutters! This is the thanks I get for canceling my date. You stay put. I mean it, Kathleen."

She stuck her tongue out and looked around for Ellie. Danny had her by the hand at the bar, and he was talking animatedly. What the hell?

The kitchen door whacked against the wall. She ground her teeth. Fantabulous. Something whispered across from her. She looked over and gave a cry of surprise. "Declan!"

He sat across from her, wearing a rumpled black shirt. "I have something I want to share with you."

"What—" She blinked and shook her head. "What the hell are you doing here?"

He pointed over her shoulder. "Please keep in mind that I had to convince your oldest brother to let me talk to you. I tracked him down to the police station. Not an easy task in Boston. Do you know how many police stations there are?"

Her head was spinning. "You talked to Robbie? Wait. You just hopped on a plane—"

"I couldn't lose you." He gripped the edge of the table between them. "Please. I want to show you— Hell, let me get it."

She shook herself as he took out a *journal* from a carry-on in the corner. He'd just crossed an ocean to see her. Her chest swelled with hurt. And hope. "Declan, I—"

"Secret number one," he said, opening the book as he walked back to the booth. "I was three years old." He sat. "I knocked over my mother's milk pitcher in the refrigerator when I was going for a snack. I buried the shards in the garden."

She shook her head, confused. "Declan, what is this?"

"I want you to trust me again." He held up the journal. "You told me you wanted me to share things with you. That love wasn't enough and you wanted that kind of a relationship. So I'm trusting you with every secret I have. I wrote them down on the plane ride here."

Love squeezed her rapidly beating heart. "*Every secret? How many are there?*"

His mouth was a flat line. "I stopped at one hundred. I might have forgotten a few. Secret number two: I took Brady's new football to the sea and lost it in the waves."

She started to slowly melt, all the hurt in her muscles melting like wax. "How old were you?"

"Four." He took a breath and gave a brief smile, obviously still filled with tension. Perhaps that was because she could feel her brothers looming behind them.

When she looked over her shoulder again, all seven of them were standing there, arms crossed, looking as tough as ever. Ellie stood in the middle of them, tears shining in her eyes. They shared a look, and Kathleen nodded. Her best friend wiped her tears and then mumbled something to Danny, who nodded as well.

She watched her brother slip behind the bar again and pull down their favorite whiskey, the kind for special family occasions. Lagavulin 16 Years. She wouldn't tell Declan it wasn't Irish.

Turning back to him, she saw he was waiting for her. Their eyes met. He smiled at last. "Ready for the next one?"

"Yeah," she whispered, her throat thick with emotion. He went through the next twenty secrets without interruption, mostly the kid variety. Where he'd hidden his favorite toy or car magazine. The first and second times he'd kissed a girl. Morag had been the first and second, which she hadn't known.

Danny came and set down two whiskeys in front of them and ruffled her hair as he left. God, she loved those idiots. They were still watching from the bar, but they'd lost the air of menace.

"Just out of curiosity," she asked when he reached the fortieth secret and his twelfth year. "Which number is the one about Jimmy and Morag?"

He ruffled through his remaining pages. "Ninety-two. I don't have many secrets as an adult, Kathleen."

She extended her hand to him. "That's good. I wouldn't want to be with anyone who had a ton of secrets. Tell me a recent one. Like number ninety-seven."

He lowered his head and read, "A dog that came in with one of the old ladies in town got behind the butcher counter and jumped up. He devoured two steaks before I could pull him down. The older woman was mortified. She asked me to swear not to tell anyone. I think she was scared her family might say her dog was getting out of hand and she was frail. I let her pay for the steaks, but I didn't tell anyone. Not even Seamus."

"That was rather nice of you." She felt her eyes burn. This was the man she'd fallen in love with.

"She's passed on now, so I didn't think she'd mind me telling you." His eyes gleamed with emotion. "But I don't let her niece bring the dog into the shop. I learned my lesson there."

They were both learning their lessons, it seemed. "I like you sharing your secrets with me."

"I've never told them to anyone else." He handed the journal over to her. "I love you. I want you to trust me, and I want you to know I do trust you. With everything. I'm used to keeping things to myself, but I understand you wanting to know things. I want to know things about you too. If you call it sharing, I'll do it. I can't promise it'll always be easy for me. It wasn't easy to write these pages."

She could see him huddled over them, scrawling out his secrets next to a stranger on the plane. "No, I imagine it wasn't."

"But there was also a sense of relief." He exhaled with a wry smile. "Some of them seem downright silly now. But it felt important to keep quiet about them at the time. A man has to honor that. I promise you right now, though, that's over. You want to know everything, I'll tell you. If you'll forgive me for hurting you and making you lose faith in me. Kathleen, I'm sorry. More than I could ever say."

The hurt welled like a lanced wound and poured out. She let it rain down her face. He reached over and brushed aside her tears with his thumb, his blue eyes narrowed with their own pain. "You're forgiven. Let's start again, shall we? I'm Kathleen O'Connor, and this is my family's bar."

"I'm Declan McGrath, newly arrived from Ireland." He held out his hand. "I was wondering what you were doing for the rest of your life? I was hoping you might marry me."

She blew out a slow breath and took his hand. "Marry you, huh? That sounds interesting. When were you thinking?"

He raised her hand to his lips. "Well, your entire family is here. Maybe in a few days? We could have another ceremony when we go back to Ireland."

She leaned forward. "I think that's an excellent idea."

"I was going to buy you a ring except I know how treasured your mother's ring is. The Claddagh ring is traditional Irish, you know."

She lifted out the necklace. She hadn't been able to take it off. "I was hoping you would be of that mind."

He scooted over to the bench she was sitting on and helped her unclasp the necklace. "I know it makes this particular Irishman very happy indeed."

She held out her left hand and he slid the ring on it. *Oh, Mom, I hope you're watching all this.*

Ellie let out a shriek, which stopped every patron in their tracks. Heads swung their way, her seven brothers included. The lot of them exchanged looks, and then Robbie nodded.

"Someone had better call Pop," Billie shouted.

Ah, Pop. She couldn't wait for him to meet Declan.

He took her hand and set it against his chest. "The Claddagh looks good on your finger. Love, loyalty, and friendship. I promise them all to you. I love you, *mo chroí*."

"I promise them right back." She leaned in until their mouths were inches away. "And I love you too, Declan McGrath. Now kiss me."

He grimaced, his gaze looking past her shoulder. "I might need to ask your brothers' permission. One of the rules was about me not touching you."

Snorting, she wiggled the hand he was holding. "You're already touching me, you idiot."

He smiled. "Yeah, but kissing might be different. Broken bones and death were mentioned if I did. The first I can handle. The second..."

She rolled her eyes. Later, she would ask him about the other rules her numbskull brothers had concocted. "I can't imagine them having any issue with me kissing my fiancé."

He made a rude noise. "Your brother put me in the interrogation room at the police station."

She tried and failed to muffle her laughter. "Okay, I see your point. I'll defend you if necessary."

"Like I'd let you," he said, shooting her a look.

The scent of oranges surrounded them.

She jerked back. "Sorcha's *here*?"

They both craned their heads looking, but they didn't see her. Suddenly her quiet laughter reached Kathleen's ears.

Something crashed in the kitchen.

The cook ran out, his hairnet askew. "Danny! There's a fucking ghost in my kitchen. I don't care that she's gorgeous. Get the baseball bat."

Kathleen pressed her hand to her mouth, laughing. Declan only shook his head as Danny barreled past them, following the cook back in. More crashing sounded.

"Well, we know she can cross oceans now, don't we?" Kathleen said.

Ellie ran over. "Is that Sorcha? Oh my God! What does that mean, her being here?"

Kathleen wouldn't presume to guess when it came to Sorcha. "I'd say she's fulfilled her mission when it comes to us."

"Soulmates," Declan said softly. "Seems she was right. Of course, we won't be able to live with her after this."

"Isn't she dead?" Ellie asked, which made them all laugh.

Her brothers edged over as more crashes and curses came from the kitchen, Robbie leading the way.

"You're Irish." He gestured to Declan. "You know how to get rid of a ghost?"

"If I did, I wouldn't be standing here," Declan said with an endearing grin.

And thank God, Kathleen thought, as her brothers

exchanged another round of looks before rushing into the kitchen like linebackers, pots clanking loudly as chaos ensued.

Said ghost appeared beside them and grinned. "It's important to have a good time while finding love. Now kiss her. I've got them good and distracted."

Then she winked and disappeared.

Having a good time while finding love. Kathleen couldn't think of anything better.

She leaned over and kissed Declan, their mouths moving slowly, relearning, rediscovering, all the while bedlam reigned in the kitchen.

When her brothers darted out of the kitchen yelling like little schoolgirls, she couldn't help but laugh gustily. Declan was grinning from ear to ear.

"Welcome to the family," she said, leaning in for another kiss.

The scent of oranges surrounded them yet again, reminding Kathleen of all the reasons home was where the heart was.

EPILOGUE

B usy, busy, busy.
That was Bets' every waking hour right now, and she loved it.

She glanced at the open newspaper on her bed featuring an article on the Sorcha Fitzgerald Arts Center that had just run—in *The New York Times*! Sophie's press release had been like Helen launching a thousand ships. The artist was the new face of the arts center worldwide at the moment. She'd be arriving in late August before school began, and Bets was fielding interviews and inquiries right and left.

When this was what she focused on, it felt like life couldn't be better.

She hummed along with some Bon Jovi she had playing as she fussed with the dress she was wearing for Kathleen and Declan's wedding. Goodness, that couple! They'd gotten married in Boston last week and then sent out hasty invitations for another ceremony with their Irish friends and family, scheduled for today. Sorcha must be pleased.

"You're not dressed yet, Mum," Liam said from the

open door of her bedroom. "We need to be at the church soon."

She gestured to the rare curlers in her hair, ones she'd decided to use in a moment of vanity. "I only have a few more minutes before I can take these out. Don't you look handsome."

He tugged on the lapel of his blue suit and shot her that endearing smile of his. "Why, thank you. We Irish clean up pretty well. You finally ready to talk to me about why you asked me to be your date today?"

No, she really wasn't.

She did her best not to scowl as she fussed with her curlers. It wasn't that she wanted to deny that she and Donal were finished. They were. Everyone in the village seemed to know. After all, he had left for another long trip, this time to France with his father. It didn't take a brainiac to figure out what that meant. Thankfully, the Irish were kind. Okay, everyone but Mary Kincaid and her lot. No one else was going to say a word to her other than the Lucky Charms—who had brought wine and comfort—and her son here, of course.

"Maybe not today," she said, reaching for the first curler and unrolling it. "The Irish would say it's bad luck to talk about a breakup on the day of a wedding."

Liam came over and wrapped his arms around her. "I thought it was going that way with you and Donal, but we can talk of it another day if you want. You know I've been waiting for you to be ready."

She loved that he never rushed her. "Thank you. I just want to focus on everything we have to do for the arts center right now and our good fortune. I mean, we have a wedding today and the baptism for Angie and Carrick's daughter next weekend. Isn't she a peach?"

"As beautiful as a star," Liam said of Emeline Fitzgerald. "Carrick is already saying she clenches her tiny fist like her mother does when she holds a paintbrush."

That got Bets to thinking. "I need to add kid paintbrushes to my list for the new children's center. You have your hands full, building all these new sheds."

He lifted a shoulder. "I have good help. We're certainly going to be busy this summer with it all, won't we?"

Yes, and Bets couldn't be more thrilled. Because then she wouldn't have to think about Linc and how much she missed him. He'd been keeping himself occupied with other things too. They'd fallen into a weird new routine of texting and emailing, and the professional tone of their exchanges was going to give her ulcers.

She told herself it was for the best. They were working on the arts center together—her baby and now his, it seemed. Being in love with him would mess all that up, especially since Donal had told her Linc didn't much think it was wise of him to press his suit with her. Besides, what did it say about her that she was already interested in another man so soon after her breakup with Donal? Maybe she wasn't a good suit for him.

But she missed him. She really loved that darn cowboy, God help her.

She tried to pull another of the curlers out, tugging her hair, and she was shocked at the sudden rush of emotion that roared through her. She started crying, and suddenly Liam's arms were around her and he was rubbing her back.

"Oh, Liam, I'm such an idiot," she whispered against his shoulder.

"I don't think so," he calmly replied. "Mum, you're really coming alive. It's incredible to see."

"But I'm in love with two men!" she blurted out and

AVA MILES

then shoved away from him, slapping her hand over her mouth. "You didn't hear that."

His mouth twitched. "Mum, you're not in love with two men."

She felt for the bed and sank down, her knees trembling. "I'm not?"

"No," he said, sitting and taking her hand. "You love Donal, but you're not *in love* with him anymore."

A woman in a white dress materialized in front of them suddenly.

Bets jumped a mile.

Sorcha!

"You have a very wise son. Then again, he was always special."

"Hello, Sorcha," Liam said calmly to the ghost in front of them.

Her dress danced as if the wind touched it. Bets glanced at the window and felt faint. It wasn't open. Jesus, this wasn't what she'd thought it would be like to see a ghost.

"Oh, my!" She scooted back on the bed and lifted up her knees.

"I'm a ghost. Not a mouse. You don't need to hide on the furniture."

She exhaled loudly. "Okay. Right. No need to hide. It's just...you've never appeared to me before. Everything is coming up roses with your arts center. Are you here about that?"

"No." Her white dress twirled against her as she swayed. "I'm not here about the arts center."

"Then what?"

Her laughter filled the air before she said, "Why do you think, Betsy O'Hanlon?"

Then she smiled.

368

And disappeared.

Liam started laughing under his breath as the scent of oranges enveloped her. The ghost's meaning finally struck her.

Well, shit.

Every time you leave a kind review, a rainbow appears in the sky.

Leave a review for After Indigo Irish Nights and get ready for a splash of color!

Will love bloom for Bets and Linc? Find out in Beyond Rosy Irish Twilight, the next Unexpected Prince Charming story!

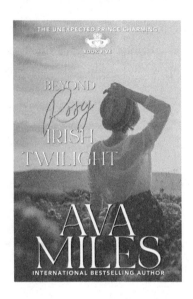

A second chance at love and a first chance at happily ever after.

"One word for Ava Miles is WOW."

MY BOOK CRAVINGS

Get Beyond Rosy Irish Twilight!

Available wherever books are sold.

ABOUT THE AUTHOR

Millions of readers have discovered International Bestselling Author Ava Miles and her powerful fiction and non-fiction books about love, happiness, and transformation. Her novels have received praise and accolades from *USA Today*, *Publisher's Weekly*, and *Women's World Magazine* in addition to being chosen as Best Books of the Year and Top Editor's picks. However, Ava's strongest praise comes directly from her readers, who call her books unforgettable and life changing.

If you'd like to connect with Ava or hear more about her upcoming books, check out the links below:

https://avamiles.com/
https://avamiles.com/newsletter/

facebook.com/AuthorAvaMiles

twitter.com/authoravamiles

instagram.com/avamiles

bookbub.com/authors/ava-miles

pinterest.com/authoravamiles

DON'T FORGET...
SIGN UP FOR AVA'S NEWSLETTER.

More great books? Check.
Fun facts? Check.
Recipes? Check.
General frivolity? DOUBLE CHECK.

https://avamiles.com/newsletter/

Made in the USA
Las Vegas, NV
26 July 2022

52149458R10225